"A wild debut about Time and War teaming up to battle the evils of eternal peace. By the time you're done you won't fear the reaper; you'll want to wrap his lonely, cross-stitch obsessed self up in a hug and never let go."

Alis Franklin, author of Liesmith

"Vivid worldbuilding of a fascinating alternate Earth, peppered with touches of whimsy. This is a promising debut!"

Emmie Mears, author of the Ayala Storme series

"The Interminables is the type of book that Angry Robot was made for."

Strange Alliances

"It will reward you with a world of wonders and horrors, alongside a tale of deep and desperate friendship: a thief and a war, trying to save as many lives and they can."

SFX magazine

"So fucking good."

The State of Blogendorff

"If you're looking for an entertaining piece of dystopian fiction, with magic and heroes and… er… a cat, then this will suit you very well indeed."

SF & F Reviews

"A dark, depressive, but beautifully imagined urban fantasy/ alternate universe. Perhaps one of the most interesting, intriguing, and rich books I've read this year."

Online Eccentric Librarian

The Interminables

PAIGE ORWIN

IMMORTAL ARCHITECTS

ANGRY
ROBOT

ANGRY ROBOT
An imprint of Watkins Media Ltd

20 Fletcher Gate,
Nottingham,
NG1 2FZ
UK

angryrobotbooks.com
twitter.com/angryrobotbooks
Stormbringers

An Angry Robot paperback original 2017

Cover by Amazing15
Set in Meridien and Sperling by Epub Services

Distributed in the United States by Penguin Random House, Inc.,
New York.

ISBN 978 0 85766 594 2
Ebook ISBN 978 0 85766 595 9

Printed in the United States of America

9 8 7 6 5 4 3 2 1

IMMORTAL ARCHITECTS

CHAPTER ONE

"Come now, it will be perfectly fine," said the ghost, his accent more than faintly reminiscent of Dracula. "Nothing to worry about. Put your hat on."

Edmund Templeton regarded his top hat steadily. It was old, like him, and didn't look it, like him. He'd bought it in the Fifties, when this had all started. He'd been thirty-five then, too.

"I don't know," he said.

"You've put on all the rest," said Istvan Czernin. "Even the cape, which I should think is the oddest."

He propped a thumb in his belt, buckled high around the waist as was proper for the uniform he wore: Austro-Hungarian infantry, circa 1915. A medic's cross banded one arm. His face was broad and bespectacled, his features a hawkish blend of Caucasian and Asiatic, the right side of his mouth twisted upwards, paralyzed in a permanent half-grin. Burn scarring tugged at the corner of his eye and plunged into his collar.

He cast no shadow. Barbed wire coiled at his feet.

"Lay off," said Edmund. He adjusted the cape, a high-collared number with a mantle, intended to make his shoulders look broader than they were.

"It is," Istvan insisted. "I'm surprised you still wear it

after that business with the tiger."

"That's why it's buttoned, not tied," Edmund grumbled.

"Yes, but…"

Just give me a moment, Edmund almost said. He didn't. He stopped himself, even though it wouldn't have mattered – not with Istvan – and again he regarded his hat. It was the last part of the full ensemble: black double-breasted suit jacket, black tie, black pants, black shoes. Black gloves. A pair of battered aviator's goggles. A silver pin at his lapel, a pair of crescent moons together forming a clock marking midnight.

It wasn't exactly a uniform, but it might as well have been.

The Hour Thief. That was how the world knew him, and he'd chosen the title for a reason. It was true. Every word of it, bare and literal.

Before, of course, he hadn't been known at all. The Twelfth Hour had been a secret, a wizard's cabal founded just before the turn of the century to carry on that old and foolish tradition of looking too deeply into things that looked back. They had all been secret, then, often even from each other.

Now the Twelfth Hour was one of the only governments left on the northeastern seaboard that could enforce anything beyond its walls.

It had been eight years since 2012. Eight years since Mexico City sank. Eight years since every major population center in the world cracked and buckled under ancient sorceries, twisting into vast stretches of what was no longer quite real: the city present juxtaposed with cities past, future, never, and alien, overrun with warping magics, shattered by the tread of rubble-born beasts like walking skylines.

2012. The Wizard War. The return of Shokat Anoushak al-Khalid, the Immortal, who might not have been killed in the fighting this time, either.

Eight years trying to pretend that the Hour Thief still moved in the dark.

Istvan strode to the door, footfalls silent despite the hobnails in his shoes. The barbed wire followed him. "Come on, now. You've put this off long enough."

"Don't remind me," Edmund told him.

"Someone ought to."

Edmund took a breath. It was nothing he hadn't done before. Nothing he couldn't do. Nothing, really. Just put the hat on and go.

He cast one last look around his living room: the green couches dusted with cat hair, the bookshelves packed with volumes in eighteen different languages, the upright radio in the corner that could only pick up one station and that only in the morning. A blue plastic barrel filled with river water sat near the three shallow stairs to the kitchen. A sheet of steel siding patched what had been the front window, cut in the center to hold a windshield removed from a pickup truck.

No pictures on the walls. No plants. Beldam was off doing the sort of things cats do. She didn't need him, really. She could find her own meals if she had to. She always forgave him, if he forgot.

Cats could take care of themselves.

"Edmund–"

"I know!"

The words emerged sharper than he intended. One hand slipped into the pocket of his suit jacket.

Istvan raised his eyebrows. "I'm going to open the

door," he said.

Edmund rubbed a thumb over cold brass. "I'll do it."

"You're certain?"

"It's my house, I'll do it."

Istvan stepped aside. The wire tangled around his feet, rusted and faded, stained with old blood. The blood was normal; rust meant he was worried.

Another breath. Edmund stared at the door handle. His hand stayed in his pocket.

"Your hat," said Istvan, gently.

Right. That.

Edmund hesitated one more moment – yet another that wasn't his, that he couldn't spare – and then donned his hat. The weight settled on his head like it belonged there.

"OK," he said. The Hour Thief said. With it all assembled, that was who he was. Who he became. That was how the world knew him. What was left of it.

He tried a smile and it fit easily into place.

"There you are," said Istvan, a note of approval in his voice. He set a hand on Edmund's shoulder, the touch freezing in a way more than physical but familiar, and endurable. "Shall we be off then?"

Edmund nodded. He reached for the door handle, and turned it.

Nothing foundered. Nothing sank. Nothing sprang at him.

He blinked at sunlight glinting off rain-slick cobbles, the road winding towards the sea, the streetlamps strung with salvaged power lines that reached from cottage to suburban rambler to the pagoda perched high on the hill. A gutted truck sat before his house, stripped of windshield and front doors. Smoke spiraled upwards from chimneys and hobo stoves. Gulls fought over a clump of tendrilled strands that came apart as it fell. A clothesline bobbed, just visible, over the hedge. Edmund tried to remember the neighboring family's name, and couldn't.

New Haven. Still home, despite the changes. His house hadn't been so close to the shore before the Wizard War – it hadn't been a free-standing structure at all, in fact – and the original city port was gone, stretches of highway and storefront drowned along with it. The new docks were visible just down the street, piers cobbled together from scrap, rubble dumped into the water to form boat ramps.

Across the grey waters of the sound rose a twisted spire, three miles high, marking the deadly remnants of New York City. The Black Building. Auroras crackled at its peak.

Istvan stepped out beside him. "There. Not so difficult, was it?"

Edmund looked away from the horizon. He didn't need any reminders about New York. A nearby window caught his eye: a round face peering out, a hand raised to wave – and then another figure that rushed over and whisked the curtains shut.

He sighed. He closed his fingers around brass, warm now, and drew out his pocket watch. The embossed hourglass on the front was almost worn off again. He flipped it open. "You know, Istvan, I think it was better when I was just that strange old-fashioned bachelor at the end of the block."

"I'm sure they appreciate knowing the truth," Istvan replied.

"They already knew the truth."

"But now they can know it openly, and I imagine they

do feel safer with you about, even if they don't show it."
The ghost glanced up at the window, then away. Bone
flickered beneath his skin. "It's mostly me, anyhow," he
added, "frightening them."

"It's not mostly you."

Istvan started down the drive. He left no footprints.
"Come on, then."

Edmund eyed his pocket watch. Just past noon. He'd
checked his ledger this morning, again, even though
there was nothing to note save the usual drain. One
more day to replenish. Twenty-four hours.

He snapped the watch shut and dropped it in his
pocket. He made sure his hat was on straight. He checked
that Beldam hadn't escaped (as cats do) and that the
wards etched beneath his welcome mat were still true.
He closed and locked his door.

Then he followed Istvan.

"We aren't going to see the Magister?"

Istvan shook his head. "No."

"Barrio Libertad?"

"No."

Edmund shoved his hands in his pockets, stepping
around whatever it was the gulls had dropped in the
snow. "New headquarters site?"

"I, ah… thought we might go for a walk."

"A walk."

"First," Istvan amended. "A walk first, and then…"

This again. This was the second time this week.
Edmund hunched his shoulders and walked faster.
"Istvan, you know I haven't figured out what we'll need.
You've seen the lists. With as hard as it is to get anything
now, and trying to convince anyone in the area to go
along with it, and trying not to rely on Barrio Libertad…"

He shot a glance around, just in case anything was listening, anything at all, even the dust. "Istvan, the labor alone – the food, the water–"

"Edmund–"

"Do you know how hard it is to find anywhere with clean water?"

"Edmund, I–"

"I can't bring it all in myself, and we'll have no power, and no defenses, and–"

A bony vulture's wing snapped open before him, scattering rotten feathers and loops of faded wire. Hollow eye sockets regarded him through mists that stank of chlorine and mustard gas. "Edmund," said Istvan, apparently oblivious to the bloodied bullet holes torn in his uniform, "Please remember that I'm quite accustomed to that sort of privation."

Edmund spent a moment to calm his racing heart. Just Istvan. It was just Istvan. He pushed away skeletal phalanges. "I know."

"And that I've offered to help."

"You're busy."

The specter darted before him again, awful wings flaring. "You've a standing order!"

Edmund almost walked through him. He could have – easily, too – but Istvan was a friend, his closest friend in all the world, and treating him like he was no more substantial than he was emphasized that he wasn't human, and Edmund didn't want any more reminders of that. No more than the unavoidable.

"Please cut it out," he said.

Distant artillery hammered. "But I–"

Edmund drew a hand across his lapel.

The specter paused. He glanced down, cursed softly to

himself in Hungarian, and brushed away a line of bullet holes ripped into his chest. The wings dissipated. Flesh returned, scarred and pearlescent and unreal as it was. He fiddled with his wedding ring. "It's getting worse, isn't it," he said.

"It's not."

"I'm doing it more than usual, I know it."

"I'm sure it's nothing," Edmund lied.

Istvan peered at him, gaze sharp behind his spectacles. "You don't believe that."

Edmund shrugged. "I'd like to."

He meant it. He really did.

Unfortunately, Istvan was a sundered spirit, a human soul torn to pieces and then merged with the horrific energies of disaster: anything from earthquakes to plagues, famine and war. They were rare – Edmund knew of only three others – and a class of ghosts unlike any other, more attached to a historical event than any place.

In Istvan's case, the First World War.

He was bound to it. Made up by it. Its violence seethed within him, and its power had brought him back. He remembered not only his own experience in the war but that of everything and everyone that participated. After it was over, he'd fought all over the world for almost eighty years, a cryptid caught in blurred photographs and depicted in unit insignia, driven by the bloodlust that was now a fundamental part of his nature.

The Twelfth Hour had caught him in the Persian Gulf. He was the most dangerous prisoner they had ever kept. Now, freed, he was the most dangerous entity on roster. He hadn't done anything terrible yet, but no one could guarantee that who he'd been in life was always enough to override what he had become. It was enough to make anyone worry.

Edmund had used him, and though Istvan had accepted more than one apology, Edmund feared that he still wasn't forgiven. Might not ever be.

He nodded at the road, cobbles winding downwards toward the beach and the rickety docks. Any eavesdroppers were keeping themselves well-hidden. "Were we going to take that walk or not?"

Istvan stood there a moment longer. Then he brushed away the last of the bloodstains, resettled his glasses, and started back along the path. Edmund stepped around the trailing wire and followed.

A team of ragged fishermen and women were hauling a boat onto the jetty as they approached, rents ripped into its aluminum sides and part of its canopy torn off. One man sat on the pier, shaking, trying to untangle a snarl of lines and netting. No haul.

Edmund tipped his hat at them, wishing he knew how many might go hungry. Eight years he'd lived here – since the eastern seaboard from Boston to Washington DC became the twisted fracture zone of "Big East," since desperate bands of survivors first poured in to shield under the aegis of the Twelfth Hour, which, for a time, he'd led – and he still couldn't place any names or faces in his own neighborhood.

"Hard sailing?" he tried.

"Some," one replied, a taciturn man who looked to be prying a hook out of one arm.

Istvan squinted at the damaged boat. "Did you run afoul of a kraken, then?"

No response. The fishermen exchanged weary glances.

"Well," Edmund said, "if you need anything, let me know."

"Edmund, there are krakens here? You never told me there were krakens here."

"Come on, Istvan."

The beach wasn't deserted, but it soon became that way. A pair of children that had been throwing rocks in the water now hid behind a carved stone head that had appeared without explanation when the war began, whispering about the wizard that was actually Mr Templeton from down the road, the strange man who lived alone, who sometimes had fits and didn't come out.

That's the Hour Thief. The Hour Thief and his ghost.

No one had said he had grey in his hair.

"I'm thirty-five," Edmund told the stone head as they passed it.

"I've told you it looks fine," said Istvan.

Edmund dropped his hand from the grey streak shot through the jet-black he'd maintained for seventy years.

"Rakish, even," Istvan continued.

Sand shifted beneath Edmund's tread, footprints for the tide to wash away. Nothing to think about now. He coughed. "What's this new site you've found?"

Istvan bent to pick up a stone, hefting it distractedly. "Ah… you remember that ossuary cathedral I showed you?"

"We're not going back to the cathedral."

"No, no, of course not. But, yesterday, while I was making certain that nothing more had escaped from it, I found a facility that I seem to have overlooked. It's below a sort of overhang of other buildings – not easily visible from the air." He hurled the stone at the water; it passed through his hand instead and clattered down onto the beach beside him. He sighed. "Oh, I used to be so good at that."

Edmund picked up a stone of his own. "What kind of facility?"

"I was hoping we could investigate."

Right.

He angled the stone across the waves. It skipped twice, three times, and then a tentacle shot out of the water and slapped it away. He ducked; it struck the bluffs behind him like a gunshot.

"Krakens," Istvan said meditatively.

Edmund called down the beach at round faces and wide eyes, peeping out from behind the driftwood. "Do your parents know you're out here?"

They fled.

Istvan was still staring out at the water. "Do you suppose…"

Edmund gripped his pocket watch, the thought of mounting an expedition below the waves to take on tentacled horrors was nothing he wanted to consider. Never again. "I wouldn't recommend it."

"The new site is quite dry," Istvan said, casting him a worried glance.

"That's fine."

"What I saw of it, anyhow. I didn't go very far inside – I was due back at Providence, and, well…" He looked away, dragging the toe of his shoe through sand that didn't respond to his presence. "I thought you might want to come along. You've been so locked up, worrying over those lists all day, not talking to anyone, not going out except at night, like a wraith, and…"

Edmund picked up another stone. Grey, with streaks of white. Six months of the same assignment, starting everything over from scratch. He was the Hour Thief. He was the Twelfth Hour's most visible asset, most famous member: the oldest fixture of a young wizards' cabal, compared more than once to the fine china or the family dog, an elder statesman on indefinite probation for a crime no one else remembered. As far as any of the others were concerned, he had simply always been there.

There was a reason for that.

Lead the founding of another Twelfth Hour branch, the Magister had said. Keep an eye on Barrio Libertad, she'd said. You were Magister during the Wizard War, Mr Templeton, and you survived that well enough. How hard can this be?

Sometimes he still woke up shaking. Or worse.

He hadn't asked to be elected.

He'd never asked.

He threw the stone at the water. It didn't skip.

"Edmund?" asked Istvan.

"Let's go have a look at the place," Edmund replied. He pulled out his pocket watch and flipped it open, focusing on its weathered face instead of the ripples on the waves. Past noon. "Might as well. Sooner rather than later. Near that cathedral, you said?"

Istvan nodded. "Not walking distance, but I can show you."

"All right. I'll meet you there."

The specter hesitated. "Pardon?"

Edmund fixed the familiar room in his mind: upright radio, well-stocked bookshelves, green couches he'd never bothered to replace. Ineffable calculations bubbled in the back of his brain, just beyond conscious thought. Safer that way. "I have to feed the cat."

He snapped the watch closed–

– and vanished.

•••

Istvan watched golden glimmers fade, outlines that sputtered out where Edmund had been, and kicked at sand that flew only begrudgingly. Very well. If the wizard didn't arrive when and where he was expected, Istvan knew where to find him.

At least he'd agreed to the walk. Come outside, a bit, like a normal person, instead of skulking about at night, doing what he did. It was a start.

There would be no backslide, not if Istvan had any word in it. Once was enough. Once, years past, lost and drowning in the depths of those wine-rich fears...

Istvan sighed. He looked across the water, where krakens dwelled, and then up at the gulls, wheeling. A fine walk, while it lasted.

He wished it had been longer. He wished he didn't wish that.

He jogged four steps, ran two, and leapt at the water, pinions scattering bloody droplets from their tips. Poison streamed behind, barbed wire looping in glittering contrails. One shoe struck the waves. Nothing grabbed for him. Disappointing.

He skimmed the surface a moment longer, water rippling red below him, then tilted and shot upwards. The seagulls scattered. One wingbeat and he was level with the pagoda on the hill. Another and he circled it, peering through paper windows at a haze of color and motion beyond. A third and he rose above it, New Haven rendered down into features on a map, Edmund's house at the end of its road and the mountainous edifice of the Twelfth Hour – once a modest library, now mingled with the lines and stonework of a Hindu temple – overlooking fields scratched in and around Yale and its gargoyles.

To the west billowed the smoke and steam of the

Generator district. To the south a pine forest grew below a great crystal dome. To the east stretched the sea… and on the horizon, the Black Building, a mirrored spire three miles high. Its auroras crackled even in the daytime, now.

City, all of it. City where there hadn't been any before. City that shouldn't have existed, parts of it fallen to rubble or rent by enormous claws, beautiful in its very state of dissolution, its struggles, its terrors. Mixed-vintage misery was the flavor of the day: not at all unpleasant, darkened by dread, textured by small annoyances and flashes of hate or pain. Even the abandoned stretches and the wastes were grand, in their own way.

Istvan was the only one who ever saw it from this high, this far. He'd never met another flyer who wasn't trying to fight him. He hadn't seen any aircraft in years.

Oh, if only Edmund could fly as well…

Istvan shook the thought away. He rolled to place the Black Building on his right and sped northwards, wind sheeting through his ears. The Twelfth Hour's domain receded, replaced by the tenuous alliance of sheltered enclaves it oversaw. Fourth and Black. Oxus Station. The Magnolia Group and their crashed spacecraft. The Wizard War memorial, the concrete corpse of the felled beast stretching across twelve city blocks.

The ossuary cathedral lay eighty or so miles to the north. Istvan reached it in five minutes.

Edmund was there already.

Istvan alighted beside him. The man was staring at the building's stained-glass windows, their elaborate mosaics glorifying an invisible God of sun and storm, Mary the mother of sacrifice, penitent saints Istvan didn't recognize. Feathered serpents framed each panel.

"The workmanship is fine, though, isn't it?" Istvan tried.

"It wouldn't have felt right," Edmund replied. He turned, the sun overhead and the brim of his hat casting part of his lean face into shadow. His goatee and sideburns seemed neater now; his smile readier, faint but pleasant. Beneath it churned the truth, the bittersweet roil of familiar fears: fear of the task at hand, fear of past failures, fear of darker things he hadn't yet and would likely never escape.

He was, on the whole, unfairly handsome.

"Ah," Istvan said. "Shall we be off?"

A nod. "I'll follow you. Let me get on the roof."

Another snap of that pocket watch. In a moment he was gone, and a small dark figure stood on the cathedral roof, stumbling a bit on loose tiles before it straightened, cape snapping in the winds.

Istvan took to the air again, fleshless and awful. Try as he might, he couldn't fly any other way: he'd never had wings in life.

He led Edmund across a district badly rent by the recent earthquakes, abandoned like the other wastelands, great fissures plunging into the earth along with parts of roadway, tenements, overgrown parks. No dramatic maneuvering, this close to the ground. Not now. Edmund followed in flickers: atop a clock tower and then standing on a market roof and then leaping a gap between alleys, a still portrait stepping from panel to panel, just near enough to keep Istvan in sight.

It wasn't the power that had given the man his name, but sometimes Istvan wished it were. It asked so much less of him. So much less of those around him. Oh, it would take ages for him to make up the shortfall, and of the means to go about it, well… the less thought about that, the easier it was.

No better, but easier.

At least Edmund didn't kill people.

Istvan folded his wings and dropped, landing with a billow of chlorine and the booming memory of distant artillery fire. The worst faded with the feathers; only the wire remained, twisting in place of a shadow. He peered out over the edge of a stucco balcony, vines spilling down its sides in a verdant cascade.

A tiny courtyard opened below. In the center, a shaft: spiraling stairs, electric lights that guttered, walls lined with steel and glass. The buildings around it leaned inward, as though drawn towards it.

"Well?" said Edmund, appearing beside him.

Istvan nodded. "Yes, down there. Look."

Edmund glanced over the edge. "Ah. I can see how you'd miss it at first." He tugged his cape over a protruding vine. "You said you've gone inside?"

"Partway."

"Hm," said Edmund.

"I thought you might like to come along," Istvan blurted. "And I, ah… I didn't want to go any further alone. It seemed abandoned, but what if…"

Edmund waited.

Istvan rubbed at his wrists, where the chains had been. Twenty years bound. He hadn't even been able to leave the Twelfth Hour basement until the Wizard War, eight years ago. He'd been a prisoner. A trophy. They had locked him to a pillar in the Demon's Chamber, forced to his knees, barely able to move. No one had come to visit him but Edmund.

Even after, when Istvan was given more leeway,

when he had all of the Twelfth Hour's claimed territory to patrol... he had worked in the infirmary, and gone out only rarely, either to respond to disasters or to accompany Edmund. He was what he was. He was too dangerous. The wizards had seen what he'd done when they told him to fight, even if he himself couldn't remember anything but a euphoric blur, and he couldn't blame them at all, because they were right.

For twenty years he'd had his orders. Disobeying them meant agony.

"There's nothing stopping me, you know," he finally said. He realized what he was doing and crossed his arms on the balcony instead.

"You'd stop you," Edmund said.

"I haven't," Istvan told him. "Not before. You know that."

"I'm still here."

Istvan punched him in the shoulder, which had roughly the same effect as a blow from a housefly. "That doesn't count."

Edmund stood there. He rubbed his shoulder.

Then Istvan's rational self caught up to what he'd done. "Oh," he said. He coughed to stifle an idiotic chuckle. He folded his arms on the balcony again, looking down at the well.

"Are you all right?"

Istvan took off his glasses. "Oh, you oughtn't ask that of me." The lenses weren't dirty – they didn't, strictly speaking, exist, save in memory – but he wiped at them anyway. "'I'm still here.' Of course you are. Of course." He put his glasses back on. "Edmund, you're a terrific bloody cheater and I shouldn't be glad of that."

The wizard stared at him, confusion dueling self-hatred battened down by denial. "Right," he said. He flipped open his pocket watch. "Let's see about that facility."

A snap. They stood four stories below at the edge of the well of glass.

"You could have said something," said Istvan, reorienting himself. The steel railing spiraled down beside him. He trailed a hand over it. It was cold, hidden down here in the shade.

"Sorry," said Edmund. He took a step down the stairs, paused as though testing his weight, and then took another. "There's still power," he commented.

Istvan tried to focus. Electricity, yes, even though there hadn't seemed to be anyone down there before, and he couldn't make anyone out now. Anyone save Edmund.

Oh, he shouldn't have done that. Shouldn't have said that.

Cheater, indeed. Don't bloody remind him.

Shouldn't have touched him.

"I thought that was interesting," Istvan finally said. "That the power still works."

"Hm," said Edmund. He started further down the stairwell.

Istvan checked again: still no hint of any stray suffering, any human emotion he could taste. All bland and abandoned. That didn't rule out other beasts, of course, but monsters were usually easier to manage.

Edmund's apprehension suggested he didn't share that opinion.

"It isn't unheard of," Istvan said, though he wasn't quite sure that it wasn't.

"Eight years running through these kinds of

earthquakes with no maintenance?"

"Perhaps the Germans built it."

"Ha," said Edmund. His top hat vanished from sight.

Istvan rubbed at his wrists, half expecting the burn of chains that weren't there. Oh, he hated such tight quarters. One never knew what might jump out. Likely innocent, too, and only frightened.

"Coming?" called Edmund.

"Yes. Yes, of course."

Istvan flitted down the stairwell, taking the steps two and three at a time. The harsh light flickered, spiraling in glowing tubes around and around. Sometimes they ran behind the glass rather than on the outside.

Edmund stood before a steel hatch. A green light blinked above a windowed slot in it, coated in a dull patina of smoke. The labeling was no language Istvan had ever seen, hooks and horns and little squares, tiny lines pressed into the metal.

"Tocharian," said Edmund.

"Can you read–"

"No." The wizard tugged at the wheel. "And I don't think it's coming open, either."

Istvan inspected it. Someone had welded the seam between wheel and door together. "Oh." He hooked a thumb in his belt, somewhat at a loss. "I... didn't see that."

"You wouldn't." Edmund squinted through the window slot. "I think I can manage, but if this pans out we'll have to fix that."

He retrieved his pocket watch and vanished in a golden blur.

Istvan sighed. He hadn't looked. It hadn't mattered. He couldn't move anything that heavy himself, anyhow.

He stepped through the door, steel dragging through his ribs, the chill of the metal rather like stepping through a waterfall while the waterfall simultaneously stepped through him.

He almost ran into Edmund. The wizard had stopped cold on the walkway beyond, staring out at cube after cube of glass-walled hydroponics gardens, lit by great coiling arcs of those same strange tubes. Each cube could have housed a squadron of aircraft. Ventilation hummed.

"Power still works," Edmund said, weakly.

Istvan straightened his uniform, though nothing was out of place. "I did fly across it, some," he admitted. "I suppose it self-maintains somehow, or..."

Wait.

Wait, there was someone here – something–

Footsteps fell on the walkway.

Istvan whirled. He should have known it earlier – he always knew, he couldn't miss even the most banal of suffering, the smallest annoyance, the merest hint of the human condition–

– except for in one circumstance.

The woman that climbed the stairs to meet them, Oriental, clad in a belted robe of blue and silvery earrings, was a hall of mirrors. Whoever she might have been, whatever self lay beneath, now reflected her surroundings – reflected the fears and uncertainties of others, camouflaged her, hid her within the background flavor of the city above them.

It was as though she were multiple people. A city, herself.

"Afternoon," she said, in perfectly understandable English.

Edmund raised a hand to tip his hat. Istvan grabbed his wrist.

The wizard glanced back at him. "What?"

Istvan backed away, trying to look everywhere at once. It was so hard to detect them. It was like searching through static.

"Istvan, what is it?"

The woman smiled at them.

Edmund looked to her, to Istvan, then back to her. "Oh, hell," he said.

CHAPTER TWO

"You don't have to talk like that," said the woman. "Have you come for answers?"

Edmund stepped back as she walked towards him, dull thuds and booms signifying Istvan's increasing agitation. "No, thank you," he told her. "We seem to have taken a wrong turn. My apologies."

He elbowed Istvan's general vicinity.

"What?" the specter hissed. He'd gone to bone already, somehow managing to look frantic with no real expression.

Edmund indicated the woman. "We don't know if there's more of them."

"There's always more of them!"

"We can't leave her here like this, you know that."

The woman drew closer. The fabric of her robe, its bottom edge tattered, rushed against the walkway railing. Her earrings were safety pins, still bloody. "Like what?" she asked. "Knowing? I know what you kept hidden. You wizards. I know it all, now. Our Lady of Life had a plan for us, and you were too jealous to see it." She reached for Edmund. <Let me show you,> she said, Old Persian rolling from her tongue like a native. <Let me show you the truth of the sun.>

Istvan leapt between them and jammed bony phalanges through her chest.

She gasped. Phantom blood trickled from the wound. Flickerings of uniform buttons, the edges of spectacles, a field cap that wasn't hers... memories flitted across her form, as Istvan grew less distinct, more cloudy–

–and then she dropped.

Edmund caught her before her head hit the walkway. Worth a little time to prevent a concussion. Less than a second, was all. He lowered her down, gently.

Shattered. She was Shattered.

The Wizard War had birthed many horrors, but foremost among them was the Susurration: a horror from another plane of existence that could strip people of their pasts, their personalities, replace years of their lives with happy falsehoods, use them as puppets while they dreamed. The Twelfth Hour had helped put a stop to it, but finding and treating everyone it had ruined was another matter.

They were Shattered, and they wandered Big East, their sense of self destroyed, resorting to all manner of disjointed efforts to recover what they had lost. Those who had known them suddenly didn't. Those who had trusted them found that their friends, their family members, the ones they depended on for survival, could be trusted no longer. Worse, they seemed to remember things that they shouldn't: snippets of memory culled from thousands upon thousands of other victims.

The first of those – the reason the Susurration had been brought to this world at all, in the waning days of the war – was Shokat Anoushak. The Immortal. The most powerful wizard the world had ever known. She had been ancient when Rome ascended... and now, after her death, three thousand sanity-blasting years burned in innocent minds across Big East like fever dreams: the Susurration's last act of defiance before its imprisonment.

There had always been cults dedicated to her. Now they were spreading like plague.

"Bloody Susurration," Istvan said. He tottered backwards to hold onto the railing. "If I'd known it wouldn't make any difference, sealing the monster up like that, why I never would have—"

"It made a difference," Edmund replied, partly to himself. He found himself running a hand through the grey in his hair again and transferred that motion to adjusting his hat. "And you're right, there can't have been just the one."

Istvan scrubbed at his uniform sleeves, as though trying to remove stains. "Oh, Edmund, I hate it. You know I hate it."

"I know. But if you could do another flyover, just to see—"

The walkway trembled.

"Never mind," said Edmund.

A steel mantis scythe ripped through the railings. Helicopter blades tore through one of the light tubes, which blew like a firecracker. Edmund got an arm around the fallen woman, hitched her into an awkward carry, and managed to half-throw, half-fall away with her just as the walkway came apart below him with a grating metallic scream, serpentine jaws taking its place.

Just a moment. Just a moment.

Not a lot of those left to spare.

He hit the next level down back-first. Wheezed. Checked to make sure the woman was still breathing – she was – and rolled to his feet, trying to shield her from falling debris. The creature lunged over him, snapping at Istvan. Glyphs burned green along its sides. Formless horrors gusted inside its black windows. Oil drooled from its jaws.

A survivor from the Wizard War. A machine in form only, designed with such a familiar shell only to sow terror. One of Shokat Anoushak's mockeries.

It looked... patched. Dented. Like something rescued from a junkyard, like it had been revived from a dead husk...

Istvan darted deeper into the greenhouse complex. The mockery clawed its way after him, the scythes that replaced its skids shattering the glass walls in glittering cascades. Bits of palm fronds, bark, and shredded banana spattered in every direction.

Edmund dodged the worst of it – resisting the urge to dodge all of it, spend just a little time to emerge unscathed – and dashed further along the walkway. "Hey!" he called, hoping the thing could hear him. "You wouldn't happen to have a few moments for little old me, would you?"

The mockery screamed and wheeled.

Edmund retrieved his pocket watch, breathing hard. "That so? That much?"

Another light tube blew like a firecracker. Oil spattered across the walkway. He leapt over it. "The rest of your life? All to chase me?"

The thing launched itself at him.

A skeletal horror in a bloodstained First World War uniform dropped on it, the blade of a trench knife flashing, ripping through one of the thing's spotlight eyes. Vulture's wings beat at the air with a sound like distant artillery. "Get the woman out," shouted Istvan,

"Something's going to bloody fall on her!"

Edmund ducked a claw, holding onto his top hat, cape snapping in the roar from the blades. It wasn't working. He'd known it wouldn't. The mockery was a construct, not a living thing. It didn't understand him. It didn't truly have time to spend, and it wasn't self-aware enough to have any potential to refuse.

He was wasting time that wasn't his. Time he'd stolen to replace time he didn't have. Time he'd given up for a noble cause that no one in good conscience could regret.

He was thirty-five. He'd been thirty-five for seventy years.

He wanted to yell in frustration. Maybe he did.

"Edmund!"

Get the woman out. Should have done that first.

Couldn't afford to be this desperate.

Edmund got his pocket watch open. It was brass, with an etched hourglass on the front that had almost worn off again. He ran through an offering of cartographical calculations based on a planetary model proven false centuries ago, fixing himself as the logical center of the universe: all other things radiated from his location.

He snapped the watch shut, teleporting past the blades. The woman lay nearby and he crouched next to her. "Istvan, the mockery looks secondhand," he shouted. "Try to disable it, if you can. I'll be back!"

The ghost sputtered. "Disable it? How in God's name am I supposed to do that?"

"You're a doctor, Istvan, you figure it out!"

"It's a helicopter!"

"Improvise!"

Istvan did something. The mockery roared. Another glass wall exploded, flinging a cornucopia of tree branches, severed water pipes, mulched petals, and pleasant floral scents into the air, the mockery whirling in its midst like a spinning top with teeth, Istvan clinging to one of its clawed skids.

He'd be fine.

Edmund pictured the other side of the entrance hatch, estimated the woman's weight, with apologies, and sped through the required notation. A snap of the watch–

–and he propped her against a glassy wall, the sound of the fight beyond muffled through steel.

"Sorry," he told her. He wiped at his forehead and found blood. He sighed. "You're in for a hell of a shock when you wake up."

No response. She was breathing easily enough but didn't look to be regaining consciousness soon, no doubt intentional on Istvan's part. Recovery, for the Shattered, was a long, slow, painful road... and the Twelfth Hour didn't have the space or expertise for it. Edmund could find them, but couldn't do anything to help them.

Only Barrio Libertad could do that.

He'd have to take her there when this was over. Turn her in. Do his moral duty. Pretend that the "neighborhood-fortress" wasn't his least favorite place that wasn't underwater or made of bone.

Of course Barrio Libertad would get itself involved somehow. It didn't matter what he did: they were always there, waiting, trying to "help."

As if they could help him.

He stood. "Right," he muttered. "Stay put."

The Shattered woman stayed.

He went. The greenhouse he returned to was a sap-spattered shambles, a tale of wild trajectories and explosive munitions smashed into the sides of cubes four and five rows out. Sparks sputtered from broken light tubes. Sprinklers hissed over the metallic shrieks of the mockery and Istvan's own accompaniment of ghostly bombardment, thuds and booms that always sounded as though they came from the far horizon. A burning pungency to the air suggested that at some point the battle had mowed down a field of onions.

Edmund picked his way down from the walkway, more grateful than usual for the seals on his goggles. Glass crunched beneath his boots, glistening and uneven and slick with water and oil. He could barely see, save for the reflections.

Just one mockery, to do all that.

How had the cult revived it? Who had they killed? There were more of the things all over Big East, wrecked and dead. If word got out that they could be rebuilt – not revived, the things weren't really alive in the first place – everyone was in for a world of trouble.

He'd known asking it for time wouldn't work. It didn't have time to take. Asking for its whole life was a fool's errand, impossible and pointless.

He shouldn't have done it. Even in frustration, even knowing that it wouldn't matter, he still shouldn't have done it. Only a few innocent words to rip away an entire lifetime. As simple as a marriage proposal. As easy as he was willing to make it. One con, and he'd be set for the next sixty years.

Edmund swallowed. That was how it started. That was the slope.

Shouldn't have done it.

He edged into a stand of shredded palm trees, squinting at the flash and whirl of headlights in the darkness, and he thought of the fishermen on their boat. What they wouldn't have given to secure a place like this intact.

A floating sphere darted past him, disappearing into the foliage. He waited a moment, but it didn't come back. Another mockery?

He moved forward again, stepping from one pool of light to the next. Some of the glowing tubes remained, spun out at right angles to the battle's passage. The floor shook below him. The smell of chlorine joined the onion. Water ran from broken pipes, an oily river to navigate towards cornstalks that shredded and flew. Helicopter blades roared.

"Istvan," he called.

"Wait!" came the response, "I haven't–"

A spark of red. A whistling, the rustle of feathers, the serrated tip of what he knew all too well wasn't an arrow–

Edmund couldn't dodge it.

He reached for it, instead – just enough time, taken from the meager supply he'd stolen – fingers brushing the obsidian point, barely touching–

He teleported behind the mockery. The missile came with him, still set on its course.

He left it there.

He was far enough away by the time the cube exploded into a searing inferno that it didn't deafen him too much, and wet enough that his cape only smoked a little.

Very wet.

Something brushed against his cheek. He yelped and scrambled away, thrashing at whatever it was with one free hand. No, no. Not this again. Not this.

Underwater. Underwater. Couldn't breathe.

He clawed his way to shore, half-ran up it, tripped on a fallen piece of walkway, and landed hard on his side before he realized what had happened.

Fish pond. He'd landed in a fish pond.

A skid-claw whirled through the air and embedded itself into a tangle of tubing beside him, scorched and twitching. A headlight bounced into the pond. Bits of arcane etching sputtered out around him, their energies broken and dissipating.

He let out a breath and shook out his goggles.

"You could have bloody warned me," said a sour voice behind him.

Edmund rubbed at his temples, wishing the ringing would stop. "Sorry."

Istvan crouched beside him, uniform charred, bones blackened, wings stripped bare of feathers and disintegrating into ash as they folded. Smoke curled from him, wisps of his substance not yet resettled. "Sorry, indeed," he muttered. He held out a hand and stared at it as ghostly flesh re-coalesced over bare phalanges, burn scarring running into his sleeve. "I know what you were bloody thinking. Oh, it's just Istvan, he'll be fine."

"You are fine."

"It still hurts, you know!"

Edmund sighed. "I said I was sorry."

"I thought you wanted the mockery alive, anyhow. That's what you told me, before you hared off. Now look at it." The specter traced a hand across the scarred half of his face, still burnt disconcertingly down to bone. "A wonderful maneuver, though," he added. "Have I ever seen you do that before?"

Edmund shrugged.

"You caught it, didn't you? The missile?"

"Not exactly."

Istvan chuckled, looking away at the still-burning

corn stalks behind them. "Very good."

Edmund wrung water out of his cape.

Istvan sat, drawing his hands around one knee. He was close enough for the cold to be noticeable but not so close to be chilling; a fine balance he didn't always meet. "I suppose we ought to be worried," he said after a moment.

"Probably."

"Another site overrun, mockeries in the ranks, likely dozens of other cultists about." He sighed, casting a nervous glance beyond the broken glass. "I suppose I ought to go search for them."

Edmund looked around for his hat and found it floating in the pond. He picked up a length of fallen railing and prodded at it. "If you like."

Istvan stood. "I could get that for you."

"I've got it."

The specter peered at him, worrying at his wedding ring. "Edmund, you do realize that you're bleeding."

Edmund grimaced. His hat bobbed just beyond reach. "I know."

"Ah." A pause. "Ah, mind if I…?"

"I'm fine. It's just a few cuts, Istvan." The tip of the railing caught his hat brim and sent it spinning further away. He cursed under his breath.

"Edmund."

"Fine. All right." Edmund drew the railing back and tossed it down on the artificial bank, near the still-twitching skid. "I didn't have time to get out of the way," he added before he could stop himself.

No time. No time for anything but existing. Only one way to get it back…

He closed his eyes as Istvan gripped his shoulder, the

bitter chill a welcome distraction from the blind and fluttering panic that fought to claw its way up his throat. Not now. That wouldn't help anything. It never did.

The sting of the cuts on his face and forehead eased and then faded.

So did the terrors.

The chill receded, phantom pressure released, and when he opened his eyes again a skeletal terror alighted before him, holding out his somewhat sodden top hat.

Edmund took it. "Thanks."

"Of course," said Istvan.

The specter seemed chipper than the situation merited, but that was typical: he was what he was, and at least he'd put his penchant for feeding on pain and suffering to good use. Despite it all he still thought of himself as a surgeon first.

Important, how a ghost thought of himself.

"Shall I search, then?" Istvan asked.

Edmund shook out his top hat, moved to put it on... and paused. Something was moving beyond the glass.

"I don't think that will be necessary," he said.

A procession filed out across the blasted garden. At least two dozen men and women. They moved in eerie synchrony, just short of lockstep, and fanned out in silence, avoiding still-burning fires. One stopped short of the gutted helicopter hulk, shaking his head as though mourning a murder.

Edmund put on his top hat.

Shattered.

"We can't leave them here," he said, half to himself.

Istvan was already recoiling. "That's easy for you to say, now, isn't it? God knows what else they've pieced together, and you've no way to defend yourself, and you know that you'll have to go to Barrio Libertad, now, after all this."

Edmund eyed the nearest. "One step at a time."

"Oh? What will you be doing?"

"Moral support."

"Edmund!"

He tensed. If he could break them up – distract them enough for Istvan to take them down one by one...

The sphere from before came back. It darted across the field, a mechanical construct the size of a soccer ball with bright blue lenses that spun and whirled on its face. It paused in front of the Shattered cultists, who stared at it in naked confusion.

"Wait for assistance, please," it said. It spoke with a heavy Spanish accent, stuttered, shot through with static.

"What?" said Edmund.

The sphere skipped backwards. There was a clanging, a rushing and roar like a train passing–

–and then five people in riot gear folded out of the air before it. In the lead charged a figure of gold and scarlet.

Edmund wished he felt surprised.

Great. Just great.

An armored fist drove into one of the Shattered with a crack and flash; the man jerked and staggered, muscles seizing, and then fell.

"This was ours!" Istvan shouted the first thing that came to mind. "We bloody got here first!"

Grace Wu, so-called "state hero" of Barrio Libertad, whirled about and knocked a second cultist off his feet. She was built like a boxer, clad in thick-soled boots, loose pants and armored top anchored by a broad belt about her midriff. A thin band of silver encircled her cowled head, eyes just visible behind tinted goggles. Outlandish, it was... a "uniform" like Edmund's hat and cape, one that carried its own name with it, brilliant colors and instant recognition. The product of a culture Istvan still struggled to understand.

Sparks sizzled on impact.

"Yeah?" she called. "We noticed!"

"You beat us once," shouted one cultist, "but we will never falter! We are free! Our Lady will reward us, and we–"

Grace hit him in the spine. He toppled.

Her cohorts dashed after her, wielding batons that stunned. Istvan hung back, wincing at each strike, savoring the pain he knew he oughtn't, barely able to follow the dizzying multiplicity of each foe. Even their hurts were strange, split and muted. They were like human shapes mimicked by a school of fish, sides flashing almost solid, darting in a great whirl and becoming something else each moment.

He couldn't take part. He would hurt someone. One of them had been difficult enough. All he had was his knife, and...

"Bring your horsemen and your prophet," shouted another. "I am eternal! I will–"

Grace hit her, too, then spun, boots skidding through spilled water. "What's the matter, Doc?" she called, her distinctive New York accent distorting vowels in ways that Edmund had never tried to correct. "They got you spooked, or did you grow a conscience?"

Istvan bristled. "I never–!"

"Lay off," said Edmund, suddenly present again though Istvan didn't remember him leaving, evading reaching hands with cat-like ease, eerily fluid. A sign of yet more time spent that he couldn't afford. Not after...

Oh, Edmund couldn't be doing that.

Oh, it was wonderful when he did.

Istvan steeled himself – don't think about that, don't dwell on dust clinging to wet fabric, the way the wizard danced along a precipice of dread worn smooth – and turned on the nearest cultist.

"Abomination," the man hissed.

Istvan's fingers bit into his chest. The scrape of bone and the hot rush of living blood were both familiar sensations; he focused on them, the thud-thud of a racing heart, impulses firing along straining nerves. Solid. Real.

As he wasn't. As he hadn't been, since–

Istvan faltered. His vision doubled. Ghost-sheen flickered across the man's face, and Istvan saw his own in return, colorless, left side a twisted ruin, eyes wild. He sucked in a breath and his chest expanded, an unpleasant ballooning he barely remembered.

Muscle twisted in his back – or was it his own fingers, through them, a caress to reach bone? – and then a twinge of pain shot up his spine. He gasped. Words bubbled in his throat, a language he didn't know on a tongue that fluttered, and a hate that wasn't his curdled in his stomach.

How dare he.

How dare–

He was too close. He shouldn't have – oh, he couldn't – there were the right nerves, along the neck, slick and taut, and the sweet agony...

He collapsed.

No, the other man collapsed. Istvan wasn't him. Istvan was still standing, shaking, drawing too-quick breaths he couldn't feel, not anymore, and he stumbled backwards to put more distance between himself and flesh.

Oh, he hated possession. Even briefly. Even in part. Blood ran much hotter than anyone knew, and it was obscene to seek it where it dwelled without the assurance that it was necessary – he was a surgeon, this would help, this would save a life.

It thundered with each heartbeat, and he hated it.

Hated it.

"All right?" asked one of the Barrio Libertad contingent, tone a mixture of curiosity and wariness. The helmet tilted.

Istvan rubbed imaginary filth from his sleeves, his hands. He straightened his bandolier. He reflected sourly that the man asking wasn't Edmund. "Perfectly."

He took his bearings. All of the other Shattered were already dispatched, some still jerking convulsively and others battered into silence. The corn still burned. Smoke choked the light tubes, what of them remained intact. Oil spattered the rows of filters and hanging mosses over the pond. Grace Wu bounced in place, shaking out her gauntleted arms. The sphere from earlier hovered near her.

Edmund was standing next to Grace.

"This is just the pilot program," she was saying. She patted the device's round casing. "If we deploy a couple hundred of these, you could free up everything you guys have sunk into your border guard and focus on–"

"You'll have to run that by Magister Hahn," Edmund replied. He wasn't looking at her; he crouched over one of the fallen cultists, checking for breathing.

She tightened one of the straps on her armor. "What are you doing all the way out here, anyway? You're not looking for some kind of secret base, are you?"

"Don't be ridiculous."

"Have you tried finding a nice, big cave, yet? Maybe with a waterfall?"

Istvan stepped over, wishing the twist and tangle of the wire at his feet would stop betraying his agitation. The man who had spoken to him retreated a step; the other three a few more. "Edmund, perhaps you ought to retrieve the woman from earlier. The one you moved away?"

The wizard glanced up. "Right. Right, I should do that."

He vanished in a blur of gold.

Grace crossed her arms. "So. Doc."

"We could have managed," Istvan said stiffly.

"Uh-huh. How's the battlefield treatment going?"

Istvan thought of the ruin surrounding Barrio Libertad, the service he'd taken upon himself to make it right. Imprisoning the Susurration hadn't been a clean exercise. "You know very well how it's going, Miss Wu. Slowly." He crossed his arms. "I imagine you'll be claiming this area, then, too?"

She waved at the smoke billowing out from the corn as some arcane part of the helicopter popped and exploded. "We can fix it. You can't."

Istvan stared down at broken glass, his reflection misted and distorted. Another reminder. "Of course."

She sighed. "Look, the offer still stands."

"Thank you," said Edmund, "but that won't be necessary." He deposited the woman from earlier near the others, laying her down carefully. The watch went back in his pocket. "We'll manage on our own."

"Like you've been doing since Mexico City bit it?"

"We'll manage." He straightened. "Come on, Istvan. It seems we're not needed here."

Grace threw up her arms. "What part of 'we'll reconstruct New Haven' don't you understand? Don't you want working plumbing?"

The wizard smiled tightly, a thin veneer over longing and frustration. "As they say, we can handle our own crap, Grace."

"But–"

"Afternoon."

Istvan followed him around the fish pond. The man was still bleeding, and now likely even shorter on time than before. "That's all?" he asked.

"That's all. They're keeping the place?"

"Likely," said Istvan.

"Then we're leaving. They'll take care of the Shattered folks. Nothing we can do." The wizard walked faster. "You tried."

Istvan glanced back at Grace, who met his gaze. He shook his head. She shrugged in disgust, and turned to her men.

No more. No site. No progress.

Bloody Barrio Libertad. No trouble at all until the Susurration made its move, and now its people were everywhere, flaunting their superior equipment and their expertise in seemingly all things. The Twelfth Hour hadn't thought through the implications of freeing the largest settlement in Big East to pursue its own devices. Now it was as bad as the British.

Worse; the British queen had at least been human.

And Edmund... oh, Istvan had to work with them in one area, at least, but Edmund did his best to avoid them entirely, and Istvan couldn't blame him.

In its own way, it was a sort of relief.

"That's four times this month," said Edmund. He shoved his hands in his pockets. "I can't get away from her."

Istvan reached for his shoulder. "But you've said you've–"

"Don't," said the wizard. He brushed the hand away. "And I know what I said."

"Edmund–"

"It shouldn't be like this, and not finding anywhere is only making it harder. She's right about one thing, Istvan, and it's that we're a long way away from where we should be." He retrieved his pocket watch, snapping it open and then shut and then open again. "This isn't working. I can't be everywhere at once."

Istvan dropped his hand to his side. The same complaint, again and again.

There had been a time when Edmund very nearly could be everywhere at once. When he'd spent years stopping one cult or another from breaking into the public eye. When he'd led armies against Shokat Anoushak at the breaking of the world. When he'd fought the Twelfth Hour's battles all up and down the seaboard, one innocuous request at a time, on top of maintaining their library and running his own habitual patrols by night.

He'd even pursued love on the side, however inadvisable it may have been.

Now…

Well, if the man had decided to be inconsolable, so be it. Istvan would simply have to pry him out of his house to try again another day.

Grace Wu wasn't helping.

Istvan stepped over a divider, skirting the edge of falling mist. Sprinklers. "Will you be going home, then?"

"I'd like to."

"But...?"

Edmund sighed. The mist sheened his skin, droplets clinging to his goatee and sideburns. "Mercedes wants a progress report."

"Ah." Istvan considered. He'd be expected at Barrio Libertad again, soon, as he'd promised, but perhaps the meeting wouldn't take too long. "Shall I come along?"

Edmund shook his head. He reopened his pocket watch, holding it up to light that flickered. "I need to clean up. You have your own project to handle."

"You're certain?"

"The buck's got to stop somewhere, Istvan. I'll manage."

He put the watch away.

Istvan kept pace beside him as he headed for the exit. A delay, perhaps, but not an insurmountable one. At least they would finish one thing today. A walk was better than nothing.

A walk was enough.

CHAPTER THREE

Edmund appeared near the stoplight on the corner. Leaves crackled under his boots, round things, blinking weakly between red and yellow. September after the Wizard War.

The Twelfth Hour lay just across a road cracked and buckled by steel roots.

It had been a library, once. Now it rose like a mountain over Yale, a strange fusion of classical colonnade and Hindu temple, its steps marked with Roman inscriptions and its windows trimmed with inventive statuary. Cracks shot through the stonework. Pieces of fallen mortar lay in a heap beside the stairs. Skeins of cable zigzagged up the walls and trailed from its windows, strung from the Generator district and then, pole by pole, to the rest of New Haven. The wards were only visible if you weren't looking for them.

The door had a window that opened onto a very ordinary looking modern library, with metal shelves. It said "Pull."

Edmund knocked on it. "You know who I am. Let me in, please."

The lettering changed to "Push."

He did. "Thank you."

The library he stepped into was three stories high, tiled in scarlet, its mahogany shelves inlaid with barred patterns of gold and chrome that resembled opened books and splayed pages. The ceiling bore an aggressively geometric design of interlocking shapes, also gold, almost Moorish in execution and lit by round chandeliers. The crescent moons-and-clock emblem of the Twelfth Hour lay set into the floor and repeated itself at the tops of each column. The remodel had been done at the height of the Art Deco craze, and it showed.

The only jarring features were the temple stonework – seamlessly overtaking more and more of the ornamentation towards the back wall, its carvings cracked by earthquakes – and the scavenged furnishings that outnumbered the worn but still perfectly serviceable originals.

The crowds probably violated fire code but no one paid much mind to that, anymore.

"Excuse me," he said to a collection of women from the Magnolia Group poring over some kind of electronic map and taking up most of an entire aisle.

They started, recognizing him – most people did – and shifted to clear the way. They wore jumpsuits. They were all identical.

"Sorry," one of them said.

Edmund tipped his hat at her and continued on his way.

A flock of ravens descended upon him as he started through the shelves, squawking that nothing had been taken but there was that silver thing again, browsing, and they didn't like it.

He peered over his shoulder and there it was, hovering just before Symbolic Astronomy: a disc rimmed with blue lights, slim silvery tentacles sifting through pages with careful delicacy. If only everyone handled books like that.

"It isn't hurting anything," he told the ravens.

They didn't like it.

"Keep an eye on it, then, but leave it alone. It has just as much right as you do."

They still didn't like it, but he was the head librarian and so they acceded. They whirled away in a feathered cloud and settled on one of the chandeliers.

He checked to make sure everything he passed was in place. It seemed to be. The ravens were doing a decent job, with him gone now more often than not. The dangerous books, the real books, were all in the vault, anyway – nothing left to the public eye held anything more powerful than wards, all carefully vetted for display but open to general use. The Twelfth Hour owed its allies that much.

He took a turn at Inexcusable Mathematics and headed towards the Magister's office.

Cultists, she would say. Cultists again, Mr Templeton?

Cultists again. You know, Mercedes, I think we should call this off. It isn't working, and I've already told you I don't think I'm the right man for the job.

He sighed. Not a chance.

And Grace. It always had to be Grace. Shattered cultists, mockeries, and Grace. It was enough to make him miss the days when all he had to do was track down hapless conspiracy theorists in the dead of night and worry idly what the press would do if it discovered that he was the same Edmund Templeton who had been paying taxes for eighty years.

That and… other things. Things that happened when

you were the only member who could be sent on suicide missions more than once.

Had to be careful not to romanticize the past. Or be lost in it.

He came to the Magister's hall and paused at the new roster photographs for 2020, housed in an alcove that hadn't been there the year before. There were more of them, which could only be good. They included, among their members, Istvan. In color.

As requested: flesh tones filled out along with the burn discolorations, eyes a dark brown, black hair faded to steel grey – he'd been forty-four, at the end. His uniform was a jarringly cheerful sky blue with scarlet trim and silver flowers embroidered at the collar. He could have led a parade. He called it "splendid."

It was still a little disconcerting, but Istvan seemed happy with it, so it stayed.

Edmund's only change was the grey streak at his left temple.

He walked quickly past 2015 and the candles that burned there. The roster for 2010 was almost three times larger, and past that the hall continued, an alcove for every five years, his own face repeated again and again, that same fixed smile all the way back to 1955. 1950 lacked the hat. 1940 lacked the sideburns. 1945 was best not mentioned.

At the end he reached a massive oak door, just past 1895 and the Twelfth Hour's five founders. Its wood was dark and pitted; in places scorched. The Magister's office.

He didn't touch it. He tapped at it with the toe of his boot. "Mercedes?"

The door swung open with a malevolent creak.

The office beyond was empty. The desk, claw-footed and smoke-stained and belonging to the original Magister was neat, if not clean, the usual diagrammatic clutter stacked to one side. The collections of bird's wings and dusty brass instruments stayed in their corners, still not sorted. The paper lanterns overhead weren't lit.

Edmund took a careful step over the threshold. His gaze, as always, drifted inexorably to the skull of Magister Jackson, staring at him from one of the bookshelves.

You damn fool Templeton, it seemed to say.

"This is why I hung a sheet over you," he muttered.

He turned his back to it. The window was open. Breezes off the Atlantic fluttered the curtains, though the Twelfth Hour was nowhere near the ocean.

Edmund leaned over the windowsill. Waves crashed below. "Mercedes?" he called.

"Shut the door behind you," came the response. A woman's voice, low and even.

"Is this an invitation?"

"I thought you wouldn't want Magister Jackson staring you down. Shut the door."

He eyed the office door. It seemed to eye him back. "All right."

It took some doing, but he got it closed.

Nursing bruised knuckles, he swung through the window–

–and landed solidly on the upper level of a lighthouse far off the coast.

Magister Mercedes Hahn was waiting for him. She wore a grey suit two sizes too big for her gaunt frame, sleeves rolled up, the emblem of the Twelfth Hour clasped at her throat. She was brown and sharp-faced, probably Indian, though he'd never asked, pockmarked from some past sickness. Pens stuck out of her black hair, done up in a tight bun. One of her fingers was missing.

She barely came up to his collarbone.

"It's just a door, Mr Templeton," she said.

He straightened his hat, grimacing. "We have a history."

"Don't you always."

She turned and started down the spiraling stairs.

He scanned the horizon – he couldn't even see the Black Building, which dominated the horizon anywhere else he usually went – and then followed. He wondered if there were krakens out there, too.

"No luck, I'd imagine," said Mercedes.

"No luck."

"At the rate Barrio Libertad is expanding its influence, Mr Templeton, I'm going to start needing some very good excuses."

He tugged his cape over a loose nail. Barrio Libertad had been an isolated city-state a few short months ago. No one went in, no one came out. Now it was a regional power and everyone knew it, and as far as he knew they still hadn't changed their stance on magic or their plans for what future ought to await the human race, and then there was Grace…

"Shattered cultists," he said.

Mercedes didn't look back. "You've tried that one."

"Wizard War mockeries, under Shattered control."

A pause. "How many?"

"One. That I saw."

"What happened to it?"

He shoved his hands in his pockets. "It blew up."

"Mr Templeton."

"I blew it up. They're armed, Mercedes, it wasn't easy."

She said nothing.

"The facility was a hydroponics farm, still operating, and now it's a total loss. Nothing we can repair. At least a couple dozen Shattered, on top of the mockery. Too many for Istvan to handle."

She lit an oil lantern at the landing. It smelled faintly of fish.

"Grace was there," he added.

Mercedes licked a finger and pinched the match out. Her palm was heavily scarred. "Mr Templeton, I need to see progress on this and I need to see it now."

He found his pocket watch. "I know."

"We have reports of flying machines inspecting neighborhoods, squads appearing out of nowhere, strange devices building themselves overnight. We've found two more artifacts stripped of their powers. One of our best warders has been asked to leave his post, go back where he came from. Some of our allies are getting worried, Mr Templeton, and the rest are thinking of jumping ship. Barrio Libertad is more populous than us, has more resources than us, and espouses a philosophy a lot of people would like to agree with, at least on the surface. On top of that, they're the Susurration's jailers, and don't forget how insistent they've been about tying us to that."

"I haven't."

"We don't have the numbers, Mr Templeton, and I don't have the time. I would think you of all people would appreciate that."

She stalked away.

Edmund didn't know what to say, so he said nothing. He followed her down the last round of stairs, across the last landing, and into the lighthouse-keeper's quarters. She lived there, as far as he knew, and he caught glimpses of the evidence – unwashed dishes, clothes hung up to dry, a well-thumbed collection of horror novels – as Mercedes walked straight through and out the front door.

The rocks outside were razored with barnacles. Mercedes didn't seem to notice.

"I won't see the Twelfth Hour undermined by a machine," she said.

Edmund held onto his hat. "I can't blame you."

"If I had known... but too late for that, and probably just as well." She stared out at the horizon, then adjusted the emblem at her throat. "Mr Templeton, you are the best public relations resource we have. Everyone knows you. Everyone followed you, when it mattered. Once you've established yourself, you'll have no shortage of recruits, I'm sure, and then we might be able to make some headway."

"I understand that," he tried. "It's just a matter of finding somewhere to start. Istvan's been looking, and so have the others, and I do have a list of–"

"Where have you been hunting?" she asked.

He paused. "Excuse me?"

Mercedes brushed a thumb across her stump, looking at him straight on. "Your nightly patrols, Mr Templeton. Where have you been hunting?"

Edmund gripped his pocket watch. He kept his expression neutral, pleasant, unsmiling. Hunting. She could have chosen any other word. "I don't see where that's any of your business."

"I don't see where it isn't. I know how your magic works and I know how lacking you are, even now, after dealing with the Susurration. You're spending more time on trying to restock than on anything else, am I correct?"

"No."

"Mr Templeton–"

"I'm spending more time on living, actually."

She pressed her lips together. Her gaze searched him, probing, condemning, like every Magister before her. He was the Hour Thief; somewhere beyond the chain of command, the Twelfth Hour's only member on indefinite probation. He'd outlasted five Magisters now and each one had seemed more afraid of him than the last.

That was why he wore a cloak. A mask. He stood there and he waited, and he concentrated on not being Edmund Templeton.

The Hour Thief hunted, not him.

"If I gave you permission to take time from certain problematic populations," Mercedes began, "would that–"

"No."

"Mr Templeton, we don't have time for moral quandaries."

"I do. I'm not letting you legitimize it."

She regarded him a moment longer, then turned. She adjusted one of the pens in her hair. "And yet you'll keep on as you've always done."

Edmund realized he was gritting his teeth. He forced himself to relax. Couldn't force a smile. "Mercedes, I came here to report. That's all. Are we finished?"

She dropped her hand back to her side, thumb twisting between her fingers in maimed repetition. "We're finished. I expect you and your team to have a base of operations by the end of the month."

"Thank you, Mercedes."

"You're welcome to show yourself out."

"I will."

He did.

●●●

Barrio Libertad seethed.

Not the original populace, who were suspicious of Istvan, or the refugees, who were afraid of him, but the fortress itself. The plazas seethed. The terraces seethed. Every string of lights, every color of every mural, every wall of every shanty stacked atop yet more shanties made of more walls that also seethed: an inhuman anger that seeped from them like lava from the earth, viscous and choking in its intensity.

It never slowed. Never subsided.

Barrio Libertad was built like a coliseum. Its walls looked to be made of crumbling concrete and corrugated steel, rust concealed by bright red and yellow paint, badly patched and creaking... but those walls were eight hundred feet high. They were surmounted by turrets that wouldn't have been out of place on a battleship. They held enough space and resources for one and a half million people, concealed at least one superweapon, and supported a roof that could seal the fortress off from all outside assault. Part of that roof had remained closed for over a month now, locked in place, lit by floodlights.

Over its edge splayed monstrous claws of steel and serrated glass.

The creature was dead. It was also too heavy to move. The arcs of green lightning across its corpse had mostly ceased. The nightmares from proximity, less so.

Istvan wished Barrio Libertad's "People's Emergency Hospital" hadn't been built so high up, so close to it. Not that he'd had any say in the matter. No one had. The infirmary had built itself.

Barrio Libertad's master, after all, was Barrio Libertad. He called himself Diego Escarra Espinoza, but everyone knew the truth. There was no appreciable difference.

Every surface was under his direct control and every surface seethed with rage.

Istvan tried his best to ignore it.

"You've a terrible lot of scar tissue," he said to a patient trying very hard to not shiver, "but no more lesions that I can find. How is your breathing?"

"Hard," came the wheezed reply.

Istvan pulled his hand out of the man's lung, phantom blood flickering across his fingers. "Now?"

The man clutched at his chest, as though reassuring himself that his flesh was still whole, that a specter poking around in his innards hadn't just happened. He edged away, further up the bed, and Istvan couldn't blame him. He took an experimental breath. "Easier. Maybe."

He was shivering less, now. Thunder rolled outside, and he flinched.

Istvan nodded. "It will get better as time goes by. I don't know that you'll ever recover full function, but–"

"This kind of thing isn't supposed to happen." The words fell from the man in a rush. "Gassed. No one's supposed to be gassed anymore. I can't... I don't..." He coughed: a racking, painful sound that at least was no longer bloody.

Istvan wished it didn't trigger a great deal of nostalgia. "You would be surprised, I'm afraid."

"Leave me alone. I just..." Another cough. The man curled around himself, turning away, his fear a raw sweetness whorled in the warmth of the pain. "Leave me alone."

Istvan looked to his bloodied fingers. They flickered to bone.

He wiped them on his uniform sleeve and departed,

trailing barbed wire. Oh, it was only the long-term patients now. Those who were lost were lost; those whose needs were simple had departed. Each bed he passed, occupied and not, reminded him anew of the old days. How wonderful they had been. How terrible.

The annex boasted a long window, and here he paused. It overlooked a rolling field of wildflowers, mountains in the distance, sunset casting rosy fingers over their peaks.

"Don't lie to me," Istvan sighed.

The rage never changed... but the window did, its edges burnt black, rain spattering fitted glass. Outside, rimmed by a crater wall, stretched a field of muddy trenches, broken trees, and shell-pocked mires: relics of a battle fought over a century ago. Memories made solid. Ruin that couldn't be undone. Here and there flapped shreds of tattered canvas, reminders of the rows of sorry shelters that had been there before.

All changed. His fault.

Istvan crossed his arms on the sill. They were saying now that the battlefield was claiming new victims, that it wasn't static, that sometimes shells tumbled from a clear sky...

"Admiring your handiwork?"

He glanced over his shoulder. Grace Wu stood there, a messenger bag slung over one shoulder. She wore her peculiar uniform, as always: brightly colored plates buckled over that dark undersuit, a curious mix of soldier and show performer. The bag was wet, but no water seemed to have clung to her. No mud, either.

It wasn't right that she could cross such a waste and remain perfectly dry.

Istvan sighed. "What do you want?"

"Just making conversation. Finished my rounds,

thought I'd stop by. Done any embroidery lately?"

He had – he'd even taught a few patients who had nothing better to do – but he wasn't obliged to discuss that with her. He turned from the window. "Miss Wu, I've never known you to 'stop by' unless you had some pressing purpose in mind."

She hitched the bag around, casual to the point of acted intent. "Well, I was thinking about earlier, how we saved the day and all, and I thought to myself: you know, Grace, you're one person who can be in only one place at once, and the Susurration was definitely not like that." She rummaged through the bag, still talking. "It can't just have distributed the Shattered across Big East, can it? What keeps it from having agents in... I don't know–"

She produced a roll of what likely wasn't paper and snapped it open.

"–anywhere else on the planet?"

A map. Icons glowed red on three continents.

Istvan folded his arms to keep from flickering. Overseas. Away from Big East. He wasn't chained; he wasn't restricted; he could go anywhere, now. Anywhere he liked.

And the sorts of places he liked, oh...

"I do hope you aren't asking for my help," he said.

"What, me?"

"Or Edmund's, either."

She rolled the map back up, resentment bubbling into her affect. "You helped with the Susurration once, remember."

Istvan glanced at the window. The waste. The battlefield that shouldn't be. "Yes, and I bloody well know what you think of that."

She crossed her arms as well, articulated plates sliding across one another with faint clicks. She was even more afraid of him now – more than she had ever been – and yet still desperate not to show it. "Maybe it doesn't matter what I think. Maybe there's something out in, I don't know, Tornado Alley that we can't reach fast enough, and–"

"–and you want us to go do it for you?"

"Look, Doc–"

Istvan flared wings that were barely there, wisps of gas and broken feathers. "We have our own assignments, Miss Wu, and we are not retainers of Barrio Libertad. You seem to be doing perfectly well on your own."

She took a step back. She shoved the map back into the bag. It didn't crumple like paper ought. "Oh, come on, you can't still be sore about earlier."

"You 'saved the day,' didn't you?" he retorted. "You don't need us. You certainly don't want us."

She snorted. "You just now realized?"

"I've known long enough."

"Then you know that we need psychiatrists and not surgeons, right? You know that you're scaring people? You know that you're keeping Susurration victims who need help from coming in to get help?" She hitched her bag around. Motors whirred in her gauntlets. "You're sitting around here doing things we can do ourselves, and for what?"

Istvan folded his wings. "I'm volunteering my services," he muttered.

"We don't want you here."

"I don't care! I don't want to be here, either!"

"Then leave!"

"No. Not unless and until Mr Espinoza himself

deems that I ought, and I haven't noticed any signs of displeasure, Miss Wu – not yet."

They both paused. Nothing appeared on the walls. The window stayed as it was. The only sound was the faint creaking of the fortress in usual operation.

"There," said Istvan. "You see?"

Grace shot a reproachful look at the nearest surface. "Diego doesn't have anything to do with this, anyway."

"Oh, he doesn't?"

"Well, it's not like he summoned the Susurration or anything… wait, that was Magister Hahn!"

"Miss Wu–"

"'Hey,' she continued, "'let's summon something that can take over the world, to save the world and then do a bad job of it and let someone else clean it up!' Good job, wizards. Bravo."

Istvan tried to think of something to stay to that. It was, strictly speaking, true. All the same, no one else had come up with anything of use against Shokat Anoushak, and even Edmund had only managed a series of holding actions. The Magister had done what seemed best at the time.

"That's war," he said.

"It's still war, Doc."

"Then you'll have to go to Magister Hahn to request our services. Edmund, at the very least, wants nothing to do with you." Istvan hooked a thumb into his belt. "Was there anything else or ought you be on your way?"

She sighed, her disgust for him an acrid greenness that never seemed to abate no matter what he did. "You jumped awfully quick to 'we,' Doc."

Istvan turned back to the window.

What if we unchained him, Edmund had said.

He'd used Istvan. Deployed him like an artillery piece. Broken what kept him in check, in the name of what was expedient, and now this was the evidence. The Susurration locked away and a field of bloody trenches made real.

Good job, wizards. Bravo.

"We're friends," Istvan said. "Great friends. You know that."

"Uh-huh," said Grace. "Sometimes I worry about that."

Istvan took hold of his bandolier. Barbed wire twisted itself into rusty knots at his feet.

"Look," she continued, "I get what you're trying to do. I really do, all right? But you're not helping here. Not anymore."

"If you want to get rid of me," Istvan replied, "ask your council."

"I'll do that."

"I want to see a written order."

"You'll see one." She turned on her heel. "Later, Doc. Have fun body-snatching cultists."

She departed.

Istvan shuddered. She was more tolerable than she had been, but not by so great a margin. Not for the right reasons, either.

The gall. He was trying to make amends, wasn't he? He had volunteered more hours than any other person here, hadn't he? Every night, through the early morning. At least half of every day. She said that she understood it, but she didn't. She couldn't.

He set a hand against the window pane. Cold, but not so cold as his own touch. The storm outside had broken with a sudden fury that didn't seem out of place, torrents washing loose planks and rusted wire into the earth. Burying them.

He clenched the hand into a fist and drove it through the glass. Nothing shattered. Nothing happened at all.

He snarled something to himself – he wasn't sure what or why – and dove through it. Away from it. Rain sheeted through his wings as he fell, rolled, pulled up again, skimming the earth. Mud spattered in his wake, new trenches opening where they hadn't been before and then collapsing under their own instability. The thunder sounded like something else; something newer and older and better and worse all at once, something he found himself missing when he wasn't paying attention, a roar of killing shock he knew firsthand.

The walls of Barrio Libertad loomed over him, spotlights burning, their tops wreathed in mist. Even from here, he could taste the unnatural rage that boiled from them. Unchanging. Mechanical. Judgmental.

He veered away, and vaulted skyward.

Below him stretched what had been Providence, Rhode Island. The fortress crouched at the former city center. The corpse of a monstrous beast with a crest of broken towers and uprooted bridges jutting along its back lay slumped across the half-closed roof, holes blown through its skeletal body. The ocean lapped at earthen bulwarks, contaminated with storm runoff, shattered piers, and the husks of other monsters hurled away by the same force that had left a crater fifteen miles wide.

Eight years ago. The Wizard War.

Oh, he missed it. The horror. The carnage. The haze that came from massacre, the sheer joy of indulgence without doubt or shame. He hardly remembered what he'd done; another blur in a history of blurs, opening salvoes he couldn't recall and didn't regret until months later. There was nothing like it.

Nothing.

Istvan hit the cloud deck, a shock he welcomed, the flash of lightning changed to shrapnel-choked orange, mists darkened to poison. Only for a moment. Only a memory. The sun was setting, the sky lit up like a firefight across the horizon.

He wondered where Edmund was.

He feared that if he left, seeking other disasters, he would never come back.

Edmund should probably have brought Istvan with him. He knew that. With the Shattered running around, and his badly-depleted time reserves, it would have been the smart thing to do. Even Grace had to admit that.

But he hadn't. He wouldn't. He had managed just fine for decades by himself.

He didn't want Istvan to see.

He didn't want anyone to see.

He smiled, because that was what the Hour Thief did, and he said, "If you and your men will give me some time, I'll take care of it. I've dealt with constructs like that before."

"What, we show you where it is and you'll just take it out?" asked Ten-Ton, leader of the Hammers of Boston. Edmund had made sure to ask for a name, even if it wasn't a real one. Human beings had names.

"That's right."

"No questions asked?"

"Only one," said Edmund. "Are you willing?"

The gang members looked at each other. They weren't actively malicious, Edmund knew that. They were where they were and they did what they did because they knew nothing else. Victims of circumstance. Wrong place, wrong time. One bad decision that led to the next. A whole corrupt system and then the Wizard War to turn everything on its ear, making what was bad even worse.

But they weren't helping things get better, either. They'd done their fair share of evil. They maintained their hold on this bunker complex through intimidation and stolen firepower. As soon as Edmund had arrived and asked around for the local strongmen, he'd heard some stories.

They'd tried to control some things they shouldn't have.

"Yeah," said Ten-Ton. "Yeah. Just get it out of here."

Edmund tipped his hat. "Thank you."

Thank you all.

Thank you for your time.

Shokat Anoushak hadn't done this. She hadn't had to do this. Her immortality was different, and no one save perhaps the Susurration or one of the half-mad carriers of its revenge knew how.

Not that Edmund would ever ask.

He was making things better. He was this far afield because he'd exhausted all his leads closer to home, which meant crime was down. That was good. That meant he was helping. That was better than any alternative.

Ten-Ton called after him as he left the bunker. "Hey, man, you cross us, all right, you'll regret it."

The Hour Thief nodded. "I know."

CHAPTER FOUR

The first thing Edmund did in the morning was check his ledger again. The entry from the night before read "Some Time x8" in the amounts column, with the usual notations on who, where, and any hazards encountered. The running total on the far right added up to nothing he was comfortable with.

He flipped back a week, and then another. Barely holding even.

He'd have to go out again tonight.

He shut the ledger. He slid it away from him. He made sure there was no dust on the desk, anywhere, and that the locked drawers were still locked. The rows of old ledgers on the shelf above it were still in order, still distinctly uninteresting to anyone searching for them, and still intact – even the earliest.

Shokat Anoushak had survived since the days of ancient Greece. Shokat Anoushak had been mad. Pitiless. Uncaring and unyielding, like a storm.

Edmund took a breath. A nightmare was just a nightmare.

He flung the curtain open. Motes sparkled in the September sunlight, a dawn just past eight. It had rained overnight, it seemed, and wet cobbles glowed reflected orange. Masts already bobbed out to sea.

Another day.

Edmund pushed his chair back, poured himself a glass of gin from the bottle at his bedside, and went to get a shirt and pants. About three-quarters of his wardrobe was black. About half of it had been mended at least once. He wasn't as good with a needle as Istvan, maybe, but in the old days taking an opera cape to the cleaners with bullet holes in it would have raised questions.

He pushed aside the jacket with the ripped-up sleeve from the tiger attack. Still needed to figure out what to do with that one.

The glass of gin went with him when he left for the bathroom. The grey in his hair was still there. He'd have to heat more water if he wanted to take a bath and his barrels were running low, which meant another trip upriver. No working plumbing made everything take longer. He'd been there before, growing up during the Great Depression, but he didn't have to like it. Washing his face was immediately doable, at least.

He was drying his hair when the tea kettle whistled.

He spent a few moments to–

–no, he spent the normal amount of time to dress, comb, and brush, and then headed for the kitchen, where Istvan stood staring up at an enormous black cat that hissed at him from atop one of the cabinets.

Edmund set his empty glass on the table. "Beldam, come down from there."

The cat flattened her ears.

"I put the water on," said Istvan. He caught a map that drifted down from the cabinet, one of many papers now scattered across the room. "Were you ever planning to use any of this?"

Edmund glanced over the collection of survey maps, utilities diagrams, attempted census reports, notes from interested parties, and lists of necessary items, potential personnel, and assorted resources unique to various sites. Some of it – not disturbed by cat – lay in neat piles on the kitchen counters. More of it spilled over into the living room, where a scale model of a possible layout for Twelfth Hour North lay in never-reassembled pieces in a box next to the couch. "I have used it."

"To collect more of it?"

"Sometimes." Edmund reached for Beldam. "Come on, cat. I know you hate him, but you don't have to act like this."

She hissed at Istvan again, but allowed herself to be picked up and lowered from her perch.

"There we go."

Istvan set the map on the table, looking critically at the empty glass.

Edmund scratched behind Beldam's ears. "Don't worry about it."

"I would have come earlier," said Istvan.

"I'm fine," Edmund said. "How was your night?"

The specter shifted more papers aside and sat in his usual chair, turning his face to hide the scarring. He wasn't wearing his field cap or his bandolier. "The cat," he sighed, "isn't the only one who wants nothing to do with me."

Beldam squirmed; Edmund set her down. She shot into the living room.

"It isn't personal," Edmund said.

"She's a cat," Istvan replied sourly.

"And you're a doctor. You're still doing good out there, aren't you? How many people have been through that hospital now?"

"More than there ought to have been. I don't know what you thought might happen, Edmund, but that battlefield isn't going away."

Edmund picked up some of the scattered documents, stacking them in the nearest clear space. "I'm sorry."

"Don't tell me that," said Istvan.

"I am telling you that. I mean it. I wish we hadn't had to do it."

Barbed wire wrapped around the legs of Istvan's chair. The specter crossed his arms on the table, more in resignation than anger. "I know."

Edmund cleared up the last of the mess and then went to get a pan out for breakfast. No good dwelling on what they could have done better. That never made anyone an omelette.

He'd focus, today. He'd get something done.

"You're certain you're all right?" asked Istvan.

Edmund retrieved the empty gin glass. He needed to wash it, anyway. "Fine. Just fine. Mercedes gave me a deadline, Istvan, and I'm not about to slide back into the old trap." The kitchen window was closed; he opened it. Get some air. "Thank you for yesterday, by the way."

"What, for the cultists?"

"For coming by."

"Oh."

Edmund turned on the water. Still cold. "I do appreciate it, really."

The part of Istvan's face that could move bent in a faint smile. He looked away. "You are rather more interesting when you leave the house, Edmund."

"I thought I was always interesting."

"I didn't say you weren't."

Breakfast passed in a companionable silence. Edmund ate his omelette and Istvan cradled a cup of coffee that wasn't real, conjured up somehow through force of habit. A breeze blew gently through the window, carrying the pine smell of the hedge with it. There were no plants in the house, just as there were no photographs; books would do, and books in abundance, even though at the moment it was hard to see all of them under the preparatory paperwork Edmund had collected.

He'd use it. Nothing would go to waste. He had a collection of tin cans based on that same reasoning, and they'd served him well over the years.

He thought about putting the record player on but didn't want to risk the usual disagreement over jazz or waltz.

Thank you for yesterday. One of those phrases he could only use around Istvan, who had no time left to take.

"Will you be able to come to Charlie's?" he asked once he'd finished eating.

"Hm?"

Edmund pushed his chair back. "We're on deadline now, Istvan. It might be time to reassemble our little team and see if anyone else has any leads."

Istvan raised his eyebrows. "So, ready to deal with Lucy again?"

"She has her moments." Edmund pushed his chair back. "Besides, it's been over a month since I contacted any of them and that's no way to administrate. They're probably wondering where I went."

"I think that's a fine guess."

"Also, I was thinking of working out a standard set of operations for the next couple sites. I know what we need to be looking for, but if I write it down–"

Istvan sighed.

Edmund paused. "What?"

"More writing?" asked the ghost.

Edmund picked up his plate. "I don't see what's wrong with that."

Istvan pushed his cup away, where it faded and vanished. "Edmund, I don't know where you're finding all this paper. Can't we simply look? You've lists of people who might be interested – have you ever spoken to any of them?"

"Not yet."

"Then why don't we–"

"Yesterday we did it your way," Edmund interrupted, "and today I'd like to do it my way, all right?"

Istvan leaned back in his chair. Then he got up and started for the door, skipping over the shallow steps that divided the living room from the kitchen, snagging his field cap off a hook where it hadn't been hanging before. "If my way is so bad as all that…"

Edmund immediately regretted his words. "Istvan, that's not what I meant."

"I did lead us into a den of Shattered, Edmund, you're right on that."

"You couldn't have known. I know you couldn't have known. Come with me, will you? Lucy's easier to deal with when you're around, and…" He paused at the lintel between rooms. "Istvan, please, stay here. It's easier to concentrate when you're here."

Istvan stopped.

"It's true," Edmund added, because it was.

When the other man stayed only a man, when he weighed what he did over what he was, when he wasn't a human face stretched across something bloody and terrible…

When he was Istvan. Instead of... instead of what Edmund had unchained.

He liked Istvan. He played chess with Istvan. Istvan had stayed by him during those months after the Wizard War, when no one else could – or would.

"Oh, Edmund," the specter sighed, but he did step away from the door.

Beldam shot from behind the couch back into the kitchen.

"The sooner we start," Edmund reassured him, "the sooner we're finished. It will be just like the translation work we did in '95."

"You translated. I watched."

"You were good company and that was all that mattered."

Another sigh.

"Right," Edmund said. He fished his cellular phone out of a pocket. "I'll call the others and we'll meet them there as soon as we can, all right? We'll make some headway today."

Istvan hung his field cap back on its hook.

Edmund fiddled with the phone screen, a glowing panel about the size of a pack of cigarettes. He found the widget that would let him dial and punched in a number, which was a lot less satisfying when the buttons were just pictures of buttons, then held the contraption to his ear.

It rang a moment.

"Hello?" asked a woman's voice.

"Hello, Janet? This is Edmund Templeton."

A pause. "Mr Templeton? Good morning! Been a while."

"It has." He switched the phone to his other ear. "Look,

how fast do you think could you get the others together and have them at Charlie's? We've got a deadline now – a heck of a deadline – and there are some things I'd like to discuss."

Another pause.

Edmund waited. He glanced at Istvan, who seemed to have resigned himself to sticking around. Lucy really was impossible to deal with without him.

"How's two hours?" asked Janet.

"That will do." Edmund looked over the stacks of documents he'd collected. "We'll get everything together and meet you there."

Istvan wilted. "We aren't taking all the papers."

Edmund flashed him a tight smile. "Thank you, Janet."

"Sure."

She hung up. The phone screen returned to its usual parade of tiny pictures.

Edmund dropped it back in his pocket. "All right, Istvan. I'll find a box."

"Edmund–"

"Don't worry, I'll carry it."

Istvan crossed his arms over a build significantly heavier than Edmund's own. He'd spent his formative years accompanying soldiers on brutal campaigns in the Italian Alps, and looked it: in life, he would have been much stronger than a librarian who ran a lot. "Thank you ever so much."

"You're welcome."

Edmund couldn't take all the papers. They wouldn't fit in a single box.

Istvan suggested that perhaps he could take multiple

boxes, one at a time, and leave them on the street in front of Charlie's before carrying them in one by one. Perhaps Lucy could help. Perhaps Edmund could found his own delivery service.

Edmund didn't want Lucy's help and didn't want to be in charge of anything else, never mind a delivery service. He sorted out what he thought most important – slowly and carefully, checking each document over with agonizing thoroughness before nodding to himself and placing it here or there – and took only one box.

This accounted for almost the entirety of two hours.

By the time they finally departed, Istvan was certain that he should have gone to Barrio Libertad instead, even if Grace were present. Edmund didn't need him for this, not really. Edmund specialized in this sort of thing, and without going mad, too. Last time they had sorted documents together was when Istvan was chained in the Demon's Chamber and couldn't escape.

Edmund somehow managed his teleport while holding the box.

Golden edges re-outlined the world–

–and they arrived on a street corner under a clouded sky crisscrossed with precarious masses of electrical wire. White towers rose, tiled and strangely curved, and vanished into swirling fog. Pipes of all sizes grew from the ground, coiled over and through the street's rows of low buildings, or ran overhead, hissing and dripping with condensation. What structures weren't part of the tangle had been built around and under it – or, in the case of the one before them, had displaced it, cutting off pipes mid-length, the sheared ends billowing columns of steam.

Over oaken double doors swung a woodcut with

Edmund's face on it.

Charlie's, it said. *So Vintage We're the Real Deal.*

The proprietors had done rather a good job of the reproduction – the sideburns, the pleasant smile, tired eyes hinted at beneath the aviator goggles – but Istvan still wasn't certain what to make of an endorsement in exchange for bottomless gin.

Passersby halted, pointing and whispering. A baroque tank of a vehicle sat squarely in the middle of the concrete road.

"Get the door?" asked Edmund.

Istvan eyed the tank. He knew that tank. He took hold of the door handle, worn smooth by many hands, and pulled; it swung smoothly, reflections flashing across the glass portholes in its top.

Edmund edged the box through as a pair of orange-clad workers on the roof across the way waved others over to see. Istvan waited until he was clear and then let the door swing closed behind them.

The smell of tobacco came first. It was all-pervasive, lingering, powerful in a way more recent years had abandoned, seeping from every crevice in dark wood and scorched into pressed tin, burning in the hurricane lamps. Smoke-fogged chandeliers did their best but only managed a dull overhead glow. A brass footrail swept around the bar. A mechanical cash register sat above it.

The windows, through the fog, displayed trees in the first bloom of spring. Men loitered in dark suits and hats, lighting cigarettes as automobiles with rounded headlights rolled past. A newspaper boy stood at the corner.

It was always the same, through those windows. The same players, the same day, played out again and again.

April 11, 1939.

A rail-thin old man wearing a cowboy hat that had probably been black once leaned over the bar. "Templeton. Haven't seen you in a while."

"I'm here now," said Edmund. He took a step towards a particular booth opposite the piano and in easy view of the door, and then caught himself. "The others are here?"

"Back room," said the bartender. "I got the heater on, but I don't know what good it'll do. That's a hell of a cat you got there."

"Something like that," said Edmund. "Thank you."

The bartender shrugged. "Let me know if you want anything."

A pause, however brief. "Will do."

Istvan followed him down the hall, shaking his head. He'd tried to stop him, a few times, on the worst days, from fleeing here. There were better ways to manage terror: reading, chess, a hobby that wasn't late-night violence, ways that wouldn't wreck him in the morning, ways that wouldn't leave his eyes red-rimmed and his words slurred and his breath rancid, poison oozing from his pores…

…but Edmund insisted he deserved to have one vice to lose himself in, and at least he wasn't hurting anyone but himself.

An argument that had some merit.

An argument he knew Istvan couldn't counter.

Telling him that at least one person in this world didn't want him to be hurt led only to "I don't know anyone who better deserves it."

Istvan didn't like Charlie's.

The hall to the back room grew colder and colder as

they approached the lamplight leaking from under the door at the end. Mist curled along the planks at their feet.

Istvan reached for a frozen brass handle and pressed the latch. It descended with an icy crack. "Perhaps we ought to meet somewhere else," he muttered.

"The wood will be fine," said Edmund. "It's always the same day here, remember? Come half-past one, everything will go back to how it was yesterday."

"Everything."

"How did you think they have unlimited stock? It will be fine."

Istvan got the door open for him, reflecting sourly that of unlimited anything that might have appeared after the Wizard War, it had to be gin.

Snowflakes blew through him.

The chamber beyond looked as though it had been designed for fine dining – a long oval table, a tiered crystal chandelier, chairs with high ornamented backs – but the proprietor had at some point forgotten its existence. No sign of tableware. Photographs of wagon wheels and rusted vehicles abandoned in fields adorned the walls.

Frost sheened every surface, slick and glistening. A low fog hung over the floor.

"Doctor Czernin!" A Polynesian man as broad as he was tall, which was very, stood up from one end of the table, bundled in a patched jacket and knitted hat. Mr Roberts: nurse, liaison for the Twelfth Hour's infirmary, and Istvan's go-to assistant for seeing patients in that building, regrettably much less common as of late. His eyes were just visible over an upturned collar. They crinkled. "How's work at the fortress?"

Istvan got out of the way so Edmund could get the

box through. "Busy, and–"

A hurricane clatter and whirr of mechanical armor rose and clashed a gauntleted fist against its breastplate. Spiked shoulders flashed in the lamplight. A scarlet cape rippled behind golden filigree.

"Er," Istvan said. "Good morning, Miss L–"

"Hail, ravager of the pale beast, lord of the long war, ender of complacency." The voice boomed, synthesized and strangely-accented. Blood-red lights flickered behind a blank visor. "Your infirmary continues its proud tradition of service in your absence, with not a single misdeed requiring discipline. My service, as always, remains yours, viewer of my last mask."

She started towards him.

He tried to retreat but could go no further without passing partway through the wall. "No need to kneel. Please."

Another slam of gauntlet against breastplate. She turned to Edmund. "Hail, Director. Your unit awaits."

Edmund winced. "Thank you, Lucy."

Istvan wished he could regret saving someone's life, just once. He hadn't even known he was doing it. No one had known who she was, much less what she was, and the Susurration had only made things complicated, like it always did.

Although, assigning her to guard the Twelfth Hour's emergency medical teams had admittedly resulted in those teams having both someone who could punch through doors and who had a tank available, which sometimes came in handy.

A clacking came from the far corner.

White fur; blue stripes; shoulders as high as a horse; a beast that bared canines as long as a man's hand and coated in a fine layer of rime. Its massive body combined all the deadliest aspects of tiger and bear. Its mere presence caused the lacquer behind it to crack, the air to congeal, oxygen to thin and flee as though transported to the summit of the Himalayas.

It wore a screen and keyboard strapped to one arm.

William Blake, better known simply as the Tyger (both names Edmund claimed were some sort of joke on the beast's part), finished tapping at the keyboard and turned the results to show the rest of the table. Green text floated onto the screen.

apologies for the weather

"You can't help it none," said Janet Justice, a heavyset black woman who, unlike Roberts, managed to look completely comfortable in a coat and mittens. Hers was the same voice as on the telephone earlier: as one of the Twelfth Hour's technical experts, it often was. Long greying braids streamed down her back. She didn't stand. She looked to Edmund. "Though I wouldn't mind a larger venue."

Edmund set the box on the table, shivering. "That's what we're here about. Where's Vasquez?"

busy

"Right."

Istvan glanced at Lucy, who didn't seem to notice the cold at all. Her armor was probably heated somehow. Triskelion had its share of technological marvels, after all, and was the sort of place that would never spare them on its warriors.

The sort of place that he would like to but really oughtn't visit.

Edmund pulled out the last remaining chair. He glanced at Istvan.

Istvan shrugged. "You're the director of this venture."

Edmund nodded: a fair point. He waited for the others to sit down – except Lucy, who adamantly refused – and then seated himself. He started pulling papers out of the box.

"Right," he said, retrieving a notebook and a pen, "let's get down to it. Mercedes has made it very clear that, one way or another, we need to show results by the end of the month." He flipped the notebook open, deftly, and set it on the table. He wrote the date, the location, and "Opening Notes" on the first three lines in his neat, narrow, ruler-straight hand, the penmanship of a man who'd made a living writing out index cards.

The paper crackled. He smoothed it.

Then, though his breath misted in the chill air before him, he smiled. "Now, I know it's been a while, so let's hear anything you've come across before I go into details of how we're going to do this."

Istvan stared up at the chandelier. He didn't want to be here. He was of no help here. They were unlikely to get anything done here.

He didn't want to be here.

Edmund ought to have worn a coat. Too late for that now, but he ought have.

He had to be freezing half to death, and he looked it.

And yet those around the table – the team assigned to the man, the first team of any sort he'd led since the Wizard War – regarded him with the sort of automatic deference usually reserved for generals, presidents, kings; the sheer weight of his presence alone almost enough to clear any doubts about his long absence and his bureaucratic stalling.

He was doing it again. He was the Hour Thief, the

elusive Man in Black who haunted the idle hours no matter how hard Istvan tried to forget both incidents, the only one who had ever come to visit him, the one who got away... and he was doing it again.

"What?" Edmund asked.

Istvan looked back to the chandelier, reminding himself that he hated needless paperwork and didn't want to be here. "Carry on."

Edmund should have remembered to bring a coat.

He was going to catch a cold.

"The magnanimous Lord Kasimir continues to extend the hand of friendship in return for a trifling day of aid," boomed Lucy. She scythed a gauntleted hand across the table. Roberts jerked out of the way. "The passes of Triskelion yet rattle with the din of war – a din that our gracious lord would cease forever, given the might to quell it."

"Thank you," said Edmund, "but Istvan and I still aren't interested in signing on as siege-breakers. With all due respect to Lord Kasimir, of course."

Lucy's helmet turned to Istvan.

The specter shook his head. "I'm sorry," he said. He fiddled with his bandolier, twisting his fingers beneath empty ammunition loops.

Lucy bowed. That wasn't her name, strictly speaking, but her real name involved a violent title that no one could keep straight and "Lucy" had ended up being easier for everyone. "Your river-fortress awaits, should you wish it."

"I'll keep that in mind," said Edmund, resolving to do nothing of the sort. "Janet, you were saying?"

The computer expert shifted in her chair. Metallic

green disc earrings lay on the table before her, having evidently grown too cold for comfort. "The Magnolia Group's getting edgy about Barrio Libertad. Their dig has been our primary parts and pieces source since we hooked up with them, and now that the Barrio can replicate just about anything they can do, well… they don't like that at all."

Edmund nodded. "I can see that."

"The last message I got said that they'd be willing to let us look over some of their prime gear if we set up somewhere near them."

"How near?"

Janet shrugged.

Edmund shuffled through the stack before him until he came to the Magnolia Group folder. They were closer to Barrio Libertad than the Twelfth Hour, further inland, near the Wizard War memorial – they'd brought out some kind of beam cannon to help fell the beast, as he recalled, or maybe a repurposed engine. The spacecraft they occupied didn't seem crashed so much as buried, and they were the ones who maintained the Twelfth Hour's wireless and phone systems.

Nice enough people, though they seemed to come in only four or five varieties of the same mold. All more or less identical. All women, so far as he knew.

You could have worse neighbors.

"They don't happen to have any particular site in mind, do they?" he asked.

"Nothing in particular."

He rubbed at his eyes. "Of course."

All the easy places to take had already been taken. Roberts had suggested following up with the Steel City but after that incident at Oxus Station, right next door,

Edmund doubted they'd be amenable to it. Lucy had only Lord Kasimir's offer, again. The Tyger...

Edmund sighed. He'd first met "William Blake" when the beast almost bit off his arm during a starvation-fueled killing spree some months ago. The Tyger was their first evidence that some of Shokat Anoushak's monsters hadn't just been people once: that they were still people. They could still think. They'd been forced to fight under geas. Which was a damn shame, and would have been something to rectify if only there were any survivors like him remaining in Big East. Unfortunately for him, and fortunately for everyone else, there weren't.

William wanted to set up shop far away, in another fracture zone if possible. He wanted to find more like himself, learn how they were created, maybe bring them back to who they had once been. He didn't remember. If Vasquez hadn't given him that keyboard, no one would have ever known that he could think. It hadn't been a popular decision to grant a monster a chance at atonement... but, well, no one could deny that he might be useful against his own kind.

He refused to consider Barrio Libertad the bigger threat. He had his sights set firmly on the strange "children" of Shokat Anoushak, no matter what Edmund said.

It seemed to be getting colder by the minute.

Edmund rubbed his hands together, trying to warm them somewhat. He really wished he'd brought his overcoat. Istvan seemed fine, but of course he would. The ghost was wearing a military greatcoat with elaborate trim now, and Edmund doubted he'd noticed.

One step at a time.

They'd figure it out.

By the end of the month, they'd have it figured out.

He let out a breath. It floated away in a pale cloud. He'd quit smoking almost two decades ago. "Right then," he said, "this is why I'd like to come up with a new procedure for picking sites." The notebook yet lay before him, lined with notes, and he flipped to a new page. "I'd prefer it to have at least the basics: a water supply, some proximity to somewhere we can bring in food, a solid roof. Friendly neighbors is a plus. Power is a plus."

"We could bring in a generator," said Roberts.

Edmund noted down what he'd just said, dotting each with a bullet point. "I'll get to that."

Istvan fidgeted. "It's just the same as setting up a bivouac."

"I'll get to that."

The specter leaned back against the wall, arms folded, sulking.

Edmund drew a dividing line across the paper. Istvan had brought up the same point multiple times over the last two months – he knew more about setting up field camps than anyone, he'd seen men survive in the worst places under the worst conditions, of course they would have to start with modest means, what did Edmund expect? – but this was a matter of politics.

They had to be far enough away from Barrio Libertad to escape the fortress's smothering influence, but close enough to not look like they were worried about that. They had to have enough space to grow into. They had to have enough self-sufficiency not to rely on anyone who might resent them being there. They had to present a face of strength right out of the gate.

They couldn't get this wrong.

Istvan had told him that he was making excuses.

"We're going to start in a hundred-mile radius around

Barrio Libertad," Edmund began. "A preliminary survey. If we set up a master list first, then–"

His phone rang. It sounded like a submarine dive alarm. He'd never figured out how to change it.

"Excuse me."

He fished it out of his pocket. The front was a glowing panel about the size of a pack of cigarettes, currently displaying Mercedes' number.

Oh, boy.

He glanced around the table. "I'm sorry, I have to take this."

Before anyone could argue, he stepped outside, closed the door, fiddled with the screen, then held the contraption to his ear. "Good morning, Mercedes, you've reached Edmund Templeton."

"So I would hope," came the acerbic reply.

"What's going on?"

"Come to the office. Bring Dr Czernin, if he's available."

"Mercedes, I'm in the middle of–"

"This is urgent, Mr Templeton."

Edmund eyed the door. He tugged it open a crack, cursing under his breath at the freezing metal handle. William, evidently, didn't approve of this meeting at all. "Istvan?"

"What?"

"Are you available?"

A pause. "What for?"

Edmund switched the phone to his other ear. "He is."

Mercedes paused. "He's there now?"

"Yes, he is."

"I see. I expect you both shortly."

She hung up.

Edmund watched the phone screen reset to its standard configuration. If Mercedes was worried about wiretapping, this had to be something about Barrio Libertad. They were worse than the Russians.

So much for making progress.

He dropped the phone in his pocket and stepped back through the door.

Four sets of eyes and one visor looked at him expectantly.

"Meeting's canceled," Edmund sighed. He ran a hand through the grey in his hair. "Mercedes has something she wants done."

Istvan perked up. "Does she?"

Edmund started stacking papers back in the box. So close. He'd been so close. "You don't have to look so relieved."

CHAPTER FIVE

"I'm aware of the demands of your current assignment," said Magister Hahn.

"We'd just sat down."

"Something has come up, Mr Templeton. Something of your caliber, which as I'm sure you both know, isn't something I can ignore."

"I'd like to know how I'm supposed to get anything off the ground if I can't–"

The Magister leaned forward in her chair, clasping her hands together over one of her diagrams. The paper lanterns hanging above streaked red highlights across the scarred surface of her desk. "I've received a message from Landsea Cabal."

Edmund quieted.

Istvan frowned, standing at an automatic parade rest. "The Tornado Alley wizards?"

"That's right."

"I'm not teaching my teleport," said Edmund.

"That wasn't what they asked." She tapped a pen on the desk. "You're aware of the storms they face, gentlemen? Inland hurricanes, hyper-cells, 'razornadoes?'"

"I've heard of them," Istvan said, cautiously. He considered bringing up what Grace had said – the prospect of Shattered in Tornado Alley, unreachable even by Barrio Libertad – but this didn't sound like the Susurration's work. Thank goodness.

The Magister nodded. "One has gone 'smart.'"

Edmund raised his eyebrows. "Smart?"

"They've been tracking it for less than a day and it's already changed course eight times."

"Oh."

Istvan waited for him to say something more, but the man remained silent, his aspect churning. Anger over being interrupted at an important meeting. Anger over a lost day of calm. Anger over being angry.

Worry over not enough time for it all.

Istvan clasped his hands more tightly behind his back.

What could the Magister want with this storm business? Fight it? It was wind; there was nothing there to fight. And all the way out there? Yes, it was unfortunate, but Tornado Alley was at least a thousand miles away. This was an enormous country. The Twelfth Hour didn't claim close to all of it.

Besides, to reach Tornado Alley they would have to–

"I want you to intercept it," said the Magister. "Today."

Edmund's jaw tightened.

Istvan's heart dropped and leapt all at once. He swallowed. "In Tornado Alley, Magister?"

The Magister peered at him. "Where else? Besides, Doctor, I thought you would jump at the opportunity."

"Ah…"

"How long has it been since you crossed our borders?"

He saw mountains. He could hear the clatter of wheels over rocky passes, the shouts of exhausted men. Platoons picked their way over rope bridges. Snow fell gently over the fallen – or not so gently, loosed by the crack and report of cannon, a great thundering rush of smothering death.

The peaks here had no snow… but he still saw it.

"Magister," he tried to protest, but could go no further.

Triskelion. The mountains he would have to cross to reach Tornado Alley were home to the warring states of Triskelion. Lucy's homeland. It fell just on the edge of Big East and reached into the spellscars, strongholds blasted into the most inhospitable parts of what had been Pennsylvania. Its people had come from some other history, cruel and poisoned, led by warlords that swiftly subjugated everything they came across and then hired their men out to all comers in exchange for any advantage they could gain over their rivals. Even Barrio Libertad had made use of their services, hiring them to find dozens of palm-sized superweapons known as Bernault devices. They still did, for all he knew.

Istvan had fought Triskelion mercenaries. He had never fought their armies.

Oh, the mercenaries had been wonderful.

Barbed wire looped bright and bloody at his feet.

"Why do you want us out there?" asked Edmund. "Why now?"

The Magister clasped her hands together. "It's time the Twelfth Hour took a more proactive role in affairs, Mr Templeton. We've been bunkered down too long. This could be the first step towards demonstrating that we're more than a clearinghouse and artifact depot for a dozen petty city-states and skeleton crew of field agents."

Edmund turned his hat in his hands, a measured, deliberate gesture. The knot at his jaw remained. "I thought we were."

She smiled tightly. "Only because there's nothing better."

Istvan tried desperately not to think about which Triskelion warlord he ought to throw his hat in for. The only one he knew was Lord Kasimir, but it was always best to approach a war from all sides…

"I shall have to tell the emergency hospital I won't be available," he managed.

"Of course," said the Magister.

Edmund stared at her a moment longer. Then he turned, stiffly. "We'll give it our best. Come on, Istvan."

Istvan snapped a salute.

He made it until just after the Magister's door swung closed.

Then he turned and fell against the wall outside, head on an upraised arm. The wall was real. Solid. Something to distract from the wild thoughts – the improper thoughts – the gripping fever of it all – a war, a real war!

"Istvan?"

He shuddered. He beat a fist against the wood, bone and feathers flickering in and out of existence. "I can't," he said. "Edmund, I can't."

Edmund hung back. Of course he did. No need to risk it, no, not with what Istvan was. The Great War, unchained. "You can't what?"

"Go."

"It's an order."

"You don't have to tell me that! It's only… I can't…" He thought of turning, thought of facing the other man, but the actual motion was impossible. "Edmund, I can't fly over Triskelion. It's too much. It's… Edmund, it's too much."

Oh, he wouldn't come back.

Oh, he wouldn't remember anything.

"Istvan. We'll be teleporting."

Teleporting. Yes, Edmund could do that. But–

Now, Istvan turned. Partway. He peered over his own shoulder. "You've been there?"

Edmund nodded. "I have. I'll aim for a straight shot, if it makes you feel better. We won't go anywhere near the mountains."

But I want to go near the mountains, Istvan wanted to say. *I would very much like to go near the mountains, just as I would very much like you to not stand off so far away.*

He didn't say that. He leaned against the wall a moment longer – oh, he wanted to say a lot of things – and then turned, straightening a bandolier that didn't need to be straightened.

Edmund stood there, hat still in his hands. His fear had subsided to the usual unconscious wariness, an edge he never lost, a wound that wouldn't close and that no one else could see.

"I ought to notify the hospital," Istvan said.

"Then we'll do that."

"Oh, I hate it there."

It slipped out.

Edmund pulled out his pocket watch and flipped it open. "You don't have to go there all the time, you know."

Istvan shook his head. The Twelfth Hour infirmary was relatively well-equipped and well-staffed. The hospital at Barrio Libertad was new, and though the fortress supplied a good deal of equipment, it didn't have enough trained medics to account for the refugee population: some of them maimed, the vast majority with serious mental complications from years of Susurration control.

He was needed there.

Where his own patients feared him, Grace Wu

despised him, the very walls raged at him, and everyone else blamed him in hushed whispers when he turned his back. Edmund had freed them; Istvan was simply the unpleasant means.

"Right," said Edmund. "Look sharp."

He snapped his watch.

The teleport whisked them into ankle-deep mud.

"Aw, hell," said Edmund.

He'd only been to Barrio Libertad as often as he had to, which wasn't often. He could have aimed for inside, but he wasn't going inside. Not anymore. Not with them nullifying magic right and left.

Unfortunately, outside kept changing.

He put away his pocket watch, picked up his cape, and draped it over one arm, trying not to think about what else might be mixed into the morass. Istvan's battlefield. The Great War made manifest, a too-real reminder of what took down the Susurration.

"It's only mud," said Istvan. He slogged through the mess and stepped onto clear paving, completely unaffected. "Mostly," he added.

"Thanks, Istvan, you're a real help."

Edmund started walking. The entrance to Barrio Libertad loomed before them, flanked by murals: fists of every color raised against an amorphous entity of reaching tentacles and hints of human faces, a shattered lantern spilling white light from behind rose-tinted glass. Cavernous elevator doors pounded open. Turrets, high above, rumbled on their mountings. A rib cage of stone and steel lay collapsed across them, five or six clawed limbs dangling from the roof or hooked ineffectually into the walls.

The broken hulk of one of Shokat Anoushak's greatest creations.

Its body slumped across the fortress like a hybrid of snake, centipede and train; its remaining flesh composed of shattered roadways, crushed ships, rubble from fallen buildings, and stone gouged out of the earth by its passage. Towers crested its spine, leaning crazily, holes blown through them end-to-end. Wind whistled through dangling power lines. Bridge cables trailed away out of sight.

It was a nightmare straight out of the Wizard War.

It was still better than the fortress that had killed it.

Edmund stepped onto solid ground. His shoes squelched.

"I'll wait here," he said.

Istvan nodded, and stepped into the elevator. The doors thundered closed.

Edmund sat on a step and took a shoe off. The mud had seeped into his socks. "Great," he muttered.

He eyed the lay of the land, how much room there was in front of the doors, and especially where the paving ended. If he had to visit Landsea Cabal and fight a living thunderstorm to assuage Mercedes' ego, he wasn't going like this.

He returned with clean socks just as Grace skidded to a halt before the doors, muck sliding from her boots like oil from water.

"Oh," she said. "Sorry."

Edmund shook out his cape.

She reached for him, hesitated... then tapped her own shoulder. "You missed a spot."

He wiped it off. Just mud. "Morning, Grace."

She stood there a moment longer. Every quirk of her

lips, every shift of her weight, every curve below scarlet plating and dark undersuit, the whir of her gauntlets, the faint electric crackle of her hair in the wind...

Resistor Alpha. State hero. Engineer and self-proclaimed genius. A mistake, and not the first one he couldn't regret.

He hadn't known she'd survived the Wizard War. She hadn't told him.

For seven years, she hadn't told him.

"I don't see you around here often," she said. If she had an opinion on that, he couldn't hear it. She hitched the strap of a messenger bag further up her shoulder. "What's up?"

He shrugged. "Waiting for Istvan."

"Should have known. Are you free today?"

"Excuse me?"

She stepped closer. "Are you free today?"

He stayed where he was. He flicked mud off his fingers. "Actually, I'll be headed to Tornado Alley. I don't know how long."

"Great," she replied. "I'm going with you."

Going with–

He took a step backwards. Too close. She was too close, and he didn't need another complication on top of everything else. "No."

"Eddie–"

"No! Absolutely not!"

She raised her eyebrows, a flash of pain in her eyes. "You don't have to yell."

"Grace, I don't know what you're trying to do, but I've had about enough of it. If you want to muscle in on the Twelfth Hour, fine. If you want to save the world, go ahead. If you're looking for someone, I won't stop you.

Just do it somewhere else."

"I thought you might appreciate the help," she said.

"Help with what?"

"The storm, Eddie." She pointed behind him. "Watch your step."

Edmund stopped before he landed a foot in the mud again. One thing on top of another. First a month to find a workable base site and now a thousand-mile jaunt to the west to prove something that didn't need to be proved and now Grace. Every time, Grace.

He didn't know how to stop a storm, much less one that had a mind of its own.

Did Mercedes think he was superhuman?

Grace hadn't.

Grace had never–

He took a breath. Yelling wouldn't solve anything. He shouldn't have done that. He hated doing things like that.

He looked at the fortress walls that rose above them, monolithic, like the curved immensity of Hoover Dam. They looked like corrugated steel, though they were anything but. Slogans in English and Spanish splashed across their sides: *Against the Control. Free Thought Deserves Protection.*

"What are you after?" he asked under his breath.

Grace crossed her arms. "There isn't a conspiracy here, Eddie. And if you start going on about gods and horrors and the evils of the modern database again, Diego might just decide to be a little hurt."

"He's listening, isn't he?"

She shrugged.

"Edmund," said Istvan, stepping back through the doors, "I've the rest of the day, in return for–"

He saw Grace.

"Doc," she greeted him.

He shot a suspicious glance at Edmund. "Miss Wu."

"Not my idea," said Edmund.

"I shouldn't think so," said Istvan.

"She's coming with us. And this doesn't mean anything."

Grace cracked a sudden grin. "It means you've got a genius aboard, Eddie – and I'd say that improves your chances of handling that storm by a good margin."

Istvan blinked. "How does she–"

Edmund jerked his head towards the fortress.

"Oh. Of course." The specter hooked a thumb in his bandolier, not looking at either of them. Jagged tangles appeared in the wire at his feet. "Nothing but politics, then?"

Edmund got out his pocket watch. "Let's just go."

Two masses this time – Istvan weighed nothing – and he'd teleported Grace before. Some adjustment for her armor. Landsea maintained a team in that same remote station he'd visited on his mapping tour, last he'd heard. The calculations might have been called offerings, in another context, and they were more complicated for such a great distance (as a cartographer might expect), though of course all distances and indeed positions were relative. Don't think about it too hard.

No lethal mistakes; he had time.

"Hey, Eddie," said Grace, "Diego was wondering – do you know what happens every time you use that teleport trick of yours?"

"No. And I hope I can trust you not to tell me."

"Great," she said.

They were elsewhere.

CHAPTER SIX

Light. Dust. Heat that beat upon him like molten copper. Gusts blew through him, a rattling hiss from all directions, a sound wind ought not to make over such a flat, featureless expanse. Had Edmund gotten his location right?

Istvan shielded his eyes – a gesture more habitual than useful – and squinted at the endless gold that swam across his vision.

Grass. It was all grass, hazed and shimmering. The whole of the landscape rolled and heaved, looking for all the world as though it might run liquid at any moment, if it didn't catch fire first.

He'd never seen anything that wasn't water move like that. No mountains in sight at all. He wished he weren't so disappointed. "Edmund, you haven't taken us to Africa?"

Edmund shook his head, holding onto his hat. "This is as American as it gets. You didn't think 'Landsea' was a joke, did you?"

"Amber waves," said Grace. She took a deep breath, nose wrinkled. "I thought it would smell more like cows."

Istvan turned, slowly. Grass. A dirt road, stretching

away for miles. Long shadows passing over the earth, the sleek white blades of an enormous windmill spinning high above. Other machines lay toppled in a line, their pieces tossed about as though by some great beast. A squat concrete building sat behind a low fence, a pair of battered automobiles parked before it, its roof bristling with radio dishes and antennae and whirling devices facing different directions. A flag featuring a stalk of wheat bent into a lightning bolt flapped helplessly on a pole raised near its front door.

A dark smudge boiled on the horizon.

He reached for Edmund. "Do you suppose that's…?"

Edmund wasn't there. He was already striding towards the… station, Istvan supposed it was, his cape threatening to tear itself off his shoulders.

"I've never been here, either," confided Grace. She tugged at her sleeves, stopping just short of rolling them up. "Don't think I'll come back."

"No one asked you to," Istvan said.

He followed Edmund.

All the way across the mountains. How often had Edmund come here? Where else had he gone? He'd been responsible for mapping much of what remained, after the Wizard War, but Istvan had never thought much of it – the Twelfth Hour's boundaries were his own limits, and it had been easier to not dwell on how confining those limits were.

He'd crossed oceans, once, to find the next war…

Edmund knocked.

A sunburnt woman in a white cowboy hat opened the door. "Who in–" She blinked. "The Hour Thief? That was… You're as fast as they say, aren't you?"

Edmund smiled, that way he did: bland, pleasant,

and transformative, a flash of white teeth that almost made him seem like someone else. Someone larger. "Not always," he said. He stepped aside, a rush of black silk in the wind. "This is Resistor Alpha and Dr Czernin, sometimes known as the Devil's Doctor. We're here about that storm."

"Hey," said Grace.

Istvan wondered, again, if it were something about the way the man stood. It was like a switch, it truly was. "A pleasure."

The woman looked them over, started to say something to Edmund, then paused, glancing back to Istvan. Her eyebrows rose. "Wait. Is he–"

Istvan sighed. "A ghost, yes."

"No, no, the... you know..." She bared her teeth and held her arms up, fingers hooked. "*The* ghost."

Istvan stared at her.

Grace laughed. "Close enough." She pushed forward, elbowing Edmund out of the way. "Hey, do you have air conditioning in there?"

The woman backed up. "Sure. We kept one of the turbines running, didn't we? Come on in. I'll let the others know you're here."

"Thank you," said Edmund.

Istvan followed last, again, enduring another clandestine stare on the way. She didn't seem afraid of him so much as curious, which he supposed was an improvement over the usual fare. What had she heard? What had Edmund said about him?

"I thought you had wings," she said as she closed the door.

He turned. "Did I catch your name?"

"Clark."

He waited for a first name, but she didn't give one.

"I'm the bells and whistles specialist," she continued. She skipped through the short front hall and into an interior just as utilitarian as the outside. "Wait here a sec."

She disappeared down a stairwell.

Istvan crossed his arms. Panels of switches blinked and popped on each wall; blobs of blocky color stuttered over screens, overlaid on maps or grids, labeled with numbers and symbols he wasn't quite sure were meteorological. Books lay jammed anywhere that would fit them: on top of televisions, stacked in the corner, stuffed between reels of wire, a particularly thick volume propping up a chair with a short leg. A folding table sat to one side, littered with tubes and gauges and other machinery only half-assembled.

A horseshoe hung over the door.

"Eddie," said Grace, "I thought this was a wizard's cabal."

Edmund took off his hat, suddenly just Edmund again. "You said the same thing about Janet and I'll say it again: we're not anti-technology, Grace. Technology's great. It's safe. We like it just fine."

"Sure you do." She tapped one of the screens. "Good show, there, by the way. You really do put that on every time, don't you?"

Edmund didn't answer.

Istvan peered through a dirt-crusted window. The cloudy smudge was still there, dark against the sky's brilliance. Violet lightning sheeted into the ground.

Oh, it couldn't have been anything more human, could it?

He tried to make out any sign that anyone lived

nearby, but those in the building were all he could taste. Edmund, Grace, and three others. Godforsaken place. Deserted as the open ocean.

"So, what," continued Grace, "Landsea's just the news and weather folks?"

"They're the ones that keep some of the settlements out here in one piece," Edmund replied, curtly. He wasn't looking at her. "They've got some of the best warders in the business. Have you ever seen one of those storms, Grace?"

Clark's voice came from downstairs. "Yes, the Hour Thief! I'm serious!"

"Well," Grace said, "it's not acting like a storm, is it?"

Edmund scrubbed a hand across his face. "I never said–"

"And if it's not acting like one, what makes you think it actually is one?"

The wizard shoved his hands in his pockets. "Let's not jump to conclusions, all right?"

Istvan thought of snow on mountains.

Clark returned, an equally sunburned man and a somewhat shellshocked-looking woman in tow. "Rosales, Lockhart, meet the Hour Thief. And friends. Hour Thief: the team."

Edmund tipped his hat. "Thank you for having us."

"Rosales is our primary warder for this station; Lockhart handles predictions. We've got most of Iowa and part of Nebraska covered between us, and I do not envy the folks in Kansas."

"Three Force 14s in the last year," said Lockhart, staring at a box fan set into one of the windows.

Clark stepped to a panel and indicated one of the color blobs as it advanced in stop-motion. "This here's your storm. You probably saw it outside – it's not vectored towards us, but it'll be close. I assume you wanted to have a look?"

"I don't know that want plays into it," said Edmund. He was smiling again.

Rosales produced a set of keys, along which dangled a piece of petrified bone with odd coils scrimshawed onto it. "I'll go get the truck ready."

Hot air blasted into the station as he opened the door. It closed behind him with a slam and the scream of frustrated breezes.

Clark adjusted her cowboy hat. "If one of you can drive, Rosales was hoping to get some better readings. I know you can probably just pop in right next to it, but I'd like to advise against that. The storms pick up a lot of grit and rock and… other things, and I'd hate for you to lose all your skin getting in too close, too fast."

Grace smirked. "Yeah, that would be a shame."

"I can drive," said Edmund.

Istvan blinked at him. He'd never seen the man behind a wheel, ever. "You can?"

"I doubt my license is current, but yes."

"Oh, great," said Grace. "What did you learn on, a tractor?"

"We didn't have a tractor."

She shook her head. "I'm sorry, Eddie, but there's a thing called power steering now, and I really don't want to be veering all over the road, thanks. I'll drive."

Edmund gave her a look. "The roads out here are straight lines."

"Yeah, and I don't want to be poking around at old guy speed."

"I drove a car once," offered Istvan.

Neither of the two so much as glanced at him. "No."

Istvan crossed his arms. He had, briefly. The machine had sat on three wheels and moved at about ten miles an hour, but he had. That had been an exciting day. Not everyone got to drive a car. Pietro had spent ages setting up the opportunity.

"I'm driving," said Edmund. He looked to Clark. "Did you have any thoughts on the supposed intelligence of this storm?"

She shrugged. "We haven't gotten close enough to know."

"Not for lack of trying, I hope."

"Sioux City by Union," said Lockhart. Her voice echoed like an announcement in a train terminal. "Five. Eight. Three. Due north-northwest. Gale five and rising. Range Thursday-Saturday, four hours allowance. A friend in need is a friend indeed; remember to iron your pants."

She resumed staring at the wall.

Clark noted that down on a pad of paper. "Don't mind her."

Istvan frowned. Lockhart was a wizard, then, together with Rosales. There was always a price, Edmund had told him. You weren't a wizard until you regretted it. What had she done to herself?

The woman's aspect boiled, then settled, a dull worry mingled with… surprise?

"Right," said Edmund, seeming somewhat unnerved himself, "we'll take the truck and get to the bottom of this. Thank you for the help, and for all you do."

Clark touched the brim of her cowboy hat. "Likewise. It was an honor to meet you. All of you. Drive like the wind." She glanced at Istvan. "Or fly, as the case may be."

Istvan debated with himself a moment. Then he flared rotten wings, feathers scattering over the machinery. "I might."

She stumbled backwards with a curse. She pointed at him, wordlessly. Then she started laughing. "That! That's it!" She put her arms out and hooked her fingers again, a facsimile of the same wings. "That's what Rosales was talking about – he was there, in Chicago. That's what he saw!"

Istvan drew back, something almost unfamiliar bubbling in his chest. A sighting? An eyewitness? All this time and they still remembered him, possibly fondly?

Chicago. What had he done in Chicago? There was that great monster, of course, that he'd chased from further east, and that bridge…

Edmund put his hat on. "Stop terrorizing the locals, Istvan. Let's go."

"But I haven't–"

Edmund tugged the door open. Heat washed through, with the smell and grumble of an engine running. The shadows of windmill blades rolled along the grass.

"Let's go before you do."

The truck was a pickup, its bed loaded with enough equipment to make the back end sag visibly. A satellite dish made up the greater part of it – though it equally may have been a swiveling ray gun, for all Edmund could make out the finer details – and boxes of what looked like batteries lined the sides. A forest of radio antennae bristled from near the tailgate. Strings of feathers fluttered over the wheel wells. Spars welded to the cab presumably kept the vehicle from cracking in half.

"We can follow the road most of the way," said

Rosales, crouching improbably in the midst of the mess. "All you have to do is aim for the clouds." He leaned out and dangled the keys.

Edmund took them before Grace could. "Right."

Grace rolled her eyes. "Biofuels?" she asked.

"You bet," said Rosales. "Gotta get around somehow."

Edmund climbed into the cab. It still had the basics: wheel, pedals, shift. It was an automatic, but that was fine: he'd just have to remember to leave well enough alone. The rest of the console looked like something out of a fighter jet, but he didn't think he'd need all that to get moving.

It started easily enough once he found the right key.

Istvan peered through the passenger-side window. "There isn't much room, is there?"

Grace opened the door and hopped through him into the seat. "Nope."

Istvan stiffened.

She buckled her seatbelt. "You can fly, can't you?"

He opened his mouth, closed it, and then swung into the back. Ghostly barbed wire wrapped around the mirror on Edmund's side.

Edmund looked for a window crank.

"Problem?" asked Grace.

"I've got it." He found the right switch and rolled his window down. "All set?"

A thumbs-up from Rosales appeared in the mirror.

Grace rolled down her own window and propped an elbow on it, eyeing the storm that loomed in the distance. "Giddy-up, cowboy. And remember, power steering."

Edmund put the truck in gear. "Don't worry about it."

Grit blew into his goggles. The gravel beneath the tires sounded like ripping paper. The steering skidded and shuddered. A shrieking maelstrom bore down upon them, spanning more than a quarter of the horizon, a hurricane of dirt, nails, shredded plant matter, and wire. The ground at its base was a canyon in the making. Violet lightning flashed within its depths.

Edmund gripped the steering wheel grimly, knuckles white.

It was fine. It was all fine.

"Can't you go any faster?" asked Grace.

He didn't dare look at the speedometer. "No."

"OK," shouted Rosales, "we're almost ready to go off-road!"

Edmund swallowed. Great.

"There's something in there," said Rosales, once the truck had stopped and the storm boiled a safe if not comfortable distance to their left. He tapped at his equipment. "Something in the eye of it, hanging up there."

Istvan peered over his shoulder at a mass of colored lines and couldn't come to that same conclusion. "Hanging?"

"Floating. A long ways up." Rosales took hold of a pair of handles and adjusted the aim of the device, then checked the panel again. "Traveling with it."

"How big is it?" asked Grace, sitting half-in and half-out of the truck window.

Rosales shrugged. "I can't tell from this distance. I wouldn't have found it at all if we hadn't made that run."

"Do we need to take another look?" asked Edmund.

Istvan glanced back at the side mirror. Edmund was still leaning on the steering wheel, though he seemed less shaky than earlier. He had kept the vehicle more or less straight, to his credit. His hat had blown somewhere back into the cab. His face was scratched, thin lines of grit and sweat around his goggles.

"I'll drive this time," said Grace.

"I can do it," said Edmund.

Istvan swung himself onto the roof of the truck. "I'll be back," he said.

He took two steps and launched himself towards the storm.

"Wait..." called Edmund.

Istvan didn't. He couldn't hear anything after that, either, the wind picking up immediately and buffeting him sideways. He tumbled – it was like the powerful currents that circled the Earth much higher up – and righted himself, wingbeats bringing him about in a long arc towards screaming columns of grit and dust.

Then he was through, and he couldn't see.

A flash of violet, searing and jagged.

He spat a curse he couldn't hear. He covered his face.

It felt like sandpaper, tearing through him. Like bullets. It felt like he oughtn't have any feathers left; flesh already gone, uniform in tatters...

Another arc, blinding. Thunder. Sparks played across trailing streamers of wire. Oh, he hoped he was still going the right way. He thought he might be moving sideways more quickly than forward. He grasped for something familiar and found it: Edmund's worry, taut and bittersweet, and the lesser presences of Grace and Rosales. They were all much further away than he'd expected. He flapped harder.

A boulder whirled past.

Up, and up. He tried to follow the winds as best he could. Some had to be spiraling around the center, hadn't they? That was how storms worked, wasn't it?

Perhaps he should have asked.

He covered his eyes at more lightning, sparking from shreds of airborne sheet metal and tatters of iron gratings and nearly burning through a wing. He couldn't even hear the thunder anymore. He could barely hear himself think.

Oh, why was he the only one who could fly?

Perhaps he ought to go back, and–

He tumbled into total calm. No wind. No sound of wind, even. Instead, a clear shaft like that of a mine, perfectly circular, walls of whirling dust and light drawn down from a distant sun.

A small figure floated far below him, arms outstretched and head thrown back, surrounded by orbiting motes of absolute darkness.

Istvan coughed. It made no sense to cough.

A person?

It was a person?

The storm… was a person?

Then why couldn't he–

It struck him like lightning. He dove, wings folded tight. No. Oh, no.

Not one of the Shattered.

Not one like this.

He burst from the storm much faster than he'd entered it, banking wildly, half-blind and deafened. Edmund. Edmund was over there.

"Edmund!"

The wizard said something Istvan couldn't make out in response. He wasn't in the truck any longer. He stood some distance off from it, with Grace. He was holding onto his hat. His cape strained at its buttons.

"Edmund," Istvan tried again, still not touching the ground. How could he alight with news like this? Poison rolled around him in great clouds, bringing thunder of its own. "It's Shattered! It's bloody Shattered!"

What? mouthed the wizard.

"There's a person in it and he's Shattered!"

I told you, Grace probably said. That was the sort of thing she would say.

"–ever told us anything," said Edmund. He coughed, staring up at the storm. "You just came."

Istvan clutched his temples and shook his head. It felt like he was trailing pieces of himself, like he hadn't left the storm at all. Afterimages cracked across his vision.

Oh, it made no sense.

"I saw it," he said, and at least this time he could hear himself better. "There's someone in there, and I didn't know until I nearly tripped over him. He's Shattered, I'm sure of it. He's directing the storm, or making it!"

"Magic?" asked Edmund.

"Conduit," said Grace. She gazed at the storm, sparks crackling between her fingers as she drew them across one another. "I bet you it's a Conduit."

Edmund turned. "But that's–"

"Not impossible. We don't even know the limits of what is possible."

Istvan did alight, now, uncertain. Grace herself was a Conduit, of course – one of that peculiar class of individuals who had changed when the world broke, their abilities manifested or called from somewhere not yet determined. Conduits didn't seek out power, as wizards did: they channeled it through their very bones. What effect that might have on their physiology, their wellbeing, no one knew. They were so rare that no one could make an informed judgement.

Istvan suspected that the vast majority had died the moment they changed. Grace was the only one he had ever met.

He'd never heard of a Conduit powerful enough to direct a storm.

"Why do you think that?" he asked.

"We have theories." She turned away, steady in the wind. "Let's get back to the truck. We need to bring this hurricane in."

"But how–"

She grinned a faint grin. "How do you usually do it?"

"Not when they're flying," said Edmund.

Istvan tried to fold his wings tighter. He was missing even more feathers than usual, dark and jagged shadows whirling away as the wind blew.

Of course it would come to this. No one else could fly.

"Edmund, can you catch someone?" he asked, feeling altogether like he would rather be somewhere else. "Mid-fall?"

The wizard looked at him strangely. "You've seen me do it."

"Even when you can't see?"

Edmund frowned. He looked from Istvan to the storm and then back. "If you're saying what I think you're saying–"

"I can't catch anyone," Istvan told him. "You know that."

Edmund retrieved his pocket watch. "I'll try."

"Hey!" called Rosales from the back of the truck. "It's all good for another run!"

"Good," said Grace. She opened the driver-side door and jumped in. "We'll try to aim you right, Eddie."

"What?" said Rosales.

She shut the door. "We've got a wizard to launch."

Istvan exchanged glances with Edmund.

"It's better than nothing," the wizard said.

"The debris–"

"I'll be fine."

Istvan traced two fingers across his facial scarring, wishing he could think of any other way to go about it. "I saw boulders in there. I can't imagine what else it's picked up."

The wizard shoved his hands in his pockets. "I'll manage. You be careful, yourself. I don't like this."

Istvan nodded. The Susurration had never employed Conduits before. It had tried, perhaps, but none of its victims had ever demonstrated anything beyond the mundane.

Perhaps they ought to have asked why.

Grace hung out the window. "You two ready or what?"

"I'm coming," said Edmund.

Istvan took a false breath. Intercept the storm. At least this would be easier than trying to turn aside an entire weather system.

Shattered. A Conduit, and Shattered.

He leapt into the wind.

CHAPTER SEVEN

It was a boy.

Istvan tumbled into the uncanny calm at the storm's center, flayed near to nothing, and circled above him. He was more a young man, really – tall and thin and gangly, wearing a battered jacket and blue jeans more hole than fabric. He was African, or at least African-descended.

He hadn't spotted Istvan yet. Once he did, well...

Istvan glanced at one of his own skeletal hands, each wingbeat marked by the reappearance of feathers torn away by the storm. Barbed wire twisted through his bones.

Oh, there was no help for it.

He circled lower. "Excuse me," he called.

No response. The wind tore his words away.

Istvan descended still lower, trying to minimize his profile as best he could. "Excuse me!"

The boy looked up. His face was dirt-encrusted, his hair a matted nest of debris and dust. He looked faint, as though he hadn't eaten in days.

"You," he said.

The storm roared a dull thunder.

Istvan took nervous hold of his bandolier. Many of the Shattered seemed to recognize him, at least while he was like this. He was the last thing Susurration had seen before the end. The last person it had spoken to. He'd tried to help it, and couldn't, and then it was ground under by the War.

Those Shattered that seemed to know him often reacted with betrayed rage.

"I'm Doctor Czernin," Istvan replied, hovering at what he hoped was a safe distance. "I'm here to speak with you."

The boy simply stared, his eerie, multifaceted presence scattering whatever he might have felt in a thousand different directions. It was like facing a crowd. Like facing a jury. Was he a Conduit, really? Or was there some fragment of Shokat Anoushak lodged deep within his soul, teaching him the same secrets that drove her mad?

"Are you really him?" the boy asked. "Doctor Czernin?"

Istvan nodded. "Certainly."

He dared to edge somewhat closer, praying that whatever recognition the boy thought he had would keep him from panicking. Perhaps he could talk him down?

Talk him down, rather than…

Rather than…

Istvan shuddered, brushing at his sleeves. "What's your name, then?"

"Kyra," said the boy.

"That's a fine name. Is it African?"

The boy looked at him a moment longer. The storm trembled, stones dipping in broad arcs before the wind caught them up again. "You were there," he said. "You fought her. You fought it. I remember." He frowned.

"What are you?"

"Dead," said Istvan.

"Oh." A long, long pause. "Like a ghost?"

"Yes."

"That's weird." Kyra shook his head. "That's really weird. You ain't supposed to be dead."

Istvan wasn't sure what to say to that. What was he supposed to be? Alive? If he hadn't become what he was, he would have died of natural causes long ago. He hovered, fighting to stay steady. Kyra, at least, looked every bit as confused as he felt.

"How do you know me?" Istvan finally asked. "What do you remember of me?"

The boy mumbled something, inaudible in the wind. His eyelids fluttered. The stones in the storm dipped lower again, falling and then righting themselves.

Istvan thought of Edmund, far below. If the storm came apart now...

Kyra took a deep breath. "I remember this... noise," he said. "All over, that never stops and keeps getting louder and louder. And you're standing there, watching. Just like that. Wings and everything." He shook his head. "But if you're Doctor Czernin, there's... other things. I don't know." The boy balled his hands into fists, arms still outstretched. One of the cuts on his face oozed blood. "Listen," he added with sudden urgency, "I have to find some wizards. She's coming back. They got me, and they know how to make her now, and they're going to bring her back."

Istvan tried to tear his mind away from the thought of the Susurration's last moments. Pietro. Everything beloved, used against him. "Er–"

"The wizards can kill her, right?"

"Who?"

Kyra looked away. "Our Lady."

Oh. Oh, dear. Istvan had heard that phrase before.

The boy had fallen in with a Shokat Anoushak cult. He'd come from some awful coven, somewhere, that hoped to make use of her magics for their own ends – to revive the Immortal, to finish what she had begun. He wasn't out of his mind, or on some sort of rampage. He was *running*.

Or… was he?

Why create such a vast scene? He was travelling in the most obvious way imaginable. If someone were looking for him, wouldn't he want to hide? One could never be certain with the Shattered. Some could seem quite lucid.

"Well," Istvan continued, awkwardly, "it's, ah… rather loud up here, isn't it? Why don't we…"

The boy smoothed his jacket.

Was he carrying something? An artifact? Preparing some sort of spell? What if there were another mockery, hiding in the storm?

Istvan dove for him.

Kyra yelled. He tried to backpedal. He dropped, flailing.

Wind blasted Istvan sideways. Stone and pebbles and shredding grit showered through his wings. And something else – something that wasn't wind, that tugged and tore, smearing together rock, branches, brief glimpses of sun and sky–

Istvan held an arm before his eyes, beating his wings as hard as he could. "Kyra!" he called, or thought he did. He couldn't hear it. "Kyra, stop it! I only meant to talk!"

There seemed to be a flicker of terror – there – a feeling that slipped away as soon as Istvan caught hold of it, dissolving into the howl of the wind. Istvan tacked towards it–

–and ran into the boy.

Through him.

Sickening wetness, the hot rush of blood pounding through an overstressed heart, a look of horror in brown eyes, bloodshot, bruised skin and broken veins...

Istvan tumbled. The storm pressed in around him. He couldn't right himself, couldn't orient up or down. Wherever he turned, the storm had become a hall of mirrors, his vision twisted, a terrible pressure twisting through him, like hooks trying to tear out his bones. Rubble fell towards him from above and below, careening at impossible angles.

What on earth?

How could anyone rip holes in the air?

He didn't know where he was falling, or if he was moving at all.

Rock rushed towards him.

Edmund tackled the airborne figure from behind. He wasn't about to ask why the storm had twisted itself around from a spinning hurricane to a blast that left its center exposed, blazing with sheet lightning, hazed and strangely mirage-like. He was afraid he already knew the answer.

He could feel ribs beneath the jacket.

No time for courtesy: Edmund held tight, triggered the return teleport, and – as the field near the truck rushed towards them – twisted around and slammed the other man flat on his back.

The Conduit tried to yell. What emerged was more akin to the squeak of a deflating balloon. He was black.

Very black. He smelled like he hadn't bathed in weeks. He scrabbled at Edmund's jacket front, trying to either get up or pull Edmund down.

Edmund hit him in the stomach. He buckled.

"The tiara!" shouted Grace. "Get the tiara!"

Edmund snatched up the circlet she'd given him. It was hers. She'd done something to it. Be careful, she'd said. It was a trick to get it over the unkempt mane, but Edmund managed, and Grace hadn't been kidding – a flash, and it was all over.

The stormbringer toppled, limp.

Edmund stood over him, breathing hard.

"Got it?" called Grace.

Edmund swallowed. He knelt down, checking for breathing. Whatever the circlet did, it had done it: the other man was out like a light, no blunt impact needed.

The other man...

"Grace," Edmund said, going over the last few moments in his mind with a kind of dread and wondering how he'd missed something so obvious, "he's just a kid."

Grace knelt beside him. She pressed a silvery capsule against the downed Conduit's neck, paused, and then put it away in one of her many pockets. "Jeez," she said. She tapped the circlet, as though checking for something. She shook her head. "Jeez."

"That's about right," Edmund agreed.

Thunder shook the horizon. The ground trembled.

Edmund's insides froze. Not here.

He turned around. A wall of dust and grit filled the sky, rushing towards them, roaring like a wave. The storm had fallen apart.

Fallen.

He found words. "Grace, take a moment to–"

"Not taking your time!" Grace slung the kid over her shoulder like a decorative scarf and launched herself away. "Get to the truck!"

Edmund looked around. Spotted the truck. Snapped his watch.

He stood by the truck. Grace wasn't there yet.

"Get in," shouted Rosales, now in the driver's seat.

"But–"

Grace leapt into the back. "Go, go!"

Edmund swung himself into the passenger seat. The truck lunged forward as he slammed the door. The engine howled. His respect for whoever had rigged the vehicle's suspension rose significantly: he hadn't thought it could accelerate this fast over such bumpy ground without throwing riders out the back.

He twisted around to make sure Grace was still there. She was, crouched over the kid to shield him from the debris, one gauntlet locked in a death grip on an equipment handle. The lower half of her face was the only part of her left exposed; the rest, armored and buckled and booted, seemed to be holding up much better than Edmund's own ensemble. She looked like she wasn't going anywhere. She looked like, if worst came to worst, she'd uppercut the storm herself.

Her eyes caught his.

All right, he mouthed.

Her lips quirked in a faint smile. She gave him a thumbs-up.

Behind her rushed the wall of dust. It was much closer now.

Edmund turned back around, slowly. His hat rolled on the floor by his feet; he picked it up and put it on, trying not to look at the side mirror.

Where was Istvan?

"Rosales," he said, "are you sure we need the truck?"

"We need the truck," confirmed Rosales, without turning his head. He nodded: the rapid up-down-up-down affirmation of a man who had other things on his mind. "We definitely need the truck."

"I don't think we're going fast enough, then," said Edmund.

"We're going pretty fast," said Rosales.

"We are."

Rosales glanced at the rearview mirror. He paled. "Hey, Hour Thief, you think your girlfriend back there will–"

"Not my girlfriend."

"Yeah, right, right. You think she'll be OK if we try something?"

"Probably."

"OK." Rosales reached for the key in the ignition. "Don't breathe too much."

Edmund sat up. "Wait, wha–"

The key turned one notch beyond where it should have.

Edmund found himself staring at the fossil tied to the keyring. Just a bit of bone gone to rock. Strange coils scrimshawed onto it.

Back and forth it swung, twisting in the jolts that no longer came.

Dust washed over them, the engine noise gone, grit and stone and bits of torn-up wire quieted to a clouded whisper that streamed through the cab like it and all its occupants weren't there. Boulders tumbled gracefully to the earth around them, breaking to pieces. Grass whirled upwards in great rushing spirals. Topsoil followed, more and more of the earth blown away beneath them.

Edmund could feel the dust whistling through his skin.

What? he mouthed.

Orange flashed along the storm front, the crack and whistle of something familiar echoing through the muffled quiet. Broken feathers whipped past. Lengths of barbed wire tumbled away and vanished into the dust.

Edmund touched the window. "Istvan?"

His voice emerged muted.

A piece of wire caught on the mirror, winding around the frame as though seeking purchase before it, too, tore away and was gone.

Another heartbeat and the front had passed them.

The key turned back with a click.

The engine roared to full strength... and the truck dropped at least two feet. When it hit the ground, it knocked Edmund's hat off and did nothing for his tailbone, and when it took off with all its prior acceleration and almost skewed over onto its side before coming to a sudden halt, it threw him against the door.

"Sorry!" called Rosales.

Grace pounded on the back window.

Edmund rubbed at the side of his head, devoutly wishing a vehicle had never been involved and trying to remember if he had any spare jackets left. Or pants. Or shoes. Or anything else. Maybe he should have done like with his hat and left it all in the truck.

Something seemed to be smoking. The tires?

What had happened to Istvan?

Rosales rolled down his window. "Sorry!"

Grace swung down out of the back. "Some warning would've been nice."

The Tornado Alley wizard shrugged. "No time."

Grace looked to Edmund.

He held up his hands. "I didn't know."

She sighed. "Look, I've got some more tranquilizers, but I can't keep our new friend there out of it forever." She took a step onto the wheel well to peer into the truck bed, then lowered herself back to window level. "Jeez, he's like… he can't even be sixteen yet."

Edmund rubbed a hand over his eyes. "Is this why you wanted to come, Grace?"

"I've never heard of a Conduit this powerful," she said.

"You said you had theories. Would any of those happen to include a Conduit creating a superstorm and–"

"Sustaining it," said Rosales. "Not creating it. It wasn't following the normal paths, but other than that it seemed like a regular storm to me." He propped a hand on the steering wheel, watching the dust recede. "Without the kid I guess there was nothing to keep it together all the way out here."

"It doesn't matter now," said Grace. "We have to get him back to Barrio Libertad."

Edmund put his hat back on. "Excuse me?"

"What? Where else were you planning to put him?"

Nowhere came to mind.

Somewhere else. They could put the kid somewhere else. Somewhere not Barrio Libertad. Maybe the Demon's Chamber could hold him – it had held Istvan, after all.

This was his investigation. His mission. Grace wasn't even supposed to have come.

The mirror on his side seemed blown out of alignment. Edmund rolled down his window to adjust it.

"In case you forgot, Eddie," Grace continued, "I'm a Conduit, too. We've done research. Maybe we can–"

Edmund jerked around. "Research, Grace?"

"Of cour–"

"Yes, of course you've done research. Of course. Seven years of it, and not a word to anyone. Is that how you got those gauntlets tailored, Grace? Is that how Diego's always listening? What did you do, let him cut you open?"

She opened her mouth. Closed it.

Edmund pressed on, knowing he shouldn't. "Grace, when we first met, you said you'd never let anyone dissect you."

She took hold of the window frame. Pushed down. The truck tilted, creaking. "You don't know what you're talking about."

"I know what I heard."

"No one," she said, "cut me open."

She let go. The vehicle frame rocked back to an even keel. She turned around and climbed back into the truck bed.

Rosales looked at the window frame. It had dents in it. "I think we should get back to headquarters," he said, in a tone that suggested sudden, serious doubts about his traveling companions.

Edmund crossed his arms. "I agree."

"I'll drive."

"Thanks."

Rosales put the truck in gear. "No problem."

Edmund propped his elbow against the window as they started moving again, feeling sour and bruised and tired. He tasted grit in his teeth. He couldn't spit. It wouldn't be polite to spit.

Where was Istvan? He should have been back by now. Complaining about his uniform, probably, and how Edmund didn't get to his target on the first try, and about how he'd had to go all that way over a boring field to get back to them, and retorting with his own opinions whenever Grace said anything, and fussing needlessly but at least genuinely over Edmund's scrapes and other minor injuries.

It would have been easier with Istvan.

"Seatbelt," said Rosales.

Edmund sighed. "Right."

He buckled up.

Barely aware, he drifted. Flashes of memory. Mist over fields.

The storm had passed, now. Whatever strange force had torn him apart was gone. The boy. The Conduit. Kyra.

Edmund had taken him. Edmund was there, still, a lingering disquiet, rich and graceful and familiar, passing further and further away every moment.

So like someone else.

War called. Battles stalemated on a mountain, waged up and down roads blasted into its peaks. Great doors trembled under siege. The dead slid down into smog-choked dust.

Istvan followed. Drawn, inexorably, to the east.

To Triskelion.

The door to Landsea flew open as they parked the truck.

"It's gone," said Clark, running out to meet them. She waved a printed piece of paper. "The storm up and vanished! I knew you were supposed to be good, but…"

She trailed off as Grace hoisted the kid out of the back.

Edmund shut his door and walked around the tailgate, acutely aware of how he must look. Not quite a tiger attack, but close. "It's never that easy."

Clark blinked at him.

He tried a smile. "Had to get him down somehow."

"Wasn't my idea," said Rosales.

Grace lay the kid on the ground, gently. She set a hand on his forehead. She was wearing her own circlet again, reset to its usual function of countering unnatural mental influence. An important function, given that she'd spent her entire career as Resistor Alpha fighting the Susurration.

"All right?" asked Edmund.

Grace sighed. She patted at her pockets and withdrew another silvery vial, twisting at it as she kneeled. "He won't be if he wakes up here."

Clark peered into the cab. "Where's your friend? The ghost?"

Edmund's smile faded, despite himself. He glanced back at the horizon. No Istvan.

It had taken more than two hours to get back, and still no Istvan.

He couldn't have been hurt – Istvan was Istvan, after all – and he wouldn't have run off, no matter what he'd said about Triskelion and the fighting there and his worries about losing himself. Again. Like he'd done for decades before he was chained.

Edmund tried not to think about the flash of a knife in the dark, a forest littered with burning Russian tanks. "I'm sure he'll turn up."

Better than the alternative, if it came to that. If he had been hurt, somehow, if the kid's power extended to tearing apart an avatar of war itself...

Clark frowned. "What happened?"

"The boy's a Conduit," said Grace. She tucked the vial away. "He's also Shattered."

"Shattered?"

Grace shrugged. "We had a problem back East with a mind-controlling extradimensional parasite called the Susurration – tried to swamp the Earth in eternal peace and happiness, stagnate civilization and destroy free will, that kind of thing. It managed to mess up a lot of people before we put it away. Kind of a final middle finger to human decency." She brushed at the duct tape holding the kid's jacket together. "His mind's all mixed up with a thousand other people. He doesn't know who or what he is. That's what 'Shattered' means. That was him, directing the storm."

Clark crouched beside her, hesitantly. "I didn't know a Conduit could do that."

"There's a lot we're trying to figure out," said Grace. She smoothed the jacket collar, then stood. "Poor kid," she added.

There was something more behind that statement – something in her eyes, the pause between explanation and opinion – but Edmund knew better than to ask. All Conduits had manifested simultaneously. A single day and night in 2012. The start of the Wizard War, when Shokat Anoushak's ritual sacrifice of Mexico City shattered reality, and the world as it had been along with it.

The circumstances hadn't been ideal.

Grace, at least, was already a grown woman when it happened. For a kid – a little kid, at the time...

Edmund found himself dreading the inevitable next

meeting with Mercedes.

"Grace," he said. "You don't know what happened up there. You don't know what he can do. You don't know how long he's been active or where he came from – and you still want to take him to Barrio Libertad?"

"Better than the alternative," said Grace.

Edmund leaned against the tailgate, biting back a sharp retort. She always had to use that wording. Throw it back in his face. "Grace, Barrio Libertad is home to well over a million people now. Putting a Conduit like that in the middle of them doesn't seem the least bit dangerous to you?"

She jerked a thumb at her breastplate. "Eddie, I'm Resistor Alpha."

"Titles don't solve everything."

"They'll understand. Besides, you know what Diego can do. We'll take care of him."

Edmund wondered if the vault could hold a storm. If the Demon's Chamber would be a good place for a kid to wake up. If the Twelfth Hour had anyone who could handle the kind of trauma that Shattering caused.

Istvan, maybe.

Wherever he was.

"Clark, Rosales," he began, "Landsea wouldn't happen to have anywhere to house a... person of interest like this, would it?"

"There's an old missile silo across the state line, I guess," Clark said. She folded a corner of the paper over itself. "It's full of... well, missiles, but..."

Rosales, who had been inspecting the dents left in his truck, coughed.

Edmund sighed. "Right."

Grace flashed a triumphant look at him. She was

right. She knew she was right.

What did you think you were trying to do, Eddie? Barrio Libertad is clearly the best option, Eddie. I thought you were the Hour Thief: what have you done over the last few months aside from not a whole lot?

We'll do everything you can't, Eddie. Diego and I.

Everything.

Something tightened in Edmund's chest. Empty-handed, all this time. Hiding in his house. Not answering calls. Not doing anything he was supposed to, and interrupted even when he tried. One mission on top of another and all of them stalled.

Now he was supposed to go back to the Twelfth Hour – to Mercedes – admitting that he'd turned this, too, over to Barrio Libertad?

He tugged his tie straight. "Grace, I appreciate the offer, but I'm taking the kid."

Grace shook her head. "Don't be stupid."

"I've been in this business since before you were born," he retorted. "I know what I'm doing."

She raised an eyebrow. "Really, Eddie?"

"I'm the one that got us here. I was pulled out of a meeting to be here."

"Yeah, well–"

"I went through that storm to get him, and I caught him, and I'm the one who is going to decide where he ends up because, Grace, I feel like hell right now and I'm done arguing with you." He reached for his pocketwatch before he could change his mind. "I'll drop you off outside the walls."

She dodged, blurring–

He was faster.

As long as he had time, he was always faster.

When he returned, Clark was bent over the boy, checking his breathing. She startled when she saw him – only him, no Grace – and produced a nervous chuckle. "So. Uh."

"Don't worry about it," Edmund said.

"Right. Right, I won't." She stood, smoothing her jeans. She didn't seem willing to look at him anymore. "Oh," she said. "Thanks for helping to keep that tower up, by the way. Lockhart reminded me."

Edmund frowned. "Tower?"

"The cell tower. While you were out here mapping the place, oh… six years back?"

He considered. He'd covered a lot of ground, then. Mercedes had wanted to know what places were in one piece and might be helpful allies, and he'd been able to go further, faster, than anyone else in the Twelfth Hour.

"Full of those trapdoor spiders?" Clark added.

Right.

"You're welcome," he said.

A pause.

"Thank you for having us," he finished. He stepped to the kid, wondering how long he'd stay sedated. "And for driving," he added to Rosales.

Rosales gave him a thumbs-up.

"Give our regards to your Magister," said Clark.

"I will."

Edmund pictured fallen leaves of blinking red and green.

Thunder called him. It rolled from peak to peak and cliff to cliff, the echoing roar of artillery fire and the lighter patter of small arms, a pass under siege. Stray shots chipped off shards of rock. Other shots struck softer things.

It was when the rockslide fell, burying a supply convoy winding up the cliffs, that he awoke.

Blood. Agony.

A wheel, spinning down into the canyon.

Artillery crews scrambling down from the other side of the pass.

Figures in burnished armor shouting, backpedaling. Shots rang through him. Amplified voices calling demands in a language he didn't know.

Istvan hovered, above the fall, drawing in every flavor – the sweet fluttering panic of labored breathing, the rich dread of crushing darkness, the burning ecstasy of pulverised limbs – and sighed, and shuddered with the sighing (oh, it was wonderful) and wondered which side he ought to join.

This one?

The other one?

Which was it, and which was more outnumbered, and which would be more sporting?

"Who's winning?" he called.

Gunfire answered him.

He skipped down the fall, poison trailing in his wake. The air was choked here; almost orange, thick with coal smoke, acrid and burning. Fires threw odd shadows across the rocks. The artillery hadn't stopped.

Those firing at him retreated. Soot stained spiked pauldrons, spiked crests, ratcheted seams at shoulder and elbow. Scarlet lights flashed behind closed visors. Some wore capes, torn and faded.

Triskelion. Armor like that only came out of Triskelion.

Not nearly so splendid now, were they? Difficult to keep up a polish while waging a siege, wasn't it? Even if they were the winning side, would it matter?

Something buried under the rock pile shifted, sending more stone cascading into the canyon below. The warriors scrambled to keep their footing.

Istvan laughed. A shot blew through him. He spread rotten wings in the dust.

He'd just have to get a good look at the situation himself, wouldn't he?

He stepped forward – they held their ground this time, bless them – and dove sideways off the side of the road. Stones fell past him. Motor oil trickled down in thin cascades. Smoke billowed from the shattered shell of a domed spire toppled from its foundations: smoke with a thick, greasy quality to it. Bodies lay slumped beneath the twisted skeletons of iron gates.

The thunder came from further up the canyon.

Istvan snapped his wings open. Righted himself. Side-slipped around the broken pillars of a bridge, half-wishing there were something to chase him.

Brass glittered below: shells littering cracked pools of alkali.

Oh, he'd missed this.

He'd missed this so much.

Why, once he found the siege, all he'd have to do was ask to see the commander (or at the very least figure out which side was Lord Kasimir's, the only name he knew), and then he would be free to…

To…

He slowed.

There had been a boy. A Negro boy, in a battered jacket, just on the edge of manhood. Floating, amid the dust.

And the storm…

Where was Edmund?

Something exploded nearby. A searing rush of unrefined terror flooded his senses. He gasped. He almost hit a cliff. He soared in it: a brilliant, crystalline sweetness, raw and sharp, the agony of it setting his sight to spinning and his breath to a wholly unreal and involuntary catch in his throat – where was it? How many? – and when he finally managed to alight he was shaking so badly he wondered if he were a haze to outside eyes, trembling with need and frustration and awful pleasure.

There was more where that came from. Oh, so much more. Triskelion. Triskelion. A war, a real war, finally–

He could lose so many weeks here. He could lose it all, let it overcome him, wash into him, sweep away all his worries in the rush of blood and fire.

He clutched at his wrists. His forearms. Hugged his chest.

No. No, no.

Rock scraped at his back. He raised his wings to hide it – the doors set into the mountain, the armies that climbed perilous trails toward them, the flare and flash and fierce joy of it all, siege waged by vicious warlords for ends no one could say – but the feathers were transparent, and fraying.

Did they all have the same peculiar armor that blocked his blade? Did their equipment have the same protection? Did all sides know of him?

How many men could he kill before their generals took note?

He tore away. He fled back through the canyon – sometimes through rock, stone scraping through his insides as he barreled onwards, blind – and back past the fall.

He hadn't meant to come here.

He shouldn't have come here.

He couldn't stay.

He couldn't stay.

The Twelfth Hour never should have unchained him.

CHAPTER EIGHT

Edmund couldn't help but wince when he snapped on the shackles. Black iron, they were, shaped like grasping claws, clutching the boy's thin wrists with a tightness that seemed to draw blood when you weren't quite looking at them. The links that dragged after them were thick as human fingers, chains wrapped around the chamber's central column and bolted in a dozen places to the hewn stone of both the floor and the walls. Arabic calligraphy flowed across their surfaces. Steam rose from the anchor points, glowing as though backlit by flame and smelling of sandalwood.

The Demon's Chamber had been built to hold its namesake, before it held Istvan, and it looked it. Not a place for a kid who might have been barely fifteen.

The boy didn't fight back. He didn't do much of anything but droop, bonelessly, eyelids fluttering. Whatever had been in that vial was powerful stuff.

Again, Edmund wondered if he'd made the right choice.

The kid was dangerous. There was no doubt about that. He was Shattered, and a Conduit, and the most powerful Conduit anyone had ever seen. Any one of those three by themselves would have been worrying enough, and the Twelfth Hour didn't have anywhere else suited to that kind of threat. If Barrio Libertad was going to be out of the picture, the Demon's Chamber was the next best thing.

Which still left the matter of actually putting a colored kid in chains.

Edmund retrieved a cylinder of table salt from the toolbox he'd brought down the stairwell and started spilling lines of it along the paths marked on the floor.

What the kid looked like shouldn't matter. The question of segregation was long over and done with – hell, almost everyone he knew at this point had been born after the marches, and had never seen the signs in shop windows or over water fountains. Anyone could use whatever door they wanted, now. This was 2020. The Twelfth Hour's own Magister was a woman with brown skin. Edmund had thought well of the civil rights movement, and done his best all his life to treat everyone he met with equal dignity.

It shouldn't matter.

Edmund spilled the salt faster. He tried not to imagine the kid waking up suddenly and demolishing the entire Twelfth Hour basement before he could get the room warded. At least this version of the ritual wasn't the one that required an animal sacrifice. They were running low on gerbils.

Salt lines finished, he lit a match and held it to a bowl laid in a depression near the door. Its contents caught fire almost immediately, throwing the stench of burning hair into the air. He held back a sneeze. Scattering salt all over the room wouldn't do at all.

"Right," he muttered to himself.

He rose, stepped carefully over the lines, and checked

the notes written on a clipboard hung by the door. They were written in Classical Arabic, one of those languages that he knew by necessity. This was Innumerable Citadel magic. They were the mystics who had defeated Shokat Anoushak the first time, in the mid-600s. They had catalogued her works, adapted them, expanded on them, and passed them down to form over a full quarter of modern Western magical canon.

Edmund closed his eyes.

The first kind of magic was Conceptual magic, which drew on the known: perfect solids, logical extremes, ideas sharpened to a razor point. Istvan was Conceptual. The Susurration was Conceptual. Conceptual magic was dangerous, because fire burned hotter than flame.

Then there was the other kind of magic.

The words flowed easily, but not gently. They entreated the invisible and the unknowable, with such power that granting them names made the world shudder. They drew attention where attention was best not drawn at all.

His had come from the lake.

The last word left his lips. He'd said it right. He knew he'd said it right.

He still reached a hand for the wall, dizzy and dry-mouthed.

The chains clanked. The steam vanished, as though sucked in by a hungering maw. He imagined he saw eyes in the spaces of each link and hastily looked away.

A rushing, like enormous lungs drawing inward–

–and then there was only a spindly young black kid, propped on his knees, head drooping, wrists fixed by iron claws to a central column of stone.

Edmund swallowed.

This was how he'd met Istvan, the second time. After his capture. A man, however translucent, bent to his knees and chained immobile in that very same place.

You don't look at all like I remember, Edmund had told him.

The specter had smiled, then.

You do, he'd said.

Where was he? Istvan would have known what drugs Grace had used. He would have had an opinion on what to do. He would have had ideas of his own. He wouldn't have approved of this.

Too late now.

Edmund took a few steadying breaths. He bent down and closed the toolbox with a click that seemed far too loud for the space. The kid really was dangerous. No doubt about it. No matter his color. This was the best Edmund could do with what he had. It wouldn't be permanent.

He picked up the toolbox, cast one last glance at the chains – Istvan's chains, for twenty years, before the Twelfth Hour had resorted to the pure Conceptual, anchored to the pillar that rose from the room's center, bathed in hellish firelight – and then shut the door behind him.

Now to tell Mercedes what he'd done.

Istvan had figured out what happened by the time he reached New Haven. The boy in the storm – Kyra – had done something to him. Trapped him. Tore at him. Ripped away at his substance. How, he didn't know, but that he had done it was certain.

This wasn't wholly new. Istvan had been torn apart before. Once, at death, when he'd had no idea what he was doing or what he'd called up, and several more times over the course of his career, mostly struck by bombs he hadn't been expecting.

It was as close to unconsciousness as he ever came.

Kyra had reached for something, tried to do something… and Istvan had forgotten how young the boy was, and that he himself was invincible.

He swooped low over the house. No Edmund. Boats skimmed through the bay beyond, dragging nets behind them, and he wished them better luck than in the days before. The mountains rose jagged to his left. He tried not to look at them. They hadn't been so dramatic before the Wizard War. Not like the Alps at all.

He shivered at the thought. It wasn't an unpleasant shiver. He realized that he was drifting to that side and course-corrected.

Don't think of the Alps.

He whirled around the Twelfth Hour's crumbling superstructure – its earthquake-toppled facade, its cracked windows, the rows of stone dancing-girls that lined its upper stories, the wires trailing down towards New Haven – and then shot upwards, towards the mist of thin clouds that veiled the sun. They broke in a shower of bloodied droplets.

He wheeled in a slow circle, trying to gather his thoughts.

Edmund was down there, unmistakable. Was Kyra? Was Grace?

He didn't think so, but…

Oh, how was he to explain himself? He hadn't meant to leave. He hadn't meant to take so long to come to his senses. He hadn't meant any of it, and the simple fact that Edmund would likely forgive him and then do his best to forget it only made it worse.

At least he'd found the man. At least no one else had been hurt.

He hoped.

The Twelfth Hour's doors opened for him, and the crowds cleared away from his presence – as always, his reputation from the Wizard War preceding every good deed he'd done since. Did he look worse than usual? Was he having more trouble maintaining his own facade over what he truly was?

Edmund wasn't in the Magister's office. Neither had he entered the high-security vault, the other most common destination.

He seemed to be in the basement. What on Earth was in the basement, aside from unsorted archival documents and the Demon's Chamber...?

The stairwell circled round and round, cut into dusty stone; Istvan skimmed over it more than stepped down, reflexive dread rising even as he descended.

"We can try to keep him dosed," came a voice, "but I'd worry about his health. It's dangerous to keep anyone under longer than you got to. I'd have to run more tests to figure out what Barrio Libertad put into him, and... well, this isn't really the kind of place that makes caring for someone easy, y'know?"

Istvan rounded the last spiral.

And stopped.

"Istvan," said Edmund, gone suddenly pale. "I can explain." He put an arm across the doorframe, cape whirling after it, as though trying to hide the chains and the hellish light beyond. As if that could be hidden. As if either of them had forgotten that place by now.

Istvan took a step towards him. "You didn't."

"This isn't permanent."

"You bloody didn't!"

Edmund flinched. "Istvan–"

Istvan flared wings that filled the stairwell, not caring as bone scraped through solid rock. "You put him in there, didn't you?" Mud and worse things splashed across phantom bullet scarring. Gunfire rattled the hall. "You put him in there!"

Edmund held up his hands. "I didn't have time to think of anywhere else! I told you, it isn't–"

Istvan caught at his lapels, shouting now. "He's Shattered, Edmund! You should have bloody given him to Barrio Libertad!"

Edmund tried to draw away, heart racing against Istvan's grip, terror rolling off of him like overflow from a pot, and Istvan considered reaching into him – grasping that heart as the blood pounded around it – hitching fingers around the other man's ribcage and snarling at him: *This, Edmund, is what those chains felt like. This, but burning!*

Kyra was barely conscious! He slumped before that pillar, held up by nothing but iron, shackled so he couldn't stand. Couldn't bring his hands together. Couldn't turn sideways more than a few inches.

How could Edmund?

How could he?

"Dr Czernin," said Magister Hahn, "you're gassing us."

Istvan realized that Edmund was coughing, clouds of poison hazing the chamber so thickly it seemed to be underwater. Not real, any of it, but the sight, and the smell...

He let go of him. He looked to the Magister. "I hope this was your idea."

"I didn't know until the deed was done," she replied. Her eyes were watering, but she made no move to wipe the tears away. "Mr Templeton did this on his own."

Istvan whirled back to Edmund. How? How could the man do this to anyone else, after two decades of visiting another prisoner trapped in this very same chamber?

"Unchain him," Istvan snapped. "Unchain him now."

"Uh," said the first voice who had spoken. "Uh – uh…"

Then – and only then – did Istvan notice an orderly he didn't recognize cowering against the far wall, almost hidden behind the central pillar. One of the Twelfth Hour's volunteers, probably.

We can try to keep him dosed, he'd said.

More tests, he'd said.

He carried a bag sporting the red cross.

Istvan stepped toward him. "Give me that."

The man dropped it like it had caught fire.

"Now run."

The man hesitated.

Istvan charged the pillar. "Run!"

The fright was hardly worth it. Not comparable at all. Triskelion had been better. Triskelion had been marvelous.

Istvan unzipped the bag.

"You didn't have to do that," muttered Edmund. He wiped at his eyes.

"You didn't have to chain a boy up like a bloody animal," Istvan retorted. He abandoned the bag in disgust – nothing more than basic first aid – and moved towards the young prisoner. "I want a proper kit," he began, checking his pulse, "and I want Roberts here as soon as he's able, and I want something to keep Kyra from hurting himself if he starts thrashing about."

"Kyra?" asked Edmund.

The Magister adjusted one of the pens in her hair. "Dr Czernin, that boy is the most powerful Conduit anyone has ever seen, if Mr Templeton is correct. I don't find his precautions unfitting."

"If we don't keep him sedated–" Edmund began.

"Get out," Istvan told him.

"He did something to you, didn't he? That's why you didn't come back until now." The wizard crouched beside him, a rush of black silk and regret Istvan wished he couldn't detect. It would have been easier. "Istvan," Edmund continued, "I know what you're thinking, and I'm sorry, but he's dangerous. We don't know what more he can do, and Shattered or not, I didn't want Barrio Libertad getting their hands on him."

Istvan lifted Kyra's chin. Brown eyes stared through him, dully. The boy breathed like one asleep. Scrapes and cuts marred his skin, in places crusted with dried blood. The irons at his wrists were almost tight enough to cut off circulation.

"Get out," Istvan repeated.

Edmund paused, then stood. He went to the door, and Istvan tried not to remember all those times, all those years, when he'd wished he could follow him. When he'd been stuck staring at the grain as it closed, the latch echoing.

Twelve stone blocks away. Utterly unreachable.

Twenty years.

"I'll consider you re-assigned," said the Magister. "Keep 'Kyra' under."

Footsteps.

The hinges, creaking.

And then the latch.

Istvan hadn't wanted so badly to kill someone since less than an hour ago.

"The Demon's Chamber isn't designed to hold creatures like that boy," said Mercedes as they started back up the stairs.

Edmund glared at his feet. "I know it isn't."

"And yet you bound him."

"Yes."

"Did you do the one with the gerbils?"

"No."

She nodded. "Good."

They climbed a full round in silence. Edmund had been up and down those stairs thousands of times – probably tens of thousands – and he let his feet carry him while he tried to erase the last few minutes from his mind. Tried to focus on something, anything other than the choking stench of chlorine.

It didn't matter how long they'd been friends: Istvan could still scare the living daylights out of him. Out of Mercedes, even. The specter had run roughshod over her without even realizing it. Without any effort at all.

It was how he moved. What moved with him. Oppressive. Explosive. The dread certainty that he couldn't be stopped and that he would always find you, no matter where you ran.

Where had he been? What had happened to him?

Had he hurt anyone?

Edmund turned his pocket watch over and over in his fingers. No use wondering about help or forgiveness. After today, Istvan would be slow to accept or grant either, and Edmund couldn't blame him.

Worse: no one held grudges like the unquiet dead.

"You should have taken the boy to Barrio Libertad," said Mercedes.

Edmund gritted his teeth. Sure, tell him now. That would help. "I don't know what I should have done, Mercedes, because anytime I do anything I'm interrupted and told to do something else."

"That must be frustrating," came the reply.

"Yesterday you gave me a talk on how the fortress is just about the worst thing that's happened to us since the Wizard War. Today I'm supposed to have turned over this latest problem to them, no questions asked."

"You've always turned over the Shattered to them, Mr Templeton."

"Not like that."

"Even though you knew we didn't have the facilities to deal with him?"

Edmund thought of Grace, so confident that Barrio Libertad could hold a Conduit of such power. That Diego could solve anything with liberal application of who-knew-what. That everyone else living there would be perfectly fine with the arrival of such danger, just like they seemed perfectly fine with omnipresent surveillance and remote control of every surface within those walls.

The Twelfth Hour had the Demon's Chamber. And the high-security vault, but putting the kid, this "Kyra," in the same place as confiscated artifacts and mysterious devices from up and down the seaboard seemed like a remarkably bad idea.

"Mr Templeton?"

Edmund grimaced. Couldn't even spend a few moments to think. "Mercedes, if there's one thing Diego doesn't need, it's more firepower."

"Which is why I'm considering what's done to be done," she said.

"Excuse me?"

Mercedes stopped. She turned around, holding onto the rail. She was no taller than he was even two steps ahead. "Consider Kyra an addition to your merry band, Mr Templeton. Incentive to find a site, and find it quickly."

He stared at her.

It wasn't fair. It wasn't fair to drag him back into this leadership mess and then expect him to cover so many things at once with no time to do it all.

"You pulled me out of a meeting," he said. "To do just that."

"I was in the middle of yet another call about the repair of Oxus Station when it came up," she replied, "and I have both the Magnolia Group and a general citzens' strike to deal with once we're done here. Were you aware that there's a very vocal group of people who want us to open up the vault to everyone? Or that Lord Kasimir is now offering 'wealth, esteem, and vast tracts of land' to anyone willing to break a siege for him?"

"That last I knew," Edmund retorted.

"Still not willing to teach your teleportation skills to anyone else?"

"No."

She started back up the stairs. "Meetings can be rescheduled."

He caught her arm. "Why did you send us?"

She looked at him. Her eyes were very dark, almost black, and still a little red-rimmed from the gas. She'd summoned the Susurration, a literal incarnation of control and stagnation, to end the Wizard War (which it had done by killing the most powerful wizard in history), and then she had proceeded to cannibalize every other magical cabal in Big East until the Twelfth Hour became the only authority on such matters worthy of note, laying claim to the entire seaboard as a protectorate. She was missing a finger and Edmund didn't want to know why.

He let go of her.

"It was a demonstration," she said. "Now, an asset."

"Did you know the storm was a Conduit? Did you know the kid was Shattered?"

"Of course not. The Twelfth Hour is dedicated to helping our allies whenever they call, and that's the end of it."

Edmund gritted his teeth. "But–"

"Despite," she continued, "what Barrio Libertad might say. To us, to our allies, and to anyone else who will listen. You're the Hour Thief, Mr Templeton. You and Dr Czernin fought a storm today, and won. Not everyone can say that."

They reached the top of the stairs. Mercedes took hold of the trapdoor latch.

"What about the kid?" asked Edmund.

A shrug. "It seems to me like you're well on track for recruitment."

Istvan finished wiping away the last of the grit and grime that he could reach. Face, neck, hands. The chains prevented removal of Kyra's jacket, never mind arraying him in any sort of proper position for treatment.

He suspected that the boy was rather thinner than was healthy. He hadn't located any grievous injury or infection, but the drug that kept him so unaware and lethargic was a worrying matter: Istvan had encountered it before, in use by Barrio Libertad against other foes, and knew that it wouldn't last nearly so long as the Magister hoped.

The Twelfth Hour had only limited supplies of something similar.

"Never mind the side-effects," he muttered. "Keep him in a bloody coma while hung by his wrists, oh, that's a fine way to do it."

Did anyone realize how dangerous this could be to him?

Did anyone care?

Lock a fifteen year-old boy in the Demon's Chamber. Bloody wizards.

Bloody Edmund.

"Doctor? I came as quickly as I…" Roberts paused in the doorway, "…could."

Istvan got to his feet, barbed wire looping around chain links. The other man looked as though he would barely fit through the door. "Didn't they tell you?"

"They did, but then I had to convince Lucy that this was a single-man gig and that you had asked for me specifically, and that took a while." Roberts turned sideways, hefting a rather more substantial bag of supplies than the one already present, and threaded himself into the room. He set the bag down. "It's… it's a little different, seeing it."

"Oh, it's nothing, really, Edmund just took a boy down here and chained him to a pillar and put magic on. Did you see the salt?"

Roberts unzipped the bag. It held syringes, saline, tubing, vials of what anesthetics the Twelfth Hour possessed, alcohol swabs, catheters, tourniquets, gauze, scissors, tape, a blanket, and other sundries. It wasn't quite up to modern standard but neither was Istvan; nothing was, anymore.

They began setting up for fluids.

"I can't believe it," Istvan muttered. "I can't bloody believe it. Twenty years, seeing me like that, and now he does this. At least I had a reputation, Roberts. At least I'd killed people of my own bloody volition."

Roberts unrolled a length of tubing, and said nothing. Istvan had selected him as his primary assistant after the Wizard War due to the man's steadiness, dependability, and ability to manhandle what Istvan couldn't. He'd seen a lot since then. Tackled some of it.

He still seemed shaken.

"Ought to have taken him to Barrio Libertad," Istvan repeated. "Ought to have done anything else."

"What did the kid do, exactly?" asked Roberts.

Istvan drove a needle home. "Dragged a storm about. Caused a ruckus. Tore me apart when I got too close."

Roberts' eyes went wide.

"But he didn't mean any of it! He's Shattered, Roberts! God only knows how long he was in thrall. Years, maybe. Half his life, who knows? How am I supposed to help with that? What happens when he wakes up? I spoke to him before we caught him – he may have escaped a Shokat Anoushak cult, and we don't know anything at all about what's been done to him!"

He tore at a cotton ball. "But no, I'm not to allow him to wake at all. Never mind what he must have been through. Never mind that keeping him like this is cruel and inhuman, and Edmund ought to have known better."

Istvan finished fixing the IV in place and sat back, fuming at it.

"The kid tore you apart," said Roberts.

"I'm back now, aren't I?" Istvan retorted.

"Doctor–"

"Everyone is so bloody worried about what he can do that no one is worried about him. Take him, chain him, leave him to rot. He isn't a weapon, for God's sake!"

Roberts blinked at him.

Istvan busied himself with the bag again. Had to figure out dosage. Had to determine that nothing would interact poorly with the Barrio Libertad cocktail.

He wished he knew where Kyra had come from. If there were more like him. If Conduits weren't so uncommon as everyone had thought, but sequestered. Stolen away at the conclusion of the Wizard War. Stockpiled.

Kyra shifted dully in his chains, eyelids fluttering.

Istvan withdrew a vial. He hoped the boy wouldn't remember any of this.

He wished he could try talking to him again.

Roberts drew closer, a knot of apprehension swathed in forced calm. "Doctor, have you maybe considered that you're taking this... I don't know..."

"Personally?"

A shrug.

Istvan pointed at the pillar. "Twenty years."

The other man nodded. "I know. But–"

"I couldn't move for twenty years, Roberts! I went months without anyone speaking to me! I was a... a trophy, a curiosity to be brought up over dinner! 'Oh, yes, the ghost, would you like to see him? He's restrained, don't worry.'" His fingers slipped through the vial, incapable of breaking it. "How could I not take this bloody personally?"

Roberts reached over, retrieved the vial, and placed it gently on the stone. Then he set a large hand approximately on Istvan's shoulder. "Did you ever have kids, Doctor?"

Istvan stared down at Kyra. "No. I didn't."

Should have.

"Then let me tell you something," said Roberts, apprehension giving way to something else, "I had a daughter, Doctor. Before the Wizard War. And it kills me to see a kid like this – any kid, doesn't matter whose – but in this case I think Mr Templeton and the Magister have cause."

A daughter?

How old? How…

Istvan shook his head, dully. He hadn't known. He'd had no idea. "I'm sorry."

"Listen to me," Roberts continued. "Was this place the best place to take him? No. Barrio Libertad would have been better. But he's here now and this is the safest place we've got. For us, and maybe for him. If he's that powerful – if he can control storms, rip up the countryside – then I think it would have been irresponsible to put him anywhere else."

Roberts backed away, picking up the vial again. "I don't like it, and he won't like it, but not everyone can just come back from being torn apart. It's a little more permanent for the rest of us."

Istvan sat there as the other man rummaged through the bag, checking labels, an old, distant pain echoing behind each motion. Istvan hadn't thought anything of that. So many people carried that, now. Almost everyone had lost someone to the Wizard War.

That didn't mean the lost weren't of note.

Istvan looked at Kyra again. What dream was the boy living? Who was present in it that hadn't survived 2012?

More permanent for the rest of us.

Had Istvan truly lost so much perspective? Of course they feared Kyra. Of course the Twelfth Hour couldn't keep him anywhere else. Couldn't move him, for the terror.

He had hurt Istvan, after all, and everyone knew Istvan couldn't be hurt.

Istvan was invincible.

"Roberts," he said.

"Yeah?"

"We'll do our best. He'll have the very best care we can give him, despite it all."

The other man nodded. "That's what we do."

Istvan realized he was rubbing at his wrists again. He took hold of a chain instead, iron that for once imprisoned someone who didn't deserve it. A challenge. Think of it as a challenge. "Let's set him up for airway control," he said. "If we're to keep him under, we'll do it right."

CHAPTER NINE

Edmund went home. It was getting late, he was exhausted, and he wanted a chance to finally change his clothes.

He needed to find someone who could make suit jackets and wasn't Barrio Libertad. The Magnolia Group, maybe. If he set up a site "in their vicinity." If they wouldn't mind a Conduit who could destroy entire counties as a neighbor.

He was going to have a lot of adjusting to do for the next meeting. Was he ever. When Janet Justice heard about this…

Edmund pulled off his goggles and rubbed a hand over his eyes.

There was a paper stuck to the outside of his living room window.

He squinted at it for a while, trying to read what was on the other side backwards. His vision kept swimming. When was the last time he'd eaten?

Later. Get the note later.

Beldam headbutted him as he hung up coat and hat. There seemed to be even more paper strewn about than usual, which was strange given that he'd put at least half of it in that box. Some of his books had been knocked off the coffee table, too...

The cat yowled and shot into the kitchen. Edmund followed, wondering if he had any potatoes left, and then immediately found something else to occupy his mind.

Water all over the floor. Tea tin knocked over. Loose leaves floating in the water. Broken glass scattered before one of the cabinets, together with four or five pieces of plate. Wet paper tracked into both the living room and the hall.

Beldam.

He'd forgotten to feed Beldam.

Dammit.

The cat headbutted him again, meowing what was probably a snide and vociferous commentary on his competence, parentage, and upbringing.

"I'm sorry," he muttered. "Something came up."

She wasn't having it.

He fetched the bag of cat food – it was running low; he'd have to start keeping an eye out again; he hated the idea of Beldam having to eat rats and birds – and poured an even helping into her bowl.

"There. I'll try harder, all right?"

No comment: her mouth was full. Her tail switched behind her, suggesting that he wasn't yet forgiven.

She wasn't the only one.

"Sorry," he said again, and went to change his clothes. Into what, he didn't care. A bathrobe would do. And shoes, thanks to the glass.

He wasn't about to throw out all that tea. He'd been lucky to find that tea.

Bathrobe obtained, he returned to the kitchen and found a broom and dustpan. Glass first. Then some way to scoop up what remained of the tea.

He was dumping the plate pieces into the trash when a knock came at the door.

He almost spent a moment to get dressed.

Couldn't do that. Couldn't afford that. Bathrobe would have to do.

He cracked open the door and peered through. "Yes?"

A middle-aged couple stood there, a man and a woman he thought he recognized. He'd seen that red hair before. Had they helped with the tilling at Yale? They'd had some kind of cart, a trailer probably made to be pulled behind a car before conversion.

They shifted nervously. A box sat beside them. His box of documents, he realized, left at Charlie's for the others to pore over. He'd thought.

"Can I help you?" he asked.

"We were just wondering if... you know, the box," said the man, his words a hurried rush. "It's been there a long time and you don't really seem to ever go out much or open the door much and we wanted to make sure you got it."

Edmund glanced back at the note on his window.

"I put that there," said the woman. She clasped her hands together. "I... I didn't realize it was backwards. Sorry!"

Edmund imagined her skulking around the hedge, making a sudden dash for it, slapping the note on the window, and running. He sighed. "It's all right. Thank you for letting me know."

"You're welcome."

He waited for them to leave so he could open the door all the way and get the box, but they stood there awkwardly, never quite meeting his eyes.

"I'm in a bathrobe," he explained.

"Oh!"

Yes, he mentally added, *I bathe.*

"We'll leave you to it, then," said the man with a strained chuckle.

The woman nodded, managing to stare fixedly at Edmund's lapel. "If you, um, ever need anything, Mr Templeton, we're here."

Edmund shook his head. "I'm fine. Thank you."

"I thought you were older," said the man.

The woman elbowed him.

Edmund froze, wondering if the grey streak were visible and concluding that it was on the side of his head presently obscured by the door. "I am," he said.

Another strained chuckle. "Looking good."

The woman grabbed at her husband's arm, evidently trying to drag him away.

"I didn't get your names," Edmund said.

"Thompson," said the woman. "Maggie and Bill Thompson."

"A pleasure. Thank you again."

He watched them hustle off his doorstep, picking up speed as they departed. Thompson. He'd remember that.

He let the door swing open so he could get the box.

Still shouldn't have let the secret slip. It wasn't that it was a particularly well-guarded one anymore, that Edmund Templeton was the Hour Thief, but letting people know for the sake of clearing the air hadn't done anything but make life awkward.

Before, he'd been mysterious but polite, and in turn politely avoided. Now the neighbors couldn't seem to decide whether to approach him, awed and armed with effusive compliments, or just stare at him, wide-eyed, like he might burst into flames at any second.

He hefted the box.

Granted, Istvan tended to tilt the balance toward the latter.

The exhaustion hit again. He closed the door, set the box near the couch, and collapsed on the cushions, both hands over his eyes. What was he going to do about Istvan?

What was he going to do about any of it?

Find a place. Write a charter. Wrangle a team. Take care of that boy. Get more time. Figure out how in hell to make it up to Istvan. Don't think about the chains. Remember to feed the cat. Find out where to get replacement jackets and pants. Get more time. Deal with Grace. Don't think about the chains. Get more time.

Always, get more time.

Drink. He should get a drink. That would help.

Just one.

Then he'd finish up with the kitchen and go on patrol.

He'd sleep eventually.

Near to midnight, the door latch to the Demon's Chamber clicked.

Istvan didn't look up from his embroidery. "Go away."

"I brought some things," called Edmund. Something thunked. There was a muffled shuffling, like cloth sliding against the door, and then the clatter of dropped metal.

Istvan jabbed the needle into his vaguely-defined mountain pass, thread of white and blue and brown on black. Red would come later. "I said go away!"

The door burst open. A metal stool crashed onto the floor. Edmund stumbled through, carrying a mass of pillows and a picture frame, clad in civilian attire and whirling with terror.

Istvan put the embroidery down. "Edmund, what on earth do you think you're–"

"Housewarming gift," said the wizard, eyes wild.

One of the pillows fell from his grasp and landed across one of the salt-filled grooves on the floor.

It was heart-shaped.

Istvan checked to be sure Kyra hadn't stirred. Tubes ran into the boy's right arm and mouth, his jacket cut away and padding wrapped around the chains that bound him. He looked terrible, strung up like that, but the machine they had brought down continued its steady beeping: he remained well beyond hearing.

Just as well.

Istvan stood. "Edmund, I don't know what you think this is, but it isn't funny."

Edmund dropped the other pillows in a heap near the door, and righted the stool, his motions jerky, controlled to the extent that his hands didn't seem to be shaking. "Not housewarming," he said. "That's what they tried to give me. This is decor. Something to make the place a little less… demon."

Istvan frowned. "Have you been drinking?"

"Only one."

"One what?"

The wizard's legs folded under him and he sat down hard. He dropped his head in his hands. "Don't make me leave, Istvan. Please don't make me leave."

Istvan stepped over the salt lines. Strange, being able to do that. "One what, Edmund?"

"If you make me leave I'm going to Charlie's."

Not this. Not again.

Istvan crossed his arms. Who did Edmund think he

was? Coming here, after what he had done – knowing what Istvan thought of the Demon's Chamber, what he'd endured there, all those years – and then expecting to be cared for?

Here, of all places?

And Kyra chained to that pillar all the while, unseeing, like so much meat–

"Don't make me leave," Edmund repeated. Fear rolled from him, rich and dark, that subtle sweetness Istvan knew all too well. His shoulders shook. He was starting to hyperventilate.

Istvan sighed. He crouched beside him. "Edmund–"

"I'm sorry. I'm sorry for everything. I wasn't thinking. I know the kid's colored, Istvan, and I'm not racist, but I didn't want to come back empty-handed, again, and Grace was right because she's always right, Istvan. I hate that she's always right."

Grace. Of course. Always.

The man needed to get over her, was what he needed to do. This was ridiculous.

Istvan set a hand on his shoulder, begrudgingly. "It's too bloody late now. We've already arranged Kyra to stay, if you hadn't noticed."

"You have every right to be angry," Edmund said.

"Oh, I'm angry, believe me."

"I didn't have time."

"Evidently."

Edmund leaned back against the wall, staring blankly at the ceiling. "I need to get more time," he said.

Istvan patted his shoulder, drawing off as much terror as he could and wishing the feeling were more unpleasant. The audacity, coming in here and expecting care at the drop of a hat. And with a… a bloody heart pillow.

Edmund had never brought a heart pillow in here while Istvan was chained.

"I cleaned the kitchen," said Edmund.

"Good for you," Istvan replied. "I put a boy in a coma," he added.

The other man wilted. "I'm sorry."

Istvan indicated the shackles that pinned Kyra's wrists to the pillar. "Why did you put him in the solid chains, anyhow? Why not the Conceptual ones? You can do that. I know you can do that. Why didn't you start with those from the beginning?"

"Gerbils," came the reply.

"Pardon?"

Edmund put his hands over his face, slithering further down onto the floor. "We would have needed an animal sacrifice, Istvan. It's a different incantation. Harder to break. With the shackles, we'll just have to unlock him and take him out of the room."

Istvan sat back against the wall, glaring at the pillar. Another angle that seemed jarring and strange.

Oh, he hated this place. Every time he moved he was reminded that he ought to be in Kyra's position, forced to his knees, staring at a locked door. " You couldn't have simply put him in the room with the salt, alone?" he asked. "No chains?"

"Not how it works."

"Well, that seems terribly cruel and unnecessary."

Edmund shrugged. "It's from the late eighth century, Istvan, and meant to hold demons."

Istvan propped his elbows on his knees. "I don't care."

Another shrug.

They sat in silence a moment, the breathing machine beeping softly from its place propped against the far wall.

Edmund quested for his hat and found nothing. He glanced down at his own clothing, as though surprised to see a green cardigan instead of his usual black jacket. He picked up the heart pillow. "Istvan–"

"Go on and do whatever you're going to do, then," Istvan snapped. He jabbed the needle savagely into the fabric. "I'm staying here."

Edmund flinched.

Served him right, it did. What right did he have? Putting himself above others. Determining who was safe and who was too dangerous to go free, and all without any outside consultation.

This was the second time. Kyra hadn't asked to be bound; Istvan hadn't asked to be set loose. Not the way Edmund did it.

The Susurration was Conceptual. Istvan was Conceptual. Istvan was the Great War, and only the chains had maintained a degree of separation between him and it: a degree broken the moment Edmund cut them away. They had brought War to the domain of Peace, with depressingly predictable results.

Even the Susurration hadn't deserved that. Its thralls caught in the crossfire hadn't deserved that.

Go, Edmund. Go on, go get your time. Tell yourself you do it all for others.

Istvan didn't care.

"Is there anything I can do?" asked Edmund.

"No."

The wizard dropped the heart pillow. He glanced at the embroidery. "Triskelion?"

Istvan folded it over itself, hiding the siege below the mountain. "Go away."

"That's where you went?"

"What does it matter to you?"

Edmund got to his feet, leaning somewhat on the stool he had brought. "You had me worried while you were gone. That's all."

"You oughtn't worry," Istvan informed him. "I'm invincible."

A sigh. "Istvan–"

"Go." He waved a hand at the chamber door, still ajar from last night. "You've people waiting for you, I'm sure. Can't bloody deprive them of the Hour Thief. Tell them I'm being stubborn and foolish, if anyone asks."

Edmund hesitated. He swung his watch chain around his hand. He looked like one who'd slept soundly due only to exhaustion, and not for lack of worries. Some of his hair stuck out at odd angles.

Istvan was still mad at him.

"Fine," said Edmund.

"Fine," replied Istvan.

"I'll check back in a few hours."

"Don't." Istvan indicated Kyra, pinned like an insect, swathed in tubing, thin and drooping. "Go, and don't come back, and ask yourself where you're planning to put the next one."

Edmund looked away. He snapped the watch and was gone.

Served him right.

Istvan picked up the heart pillow, tossed it into the hall, and slammed the door behind it.

Edmund didn't dare call a meeting until he had time for it. He needed to – the addition of the kid was no small one, and they hadn't gotten anywhere with the last one – but time came first.

He couldn't help anyone if he were dead.

Mercedes' offer floated in the back of his mind.

Where do you hunt, Mr Templeton?

If I gave you permission to take time from certain problematic populations…

The Twelfth Hour kept a running catalogue of incidents. Once he was suited again, he picked the likeliest-looking one and took off. It was a report from the night watchman of a walled-off settlement of maybe forty people: strange liquids seeping into the ground, lights flickering in the distance, the disappearance of someone's son who wandered too far. Suspected Shokat Anoushak cult, occupying the dead hulk of one of her monsters.

Seemed clear-cut enough.

Edmund considered taking the Tyger with him, not for the first time when dealing with this kind of case. William was one of Shokat Anoushak's creatures himself. He might have some insight into the cults. If there were more of those bootleg mockeries skulking around, he might even make a decent alternative to Istvan. There were advantages to weighing a half-ton and boasting claws and saber teeth.

Edmund decided against it. This was a patrol, not a mission.

Patrols were what the Hour Thief was known for. The Hour Thief was a loner, by habit and preference.

It made it easier not to think about what he was doing, when he was alone.

The hulk in question lay due south, closer to what had been New York City than he liked. The Black Building jutted from the horizon. Big East's eclectic but otherwise survivable architecture twisted into something less as he teleported in measured steps from roof to roof. The air grew short in places, blisteringly hot in others. Crowds murmured along abandoned stretches of snowy highway. He missed one rooftop that seemed further away than it was, and had to hastily course-correct. The towers that formed the city's heart weren't constant in style or number, and they didn't act as if they were lit by the same sun, much less reflecting the same surroundings. Sometimes they weren't there at all.

New York City was a deep fracture zone, one of the epicenters of the great cracks in the world. What had been the most populous areas were always the worst. The spellscars, by comparison, were relatively solid. The spellscars only threatened to change you.

Edmund kept his distance.

He found what he was after in less than an hour. It lay toppled over several blocks, a gargantuan amalgam of crocodile, bison, and locomotive, six or seven limbs visible and part of its body still sunk into the rock. A sheen of glassy scales on its back suggested it had incorporated at least one skyscraper.

It was small, as its kind went. Dead, as much as that could be said.

It wasn't one Edmund remembered fighting, but everything had blurred together towards the end. Aside from corrosion over the last eight years, it didn't seem damaged. Weeds grew in some of the chinks between rubble.

He teleported around the perimeter, searching for a likely way in. Its mouth was open, but he dismissed that as an option: literally walking into the teeth of a beast was never a good idea.

The eye socket would do.

A trail of unlit candles across a field of mud confirmed the presence of… someone. Dusty light filtered in from above, dim but manageable. Flickerings of green lightning sparked across the opposite eye socket. Crude attempts at wards were carved into the softer materials: concrete, plastic, wood. None looked functional; true protective wards were never there when you were looking for them.

Edmund stepped softly, keeping to the shadows as best he could, and tried not to think about being inside a giant skull. The edges of it merged smoothly with the earth, sunk through rock as though it were water.

The candles led to the start of artificial vertebrae, a ridged passage considerably darker than he would have liked. Still no sign of anyone.

It was the middle of the day. What were the chances of anyone actually being here in the middle of the day? What kind of cult would meet at noon?

He got out his phone and forged ahead anyway. Maybe he'd run across a straggler or two. Special meeting. Cults were usually just groups of desperate people hoping to salvage some measure of power from the one who'd brought the world down. They weren't known for tactics.

His heart sank as he reached what had to be headquarters.

Empty.

Nothing but a few benches, more attempts at warding, salvaged bits and pieces from at least one mockery laid reverently on a cloth, and an end table holding two hammers and a chisel. A block of concrete stood in the center, tipped so it was taller than it was broad, with vague attempts at carving gouged into it.

Edmund circled it. If they had been trying to make a statue, they either hadn't been trying very hard or they had just started.

No one around to ask.

He took a measured breath. He could almost feel moments slipping away.

Maybe he should try closer to the spellscars: at least there he would probably find something, and the something would be likely to attack him, and it might even be a creature capable of giving unwitting consent to his thievery.

Or it might be a manhole cover, like last time. Istvan had asked if he'd run afoul of a bear trap and he'd said yes.

Edmund shook his head. He wasn't that desperate. Not yet.

He really wasn't.

Really.

He started back up the passage, hoping that he'd run into someone on the way out.

"The present circumstances are regrettable," boomed Lucy, "but I am certain that his most gracious Lord Kasimir would be pleased to assume the burden of this most powerful of Conduits." She spread her arms over the picnic table, armor flashing in the afternoon sun. "Never let it be said that my lord shirks from danger."

"I'll keep that in mind," said Edmund.

"Failing that, I still think we should contact Barrio Libertad," said Roberts, taking up the rest of the bench beside her. No Istvan: Edmund had asked Roberts to go see if the ghost wanted to attend, and Roberts had come back alone. "If that boy really is Shattered, that's their field. They have a dedicated mental reprogramming ward. Lucy's been through it – she can vouch for them."

"It is a most expeditious facility," agreed Lucy.

Edmund shook his head. Mental deprogramming could just as easily spin into mental programming, and while he was stuck with Lucy for the time being, at least she couldn't level towns on her own. "I don't think the Magister would agree to that. Istvan will have to do what he can."

"With all due respect," said Roberts, "Dr Czernin isn't a psychologist."

"I know."

"I mean, I know he works with you, but–"

Edmund clasped his hands on the table, pointedly. "Let's not turn this into a personal discussion."

Bad days happened. He was fine.

He eyed the crowd milling along the road to the Twelfth Hour, but they didn't seem inclined to enter the courtyard. The Yale campus was common ground now, its greens tilled and planted, and while harvest might have made a fine excuse for an interruption, the blue-striped, bear-sized big cat crouched some twenty feet from the table on a sheen of frozen cobbles did much to dissuade any attempt.

Citizens' revolt, Mercedes had said. What were they using as leverage?

Janet Justice pushed over a notebook. "I went through that box of yours before I had it dropped off," she said. Her tone of voice was carefully neutral, to the point of flatness. "Collated what seems like our best bets for the site."

Edmund took the notebook, hoping it would detail "best bets" with the kid in the picture so that he wouldn't have to ask her about it. He didn't want to ask Janet much of anything right now.

No such luck.

She kept watching him. If she had a personal opinion on the mess – which he was sure she did – she'd kept it to herself the entire meeting.

He pretended to study the notebook. "The kid?" he asked.

"The kid makes it a little harder." She shrugged. Her earrings jangled. "To be honest, Mr Templeton, I'd say it's looking like either Barrio Libertad or taking Kasimir up on that offer. We could use some tracts of land right about now."

Edmund smiled, blandly. "Mercedes doesn't want anything to do with Barrio Libertad."

Janet smiled back. "She doesn't, or you don't?"

"She told me–"

"I know what she told you. We've got that stairwell monitored."

"Templeton," rasped a voice.

Thank goodness.

Edmund turned, trying to conceal his relief at the interruption. A roughly man-sized lizard in a purple parka leaned on a cane several paces distant from the Tyger. "Vasquez. Glad you could join us."

A tongue flickered. "Went around. Didn't want to ruin the protest."

"All the same."

Vasquez pointed at the Tyger, who was typing again. One letter at a time. "We had some questions about the boy."

The Tyger turned his screen around, blocky green letters on black. A cursor blinked at the end.

is he the only one

Edmund let out a breath. There were some things he didn't want to think too much about, and that was one of them. He'd have been able to get away with that before Mercedes decided to give him a title.

"Director" Templeton had to consider all the angles.

"I don't know," he said, "but if he isn't we'll have to be ready to take in others like him. Stop them first, if we have to."

what of the mockery

"What mockery?"

The Tyger bared his canines, tapping laboriously at the keyboard. Ice cracked beneath his paws.

the one you killed.

Vasquez bobbed her head. "We were thinking: there were cults before the Shattered came along, but they never managed to bring a mockery back to life. They never had any powers. What if the old cults are taking advantage? What if they can piece together Shokat Anoushak's magic from different people?"

Edmund swallowed. "Let's not get ahead of ourselves."

The Tyger had been part of Shokat Anoushak's forces, and while no one was sure what Vasquez was, she'd taken a liking to him for understandable reasons. They were both freaks. Both monsters. If there were established cults looking to replicate Shokat Anoushak's feats in full, the Twelfth Hour might soon find itself encountering more than bootleg mockeries and strays from the spellscars.

It wasn't a surprising train of thought, all considered.

Edmund brushed at his upper arm, mostly healed, where the Tyger's over-sized canines had affixed themselves some two months past.

Using the Shattered to duplicate Shokat Anoushak's magic? Could they really piece together enough of the old rituals from the ramblings of the Susurration's last victims to make it all work? If it didn't stop with mockeries, then what?

Shokat Anoushak had done more than make monsters... *trying to cover all the angles*, typed the Tyger.

"I'll... keep that in mind," said Edmund. He looked down at the notebook Janet had passed him. Sell out to Barrio Libertad or sign on with a warlord. Not choices he liked. There had to be a third option.

He wished Istvan had come.

"Let's meet back up on Tuesday," he said.

Roberts put his elbow on the table. "I thought we were on a timetable."

"We are. Janet, make an offer to the Magnolia Group. Explain the situation. Maybe they can come up with something. Vasquez, William, go ahead and look into somewhere further afield."

"You're expecting Dr Czernin to stay down there for a week while we do research?" asked Roberts, not moving his elbow out of the way.

Edmund closed the notebook more sharply than he intended. "No one's making him stay."

"Kyra is."

"It's still Istvan's choice. You and Lucy do whatever he says."

Lucy held up a mailed fist. "The offer from Lord Kasimir yet stands."

Edmund stood. "I know. We'll decide Tuesday."

Janet took the notebook back. "What about you?"

He sighed. That was the kicker, wasn't it?

"I'll be paying a visit to Barrio Libertad," he said.

Their little group split up, each going their separate ways. Roberts to the Twelfth Hour infirmary. Janet back home (she had a sick husband to attend to, she explained). The Tyger and Vasquez to... wherever the Tyger kept himself. Maybe the Twelfth Hour's holding cells, still. Edmund hadn't asked.

Lucy made a beeline for the crowd milling on the road, drawing her saber.

Edmund stepped before her. "Let them be."

She cocked her helmet down at him. Behind that visor, grids of flashing scarlet played across the faint shadow of eyes. "The Twelfth Hour tolerates this rabble?"

"Mercedes is dealing with it. If you want to help, you need permission from her."

A slam: gauntlet against breastplate. "Understood."

Edmund watched as the Triskelion warrior-woman marched off without another word. He'd seen her out of that armor, before her treatment, still under thrall, smiling and laughing and making small talk in French. He was glad she wore the helmet, now. Made it easier not to remember.

A piece of paper blew against his pant leg, lost from somewhere in the crowd. He leaned over to pick it up.

A brochure.

"On Wizards:" it said, "The Concentration and Misapplication of Power After the End of the World." The heading repeated itself in Spanish.

He flipped it over. The rounded sigil of Barrio Libertad marked the back.

Great.

They would want him back at the fortress. Istvan knew that.

He put the final touches on an embroidered convoy, dust-coated, smoke rising from its passage. The outlining was finished; the border finished; the larger details finished. The work spilled over his knees, all the colors he himself couldn't possess.

Every day he stayed in this chamber was a day he wasn't doing his duty.

He didn't even know what day it was, anymore.

Kyra slept beside him. Istvan checked his vitals each time he finished another part of the scene. He kept an eye on the IVs: the tubing, the needles, the fluid levels. Every so often he adjusted the boy's position – what little he could – in an effort to combat chafing at his wrists and knees. He took wastes and set them outside the door. If it seemed as though the boy might wake, Istvan put him under again.

Injections. Altered dosages. Tweaks to one set of nerves or another.

Kyra was terribly thin, gaunt in the eerie light. He didn't deserve this.

Only fifteen.

Istvan finished the smoke and the wheels and the figures walking alongside their vehicles, distant caricatures of men – and women – in spiked armor. He was almost out of grey thread.

The stone pressed in around him. Twelve blocks to the door. Four major rounds of salt lines, sixteen smaller circles-within-circles, one sigil that resembled a face, another a flower. Fire-lit steam rising from the shackles, each link of each chain bearing Arabic script he could write from memory but still couldn't decipher.

He couldn't hear the beeping of the machine anymore unless he listened for it. At times Kyra breathed so shallowly Istvan had to check to be sure he still was.

Above rambled the Twelfth Hour. Minor annoyances

and gnawing fears, faint pains from the infirmary, losses of all varieties, envy of the wizards' comfort, anger at a cruel world or a traitorous friend or one's own failings... all of it, the lives of everyone who passed through its doors, trickled down through the rock.

More variety usually meant it was day. Less, night. Sometimes Istvan could trace specific emergencies from one side of the building to the other, different worries rising and falling as the situation changed.

He was out of grey thread. He substituted blue.

Roberts came by to ask how the boy was doing; Istvan asked for more saline. Kyra's chances of emerging from the sleep unscathed dropped by the day.

Istvan was doing fine. Tell Barrio Libertad that he would be unavailable until further notice. Tell them he was making a foolish point. Tell them he was holding grudges. Tell them it was Edmund's fault.

The infirmary staff – Roberts, Parker, Mendoza, Dr Orlean, the three roving emergency teams and Lucy, assistants and volunteers that came and went as the situation merited – flowed in and out like a tide. The Magister remained in her office, except when she disappeared. Edmund came through the building intermittently, less and less often. Sometimes to wander the shelves. Sometimes to visit the Magister. Sometimes to approach the basement stairwell, and hesitate, and pace in circles, and depart.

All others remained jumbled together, coming and going, groups migrating from one space to another, growing closer or more distant as they travelled up or down stairways, bearing stories in their worries and pains he could only guess at. No faces, no names.

Istvan speculated. Perhaps that large gathering was

from the Magnolia Group. Perhaps that odd one wasn't human. Perhaps that particularly angry person was here to ask about Dr Czernin, and where he was, and why he wasn't doing what he'd promised.

It was like tracking shadows by where the sun's heat didn't reach.

For twenty years he had done almost nothing else.

Edmund's fault.

It was Edmund who had helped to chain him in the first place. If Istvan hadn't recognized him – a face, just the same, from sixty years earlier – the attempt would never have worked. Other wizards had tried before, and none of them had survived to try a second time… except one.

Istvan had told himself it was only the shock of such an impossible reunion that let them take advantage. He had been certain that, if the opportunity presented itself, he would be more than willing to combat his seemingly ageless foe once again. Perhaps even finally kill him.

Now he knew that he would never be able to do that.

Edmund would simply continue to do as Edmund had always done, remaining blissfully ignorant of the absurd notion that a World War had come to love him beyond all reason or righteousness and would do anything for him – anything – to the point of sparing him the embarrassment of knowing anything of the sort for the last thirty years.

He didn't know what had driven Istvan towards the mistakes that had made him what he was, made him into that terrible scourge that deserved capture and imprisonment. He didn't know about the happiest years of Istvan's life, when he was still flesh and blood. He didn't know about his own similarity to a man long-dead, that he and Pietro would have gotten on famously, that Istvan had married under terrible pressure and never had children for a reason.

It was best for everyone that he never know. Even when the Susurration sought to use Pietro's memory as a weapon, Istvan had never explained a word – and Edmund had never asked about the brief lapse since. Not once. Not ever.

Instead, he had returned the favor by locking a second prisoner in the same chains that had once held his best friend.

His best friend.

Istvan finished the scene he had set out for himself. A mountain pass, under siege. A tapestry just under his own height, an arm's length wide, every inch bearing as much detail as he could manage. How many hours had gone into it, he had no idea.

Beside him, Kyra slept.

He slept, and Istvan wondered: what would happen if he woke him? What was the worst the boy could do? No one had bothered asking him, testing him, giving him any chance to defend himself. Kyra was bound, hand and foot. What would be the harm?

Aside from to his psyche. To his spirit.

Istvan wished he could unlock the boy and carry him up the stairs and out the door and away to a serene cottage, perhaps, or a field of flowers, and wake him there. Then Kyra would only have to face a dead man, and the destruction of everything he thought he remembered.

Istvan asked for another canvas, and more thread.

CHAPTER ELEVEN

"No," said Istvan, standing up from the table, "I'm going away. You shall simply have to be by yourself forever."

"But we weren't finished with the game," said Edmund. He pointed at the chessboard, furnished with pawns and rooks and bishops and plastic battleships and Monopoly cannons. A zeppelin hung from the ceiling. "You were winning."

Istvan went for the door. "I don't care."

Edmund chased after him. "Wait! If you leave, who am I supposed to play chess with?"

"Go find a nice table in a park somewhere and play by yourself," said the ghost. He put his cap on and peered disdainfully at Edmund over his glasses. "That's what old men are supposed to do."

"I'm thirty-five."

"No, you aren't. You spent all of your time, remember?"

Istvan produced a mirror and held it up.

Edmund woke. He clawed for his pillow. He clung to it, halfway under sweat-soaked sheets, staring at the still-dark window and counting each breath until he could stop shaking.

Then he reached for the bottle of gin on his bedside

table and spilled it anyway.

He pulled his pillow over his head.

Dammit.

Dammit.

I'm sorry, Istvan.

I made a mistake, Istvan.

I'll be going to Barrio Libertad today, Istvan, I promise, and I was wondering if you'd like to come along.

What can I do to make this up to you?

It's been a while since we played chess, Istvan…

Three days to Tuesday.

Edmund had managed to patrol every night but one. He had gone to the Twelfth Hour two days out of four. He had managed to take one walk. He had fed Beldam every day and counted that a victory.

Still no visit to Barrio Libertad.

The place hated wizards. The place could negate his magic at will. The place scared the hell out of him. Nothing but a verbal agreement held Diego in check, and, according to Grace, this was a being whose thoughts flowed so quickly that every pause between words in conversation lasted a relative eternity: a being whose existence was an abyss of perpetual boredom, his stilted communication the result of a gulf so vast it was a wonder he bothered to speak with anyone at all. He could see the worlds within atoms, she said, the past and the future. He had a plan, and the curiously ramshackle design of Barrio Libertad was the result of a vast and benign intelligence deliberately presenting itself as less frightening than it was.

Diego could see magic, she said, and that was how he could negate it. What wizards did wasn't really magic at all, she said, but a branch of science so complex that the merely human mind couldn't grasp its most fundamental truths.

There was no way to know. Nothing human could see magic – nothing that wasn't crushing and mad and incomprehensible, beyond the world, like gods – and Edmund knew better than to pry too closely. Everything Grace had said about Diego sounded like religion, even if she laughed to Edmund's face when he said so.

She would be mad at him, too. Everyone was mad at him.

He didn't want to go by himself.

Everyone expected him to know what he was doing and he never felt like he did. Just like during the Wizard War. Just like when he was made Magister because everyone else thought it was a good idea. Just like when he finally broke, completely, and vanished from the public eye.

He'd barely been able to get out of his house. He'd been useless for over a year.

He pulled his sheets up, telling himself he was only cold and not hiding.

What if it happened again?

The silvery disc was back. It had browsed through every book in the Symbolic Astronomy section, the ravens informed him, and then had selected a pile of them and transferred itself to a corner, where it remained even now, flipping pages with slender tendrils and blinking its lights to itself.

It still wasn't hurting anything. It was fine.

Edmund waved the ravens away so he could pace the shelves in peace. The crowd outside wanted access to the high-security vault, but the library was already open; he had vetted each volume himself to make sure that nothing on display could be used to cause too much trouble. He still liked to make sure everything was in order.

He knew that Mercedes would never agree to open the vault to the public. Some things were better kept unknown.

He knew he was stalling.

He straightened the books jostled by the disc's selection, focusing on the weight of his hat on his head, his cape on his shoulders. He was the Hour Thief. The Hour Thief had been to Barrio Libertad before and would manage just fine going there again.

As soon as he finished with this shelf...

A buzzer sounded.

He frowned. That was the door alarm. Had someone tried something?

A return to the entrance revealed an uncertain door guard – he'd set off the alarm, he wasn't sure what else to do – and Grace Wu.

She was outside, of course. She stood before the door, one hand pressed against the glass, peering through it blindly and shouting, her voice silenced by the wards. The crowd that had gathered that morning milled behind her, also silent.

"She hit the door," the guard explained. "And look at her badge."

Edmund didn't need to look. "I know who it is," he said, waving off the curious that had begun to gather on their own side, "I'll handle it."

He steeled himself. He knew what was coming. He opened the door.

"...bassadors like this?" shouted Grace. She blinked. She stepped backwards, peering around him at the suddenly visible Twelfth Hour library stacks revealed through the open entrance, then crossed her arms. "You don't even have a doorbell," she said.

Edmund pulled the door closed behind him. It latched. "I'm sorry."

The crowd buzzed.

"Hey," called someone. "About time we got some answers!"

Edmund didn't look at them. Not his job. "So. Grace. What can I do for you?"

"How many out there?" shouted the crowd. "How many victims?"

"You helped take it down, they said! Why didn't the Magister say anything?"

"I heard she was responsible for it!"

Grace stepped aside, waving at the packed road. "Planning to deal with this?"

"Hey," came more shouts, "hey, why didn't anyone tell us that the Susurration was out there?"

"Is the Magister ever going to let anyone else learn magic?"

"We need to be able to defend ourselves!"

Edmund swallowed. "Uh," he said.

"When will you be up for re-election?"

"–Twelfth Hour doesn't do elections!"

"–a dictatorship–"

"Wizard duel!"

Grace stood there and watched him, inscrutable. She was still mad at him. She had to still be mad at him. This crowd was probably her fault. Who else would have distributed those fliers? Mercedes had never said a word about the Susurration to anyone, not even after she had helped defeat it. She'd said nothing about the Shattered, either.

Barrio Libertad. All they ever did was make things harder.

These people had no idea what a wizard duel was like.

"Go on," said Grace.

He could run. He could go back inside, right now.

Edmund took a breath. He held up a hand.

The crowd quieted, instantly, and his stomach twisted. He was a hero now, sure. That kind of thing only lasted until you lived long enough to make a mistake.

"I stand by the Magister's decisions," he said. "I won't speak for her."

The crowd rumbled.

"I'm sorry. I can't tell you anything else." He took Grace's arm. "Excuse us, please."

He snapped his watch.

He and Grace reappeared on the roof.

"Bravo," said Grace. She tugged her arm out of his grip and clapped. Once, twice. "You're about as good a politician as I am."

"Thanks." Edmund put his watch away. "What can I do for you this time?"

"An apology would be–"

"I'm sorry."

She searched him. "Right."

"I am," he said, wishing he hadn't answered so quickly. "Getting rid of you like that was a petty thing to do, and I shouldn't have done it."

"Like you shouldn't have taken the kid?"

He wanted to turn away. He shrugged. "I've made better decisions."

"Where is he, Eddie?"

He tried to tell her. He did.

It caught in his throat.

He turned away. They were twelve stories up, too high to make out voices from below, but what sound did filter up seemed displeased. Rightly so.

He wasn't taking her to the Demon's Chamber. Never mind the question of whether or not Istvan would even let them in.

Edmund crossed his arms on the low stone wall that ran around the roof's edge, ignoring the exuberant scenes of dancing girls and other things carved into its surface.

"Eddie," Grace said.

"He's here," Edmund answered. "We have him in a safe place."

Grace leaned on the wall beside him. Close, but not too close. Not close enough. "I tried to get the People's Council to demand custody," she said. "I asked them to bring down you have no idea what kind of justice on this place, so we could get him somewhere actually safe."

Edmund hunched his shoulders, reflexively. "You don't want to attack the Twelfth Hour, Grace. You really don't."

"Yeah, well, they turned me down, so you don't have to worry about that."

"Oh, good."

Grace snorted. "Didn't want to deal with it. Didn't want to worry about anything else. 'Let the wizards inflict on themselves whatever they want,' and so on. It's not like the kid's a person or anything and it's not like there might be more like him."

"You're sounding exactly like Istvan," Edmund told her.

She paused.

She started to say something else, then stopped.

Edmund stared out at New Haven, trying not to think about a Barrio Libertad-Twelfth Hour war. That was the last thing anyone needed.

"I'm nothing like spook Dracula," Grace said, finally. She pushed away from the wall. "He's helping you keep the kid here, isn't he? Probably assigned to make sure he doesn't up and die from mistreatment."

Edmund gritted his teeth. "Grace, what do you want?"

"Keep him just on the edge, yeah? He'd have a lot of experience with that."

"Grace–"

"What's it like, having your own personal Meng–"

Edmund whirled. "Grace, stop it!"

"What, going to get rid of me again?" She dropped into a fighting stance, gauntlets snapping with static. "Good luck."

Edmund backed up. He knew the kind of voltage she could put out, given a chance.

Istvan wasn't like that. Edmund wouldn't associate with anyone like that. Yes, the ghost had fought with the Nazis. He was Hungarian. Hungary had been with the Axis. That was the only reason.

It was all a long time ago.

"I'm here to help," Grace said. "Is that so hard? I'm here to make sure your prisoner is treated decently and that you find somewhere for him that isn't a cell. I'm here to hunt down any others like him, and do the same for them."

Edmund stared at her.

"What?" she asked.

"That's... different," he said.

She jerked a thumb at her breastplate. "I'm the only other Conduit in the area, Eddie – and I'm an engineer. I figured out my own powers years ago. I can help that kid better than anyone else. Don't act all surprised."

Well. Well, then.

Edmund wouldn't have pegged Grace for the mothering type. If she'd seemed that way during the Wizard War, he would have tried harder to keep his distance. Never mind that he should have done that to begin with. Would have made everything easier. Fling and forget, like all the others.

Too late, now.

He shook his head. No, this was Grace. This sounded like an excuse for a science experiment. Cut the kid open, just like she'd done to herself. Her and Diego. She insisted that they weren't an item, that Diego couldn't care any less and that she didn't love science *that* much, but Edmund couldn't help but harbor his bitter suspicions.

He stuck to the safe question. "What about the People's Council?"

"They don't know what they're doing," she said. "They don't care, they won't listen to me, and Diego refuses to do anything outside the fortress without their go-ahead." She snarled to herself. "You have no idea how long I argued with them. With him."

Edmund plastered a pleasant smile on his face. He didn't want any more information on that front, thanks. "I see."

"So are you going to take me to the kid, or what?"

His smile faded.

The blade almost took his ear off.

Edmund slammed the door shut. "Now isn't a good time."

"Were those flowers?" asked Grace.

Istvan's trench knife skidded across the stone, clattered against the base of the stairwell, and then vanished.

"I don't know," said Edmund, "and I'm not asking."

He locked the door again. The key, heavy brass, went back in his pocket.

"Give me that," said Grace.

"No."

She approached him. "If you're too scared to—"

"Grace, he does not want company right now and if he doesn't want company, no one is going in there." Edmund shoved past her, hoping he looked less shaky than he felt. "You of all people should remember what he is and what he can do."

He started up the stairs.

Grace, after a moment, followed him.

Istvan waited for them both to leave.

Edmund. Grace Wu. Conspiring.

Just as it had been.

At the start of the Wizard War, on Edmund's order, the Twelfth Hour had loosened Istvan's chains. Then-Magister Templeton had spilled his own blood – calmly, willingly – as part of the ritual, replacing links of iron with links of Contractual parchment. They'd done it so Istvan could fight. So he could helm what was left of the infirmary. So he could help turn the tide.

Just in time for Edmund to ignore him utterly. To spend every quiet moment with *her*.

Not that it mattered. They had wanted Istvan to fight, and he had, gladly, and he remembered so very, very little of it.

He waited for the two to leave – vanishing, together, to who knew where – and then he returned to work. Let them do as they liked.

Hours slid into one another. Presences came and went and gradually most trickled away, one by one, leaving only that thin watch that stood vigil over the night. Perhaps a few dozen souls, some he thought he almost recognized. He'd worked through enough dark shifts to know.

He'd waited for enough nights.

Istvan crouched beside Kyra, the boy still transfixed in iron shackles. Clear tubing, removed and coiled, lay beside him on the stone. Bandaging wound about Kyra's arms, covering injection sites. The life-support machine sat silently, disconnected. Kyra breathed on his own for the first time in four days.

Across his knees lay a spread of stitched wildflowers.

One IV left.

Gently. Gently, now.

Istvan slid the needle free. Still Kyra slept, dreamlessly, painlessly, but that would change soon.

"Hello," Istvan said to himself. "Hello. I know that you're frightened, but…"

No. No, not a good start.

"Please, don't worry," he tried. He thought of Dracula. "Please, don't worry," he repeated, struggling to bend the vowels into their proper shapes, "I'm Doctor Czernin. I'm… I've… I know what this sounds like."

Again, he thought of perhaps leaving a note instead. Coming in later, to space out the shocks. A knock at the door – a friendly sort of knock – and then the introduction.

Again, he worried that Kyra might remember their first meeting, and resent it, and resent him for it. It could have gone so much better.

"Hello, Mr Kyra," Istvan muttered, putting the needle and tubing away. "I'm Doctor Czernin. You recognized me in Tornado Alley. I'm sorry for the facilities, but we'll have you out of here soon."

He cleaned and bandaged Kyra's arm, then stepped back and checked to make certain that the "decorations" Edmund had brought in were arranged well within the boy's view. The pillows. The lamp. After a moment, Istvan removed the flower-stitched fabric from Kyra's knees and draped it over the stool.

Then he retreated behind them, still within view, and sat down, drawing his knees up nervously. Back against the wall, as far away as he could be.

He glanced at a hand, then brushed at his face. Not skeletal. He turned to the side to better hide the scarring. Barbed wire coiled around the stool legs despite himself.

The taste of the air changed. Confusion, diluted and uncertain.

Kyra shifted.

Istvan checked his hand again. Still not skeletal.

Kyra's eyelids fluttered, then closed again. His mouth worked, probably trying to recover lost moisture. His fingers twitched. One wrist tugged against its shackles, rattling one length of chain against another.

He froze. He opened his eyes again. He seemed to be having trouble focusing, and trouble moving his head, but he managed to get a look at the offending chain.

The sound he made was somewhere between a sob and a whimper.

Istvan wished he could risk being any closer. "Er–"

Kyra's head snapped towards him. Too quickly – he reeled, brought up short by the chains – a shriek cut off by the band around his neck–

Istvan held up his hands, edging so far away he could feel his back scraping through the wall. "Hello! Hello, and I'm sorry, I didn't mean to–"

Kyra slammed his head back against the pillar, fortunately where Roberts had placed some padding. Arabic calligraphy flashed in the fire-orange light. The clank and slither of metal on metal echoed horribly in Istvan's ears.

"Please, I'm Doctor Czernin. I–"

Kyra screamed.

Salt grains whipped from the grooves in the floor, bouncing and then drawn aloft, whirled into a sudden wind. The chains clattered sideways, straining at their moorings.

Istvan covered his face.

The stool fell over. The floor cracked. There was a trembling to the walls, dust shaking from the mortar between stones and added to the wind. The embroidery he'd spent so many hours finishing tore away, whipped in circles, hurtling like a bat.

He'd tried.

He'd tried so hard.

The boy threw himself against the pillar again and again in futile struggle, terror warring with shock and further terror, raw sweetness compounded by verdant disbelief and incomprehension, a mélange that tore through the air with the wind and rose as it did. He didn't understand what was happening. He didn't know where he was, or why he was chained, or what he was doing.

Had he no memory of his own power at all? Had Edmund, or Grace, done something to lift that multitudinous fog from his being, to bring him back to himself with a shock, still burdened with what he shouldn't remember?

The circlet. Had Grace Wu used that circlet on him?

The angles between pillar and chains and ceiling curved sickeningly. A stone wrenched itself free of the wall, wind of a different sort whistling from beyond. A blackness–

A blackness that watched–

Istvan looked hurriedly away. Kyra was going to bring the roof down before he ever broke those chains. He was going to bring down the Demon's Chamber, and Istvan had no idea what lent it its power.

Not even the flowers had worked. Not even the flowers...

Istvan darted for the boy, catching hold of hanging chains as the wind swept him sideways, beating wings he'd meant to keep hidden. Smoke seeped from the cracks in the floor.

Kyra saw him. He tried to scream again. He choked, drawing breath in a gasping stutter. He pulled away as far as he could. Tears streamed into his collar.

Istvan clung to the pillar. "I want to help you," he shouted over the crack and rumble of more stones falling, "I'm here to help you. I'm sorry it happened like this, I truly am. I'm Dracula. I'm... I..." He cursed. "I'm Doctor Czernin. You're Kyra, aren't you? Kyra? We talked, didn't we?"

He couldn't hide his own thunder. His bloodied hands. The feathers torn from him, barbed wire coiling down the chains to wrap around one of Kyra's wrists.

It was too much. Istvan knew it was all too much.

The light snapped back to normal. The wind fell, salt and mortar pattering like rain. The boy collapsed, breath heaving, wrists raw, shaking in convulsive spasms of anguish that tore through his whole body.

"What did I do?" he sobbed. "What did I do?"

Istvan found purchase on the floor again. He didn't dare look for fallen stones. He wished he didn't feel so emboldened by the boy's terror – that he wasn't tempted to shout again, to posture, to laugh – of course he frightened him; he frightened everyone! – and he stopped himself from touching him even though that may have helped because it likely wouldn't.

"You didn't," he said. "You haven't done anything."

Kyra hunched his shoulders as though trying to huddle inwards; the chains brought him up short. He said nothing more.

He wept.

A cold wind hissed across the stones.

Istvan stood, locked in place, not knowing whether to go to him or stay away from him or to depart the room entirely. He folded his wings; they dissipated in wisps of gas and wire, streamers drawn to the gaps in the walls before fading.

The high security vault lay in a realm beyond the world, carved into a space larger than the whole of the Twelfth Hour and the city that held it. Dead bone the size of continents, drifting. Was the Demon's Chamber the same? Was something beyond it?

Could that something emerge? Could it slither through those holes, and–

They couldn't stay in here.

Istvan drew his knife.

A clatter: Kyra gasped a strangled breath.

Istvan held up a hand, knowing the gesture to be less reassuring than he hoped. "I'm going to get you out of here," he said. He flipped the knife around, blade downwards.

The nearest chain burned when he touched it. He cursed.

Kyra jerked away. Dust sifted from the ceiling. Salt whirled across the floor in scattered arcs.

Istvan turned the chain, gingerly, and slid his blade into the center of one of the links. He'd never had leverage before to try cutting them. He wasn't sure if it would work.

"Did I hurt someone?" asked Kyra. The boy's voice was hoarse. "Is that why I'm here?"

"You're here because people are foolish and afraid," Istvan replied, more harshly than he'd intended. Yes, Kyra had torn him apart. But the boy had looked as though he hadn't eaten or slept in days, and he'd been worried about a cult. He'd been more than willing to speak! He hadn't tried to attack until Istvan had startled him. He knew Istvan, somehow, thanks to the Susurration, and they had nearly had a pleasant conversation. It could have gone so much better.

Istvan shifted his grip on the chain. "You haven't done anything," he repeated, "and it isn't fair, and I'm sorry it ever happened. You won't be staying." A thought struck him. "Er – where are you from?"

Kyra mumbled something.

"Pardon?"

"Rochester," came the quiet response.

Istvan had no idea where that was. "We're in New Haven," he said. "Massachusetts. Is Rochester closer to that, or to Kansas?"

Kyra shook his head, an almost imperceptible gesture. "It's in New York. The state, not the city. Everyone always gets that wrong. It's on Lake Ontario."

Istvan tried to remember what went where on the map. New York City was near enough, and it did lie within a state of the same name, which stretched over to the Great Lakes, which were...

...part of the spellscars, now.

Rochester would have been consumed when the Wizard War broke. Either Kyra hadn't been there at the time, or he wasn't truly from that city at all. The Susurration had gripped him, and – ever well-meaning, in its blind, cruel way – the Susurration could rewrite a person's past as thoroughly as it deemed necessary for their happiness. Kyra would know only what it had decided to "gift" him.

Did he remember the Wizard War? Did he know that his memory of the past eight years was a pleasant fiction? His life, his home, his family... not only gone, but never real?

Why had he been in Tornado Alley?

Istvan shot a glance at the edge of the chamber, the missing bricks, the hissing from beyond the world, and then hastily looked away again. Oh, they couldn't wait any longer. "Well, Mr Kyra, I–"

"Miss."

"Excuse me?"

The boy nodded at him. "Miss Kyra."

Istvan stared at him. He stared back.

Shattered. How much of Shokat Anoushak's memory did he carry? How many lives now swam in his head, male and female both? How long would it take him to recover?

"Well," Istvan finally said. He fixed his blade more firmly into the chain link, and braced himself. "I do need to get you out of here. I'm going to try cutting this, all right?"

Kyra gritted his teeth. "OK."

Istvan drew a false breath – he could do this, he'd sliced apart tank armor before, somehow – then tore at the link as hard as he could. His blade bit into it with an unnatural shriek. Sparks showered across the floor. The chain's calligraphy flared into burning scarlet, the hiss of the wind louder, the urge to look back at the gaps in the walls more powerful than ever–

He was scratching the iron. It was faint. It was working.

"Wait," gasped Kyra. "Wait."

Istvan paused, gasping a bit himself. "What?"

Kyra looked at him, eyes wide. "It's magic. This stuff is magic."

"Er, yes, that's–"

"It's actually magic! You ain't never said you had wizards, Doctor Czernin! You gotta tell them! She's coming back, OK? Our Lady. Shokat Anoushak. They figured it out, and she's coming back." He twisted around, trying to get a closer look at the calligraphy on the chains. "I was looking for wizards," he continued, "I… I just got lost, is all. They got her last time, right? They can do it again!"

Istvan hesitated. No cult he knew of had ever come close to such a feat as resurrection, and while Kyra seemed sincere, the boy was also quite clearly confused. "That's all very well," Istvan told him, "but this chamber might collapse and I would rather we not be here, first."

Kyra closed his eyes. "OK. OK, do it."

Istvan nodded. He set his blade against the scratches and drew it across with another grating shriek. Deeper.

It was working. "Hold on," he told Kyra, and then he began in earnest, sawing at the metal, the flesh of his gripping hand burned away, bones blackening, salt whirling around him, and all the while he tried to ignore the strangled keening of a boy trying not to scream.

It was working. It was working.

The door burst.

Splinters sailed away from its upper hinges. A kick twisted it off the lower ones. A blurred figure of red and yellow hurtled through the gap, electricity crackling around her armored fists.

"The chains," Istvan started. *They're metal, they're conductive, please, be–*

Grace Wu hit him like a thunderbolt.

Everything went white. He dropped his knife. He couldn't see, couldn't hear, couldn't think of anything but the mistake he'd made, long ago, morphine-addled and fast-weakened and hopeless, with those pagan tales and that generator. Electricity was the future. Electricity could do anything. Electricity could let a man talk to God.

He'd burned to death.

"Get away from the kid!" Grace shouted.

Istvan found a wall. Cold winds whistled through him.

Other people arrived, two or three of them. They milled around the pillar.

Istvan sat, or tried to. He seemed to be missing most of his ribcage. Blown apart. He prodded gingerly at where his heart should have been, bleeding mist and poison. There was barbed wire wrapped around his spine.

"Get him out," he managed to say. "Find a wizard."

"Found one," replied the Magister.

Istvan looked up, still clutching at his ruined chest. Kyra hung motionless in his bonds, the others standing around him, steam wisping from the chains. His head lolled sideways. Burns, bubbled and raw, stretched across his neck.

Grace knelt beside him, tucking a silvery vial back into her belt.

The Magister moved to block his view. She carried a leather bag over one shoulder. "Thank you, Doctor Czernin, but we won't be requiring your services."

"But–"

"I've notified the infirmary and help will be here soon. The members of your staff are competent, aren't they?"

Istvan coughed. He put a hand to the floor, trying to stand, and touched fabric. Stitched flowers, spread in a field with a small cottage atop a hill.

The Magister eyed the artwork. She bent to pick it up. "I'll see that he gets this," she said, folding the cloth and tucking it under an arm. "Now go."

Istvan stood, twisting his fingers through his own reforming ribs. "I wasn't trying to hurt him."

Magister Hahn turned from him. "Ms Wu," she said, "I'm going to need some space."

"I'm going to need some answers," snapped Grace.

The Magister produced a key of rusted iron. "Space first."

"And what do gerbils have to do with anything, anyway?"

Istvan departed like the shade he was.

CHAPTER TWELVE

Edmund wasn't home.

It was three-twenty in the morning, according to the clock on the wizard's kitchen wall. The box of documents sat on the couch in the living room. A stack of dirty dishes rested in the sink. The table bore a half-assembled chessboard, its pieces mixed with plastic battleships, a paper zeppelin taped to the ceiling. Beldam hissed from somewhere in the bathroom. A bottle of gin lay beside the bed, open and emptied into the carpet, abandoned where it had fallen.

The man's ledger lay open on his desk.

Istvan switched on a lamp. Each page was laid out in columns, notated in increasingly shaky handwriting until the latest: little more than a scrawl, pressed hard enough to bleed through the paper.

"Some time." "A few moments." "A little while."

He'd gone as far as Chicago. He was ranging over a wider area than he ever had.

He wasn't here.

Istvan had no idea where to find him.

It shouldn't have mattered. This was all Edmund's fault. If he hadn't put the boy – put Kyra – in the Demon's Chamber, if he hadn't assumed the very worst, if he hadn't made a habit of treating other people like tools, like weapons, like…

Istvan slapped the ledger closed. "Vampire," he told it.

If only it were Edmund who craved blood.

Istvan sat on the bed, fuming.

Edmund got back home just as the sun began to rise. He had the presence of mind to hang his hat on its hook and take off his cape; past that, he could handle later. Sleep first. Not enough time for anything else.

Not enough time for anything.

He meandered down the hall to the bedroom and pushed open the door.

A pale figment rose from the foot of the bed.

Edmund yelped. He slammed the door.

Bloodstains blossomed across the wood, the grain gone muddy and brittle, bullet holes punched through it without any sign of the bullets–

Istvan stepped through it. "Good morning to you, too," he said. His skull and jawbone grinned visibly beneath his skin. His eyes flickered between anger and empty sockets. "Ought I leave, then?"

Edmund caught his breath. "Istvan, you're doing it again."

The specter glanced at one of his own hands, bloodied and skeletal, then back to Edmund. "It bothers you?"

"It bothers me when you're in my house, Istvan. In my room."

Istvan stepped past him, trailing gas and thunder.

Edmund blocked the hallway. "What were you doing in my room?"

Barbed wire looped around his pant leg. "I was waiting for you," said Istvan. He touched the wall beside the bathroom. A line of bullet holes arced across it. "I didn't want to roam the house, and scare the cat."

Edmund tried to shake the wire away. It clung stubbornly, opening phantom tears in the fabric. He gave up and pushed the bedroom door back open.

He did not need this right now. He could not do this right now.

"I'm going to bed," he announced.

Istvan turned, a whirl of rotten feathers. "Oh, yes," he snapped. "Run. You've always time for that, don't you?"

Edmund took a deep breath. He'd gotten into a fistfight with Istvan once and it hadn't worked and it hadn't solved anything. "I'm going to bed," he repeated.

He stepped into his room and closed the door, glancing around to make sure everything was where he'd left it. Bed, ledger, bottle...

He picked up the bottle.

"And when you wake?" came Istvan's voice from beyond the door. "Where will you go, then? Because I've thought of that already, what we ought to do, and after what's happened I think you might agree."

"Later," said Edmund.

He put the bottle on the nightstand. He'd have to figure out how to clean the carpet when he got the chance. It was going to smell.

Poison rolled under the door, pale wisps seeping through holes that weren't real. "The Demon's Chamber is broken, Edmund," said Istvan. "Kyra will have to be moved elsewhere, immediately – and I know where we can put him." Barbed wire coiled up the bedstand, flashing bloody. "Edmund, I know where you can get all the time you need."

The lamp was on.

Edmund hadn't left the lamp on.

And beside it, pulled closer to the edge of the desk–

He spun. "You went through my ledger."

"You left it open," came the reply.

"You went through my ledger!"

Istvan brushed through the door as though it were a curtain. "And you," he said, broken feathers coalescing from the mists, "are at the end of your wits!"

Edmund slid the ledger further behind him. Istvan wouldn't have even noticed it if he'd remembered to close it, but even if he had left it open, Istvan shouldn't have been poking through it. It wasn't his business.

None of this was his business.

This wasn't his house.

"Istvan, did I say you could come in?"

Wingtips brushed opposite walls. "You can't stop me."

Edmund grinned a tight smile. "That eager?"

Istvan drew up short. His hands trembled, then curled into fists. His features flickered, avatar to man and back again.

"Didn't think so," said Edmund.

Istvan turned, wire tangling across the carpet. "I'm going to Triskelion at noon today," he said. "I'm going to contact Lord Kasimir and break that siege. If you want time, Edmund, you can rip it from the defenders before I kill them."

A wingbeat – artillery flashing through poison – and he was gone.

Edmund made it to the bathroom before he threw up.

He didn't want to risk the crowds again. He didn't want to be stared at, or interrogated, or asked what to do, and he couldn't handle the day as anything other than the

Hour Thief, which left only so many options. Edmund paced the bluffs above his house, steering clear of the pagoda out of early morning courtesy. The fishing boats had already launched. His phone still worked.

He punched in a number and waited for the other end to pick up.

"Mr Templeton," said Mercedes.

"Why didn't you call me?" he demanded.

"Would you have answered?"

"Mercedes, I hate to say it, but you seem to have forgotten who you're talking to. I've answered since before the Twelfth Hour had a telephone installed. I've dedicated more years to the cabal than–"

"Whose years, Mr Templeton?"

He briefly considered throwing the phone off the bluffs. Watch it tumble. "Don't."

"You were on patrol," she said, "we both know that."

"I would have answered, Mercedes."

"I don't think so."

He turned his pocket watch over in his other hand. "You're wrong."

The line fell silent, and for a moment Edmund could only hear his own breathing, the waves on the rocks, the birds. He would have answered. He took the phone everywhere he went, just for that reason. He might not have answered immediately, and he might have had the contraption off at the time, but that was what voice mail was for.

No one wanted to bother with voice mail anymore.

He would have answered.

"Barrio Libertad," said Mercedes, her tone acid, "has kindly extended the offer to house our young Conduit for the time being. Temporarily. As a gesture of goodwill."

Change the subject. Sure.

"This is going to go in those pamphlets, isn't it?" he asked.

"That, Mr Templeton, isn't your problem. Grace Wu recalled with the boy last night."

Grace.

Grace had refused to let him take her back to the fortress yesterday evening, and he wasn't going to let her stay in his house, not ever again, after what she'd done. He'd offered somewhere on Yale campus, and she hadn't taken that, either. Twelfth Hour or nothing. *I'll sleep on a chair, Eddie.*

She'd been looking for nothing more than a chance to get close enough to the kid.

"Is Grace the one that broke the Demon's Chamber?" he asked.

"Ask Dr Czernin."

Edmund felt bile rising again. What had Istvan done?

"In fact," Mercedes continued, "ask him how he expected his little escapade to reflect on the Twelfth Hour's reputation. It will be appearing in those pamphlets, Mr Templeton, I'm sure of that."

"I thought those weren't my problem," Edmund said.

"They would be," she snapped, "if I could trust you."

He stopped. His breath misted in the morning air.

How could she–

Edmund switched the phone to his other ear, trying to keep his voice level. "I never asked for this promotion, Mercedes. I'm not the one that–"

"You're supposed to be the Hour Thief, Mr Templeton," she interrupted. "The best we have to offer. Professional in your dealings, legendary in your exploits, charming and photogenic: a wizard to represent all wizards at a time we desperately need support. In the public imagination, you are the Twelfth Hour, far more than I, far more than anyone. But now – now that you have duties matching your ability, now that you have responsibility beyond yourself and your own recovery – what do they see, Mr Templeton?"

He clutched his pocket watch more tightly. "I was asked when I would be up for re-election, Mercedes."

"And I would be thrilled to face you," she responded. "If you could bear it."

"I'm doing the best I can."

"No. You're not. You're doing the same things you've always done, and that might have served you well, once, but that world ended eight years ago. If you don't have time, Mr Templeton, go find it."

"Mercedes, I am not–"

The line went dead.

Edmund threw the phone off the edge.

He immediately regretted it. He spent a moment to teleport, catch the contraption mid-air, and return to the edge of the bluff.

He shoved the phone in his pocket. More time, gone.

He had until noon to find a better option.

He had a sinking feeling that he wouldn't.

Istvan stepped through the door at Charlie's, mud and shrapnel spattering across the wood. An engine idled in the street behind him. He knew exactly where to look.

Edmund sat at his usual booth: far wall, opposite the piano, with a clear view of the door. He wore his full Hour Thief regalia, his arms crossed on the table. He stared down at his hat.

He didn't look up at the thunder.

Istvan glanced at the bartender.

The old man shrugged, focusing on the sweep of a polishing rag across the keys of the antique register rather than meeting Istvan's empty gaze. "Just came in and sat down. Hours ago. No requests."

So, he wanted to be in fighting shape.

All for the better.

Istvan swept towards the booth. Poison dimmed the lights.

Edmund still didn't look up. "I haven't been to Triskelion before," he said, voice flat. "I can't teleport us without a lot of trouble."

"I've an arrangement," Istvan replied.

"How?" asked Edmund.

"Outside."

Edmund didn't reply. He exhaled a shaking breath.

Istvan offered him a hand. Phantom blood dripped onto the table.

Edmund put his hat on. Then he took the hand, or at least pantomimed it – oh, he knew his manners – and stood. The brim of his hat shadowed his eyes.

He regretted this already, Istvan knew. Just as Istvan himself would regret it later, as he always did.

But that was later.

Now... oh, the now was easier, and brighter, and so very promising of all that he'd denied himself for much too long. He was what he was. If that was all anyone wanted to see, let them see it – and run, or tremble, or follow in his wake, as they pleased. He didn't care. Not anymore.

He wove between the tables, Edmund in tow.

The bartender again averted his eyes.

Lucy waited outside. Her baroque monstrosity of a tank idled behind her, billowing black smoke from slatted vents. As Istvan approached, she saluted, gauntlet crashing against breastplate, and dropped to a knee. "Hail, ravager of the pale beast, lord of the long war, ender of complacency. Your conveyance is ready. My Lord Kasimir awaits your mighty presence, and wishes to offer his sincerest thanks."

Istvan chuckled. "Oh, we'll see."

Edmund said nothing.

Istvan skipped to the side of the vehicle, which had one of its hatches open, and peered inside. Not so different from the other tanks he'd known; the men of Triskelion were still human, after all. "Come on, then, Edmund, get in."

"We're driving," said Edmund, more a statement of resignation than a question.

Lucy stood. "The gifts of He-Who-Watches-in-Walls are many and potent," she said, slamming open another hatch, "and the most cunning Lord Kasimir has realized the full extent of their use. We make for the capital beacon."

"The teleportation method they received from Barrio Libertad for their mercenary services," explained Istvan. "You didn't think they wouldn't keep it?"

Edmund still stood some distance away with his hands in his pockets. "He-Who-Watches-in-Walls," he repeated.

"It doesn't matter what they call him," said Istvan. "Get in."

The wizard approached the vehicle, each step a trial, and reached for its chassis like he expected it to burn him. When it didn't, he grasped the handles to either side and pulled himself through the hatch.

Istvan swung through after him. The claustrophobic interior boasted four seats at four positions, crowded between loading mechanisms, ammunition storage, turret supports, racks for rifles, and bins for rations. Switches and levers and cable housings and other protrusions threatened his head wherever he turned. All of the same basic design elements, in roughly the same configuration as the eight-man British contraption that had started it all in Istvan's war.

Oh, he had gutted more of the Russian ones than he could count. It was like coming home, even if home now had computer screens on every surface and a place to boil tea and no longer tried to gas you to death with engine fumes.

Istvan seated himself in the commander's chair and grinned at Edmund, who had gravitated, white-knuckled, towards the loader position and now stared fixedly out one of the machine-gun hatches. His hands shook. It was the close quarters, Istvan knew – Edmund had been a navy man, but it wasn't so different – and so he leaned sideways to grasp Edmund's shoulder, and draw off sweet panic.

"I'm sure it will be over soon," he said. Then, inevitably: "Perhaps even by Christmas!"

"Stop it," Edmund mumbled.

A chuckle burst in Istvan's throat. "Christmas," he repeated. Oh, it shouldn't have been as funny as it was. They'd said it sincerely, once, before realizing that "home by Christmas" meant embarking on a multi-year campaign in more foreign countries than expected and perhaps not coming home after all. Not that anything ever changed. "That's only a few months away, you know."

The tank shook as Lucy took her place in the driver's position, leaning far back under an array of periscopes. She no longer wore her spiked pauldrons. The crest of her helmet was missing, as was her cape: likely detached and stowed somewhere. The rest of her armor stayed, and Istvan found himself wondering if perhaps the armies of Triskelion didn't care so much after all about engine fumes venting into the crew compartment.

"Hold fast," she ordered. She reached up to draw gauntleted fingers across a grooved panel, then pulled back a lever at her side.

The engine jumped from idle to a roar.

Edmund flinched. Istvan kept a grip on him. There was no getting out of this now – oh, no – not even through panic and visions, understandable as they might be. No retreating. No running. If Edmund felt like he was drowning again, well, he would simply have to drown.

Treads crunched below them. The whine of gearing filled the air. The tank shook.

"I can't," said Edmund, his voice a hoarse near-whisper. "Istvan, I can't."

He reached for his jacket pocket.

Oh, he was so predictable. Poor Edmund. He'd spent all this time trying to avoid this, and now it was all he had left. Of course he wanted to escape.

Istvan left his chair. He didn't need to be buckled in, after all. He placed himself directly behind Edmund's position, propped sideways and somewhat awkwardly against an ammunition compartment, and reached an arm around him in a half-embrace.

"It will be all right," he said, kindly. He rested the wooden handle of his knife against the other man's sternum. "I'm certain that it will be all right."

Edmund froze. His heartbeat fluttered beneath Istvan's fingers.

"After all," Istvan reminded him, "you brought this on yourself."

Lucy flipped a switch overhead. "The capital beacon has accepted our hail. Transit in two. Gird yourselves, and prepare for an audience."

"We are well-girded," Istvan called back. "Aren't we, Edmund?"

The wizard simply trembled.

Istvan grinned to himself. Oh, this was a much better way to ride.

A clanging, distant and mechanical, swept up and towards them, and the hatches flashed with a light like that of an oncoming train.

CHAPTER THIRTEEN

Metal walls pressed in at him, jolting and clattering. The taste of oil bubbled in the back of his throat. It was impossible not to imagine waves outside, saltwater bursting through the hatches and pooling around his legs. The air was close, and stifling, and smog-choked.

Edmund shouldn't have been able to stay where he was. The second that engine started, he should have succumbed to flat panic, no longer able to think straight, seeing things that happened a long time ago and fleeing as best he could. That was how it went. He knew his own weaknesses.

The weight of Istvan's knife pressed against his chest.

Edmund stared at it, at his own distorted face reflected in a blade that pointed downwards and away. The hand that gripped it did so lightly, casually, bare phalanges smeared with blood, radiating a chill that sank into his heart and slowed it. The same cold stretched across his chest and shoulder, accompanied by the faintest pressure: Istvan's arm, draped over him.

He should have been panicking. That he wasn't, he knew, was Istvan's doing.

It wasn't a matter of comfort or solidarity – it was a matter of outright being denied what he should have been feeling. Not a presence so much as an absence. Istvan drank terror like wine. Istvan was undoubtedly enjoying this.

Edmund had brought it all on himself.

He stared down at the knife on his chest and tried not to think about the notches carved into its handle. Istvan must have given up on keeping track long ago.

"How much further?" the ghost called.

"The capital beacon lies a mere two ridges distant from mighty Lord Kasimir's fortress," replied Lucy. The electronic edge to her voice cut through the roar of the engine. "Expect disembarkation shortly."

"Oh, good," said Istvan. He squeezed Edmund's shoulders tighter, which didn't amount to much, and pounded the knife handle against Edmund's sternum. "Not long now," he said, his voice too close and too loud for comfort. "A little audience and fanfare, and then we're on our way, hm? Oh, I haven't seen a parade in ages!"

"Sure," said Edmund.

"The parade is not for your viewing," Lucy said.

Istvan leaned over. "Come now–"

"You are to be its centerpiece, and the guests of honor, by Lord Kasimir's grace."

A laugh. "That's more the tune of it!"

Edmund closed his eyes, wondering if this was what one of the layers of Hell was like. Dante's version of it was imaginative, but hardly authoritative, and any speculation on what lay beyond the bounds of existence was speculation alone – you couldn't go there to see for yourself and come back with photographs.

You couldn't come back. Even Istvan hadn't ever really left.

"Edmund," the ghost continued, "have you ever been in a parade before?"

"Y–"

"I have. All you must do is sit beside me and wave, and then it shall be over and we can be on to business. Oh," he added, "I wonder if we might be attacked during it!"

"The cunning Lord Kasimir's security is unparalleled," said Lucy.

Istvan leered. "But not perfect?"

"I charge you not to raise such a question during the festivities."

"Oh, of course not. But one can hope! Right, Edmund?"

"Mm," said Edmund. He couldn't feel his shoulder anymore; he wished Istvan would back off, but dreaded what would happen if he did.

He swallowed back oil.

The jolting slowed. The light filtering through the hatches grew steadily dimmer, and greyer. It smelled of smoke: the greasy, unfiltered, sooty smoke Edmund remembered from his early days, before anyone ever thought of environmental regulations.

"Isn't it wonderful?" asked Istvan.

"I'd rather go home," said Edmund.

"You will!" The ghost ruffled his hair. "Later."

"Don't do that."

A pause; Istvan did stop, and drew back somewhat, but didn't let him go. "Sorry."

Edmund shook his head. "It's fine."

It wasn't.

Triskelion! Home of armies!

Istvan leapt out of the tank hatch. A parade ground greeted him, poured concrete laid out with guiding gridlines. Smoke billowed into the heavens from dismal factories along the perimeter. Two rows of guards in burnished golden armor stood at attention along the path to a soot-stained bunker complex dug into the rock, its walls slanted, a strange mirage-like shimmer hazing the air above it.

The mighty slopes of encircling mountains gleamed with snow. It seemed so pristine, from a distance. Istvan fancied he could hear the artillery fire.

Oh – no... that was only him.

He stepped out along the tank's main gun as Lucy climbed out of her own, driver-side hatch. "Waiting for us?" he called to the guard.

As one, they dropped to a knee. The shout of two dozen men echoed across the grounds, indecipherable but enthusiastic.

Istvan clapped his hands together. He had never enjoyed so much reverence before. "Bravo!" he called. "We shall only be a moment!"

He hopped off the gun, landed easily, and skipped over to find Edmund leaning against the back of the tank, breathing hard. Istvan clapped a hand on the man's shoulder. "Come on, Edmund – they're expecting us."

"I know," came the reply.

"Well, come on!"

Edmund looked up at him with the dull, hopeless expression of a man facing execution, and Istvan had to stop himself from ruffling his hair again. Oh, the wizard was wonderful. He didn't want to be here at all, and yet he was here. He was regretting it already, just as Istvan would, later. His fears were deep, and rich, and utterly unique – so old, yet human – and in that frailty there was immense strength. Istvan loved him tremendously, and it was so difficult to stay angry at him even though he bloody well deserved it.

It was only them, alone, now. No Grace or anyone else. Just Edmund, Istvan, the mercenaries, and the siege. It really was a fine day for a siege.

"We don't have a choice," said Edmund, as though trying to convince himself. He turned his hat around in his hands.

"Not at all," said Istvan. He grinned, or perhaps he had already been grinning. "Besides, you need time, don't you?"

Edmund sighed. He put his hat back on.

Istvan led the Hour Thief back towards Lucy and the waiting guard, feeling lighter than he had in years. Pietro would never have approved, of course. No, he would have run away in the other direction, not recognizing Istvan at all. So long ago. Things were different, now.

"Way!" called Lucy, and the guard fell back, bowing their heads. The path to Lord Kasimir's compound lay open.

"I don't suppose the parade is inside?" Istvan asked. "For fear of mortars?"

Lucy held up a fist; the blunt muzzles of cannons on the battlements swiveled away from their passage. She started towards the compound. Her cape swept behind her; her pauldrons re-attached to her shoulders. "Much celebration awaits your triumphant return," she replied.

Istvan strolled after her. "Our return? That's a bit backwards, isn't it?"

"The most magnanimous Lord Kasimir offers you his blessing," she replied, "and the honor of his presence."

"Yes, well, the Lord of the Long War merits somewhat more than that, I should think," Istvan said. He indicated the last of the guard as they passed them. "An accompanying procession, at least."

Lucy came to a halt.

"What was the rest?" asked Istvan. "The rest of those titles?"

"Ravager of the pale beast," the armored woman replied. She turned to regard the guards in their lines, still standing with heads bowed. "Ender of complacency."

"We don't need a procession," muttered Edmund from behind them.

Istvan ignored him. "And?"

"Viewer of my last mask," Lucy finished, somewhat reluctantly. She inclined her own head, setting a fist to her breastplate. "My sincerest apologies, Devil's Doctor. If it is a procession that pleases you, a procession you shall have."

"Splendid."

A gesture; a shout; another sigh from Edmund–

–and two dozen armored guardsmen (and possibly guardswomen) fell in before and behind them, gilded detailing flashing thin ribbons of light across sooty concrete. They marched with the steady rhythm of those long-trained, carrying their weapons to best show off their craftsmanship. None complained.

They were all exhausted, of course, and the beat of their boots loud in Lord Kasimir's bare halls, Lucy resignedly carrying a banner at their head... but if they were going to give Istvan titles in exchange for murder, well, let them treat him as grandly as they were able. Kasimir was, after all, just as mortal as the rest of them.

A dead mockery hung from the ceiling in the warlord's throne room.

Their procession came to a halt just below it. Istvan

peered upwards as the shout to halt echoed around the chamber. It was a great rusted-orange serpent, its "flesh" stripped away, strange glyphs carved along the length of its ribs. It didn't resemble any machine of war Istvan recognized. It might have been only a small part of one of the greater monsters that now lay like mountains across the remnants of cities. He himself might have hewn it from its origin.

The rest of the throne room was curiously bare. More concrete formed the walls. Black cables ran between banks of harsh reddish lights, with no effort made to conceal them. A dais occupied the far end, certainly, but it was simply a raised platform, three steps high with no ornamentation: a tattered banner hung behind it, and that was all. The throne was a simple block of stone without even a back to it.

It was as though all of the splendor was reserved for Lord Kasimir himself.

The warlord sat stiffly, leaning forward with his hands on his knees. A broadsword lay propped on the stone beside him. Like his men, he wore elaborate armor with golden filigree; shoulderplates with wholly impractical spikes; a scarlet cape over a long coat, itself placed over what might have been yet another coat buckled below a steel breastplate. His helmet boasted a long plume of horsehair and a faceplate fitted with what may have been the front of an actual human skull. Scarlet lights flickered behind his visor.

If Istvan weren't mistaken, he seemed rather... subdued, for a brutal despot. Wary. Nervous, even, with a verdant edge that suggested buried jealousy. Perhaps that siege was going more badly than he wanted to admit. Perhaps he saw in Istvan the kind of power he desperately desired to possess. The man had, after all, once contracted his forces to Barrio Libertad. He knew what had happened there.

A single, somewhat less elaborately-clad warrior stood to his left, a sabre at his side. No one else guarded the dais.

Lucy approached the edge of the dais and knelt, propping the banner-pole on the bare concrete floor. The rest of the procession divided itself once more into two lines, one on either side of Edmund and Istvan, likewise dropping to their knees.

Istvan glanced at Edmund, who remained standing. Unhappy, but standing. Oh, good.

"So," he began.

The man standing beside Kasimir held up a fist. "Hail, Devil's Doctor, Lord of the Long War, Ravager of the Pale Beast, Ender of Complacency," he boomed, his accented voice amplified and electronic. "Hail, Hour Thief, of the Twelfth Hour and its mysteries. The mighty Lord Kasimir has returned from the storm with dust on his boots and blood on his blade to welcome you to his domain, and once we have concluded here, to the storm he shall return."

The broadsword didn't seem to have blood on it, but Istvan could forgive that much in the name of hygiene. "Well," he said. He stepped forward to stand near Lucy, who still hadn't risen. "I suppose I should thank you for having us."

Lucy's helmet tilted fractionally, dismay filtering into her presence.

Edmund edged closer to him. "Istvan–"

"Where's the fighting, then?" Istvan continued. "Where do you need us?"

Lord Kasimir twitched two fingers. His spokesman swept an arm in a grand, demonstrative arc, his amplified voice only somewhat too loud for the space. "Our need is not so dire as to forego civility, Devil's Doctor."

Lucy murmured something in the Triskelion tongue. A plea, perhaps. Kasimir's spokesman fired back something else, channeling anger that Istvan knew he didn't really feel. The exchange gave the distinct impression of two people who didn't want to be there arguing for the benefit of someone else who also didn't want to be there.

Istvan sighed. He had agreed to siege-breaking, not frivolities.

He turned. "Don't worry, I'm sure we can find the siege ourselves," he said. "I've been there once, already. Come along, Edmund – we've work to do."

Edmund didn't budge. "You wanted a parade," he said.

"Oh, that's over with. Come on!"

"Silence!" shouted Kasimir's spokesman.

Istvan looked back at him, allowing wings, bone, and poison to flicker into existence. Phantom artillery echoed through the throne room. The spokesman wavered on his feet.

No one said anything for several moments. Silence, indeed.

"That's fine," sighed Edmund. He walked past Istvan, ignoring the barbed wire that snagged at his pant legs. He carried himself as though he had been born a diplomat. He came to a stop just behind and to the right of Lucy, and then doffed his hat, holding it politely in both hands. "Lord Kasimir," he continued, "if I may?"

The warlord shifted on his block of stone, strands of his horsehair plume spilling over one shoulder as he leaned forward further. He gave a curt nod.

"You may speak," boomed his spokesman.

Edmund took a breath. "Thank you. Before we do anything, I'd like to know just what it is that we can expect to gain from this deal. Where are these 'vast tracts of land' that you're offering?"

"Oh, that's a good idea," said Istvan. "Asking that."

Edmund's mouth twitched.

Istvan closed the distance to stand beside him, doing his best to restrain the worst of the thunder. He hadn't thought to ask about the prize itself. He'd known that Kasimir had it, and that seemed fine enough. He and Edmund could go anywhere, after all. It hadn't seemed to matter where it was.

But, oh, if they were placed in an embattled position, or...

"A land of seas, strung along a great river, lies to the east of dread Chicago," the spokesman intoned. "Between two of these seas, along this river, there lies a city in ruin, a city raised around two mighty waterfalls which have fallen silent. The cunning Lord Kasimir saw fit to conquer the dams and generators of this city, three years ago. It is these that he will exchange for your service."

"Niagara?" asked Edmund. "Niagara Falls?"

"If that is what you call this place of harnessed waters." The spokesman nodded, gravely. "This is acceptable?"

Edmund hesitated – it wasn't really, Istvan knew; anything near those enormous lakes was much too far away to keep any sort of watch on Barrio Libertad – and then nodded back. "It will do."

Kasimir straightened, held out his hands in the same manner as one offering up a sword, and waited expectantly for Edmund to copy the gesture. When he did, the warlord stood, brusquely took up his sword, and strode out of the room with the air of a man who just wanted things to be over with. Lucy got to her feet again, along with the two rows of guardsmen.

"See to your conveyance," ordered Kasimir's spokesman.

Edmund shook his head. "I'm not riding again. We'll find the place on our own, like Istvan said."

The spokesman and Lucy exchanged glances.

"If it pleases you," the spokesman said.

"Oh, it does," said Istvan. "It pleases us very much."

It was all Edmund could do to keep up.

Triskelion was unknown territory. He'd never had any reason to visit it before. The best he could do was follow Istvan, one short teleport after another, up and down sharp ridges and across cracked valley floors, boots crunching through dirt and alkali. It was hot – hotter than any mountains should have been at this time of year – and the smoke never seemed to settle. The region sat directly over Pennsylvania coal beds, and Edmund suspected at least some of them were on fire.

His breath came hard. The air was almost orange in places, and it was too easy to imagine it eating through his skin.

Istvan – being Istvan – flitted from ruin to ruin. Abandoned towers. Empty base camps. Mines with collapsed entrances. Coal towns with homes smashed to matchsticks, churches missing steeples, even the rubble stripped of anything metal or perishable. If anyone had survived there after the Wizard War, they didn't anymore. It was best to pretend that they had fled.

The working mines proved otherwise.

"Oh, we're close, now!" shouted Istvan, zipping past Edmund for the fourth or fifth time and looping back away, over another ridge.

A third cart emerged from the blackness cut into the mountain, hitched to a spindly human shape bent over like a spider. The shaft wasn't vertical, but it was close. The laborers crawled. Guards watched from rickety towers. The cart wasn't adult-sized.

Edmund turned away. Pretend that they had fled. Pretend that he was surprised. Barrio Libertad had worked with the warlords, contracting them out as mercenaries to find artifacts. He wondered if Grace had known.

He heard the siege before he saw it.

When he crested the last ridge, he realized he'd seen it before.

Vast metal doors set into the side of a mountain. A road blasted into the rock of the opposite cliff face, carrying supplies and more men to the emplacements in the valley. Smoke billowing from baroque stacks. The flash of artillery rounds beating on defenders that refused to yield. Suspended wires running from peak to peak.

He'd seen it in thread. Istvan had copied it faithfully. Istvan was, along with everything else, a remarkable artist in his own way.

It smelled like cordite, tar, and burnt meat.

Edmund swallowed.

He'd agreed to this.

Istvan landed beside him, grinning. A skull was always grinning. "You'll follow me, then," he said. He pointed at the doors and the tiny figures that swarmed up steep and jagged rock towards them. "If you can't get through, I'll make a way, and then you're free to take what time you like from anyone. You won't have any shortage after today!"

Edmund's fingers closed around his pocket watch. He'd told Mercedes he wouldn't take time from targets she chose. He would never focus on specific populations.

Yet here he was.

Istvan drew closer to him. "Oh, don't be like that, Edmund. We had to solve it one way or another, and besides, afterwards, you can go back to what you did before." He chuckled. "Unless you take a liking to this, of course."

A skeletal hand reached out to caress the lapel of Edmund's suit jacket. One finger slipped down to curl beneath his tie.

Istvan wasn't thinking straight. The fighting was getting to him. He got... strange, when he wasn't thinking straight. It wasn't his fault.

"Just go," Edmund managed.

The ghost leaned even closer, bare teeth near to Edmund's ear. "I'll leave some for you," he whispered conspiratorially. Then he turned, wings snapping open in a dark flurry, and sped off over the battlefield, leaving behind only wisps of poison and the unnerving memory of laughter.

Edmund shuddered. Not his fault. That wasn't the Istvan he knew. He wasn't sure, anymore, if he'd ever known the real man at all.

A faint cheer came up from the valley. Lord Kasimir's men were expecting them.

OK. OK.

There was nothing else for it.

Edmund eyed the doors, promised himself a night of oblivion, and snapped his pocket watch shut.

•••

Istvan swooped low over the back line of artillery, zipping through plumes of smoke and up and over a trench line. Kasimir's forces had just begun a fresh assault, likely to coincide with his own arrival, and the mountain fortress made a wonderful centerpiece. Forcing your enemies to fight uphill while you rained down fire was never a poor strategy.

How long had this siege lasted? A month? Two? What would the warlords do once they ran out of precious heavy munitions? Those weren't easy to make, especially now. Kasimir must be convinced that his enemies held something of immense value. Worth dying for? Oh, he had people for that.

Istvan crossed the valley floor and swept up the embattled mountainside.Dust from the recent bombardment hazed the air. Climbers raised ice axes to him. Holes drilled to seat explosives pockmarked the rock. He rose higher. Scorched bunkers crouched along the narrow path upwards. Gunfire blazed at him as he approached.

"Ah," he called, laughing. "You've seen me! That's good!"

He darted towards the nearest. Shouting met him. Probing gun barrels protruded from rifle slits, their owners trying to fire upwards as best as they were able.

Istvan dropped through the concrete and tore through the nearest body lengthwise like livestock, or perhaps a fish. There were four of them. Uneaten rations lay abandoned on a small table beside playing cards, a roll of tape, and an unfinished portrait etched into a shell casing. One of the defenders tried to stab him with a bayonet, which was quite brave.

Istvan killed them all and moved on to the next.

Six bunkers later, he reached the fortress's vast and improbable doors. They were made of some metal that remained bright and gleaming despite all of the punishment it had endured, pressed into peculiar patterned waves and whorls. Part of their frame protruded from the rock, blown away by artillery, revealing sunken support beams. Fallen rubble lay heaped man-high before them. No obstacle. Not to a ghost. Not to the Great War.

But to Edmund! Oh, it would do no good at all, forcing Edmund to find his own way, when a perfectly serviceable way could be made. Then he and Istvan wouldn't be fighting together, and that would ruin the poetry.

Istvan touched the doors. The metal tingled, its pressed patterns seeming to ripple outwards from his fingers. He drew back and peered up at where a direct strike had gouged a shallow cave just over the frame. That would do. He leapt, hovered, and then dove through shattered rock.

The hall beyond had its defenders: they hid behind dozens of stacked bulwarks placed for that purpose, and they made a fine attempt at covering fire. They even had a medic.

Istvan flicked bile and stomach acid onto one of the odd mosaics that lined the walls. "You do have water with you, don't you?" he asked.

The medic slid down against the wall, hugging his bag to his chest. His armor was blue, probably; it was difficult to tell.

"They will be asking for water," Istvan told him, just loud enough to be heard over pained wheezing and moans, the faint scraping of armor plate against stone, and a mumbled strain of what might have been prayer. "Sepsis is rather difficult to treat, I'm afraid. I wish you the very best of luck."

Shouting came from down below.

Istvan inspected the doors again, barred as they were with two great beams. They seemed to open using a chain-winch mechanism he was certain he couldn't budge. The hinges, however…

The first door struck a corner on the ground with a thunderous boom, twisting on its axis. Istvan cut through another hinge, started on the second door, and then darted out of the way as both multi-ton panels toppled inwards. Wounded men cried out. Dust billowed across pools of blood.

"Go on, then," Istvan encouraged the medic, "get started!"

He looked around for a way down – such a strange building, like a monastery more than a fortress – and then darted for a likely annex. "Oh," he called over his shoulder, "and if you see a man in black, tell him I took the left stairwell!"

Perhaps they would have flamethrowers. He should like to fight someone with a flamethrower again. It had been so long. They were wonderful in close quarters.

The doors were warded. No design Edmund had seen before, which meant it was powerful magic: those long ago put into common use were little good as anything more than decorative elements even when they did work, plagued by interference. All modern cities had come to bear a morass of traditional protections, the vast majority incorrectly drawn and denied the sacrifices required to satisfy them.

These must have taken several lives to place, to resist an artillery bombardment.

They hadn't helped against Istvan.

It took a moment for Edmund's eyes to adjust. His nose needed no such thing. His stomach twisted; the urge to vomit held back only by the knowledge that doing so wouldn't make it smell any better.

His boot slipped. He looked down. A severed gauntlet still clutched the grip of half a rifle, blood pooling beneath splintered bone. The person it belonged to lay not far away, curled in a twitching ball. Behind him, someone else sat staring dully down at their own intestines. More blood seeped from beneath the fallen doors.

The entire hall was littered with still-moving bodies.

I'll leave some for you.

Edmund retched. He retreated, back into the smog-choked air and the light, and slammed his back against rock, not caring if something hit him.

Istvan hadn't killed all those people. He had maimed them. He had left them dying slowly, abandoned them without a second thought, crushed those that couldn't escape to clear the way to the rest. Istvan knew that Edmund needed time, and had left as many defenders alive as possible so that Edmund could finish the job. Even the dying still had time. Some of them might linger for weeks, or months, if given care. It wasn't over until it was over.

Carrion crows, too, wore black.

CHAPTER FOURTEEN

"Niagara Falls," said Mercedes. She peered over the edge of the dam, where water trickled into the sluggish river far, far below. The collapsed span of a pedestrian bridge blocked part of the flow, one of many obstacles that would need to be dredged out of the way eventually. The city of Niagara Falls itself – both the US and the Canadian side – lay out of sight further upstream, together with the famous landmark. "I knew you would find something once you put your mind to it, Mr Templeton."

"Mm," said Edmund.

Mercedes walked further along the edge, commenting on bedraggled landscaping and the sorry state of the power lines overhead. They had already toured the road Edmund had taken to get here and the edges of the encampment still occupied by Kasimir's forces, a sullen crew who acted like Edmund and Mercedes weren't there as they prepared to return to Triskelion. The camp had clearly been intended to support a much larger contingent than worked there now: it was made of materials more permanent than canvas, took up most of the central island, and ran along the reservoir's edge to the west. There were even fields slashed and burned into the surrounding forest.

Lord Kasimir, it was very clear, hadn't been interested in the city or the falls themselves. He'd come for the dams. There were four of them, which Edmund wasn't sure had been the case before the Wizard War or not, and they were enormous. They also hadn't been fully repaired, were running well below capacity, didn't have much in the way of amenities, and were frighteningly close to Lake Ontario and the monster-filled Greater Great Lakes fracture zone, which probably explained why Kasimir was willing to give them up in the first place.

Edmund should have known. Couldn't trust despots to do anything but look out for their own interest. Too bad it had stopped being his decision the second Istvan showed up in his room, snooping in his ledger, getting bullet holes all over everything. Let's be mercenaries, Edmund. Let's solve this the violent way.

Edmund hadn't stayed for the parade. If Istvan had, good for him. Edmund didn't want any parades in his honor, thanks. Not now, not ever.

Mercedes turned from the river and headed for a squat building atop the center of the dam that they hadn't toured yet. "Niagara Falls," she repeated. "Niagara Falls. Mr Templeton, this is much further away than you had planned."

Edmund followed her. "It is."

"But," she continued, "that might not be an obstacle."

She still hadn't asked how he'd gotten this place. She'd talk about plans for it, but not how he'd gotten it. She hadn't said a word when they'd checked out Kasimir's camp.

"Oh?" he asked.

She ran a thumb over the stump of her ring finger.

"When you go to meet with the Barrio Libertad People's Council, stress that this is a secure facility. It's well away from any population centers. It's surrounded on almost all sides by spellscars, in a stable 'island' between the effects of Big East and the Greater Great Lakes. If anyone intends to escape, they'll have to cross at least five hundred miles of impossible terrain." She glanced over her shoulder. "That's security, Mr Templeton."

Of course he was meeting with the People's Council. Of course. "Right."

"We'll need somewhere to place a vault portal," mused Mercedes. "To close the distance."

He nodded. "Right." Then he realized what she'd just said. "Wait. The vault? We can't make another seal for the vault."

"We also can't rely on you and your teleportation for everything."

Edmund shook his head. The seal on the Twelfth Hour's high security vault was a masterpiece of mixed craftsmanship; nothing less would satisfy the dead corridors of the beast slumbering behind it. "Where are we going to find whalebone, Mercedes?"

"You aren't," she replied. "You focus on getting this place running and on the Conduit, once you get him back."

She reached for the metal handle of a mostly intact glass door. Edmund stepped over and pulled it open for her. "So I'm not keeping an eye on Barrio Libertad, then?"

Mercedes smiled an acid smile. "We can do better than that."

They walked into a museum. A ticket-taker's booth sat to the left of the entrance. A hanging sign welcomed them to the "History of Niagara Falls." Photographs of dams large and small graced the walls, together with portraits of prominent dam-builders – including a family of beavers. A scale model of one of the Niagara dams sat on a broad, low table, surrounded by explanatory plaques. One of them stated that construction had been completed in 2016, well after the Wizard War had left the area in shambles. There was even a gift shop.

"Headquarters?" Mercedes asked dryly.

Edmund spotted a restroom sign and wondered if they had working plumbing. He'd gladly set up in a gift shop if it meant having access to working plumbing. "Maybe."

She clasped her hands behind her back and strolled over to inspect the plaques.

"Excuse me a moment," Edmund said. He edged around the table and a display of Niagara Falls keychains. He stuck his head around the corner, located the men's room, and pushed open the door so he could flip on the light. The light worked. He tried turning the tap on the sink.

The water flowed.

He'd done mercenary work for a warlord. He'd inflicted the ghost of the Great War on a group of people he knew nothing about, for a cause he knew nothing about, for no better reason than making up for his own poor attempts at administration. He'd taken time from dying men and women, mutilated for that very purpose. He'd left early so he wouldn't have to face the suicides.

Now he'd have running water.

He shut it off.

"Mercedes," he said, returning to the museum proper, "I don't know if you were ever planning to ask where this place came from, but I can tell you right now that I don't know when or if Istvan is going to be back."

The Magister stood behind the gift shop counter. She had somehow jimmied the cash register open, and was inspecting bills with faces on them that Edmund didn't recognize. "Isn't that interesting," she said.

"I won't have to patrol again for over a year."

"Look at this – they elected someone else Prime Minister the year the robots came."

Edmund sighed. Silence it was. "Robots, Mercedes?"

"I hope he did better than ours did." She pocketed the bill. "Now, Mr Templeton, ask yourself this: if you aren't going to be keeping an eye on Barrio Libertad, what do you think you might be doing here?"

"Fixing the place," he replied.

"And?"

"Keeping an eye on the kid."

"And?"

"Mercedes, I am not teaching my teleport. That's not on the table."

She shut the cash register and walked out from behind the counter. "You aren't thinking big enough. What does the Twelfth Hour still hold over Barrio Libertad, Mr Templeton? What do we still do better?"

"Aside from magic," he began–

He stopped.

Not just magic. Anything strange. Anything that no one else knew how to handle. Istvan might be a sort of magical being, but he was more like a mobile disaster. The Tyger fell in the same camp. And the kid, the Conduit…

"You want me to collect them," he said. He looked around the museum. It wasn't nearly big enough. Hydroelectric dams weren't known for their spacious accommodations. "The kid's only the first, isn't he?"

"Security," she said. "We can offer security. Niagara will be a safe place, Mr Templeton, for everyone."

"I'm not a jailer."

"I never said you were. Besides, we've needed somewhere to train new wizards for some time."

Edmund stared at her. You didn't just "train" new wizards. Magic was a deadly dangerous, corrosive, mind-breaking thing. People turned to it because they were either stupid or desperate, and there was precious little in-between. There was plenty of literature, sure. Plenty of theory, sure. But actually learning something? Actually doing something that would draw attention – Conceptual or otherwise – and surviving the results?

You weren't a wizard until you regretted it. Anyone who claimed to be taking an apprentice was assumed to be up to something.

Edmund himself had never had any kind of teacher. He'd stumbled across something he shouldn't have, and they'd told him he could either keep his mouth shut for the rest of his life (which, they hinted, might be short) or go with them, and help them put away the real bad guys, and keep his mouth shut for the rest of his life (which might be longer). He'd chosen the latter. Most of the Twelfth Hour's membership, even in those days, had been supporting staff and co-conspirators rather than actual wizards. You had to be a special kind of depraved to be a wizard.

And then... then he'd stolen that book, and he could never go back.

He drew a steadying breath. "Mercedes, I'm not overseeing anywhere that we send people to die."

She searched his face. She had to look up a fair distance. "The old way of doing things isn't the only way," she said.

"I know that it isn't the only way. There are plenty of other ways. I've read all about them and they're all just as – if not more – dangerous. You can't produce wizards on an assembly line, Mercedes. You can't open those books to anyone who wants to give it a shot. Do you know what happened to the Innumerable Citadel? They tried opening a college, and to this day no one knows where it went."

"I'll be choosing candidates," said Mercedes. "We won't be taking just anyone. We won't be promoting it to the public at all. There are far more cults than ever before, Mr Templeton – and anyone that comes to you will already be broken."

Edmund clenched his teeth. "We can't do that."

"We can't rehabilitate people? We can't teach the lost and angry to do good?"

That wasn't what it was. He couldn't do that. He wasn't a role model. He'd let Istvan drag him into a war and hack people almost to death so he could steal what was left of their lifespans. All he could do was tell people what not to do, even as he did it himself, even as he kept doing it forever.

He was a hypocrite. An unkillable hypocrite.

Maybe that was why Mercedes was putting him in charge of the world's first-ever prison for the exceptionally strange and dangerous.

"I'm glad you understand," she said. She flicked a pinwheel with a turbine design stenciled across its wings. "I'd like to check the generator room. After that, I'd suggest you prepare for your visit to Barrio Libertad. They'll be expecting you – and Dr Czernin, if he's available – tomorrow morning."

"He won't be," said Edmund.

Mercedes started towards the back of the building. "It's interesting to think," she said, "the flow of water over the falls is completely controlled by these dams. You could shut off one of the most spectacular sights in the world any time you liked."

Edmund shoved his hands in his pockets.

The parade began at Kasimir's drab fortress and wound down through the worker's barracks and the factories and the sharp fences that kept anyone from escaping either of them. It was grey and sooty, the sides of the road packed with gaunt crowds celebrating a brief respite from labor, but the greater part of Triskelion's splendor was concentrated in its armor and its weaponry – and now everything that could be spared from the siege was on brilliant display.

A band preceded the grinding treads of burnished tanks. High-ranking warriors led captured prisoners on ropes. Enemy flags burned overhead, run up just for the occasion and coated in some odd substance that ensured they would smolder most of the night. It created a merry crackling sort of light that was most agreeable.

Istvan rode part of the route atop Lucy's tank, now festooned with empty helmets, and when he grew bored of that, he leapt skyward to show off some proper aerobatics, flitting through the beams of spotlights that struggled to track his passage. When Kasimir's spokesman asked him to cut apart a captured piece of artillery for the crowd's benefit, he chopped off part of the man's helmet crest and laughed. He was War! He was the Great War! He was attrition's revelry, death and carrion, battle waged in open graves from peak to field to tundra!

They couldn't do anything to him. No one could.

After the parade was over, Kasimir invited him to his hall for a feast, and… well, Istvan couldn't say no to that, now could he?

A roasted creature of some unknown persuasion served as the centerpiece. Favored warriors sat on cushions along either side of a long, low table cast of concrete, helmets removed. They were uniformly dark-haired, their skin smooth and pale. None of them seemed to have ever spent much time exposed to the elements. Kasimir himself sat at the table's head. He kept his helmet on. Perhaps he had eaten earlier, or planned to eat later, or there was a cleverly-disguised straw somewhere.

Istvan was ushered to sit at the warlord's right – opposite his ever-present spokesman – and when he asked for Lucy, she was brought in as well, and placed beside him. The feast began with a speech, as all good feasts do, and then those in attendance started delicately upon their meal with a sort of long fork.

Kasimir boasted, through his spokesman: he would now have unquestioned control over the passes. He could raid into both Big East and the refugee-choked regions beyond with impunity. He could carve out greater and greater stretches of the spellscars, burning everything living to bare rock and then setting off Bernault devices to quiet the earth once and for all. In his wisdom, he had stockpiled enough of the strange, near-nuclear-level artifacts to rid an entire kingdom of Shokat Anoushak's taint.

Istvan asked why he hadn't used the devices during the siege… but of course Kasimir wanted the place intact. There had been rather an odd blue-white glow in the lower levels, come to think of it. Bernault devices glowed that same blue.

Ah, well. Edmund had left long before that. If Edmund didn't care, there was probably nothing for Istvan to worry about.

Kasimir repeated a great deal how impressed he was with Istvan's service, how honored he would be to have such an ally in future battles, and Istvan told him that of course he would be. Who wouldn't?

Lucy stayed close to him all night, listening as the fires burned down.

The feast was over when the last of the guests had excused themselves, one by one, and Kasimir retired to (presumably) his own repast, leaving a great deal of the food still on the table. Istvan wished everything he tried didn't taste like ash. He tried picking up one of the long forks; it had only two tines, and felt more like a rapier than any utensil he had ever used.

"You will stay, then?" Lucy asked.

"Oh, I can't," Istvan said. He managed to pick up the fork somewhat, but could only manage a few inches before it tumbled through his hand again. He had never been able to handle anything like a rapier.

Lucy prodded at the last of the beast on her plate. "The wizards do not laud you as we do, Devil's Doctor."

"Well, they can hardly afford to do that." He vaguely remembered a crowd, along the route; men and women not granted splendid armor, who seemed malnourished. The Twelfth Hour didn't have nearly so many laborers, certainly. "Besides, Edmund will be expecting me back, you know."

Lucy leaned towards him. "Was it not they who entrapped you? Was it not they who commanded you like a slave? You should head a mighty kingdom, not answer to the whims of those who abused you so. Even our mighty Lord–"

"Yes?"

Lucy looked around, furtively. "We must retire," she said.

Istvan nodded. He put the fork down. Oh, he had to remind Edmund that the man had missed his own party – and wasted a good meal, besides. It was a shame that he had left so early. Istvan had hoped to tour Niagara with him, afterwards. It would have been a fine capstone to the campaign.

Lucy led him out of the fortress and onto the parade ground, littered with cinders and scorch marks. Her tank was there, parked where it had been left after its role in the parade was over; she waved him towards it and bade him climb inside. Surely they weren't going to ride all the way back?

"Thank you," he said as he seated himself back in the commander's chair, "but you know that I can fly back to–"

Lucy swung in beside him with a clang. "You are war," she hissed.

Istvan blinked at her. "Yes," he said. "Yes, I am. The Great War. Yes."

"You are invincible," she said.

He thought of Kyra and the storm. "Well, yes, but–"

"Lord Kasimir fears you, Devil's Doctor, just as the wizards do. He has seen what you are and he knows that he – mighty as he might be – is only a man. But you!"

She dropped to a knee. There wasn't much room in the tank, but she managed. Why she was telling him the obvious was another matter. Istvan leaned away from her. "Er–"

"You have proven yourself this day, free of chains and contracts," she continued. "The face you bear is a mask over your true being. You are an ending spirit, Devil's Doctor, the first we have found in this world. Whether Lord Kasimir wills it or not, it is your right and duty to claim dominion over all warriors, living and dead. Their voices granted you wisdom. Their sacrifice granted you power. You are War, and nothing and no one shall stand above you."

Istvan sat there a moment. An ending spirit? An avatar, who ought to bear the authority to match? A mask over something almost divine, channeled through the shell of a mortal man long dead... was that really what he was? He'd never thought of the memories as wisdom, before.

Istvan peered through one of the gun ports at the charred parade ground. "You're suggesting that I ought to conquer everyone, then?"

"If it pleases you," Lucy replied.

He wasn't sure that it would; it seemed a great deal of trouble. People didn't like to be conquered. "How do you know all of this?"

She closed a fist over her chest. "I am Banner-Bearer. I carry the standard, the stories, the founding. Lord Kasimir would have you as ally, true – but he has grown bold in this place, and forgotten his obligations. He boasts before you. He grants you your titles, and little else. It is the task of those who remember to set things right."

"You're a... priest?"

"I am Banner-Bearer, Lord."

"Oh, good heavens," Istvan said.

CHAPTER FIFTEEN

Edmund sat at a round table in an equally round, airy room which was covered with murals. He tried not to look at them. He kept his hands folded. Before him was a false window that looked into a garden with climbing vines and tropical birds, silent but full of simulated motion. He'd been in here before. The design on the ceiling was a circle of interlocking hands. He knew that, at any moment, the floor might move, or the magic that kept him alive might suddenly fade and die. Diego could do that. Just because he hadn't yet didn't mean he wouldn't.

The nine current members of the Barrio Libertad's People's Council sat evenly spaced around the perimeter, consulting the surface before them. Occasionally they exchanged brief mutters. None of them seemed to hold a clear leadership position over the others – Diego, always watching, already filled that post – and none of them seemed pleased to see Edmund, despite the fact that he'd once saved them from being forced to watch the mass murder of the half-million people that now formed the majority of their populace. They probably had been just as pleased to see who Grace had brought home.

Kyra. Kyra Stewart.

They were voting now to see what would be done with the kid, which they wouldn't have had to do in the first place if Istvan hadn't done whatever he did to the Demon's Chamber and Grace hadn't butted in where she didn't belong.

Edmund maintained a tight, pleasant smile. The balcony level, crowded with spectators, remained mercifully quiet.

As Mercedes instructed, he'd begun by reminding the People's Council of the scope of their own population: the largest, by far, in Big East. If Kyra somehow got out of control, those people would be at risk. Diego was powerful, sure, but they couldn't rely on him for everything. They had to act on their own judgement, and, regardless of Kyra's age or condition, the kid was the kind of threat best kept far away from major population centers. He belonged somewhere he wouldn't pose a danger, kept under constant watch by an agent that couldn't be accidentally killed. Somewhere secure and, above all, remote.

Somewhere like Niagara.

The Twelfth Hour had been secretly working on getting such a place operational all this time, keeping quiet to avoid anyone – or anything – taking advantage during reconstruction. The Demon's Chamber had been an unfortunate stop-gap and nothing more. It was after the end of the world, after all. Edmund had done the best he could with what he had. Now that Niagara was ready, the Twelfth Hour could handle people like Kyra properly, and they were more than willing to assist Barrio Libertad.

After all, the fortress had never asked for this. Grace Wu was never officially dispatched to deal with the storm in Tornado Alley. The problem was a Twelfth Hour problem first and foremost.

The lies ate at him less than the truth.

He knew that the birds in the murals were watching.

Finally, Councilor Rothchild slid her hand across the unseen display on the table before her. "The vote is clear," she said. "Resistor Alpha acted on her own initiative to secure Kyra Stewart from a foreign power, knowingly bringing a significant public threat into our city. Such an action was never within the scope of her duties."

Edmund nodded. A bit legalistic, but workable.

The councilor went on. "Additionally, we have a vested interest in maintaining mutually beneficial cooperation with the Twelfth Hour. We would like to reiterate that the recent distribution of brochures in your jurisdiction was the doing of a splinter group not affiliated with the People's Council."

A splinter group. Right. He'd believe that when they turned the perpetrators over and stopped doing their damnedest to replace the Twelfth Hour's curation and peacekeeping duties with artifact destruction and propaganda.

"Thank you," he said.

"However," Rothchild continued, "due to Kyra Stewart's treatment at your hands, we cannot in good conscience release him to you."

Edmund spent a moment to gather his thoughts. He could afford that now. He could cheat to maintain his composure, to come up with an on-the-nose and compelling counterargument, and no one would ever know.

He didn't have a compelling counterargument. "I understand," he said.

"Let us remind you…" began an ancient black man sitting across the table.

Great. Edmund tried not to be too obvious about squinting at the man's placard. Councilor Durand. They'd probably planned for him to speak.

Durand held up a withered finger. "First, you knowingly took a Shattered boy somewhere you knew he couldn't be treated." Another finger. "Second, you kept that boy in a forced coma for several days. Third, you left him open to attack by one of your associates."

"Actually–"

"Let me finish. Fourth, you physically restrained him in an underground stone chamber with no amenities. Fifth…" Councilor Durand shook his head. "Mr Templeton, I don't care who you are. You put a child – a black child – in shackles, and you ought to be ashamed for not knowing your history."

"I was there for the Civil Rights movement," said Edmund.

"Not if you could bring yourself to do that, you weren't." Durand folded hands that trembled. A hummingbird whirred around its perch on the seat beside him, its feathers shimmering iridescent blue. "The Twelfth Hour might not have the facilities, Mr Templeton, but at Barrio Libertad, we can always afford luxuries like basic human decency."

Edmund looked down at his own hands. He was probably older than Durand. He'd slept maybe three hours last night. He had no idea where Istvan was or what he might be doing. Mercedes had been so sure that the People's Council would give Kyra up. Things had changed, after the Wizard War. Times were hard. You did what you had to do.

Unless you were Barrio Libertad. They were the richest enclave in Big East. They could afford whatever they wanted. Edmund wouldn't have done what he did if the Twelfth Hour had any other options. If Grace hadn't been there.

He wasn't any good at politics. He wasn't racist. He was doing the best he could. This was Grace's fault for pressuring him.

His phone went off like a submarine dive alarm. The People's Council stared at him. He found the "off" button and held it down. "Sorry."

"We are finished here," a rasping voice replied, somehow carried along in the hum of wings. "Diego will show you the way out."

"Right," he said. That was it. That was all. If something happened to Barrio Libertad, at least he couldn't be blamed.

He gathered himself and stood. "Thank you for having me."

"Of course," said Councilor Rothchild.

Edmund put his hat on, turned, and strode from the chamber. The doors opened at the slightest touch: a courtesy, maybe, from the one who controlled it. That was how Diego made his presence known, usually. Small reminders that you were watched.

Edmund switched his phone back on as he descended the broad flight of steps outside. Strings of lights hung between Spanish-styled colonial buildings in a broad plaza far below. More ran upwards in an elaborate web that lit tier after massive circular tier of brightly painted shanties, streets so steep that they mingled seamlessly with stairways. Fields sheltered under transparent canopies. Gantry cranes shuttled boxes from one level to another. Cable cars slid precariously along paired wires that dangled hundreds of feet in the air. Above it all rose fortress walls, their buttresses the size of neighborhoods, reducing the sky to a grey afterthought above the half-closed roof and the dead horror that clung to it.

Most of the buildings looked to be made of wood, plaster, and corrugated steel, built piecemeal and worn with hard use. Wires creaked and swayed. Rust spotted the enormous wheels and bearings that supported the roof. It seemed like it might all tumble down at any moment.

It was the most advanced city in Big East. Maybe anywhere. Maybe ever.

"Missed Call," read the warning on his phone screen, which wasn't a sentence he ever thought he'd deal with in the Fifties. It listed Janet Justice's number.

He dialed back. What did she want? If it was about the kid, he wasn't having it. "Hello, this is Edmund Templeton. Sorry about the delay, I was in a–"

"Edmund!" came Istvan's distinctive accent.

Edmund ducked.

A flurry of dark wings and wire shot past him. The specter quickly corrected course, wheeling around above Barrio Libertad's lower tiers, and landed on the stairway beside him with a crash like thunder. "Edmund, you missed it!"

"I was trying to take a call," Edmund informed him. The line had gone dead; whatever Janet had to say, she wasn't saying it now. He dropped the phone back into his pocket. "What are you doing? Why are you here?"

"I had to find you," Istvan replied. "I went to the parade, and the feast, and then Niagara, and then I came back and you weren't at home, and you were so angry the last time I waited for you, so I flew about for a few hours and then just a little while ago I asked Miss Justice where you were, and she knew how to find you by your telephone, and so I came straightaway."

"Right."

"Oh, Edmund, you ought to have stayed!" The specter threw himself back against the railing beside him, far too close for comfort. "They had fires, and food, and I couldn't eat it so you could have had my portion, and–"

"Istvan, can this wait?"

"–I've started a religion, as well, and–"

The weight in Edmund's chest hit rock-bottom. Oh, hell. "You what?"

"Lucy thinks I'm some sort of god-king, can you imagine?" The specter laughed. "Says I ought to conquer everything, and–"

"Later," Edmund said, quickly. He glanced around: the walls were listening, always, and whatever they heard, they told Grace. "Istvan, we can talk about this later."

"But–"

"Later."

A line of blue light appeared beneath their feet. It glowed through a thin layer of what had seemed to be concrete moments earlier and now more resembled glass. That was the cue. Edmund hoped that Istvan hadn't said too much already.

"What's that?" Istvan asked. "Where are we going?"

Edmund followed the path down the stairs. "Out."

Istvan trailed after him. "Lucy asked why I put up with you at all, you know. She said that you order me about, and don't listen, and that while you're a fine enough warrior, you're a poor statesman and rely far too much on your reputation. You oughtn't have imprisoned a god-king, either."

Edmund walked faster. "We're not talking about this right now."

The ghost kept up easily, flitting from stair to stair. "Do you think I ought to take some sort of revenge?" he asked. "I thought I might have deserved being chained up, but what if I didn't? What should I do?"

This wasn't good. If Istvan returned to the way he'd been, hopping from war to war, that would be bad enough. With some kind of mercenary cult backing him up, putting ideas into his head…

Edmund pulled open the door to a cable car, focusing on the faint creak of hinges that no doubt had been added for the aesthetic. Istvan was still drunk, he told himself. The specter wouldn't be asking questions like that if he wasn't drunk. He'd come to his senses, eventually. Istvan had been the one to argue against violence when they'd dealt with the Susurration: he wasn't like this, not at heart.

"I can't kill you, after all," the specter continued, skipping after him. "I've tried already, and while I suppose I could again, and it would be marvelous, I love you far too much to ever risk it. Lucy said that I ought to renounce attachments, but I'm not a Buddhist, Edmund – I'm certainly not doing that."

He swung in through one of the windows rather than use the door and leaned back shoulder to shoulder beside Edmund – again – with the contented air of an undead horror who had murdered possibly thousands of people over his long career and was, for the moment, perfectly fine with that. He seemed completely oblivious to the stench of chlorine filling the cable car.

"Have you any ideas?" he asked.

Drunk, Edmund reminded himself. Very drunk.

"Not at the moment," he said.

Istvan sighed. "Well, do tell me if you come up with something. I'm not about to go after the Magister, Grace is all full of lightning, and it seems terribly petty to kill Beldam, even if she doesn't like me at all."

"Very petty," agreed Edmund. He kept his voice level. No one was touching his cat.

Edmund didn't want to talk about Triskelion. He didn't want to talk about Lucy, either, or ending spirits, or the statue in the mountain, or how careful Istvan had been to leave him people with enough time to take. The man wasn't interested in hearing about the feast, or Kasimir's plans, either.

"You can't pretend that nothing ever happened," Istvan told him.

"I'm not," said Edmund, but he was. He couldn't hide it. Not from Istvan. Oh, it was wonderful, the guilt. It cut through Barrio Libertad's usual flat rage in the most pleasing way, like a chaser.

They reached the elevator; a thunderous, industrial thing with flashing scarlet caution lights. When the doors closed, Edmund went directly to the far end and put his hands in his pockets, leaning his head back against the wall. Istvan followed him. Edmund edged away along the rail.

Istvan humored him. It was odd for him to be here in the first place: Edmund hated Barrio Libertad. Istvan hadn't seen him inside in months and months, not since they had dealt with the Susurration.

"Why were you here, anyhow?" he asked.

"Magister's orders," came the curt reply.

The elevator rumbled. The floor jerked and then began moving smoothly upwards.

"But you're Director, now," said Istvan. "You can refuse."

"No, I can't."

"Yes, you could. You're the Hour Thief, aren't you? You can do anything you like, and no one can stop you."

"Istvan–"

"Unless, of course, that skull on the bookshelf in the Magister's office does do something, after all, in which case perhaps Magister Hahn could stop you, but you don't know for certain that it does anything, hm?" Istvan edged close enough to elbow him. "Have you ever tried testing it?"

"No."

"What were you ordered to do, then? It isn't about Grace, is it?"

Edmund hunched his shoulders. "Kyra."

"Oh!" Istvan had almost forgotten about him: the storm-bringer, the one who'd torn him apart. Quite a feat, that. They might have to see if he could do that again or if it were an odd fluke – it would be good to know, either way. "Are we getting him back, then?" he asked. "We had only begun talking when Grace came in and exploded my ribcage and took him away. I was going to get him out, you know – I wasn't hurting him, not on purpose, and he was looking for wizards, Edmund. Did you know that he's running from a Shokat Anoushak cult?"

"I'm not surprised," said Edmund.

"She really is terrible," Istvan continued. "Grace. She never asks about anything before charging into it, all lightning. I'm glad that you two are finished."

The wizard stared at the opposite wall and said nothing. He was always irritated when it came to discussing Grace, for no real reason: it had been years since their affair, after all, even if she had faked her death and then he had only discovered it a matter of months ago. They had only gotten together because of the Wizard War. They weren't actually compatible in any way.

"She wasn't good for you," Istvan added. "And you knew it wouldn't last, anyhow – that's how you've always gone about things. You've never been in a committed relationship once in your life."

Edmund gritted his teeth.

Istvan sighed. "At least not that you–"

The elevator stopped. Something crashed beyond the walls.

Surely they weren't at ground level already? It had only been a matter of moments.

Istvan looked around. "Edmund, you were leaving, weren't you?"

The wizard tensed. He was holding his pocket watch now. "I was."

Nothing opened. Nothing started moving again. Istvan checked to be certain that the door hadn't changed places somehow. It hadn't. He stepped to the other side of the elevator – what if the floor opened into a chute? – and waited.

Nothing.

"Mr Espinoza," he called to the walls and their paint-and-paper announcements, "Edmund did say that he was leaving, and if you mean to keep him, you and I will have words, I promise you. Don't you know who I am?"

"Wait," ordered the accented voice of Diego Escarra Espinoza.

"For what?" Istvan demanded. "We have important things to do! We're important people!"

Edmund pressed himself against one of the walls. His eyes darted around the elevator, uncertainty flowing smoothly into worry, sweet panic clawing at the periphery.

"Don't worry," Istvan told him. "If Diego takes away your magic and kills you, he'll have me to reckon with." He set a hand against the wall and tried to push through it. The metal remained stubbornly solid. Hm. A new form of reckoning would be in order, one that didn't rely on cutting his way in.

Perhaps the battlefield…

He stepped back. He knew it was out there – the wastes, the echoes, the forcible imprinting of the past on the present, where shells fell from empty skies – and if Lucy were correct, well, he was more than only himself, wasn't he?

"Edmund," he began, "you won't believe this, but I'm terribly dangerous."

The wizard recoiled. "Istvan, whatever you're thinking, don't–"

Another crash came from beyond, followed by a slow churning – like gears crunching against one another, drawing closer, wheeling something into place. It was coming from the opposite side.

Istvan turned. "Ah! There we are!"

The clunk of a latch. The elevator trembled. Blue lights scribbled themselves across the wall, outlining sketched details: a blinking indicator above two large panels, a pair of circular windows, a warning to watch one's step, a wash of paint that faded from blue to striped red and yellow and then ceased to glow at all.

The new doors opened.

Kyra flashed a wide grin. "Dr Czernin!"

Words fled Istvan's tongue.

The boy was tall. Much taller than Istvan. It hadn't been nearly so obvious while he was shackled, or floating. He looked somewhat healthier than before, but still thin to the point of starvation. Circular prongs pressed against each of his temples, etched with silver detailing, attached to a milky-white band that vanished into his roughly-braided mass of gravity-defying hair. Burns marked his neck and wrists.

He stepped into the elevator from a small elevator of his own, a floor-length red skirt over black leggings swirling in his wake.

"I ain't staying," he said. "I know they wanna keep me, but they ain't listening to me about Shokat Anoushak and there ain't nothing wrong with me and the AI – Mr Espinoza – says he don't never keep anyone against their will." He squinted through Istvan. "Who's that guy?"

Edmund looked away.

"Cool hat," said Kyra.

"'Don't ever,'" muttered Edmund. "It's 'don't ever.'"

Istvan stepped sideways so the boy wouldn't be looking through him. Dreadfully impolite, looking through people. "Why are you wearing a dress?"

Kyra grabbed hold of the elevator rail. "They incinerated my other stuff," he said. "They didn't even ask – they just took it and burned it." He brushed at the fabric. "This looks OK, though, right?"

"It might, on a woman," said Istvan.

Kyra stared down at him a moment, something faltering behind his gaze. The boy's aspect was still faint, scattered, difficult to make out properly. Any procedures

Barrio Libertad might have done to treat his condition didn't seem to have worked. Even they couldn't cure the Shattered in a matter of days.

"I am, though," he said. "I told you."

"Told me what?"

"Miss Kyra, remember? When you were trying to get me out of that... that dungeon, at the Twelfth Hour." He rubbed at his wrists, and the burns that still marked them. "That place is messed up," he added. "I hope there's some other wizards we can talk to."

The elevator began moving again. Its smaller counterpart receded downwards, its doorway already melting back into blank metal.

Istvan rubbed at his own wrists. "Actually–"

"We're with the Twelfth Hour," said Edmund.

"You are the Twelfth Hour," Istvan corrected him.

"I am not."

Kyra stared at them. The taste could have been dismay, or surprise, or disgust; some mixture of all three, perhaps, filtered through alien experiences and muddled beyond easy recognition. It was like trying to sift between the reactions of a dozen different people, mired in the rage of Barrio Libertad, to boot. "You're what?"

"I'm–" Edmund began.

"This is Edmund Templeton," said Istvan. "The Hour Thief, he calls himself." He threw an arm around the other man's shoulders, a wild feeling gripping him: a recklessness, an opportunity. "He's the one who put you in chains, just as he did to me. The same ones, even. Isn't that something?"

Kyra shot a look at the ceiling, or perhaps one of the elevator's upper corners. He edged away. "Uh," he said.

"Twenty years," Istvan added. "Twenty years down

there. You're lucky – you only stayed five days or so, and you had the best doctor in the world to mind you."

"I said I was sorry," muttered Edmund.

"Oh, I know. But you can always say it again." Istvan grinned at the wizard: his discomfort, his shame, his impotent anger at being caught out and being unable to defend himself; Istvan, at least, had a proven record of massacre, while Kyra had nothing of the sort. It was wonderful. Oh, it was almost a shame the Demon's Chamber was broken, now, and couldn't be used for further abuse.

Almost.

Istvan turned back to Kyra, the shadow of wings flickering in the air. "I've been considering revenge, you know," he told him. "Would you like to help me plan it?"

Kyra swallowed. He looked as though he were trying to sink through the wall himself, solid or not, dress and all. "You're not Dr Czernin," he said.

Istvan tilted his head. His surname was far from common, here. He was reasonably sure that he was unmistakable. "Oh?"

"You're not the same guy," Kyra said. "You can't be the same guy. I... I remember..." His eyes flickered from Istvan to Edmund to Istvan again, and every so often upwards. Perhaps seeking affirmation from an uncaring God that wouldn't answer? "Before the noise started, there was this church, and... and dancing, and Mr Koller, and–"

He yelped.

Shattered, the boy was. Memories not his own scattered in a wild jumble through his head. A victim of the only enemy Istvan had faced in over a hundred years that had ever – ever – mentioned Pietro Koller by name. If he knew...

If he knew *anything*...

Istvan leaned on the wall beside him, knife half-drawn. "Go on."

Kyra trembled. The elevator trembled. Metal creaked. The air grew uncomfortably close. It wasn't heat, or humidity. It was something subtler, a stirring and a drawing-down, a pressure that clung and smothered.

"OK," said Edmund, "That's far enough."

"Yes," agreed Diego.

A panel sprang from the wall and slammed into the opposite side, cutting the space in half. The elevator jolted to a halt. Edmund caught his breath – he was on the same side as Istvan, the walls weren't moving any further, there was no water flooding in – and then flipped his pocket watch open.

He was done. It was time to go.

"Wait for the d- deliberation," ordered Diego. He spoke with a steady, if heavily accented baritone, and would have made a good show of sounding human if he didn't stutter at odd junctures and forever seem filtered through three different intercoms – even in person.

"I will not!" shouted Istvan. He slashed at the panel, blade trailing jagged rents that closed themselves again in traceries of glowing blue. Sparks tumbled across Edmund's shoes. "I need to know what he knows!"

Edmund pictured his own house, made the requisite calculated offering – sans Istvan; Istvan could stay at Barrio Libertad – and snapped his pocket watch shut.

Nothing happened.

He tried again. Same result.

"I can't teleport," he said.

Istvan continued battering at the wall.

"I can't teleport," Edmund repeated, trying to choke

down panic. It had always worked before. Diego had been able to block Shokat Anoushak's branch of magic, but not most of Edmund's. Evidently, not yet.

Of course he'd figure it out. Of course he'd–

Edmund struck the nearest wall with a fist, knowing intellectually that they weren't moving but feeling like they might any second. It was getting harder and harder to breathe. "Istvan," he hissed through clenched teeth, "you've done it now."

"I haven't," the specter shot back, inanely.

"You have! There isn't anything you can't make worse, is there?"

Istvan turned on him, hazed and bloodied, a horror half-veiled in mist that burned. Rotten feathers pressed in around him, cracking and splintering: wings, suddenly manifest, unable to pass through Barrio Libertad's unnatural materials. "Me?" he demanded, "I make anything worse?"

Edmund stuffed his pocket watch back in its place, trying not to think of that same horror waltzing over slick and stinking corpses. "I didn't ask for your help with Niagara," he informed the one who all but existed to make things worse. "I didn't want your help. I didn't need your help, no matter what you say, and now I'm going to have to live with what we did. Forever."

"You had no better–"

"Forever! That's a hell of a long time, Istvan!"

"It wouldn't matter if you stopped stealing time," Istvan snapped.

Edmund could work on that level. "I thought you loved me too much to risk losing me," he rebutted.

The mists grew close, and choking. "I never said that."

"You did."

"I never said that!"

Edmund flashed a grin, well aware of the likely results. "Truth hurts, doesn't it?"

Istvan lunged for him.

Paint rippled along the rusted metal of the barricade, slithering across the surface the way no real paint should do. It formed an image. A painting that moved. A window. A short, stocky man, emaciated, who turned from whatever project had occupied his attention, a red T-shirt hanging loosely from his shoulders. Faded tattoos of flowers and hummingbirds covered brown arms and hands marred by extensive scarring.

He had no face. Instead, a set of four mismatched sky-blue lenses clicked and turned in a dented frame, a roughly skull-sized apparatus of squared steel with fans whirring to either side, struts and tubing plunged into his neck and collarbones. A speaker grill occupied where his vocal cords should have been.

"A r- request," said Diego Escarra Espinoza.

Istvan's knife clanged into the side of the elevator, a hair's breadth from Edmund's neck. Edmund had time, now. The specter should have known better than to try.

It hadn't worked in 1941, either.

Istvan spun around to face the painted image. "For what?" he demanded.

Diego's image shifted sideways, a view of the other side of the elevator appearing beside it. No sign of Kyra. If the kid were there, he was standing or sitting somewhere out of sight.

So that was what this was about. There was no way Kyra had snuck out on his own: Barrio Libertad didn't work like that.

Edmund crossed his arms, trembling only a little.

"Diego, your own People's Council already voted," he said. "I don't know what your stake is in this, but I'm inclined to listen to them. We're not taking the kid."

"Interrogation one," came the reply, which wasn't much of a reply at all. "Are there – other – wizards who can be reached within Big East?"

"Not at all," grumbled Istvan. He put his knife away. He retreated to the other side of the elevator, not looking at Edmund.

"We're not taking the kid," Edmund repeated.

"Interrogation two," Diego continued. "Are you willing to visit Toronto, in the Greater Great Lakes fracture?"

Istvan frowned. "Toronto?"

"It's a city in Canada," said Edmund.

"I've never been to Canada."

"You wouldn't have."

The speakers crackled. "Are you willing to visit Toronto, in the Greater Great Lakes fracture?"

Edmund rubbed at his eyes. They'd found Kyra in Tornado Alley, a thousand miles off from Toronto. Was he not from there? "We're not–"

"There isn't any reason not to," Istvan huffed. "If it's Kyra asking, and he came all this way for it, why wouldn't you? It's a chance to redeem yourself!"

"You just want to go fight whatever's there."

The specter sprouted wings. "Did I say that? I didn't say that."

The speakers crackled again. "Are you willing–"

"Yes," said Edmund. "Fine. We're willing." Like all fracture zones that weren't Big East, the Greater Great Lakes still had monsters in it. Lake Ontario itself was probably full of monsters. Edmund had never had good experiences with things that came out of lakes. "Toronto's particularly stunning this time of year, I'm told," he added.

Beside the false window, Diego's mismatched lenses whirred and spun in their mountings. He stood as though he were about to throttle someone, and his every motion was a lunging jerk, just on the edge of coordination, as though the connection between machine and body only functioned half the time. It was impossible to make out what exactly lay behind him: a vast sheet of ribbed metal, and little else.

"Interrogation three," he began.

"The Council voted against handing Kyra over, Diego," Edmund reminded him. "Your own Council. I thought you listened to your people."

The cyborg ignored him. "If the Shokat Anoushak has r- returned, can you stop her?"

Edmund opened his mouth. He closed it.

Shokat Anoushak.

It had only been eight years since the Wizard War. Almost nine. They were standing, even now, over the very place that the Immortal had been defeated. Destroyed. The mystics of the Innumerable Citadel, fifteen hundred years ago, hadn't had access to weapons that could leave a crater like Providence. Her latest death had to have been final, no matter what the cults believed – no matter if they had figured out how to animate mockeries and whatever else. Shokat Anoushak was beyond the pale. She had to be.

That hadn't been true, at least once before.

"It would be a pleasure," said Istvan.

"You were serious," Edmund muttered. "The kid's serious, isn't he?"

Unseen speakers crackled: a different voice, whispery and wavering. Kyra's. "She."

"Fine. She." Edmund took a breath. This was a fool's errand, even if Diego and the kid both refused to acknowledge it. If this cult, alone, had somehow hit on a method to return Shokat Anoushak to life, putting a fifteen year-old in the middle of it seemed like the worst idea imaginable. If it wasn't true, which was far more likely, setting loose a powerful Conduit like this without dealing with his delusions and strange behavior wouldn't do anyone any good.

Shokat Anoushak couldn't be brought back. She couldn't.

Edmund looked up at the roof. "If you can hear us, Kyra, then you should know: you're what we call Shattered. It's a mental condition. You might remember a lot of things, but those memories aren't all yours, and–"

"That's what they said," said Kyra. "That ain't how it is."

"Listen to me. The world outside isn't what you remember. This place is the only place that can help you. That's why they want to keep you."

"I ain't staying."

"I would, if I were you."

"You ain't!"

Metal groaned, popping and resettling. Edmund flinched away. The kid was going to break something. "Aren't," he corrected him. "It's 'you aren't.'"

"I ain't making fun of *your* accent," Kyra retorted.

Edmund didn't have an accent. He spoke the same way everyone else in Massachusetts spoke, unless he was putting on the Hour Thief, who used the cultivated Eastern Standard characteristic of President Roosevelt and Hollywood for effect. There was a difference between a style of speech and being wrong, and the kid was wrong. Ill-educated. Not a surprise, considering.

He wished his teleport would work. He wished he could at least try again without being called out on it. He could swear the walls were getting closer. Something about the combined stench of chlorine and the sudden weight of the air dragged at him: he hadn't been trapped like this for decades. Not since...

Edmund swallowed.

"He's corrected me for thirty years," grumbled Istvan from his side of the elevator.

"Quiet," said Edmund, knowing the implications and not caring. They'd have to have a talk later. A long talk.

"The decision," demanded Diego.

Edmund wetted his lips. "I've told you, we're–"

Sound stopped. His voice vibrated in his throat – he could feel it – but the words seemed to dissipate before they got anywhere. Something about the acoustics. Something about the walls. Diego's work.

He glanced at Istvan, whose bindings had choked him into painful silence on command many, many times over the years. The specter only grinned at him.

"I guess there's no one else," came Kyra's voice, after a moment.

"Yes," agreed Diego.

"OK. Please let us go. Thank you, Mr Espinoza."

No reply. Brushstrokes painted over Diego's image, somehow leaving only bare metal. The barrier wall retracted with a clang. The elevator started moving again.

Kyra – the kid, the Conduit, Shattered – sat against the far wall, arms hugging his knees, skirt just brushing the floor. "You're pretty bad guys, then," he said.

Edmund tested his voice. "We're something."

"The worst," said Istvan.

CHAPTER SIXTEEN

They rode up towards ground level in an uncertain, stilted quiet. The elevator had four corners, and Edmund occupied one of them, Istvan another, and Kyra a third. Istvan was certain that Edmund was trying very hard not to comment on this. After all, if he did, perhaps Diego would silence him again.

It was difficult not to be smug about the possibility.

And Kyra! Oh, what a decision! The boy couldn't know what he'd signed himself up for, agreeing to leave a fortress that could leap to his defense – however unwanted – in favor of the outside world, where he would most certainly be hurt, and not always at the hands of enemies, either. "She," indeed. This was no time for nonsense.

Istvan watched him speculatively. As for what he might know about what he oughtn't, well... they would have to talk about that. Later. Alone.

Kyra couldn't quite seem to make proper eye contact with either of them.

"So," said Edmund. Something about his tone suggested dragging the word forth with a hook. "What's this about Shokat Anoushak?"

"She's coming back," said Kyra.

Edmund sighed. "Yes, you've said that. I need more than that if we're going to do anything about it. Is this why you want us to go to Toronto?"

The boy nodded.

Timidity didn't become someone so tall as Kyra, attempted girlishness or not. Istvan crossed his arms. "You can talk, you know," he said. "I'll make certain that Edmund won't interrupt you."

Edmund gave him a look.

"Even if he doesn't," Istvan continued, "I'm certain that Diego would. He's still here, after all. He's never not here."

An easy thing to forget, perhaps, if one couldn't taste the rage leaking from the walls at all hours. Barrio Libertad's architect was omnipresent. If the very structure of the fortress itself was willing, at any moment, to go against the edicts of the elected People's Council...

Istvan grinned to himself. Grace Wu was probably having fits.

Kyra looked back and forth between Edmund and Istvan.

"Go on," said Edmund. "Contrary to popular belief, I can listen."

Kyra closed his eyes. He wrapped his arms more tightly around his knees. Then, he let out a breath, released his grip and stood. "She knew how to do it," he said. "Our Lady. It wasn't the cult that learned it, or invented it. It's her. She already knew how to bring herself back. That's why–"

"But she's dead," said Istvan. "What would it matter, what she knew?"

Kyra fell silent. His fingers closed more tightly on the handrail behind him.

"Istvan," said Edmund.

"What? I'm listening!"

Edmund rolled his eyes. "That's why what, Kyra?"

The Conduit mumbled something.

"What?"

"'s why the monsters took me," Kyra repeated. "I remember. I used to. All the... the things, how to do it. How to come back to life, if you got people to help you. It's..." He looked down, closing his eyes again. "I remember a lot, and a lot of it is her. They took all the bits they wanted."

Shattered. Kidnapped by monsters.

Shokat Anoushak's creatures had cults of their own?

Istvan looked to Edmund, who had leaned back against the wall rather heavily.

"I know about the Susurration," Kyra continued. "I know what it did. I know it had me, and that... that nothing was real. Ms Wu told me that." He swallowed, hugging one arm around his middle. "Anyway, after my... after the Susurration went away, I woke up in this little town somewhere. I'm talking shacks. I was carrying water, and I spilled it everywhere. I don't know how I got there. Me and like ten other people, going on about all these crazy things. We couldn't figure out what happened. Some of them got into a fight, and I ran away, and... yeah. The monsters got me after that."

"I'm sorry," said Edmund.

The boy pressed his lips together, looking away from them. The hand that had clutched the rail crept up to his chest, as though grasping his heart. "It don't matter," he said.

Istvan thought back to his own sudden awakening. Not dead after all. Or, not as dead as he had expected. It was winter, and it hadn't been winter, not last he knew, not before the terrible cries and the tearing, like claws. The snow fell through him as much as he stumbled through it, blinded, bombarded by flashes of places and experiences utterly foreign, unable to concentrate on what was before him amidst the chaos around and inside of him: an entire continent, newly at war, flooding into his head all at once.

What if those flashes – those experiences, those memories – had belonged to someone so old, so mad, so lost, that she hardly counted as human at all?

"But the monsters took some of it?" Istvan asked. "The monsters took some of those memories, the ones they wanted, so that they could learn how to resurrect her?"

Kyra wiped at his eyes. He turned back to them, blinking.

"You don't have to answer that," said Edmund. He had both hands in his pockets, now. The brass chain that hung from a bottom jacket button and then disappeared into the right pocket trembled. "It's fine. We don't have to know how she did it."

"Statues," whispered Kyra.

The elevator shuddered to a halt. A light blinked on above the doors. A tone sounded, low and harsh. "Caution," said Diego.

None of them moved.

"I was an idiot," said Edmund.

Istvan wondered if he'd heard correctly. That made no sense at all. How would a statue do that? Even if it sprang to life – much of Shokat Anoushak's magic revolved around that sort of thing, after all – it wouldn't be her, would it? Only a mockery, like the others.

Unless she could somehow move her soul, perhaps. Like a ghost. Like... well, him. But wouldn't someone have seen her by now? Was it even possible, to become a ghost on purpose? He had never met any others.

"Statues?" he asked.

"They have to be perfect," Kyra said.

Edmund swallowed. "Let's not talk about this here." He stood up from the wall, adjusted his hat, and walked out of the elevator.

Istvan looked at Kyra. "That's how you know that he's a wizard."

"I heard that," said Edmund.

Istvan followed him out. It was just past midday now, and a cold breeze blew across the crater, carrying the smell of mud and rot. There seemed to be a rime of frost on the battlefield today. A hint, perhaps, of the other fronts. Russia. The Italian Alps. Would it change with the seasons? Would there be mountains here, someday?

It felt so right. He could sense it taking hold again: that sense of ease, of joy, of fierce and uncaring invincibility. Kyra didn't have to be his problem. Neither did Edmund. If the world burned again, under a resurgent Shokat Anoushak, that would be simply more fighting, and an endless supply of targets.

It would be easier than being angry.

He turned, clapping his hands together. "So! Where are we going, then?"

Edmund checked his pocket watch. Kyra hadn't even let go of the rail, yet, much less left the elevator, and merely hung back, eyes wide.

Istvan glanced behind himself. It was only trenches. Some smoke. The wreckage of what might have been a shelter, half-sunk in the mud, torn canvas fluttering.

There weren't even any bodies, and barbed wire only looped here and there in broken, orphaned segments: hardly a barrier to be feared.

"Is it... all like that?" asked Kyra.

"No," said Edmund.

"Of course not," said Istvan. "This is the only place like this. It's my fault, really – there used to be nearly half a million people living here, but not since Edmund decided that the Great War would be a fine thing to pit against the Susurration."

Kyra stared at him.

Edmund sighed. "Istvan–"

"They're still alive! Most of them. They've moved into Barrio Libertad – that's why there are so many people there. Didn't they tell you? You aren't the only person the Susurration took, not at all. Why, Edmund himself almost fell to it."

Oh, that had been a travesty. Poor Lucy.

"Anyhow," Istvan finished, "there are usually more ruins."

"Oh," said Kyra. He squeezed his eyes shut again, swaying slightly on his feet.

Istvan tilted his head. The boy knew, didn't he? If he knew about Shokat Anoushak, how could he not know what she had done? Even if what he'd seen in Tornado Alley was more wilderness and spellscar than city, he couldn't possibly deny that the world must be quite different from whatever he remembered. "What's in Toronto, anyhow?"

Edmund strode between them, pocket watch in hand. "That's enough. We'll head to Niagara and sort this out from there."

"Niagara?" asked Istvan. "Oughtn't we go show

the Magister that we've gotten Kyra back from Barrio Libertad?"

"No. We're not showing Mercedes anything until we know what's going on, and–" Edmund held up a hand before Istvan could interrupt, "–I like keeping my house intact, Istvan. We're staying away from New Haven."

The wizard snapped his pocket watch.

Niagara. A sullen rain drizzled from grey skies. They stood just in front of the peculiar little building atop one of the dams, a place that Istvan had flown over but not inspected.

Gunfire rattled from Kasimir's camp.

"Ah!" said Istvan. "They were right! The mockeries did–"

A twin-rotor helicopter plunged out of the sky with an unearthly shriek, struck the earth nose-first, and skidded thirty feet across concrete before catching fire.

"–come back."

Kyra stumbled away with a cry. He tripped over his own feet, trying to watch the sky and the ground at the same time, and then bolted for the building.

"Dammit, Istvan," snarled Edmund, uncovering his head. He propped an elbow on the grass where he'd flung himself prone. "Dammit," he repeated.

The mockery slid off the edge of the dam.

"You could have said something," Edmund added.

"You wouldn't have been surprised if you'd stayed for the festivities instead of running off," Istvan informed him. "I wanted to tour Niagara together. It's your own fault." He spread his wings. "Now, you watch Kyra, hm? You're quite useless in the air, you know."

He took flight before the wizard could respond.

Edmund's dismay and Kyra's peculiar multifaceted

panic, together... oh, having the boy along would be a joy. Istvan had never spent time around anyone both friendly and Shattered.

He climbed to a suitable altitude to assess the situation. Kasimir's camp was in terrible condition, badly undermanned and with a great deal of their weaponry depleted or shipped away, but they had done their best: another mockery lay half-on and half-off the banks of transformers on the artificial lake's central island, crackling and buzzing. Snapped power lines dangled from bent towers. Oil leaked into the water, swirling around wreckage that jutted up from somewhere near the turbine entrances. A plume of smoke rose from the woods.

More mockeries circled overhead. Strange beasts, most of them, patchwork creatures that didn't look like they ought to fly at all. Some bore ugly seams, crushed sides, and discolored flanks. Many sparked with uncontrolled lightning. One of them even had canvas wings. Its frame looked to be taken from an automobile. The group wasn't in formation but they did keep to much the same altitude: were they together?

Istvan squinted up at the clouds. Together, except for that one. A loner, so high up it was little more than a strange broad speck.

Ah, well. The others were closer.

A cheer rose from Kasimir's camp as he came into view. He glanced down. Less than three dozen warriors remained there, now. Had this assault gone on all night? Had Edmund abandoned them to the beasts? That wouldn't do.

He tossed them a wave. They were his people, according to Lucy, and so he couldn't help but feel a certain responsibility for them. "Don't worry!" he called, "I'll cover your retreat!"

Another cheer. Oh, he could get used to that.

He charged.

The first mockery rather resembled a small airplane with propellers. Dozens of eyes stenciled in jagged lines blinked across its sides, glowing red and blue like hazard lights. It dipped to meet him, brandishing curved talons.

Istvan darted up and over it and cut off its left tail stabilizer.

It keened. Lightning streamed from the wound. It tried to turn to meet him again, but could only maneuver in one direction, wobbling along its flight path, and Istvan took the opportunity to slash at its sides as it keeled slowly over, tilting into a spiral that became a stall and then a sideways tumble. It wouldn't hit the dams. Probably.

Istvan wheeled to find the next one… and discovered that there was no next one. The mockeries were gone. Fleeing. A single one of their number down, and they were all running away?

"I'm not finished!" he called after retreating specks. North. They were going north. He sped after them. Forest blurred below, a winding road following the river. The feverish haze of the spellscars simmered in the distance. It took him almost a full minute to catch up, even to the canvas-winged one, which would have been embarrassing if they weren't magical.

"What do you think you're doing?" he asked the nearest, drawing even beside it.

Its engine popped and sputtered. Formless mists gusted within its cockpit windows. It rolled away and dove at a surprisingly steep angle, vanishing into the mist that now seeped across the landscape.

"That isn't going to work," Istvan called after it. He rolled over himself, plunging into the mist – and somehow found himself over water. Endless water.

He pulled up, startled. The ocean? How could they have reached the ocean?

The mockery struck the water with a wing, wobbled, righted itself, and sped away. He let it go. How could there be… unless…

The lake. Was this Lake Ontario? It was that big? How far north had he gone?

Istvan turned around, orienting himself by the distant curve of the shoreline. Had it all been a diversion? Was the other mockery, the loner, still up there?

He climbed above the clouds to check, but it, too, seemed to have fled.

Hm. Perhaps it was just as well: now the mockeries could tell their friends that there was a new no-fly zone over the Niagara dams. Unlike Kasimir's forces, Istvan never ran out of ammunition. And if the mockeries came back with reinforcements, well… it would be like the Wizard War all over again.

Both Edmund and Kyra were inside that small building when he returned. Istvan dropped through the roof. "I chased them all up towards the lake," he announced, landing atop some sort of model display. He hopped off of it. "There's a tremendous lake to the north of here, did you know that?"

"I'm aware," Edmund replied sourly. He crouched near the door. The building seemed to be some sort of combination shop and museum, for tourists. "How many mockeries were there?"

Istvan looked around for Kyra. "Perhaps a dozen. I

expect that they'll be back soon enough."

"Great," said Edmund. The wizard rose to his feet, shaking only slightly.

Ah, Kyra seemed to be behind the teller's counter. Terror rolled from him... and was that a light dusting of shock, intermingled with confusion and dismay and perhaps a sweet, if muddied, hint of anger? Oh, the boy was realizing the magnitude of his mistake, now. Too late. No going back.

"What were you expecting, Kyra?" called Istvan. "Roses?"

No response.

Istvan found himself grinning. First the altercation in the elevator, then the battlefield, then the monsters. It wasn't going to get any better. "A parade, perhaps?"

Edmund elbowed past him. "Cut it out."

Istvan pressed a hand to his breast. "He needs to know, Edmund! It's a cruel world out here. He's Shattered, remember? Everything he knows isn't real and never was. Rochester is gone, isn't it? Buried under spellscars?" Edmund crossed into the gift shop; Istvan followed, skipping over the low divider that separated them. "The Susurration probably invented his family, invented friends and parties, gave him happy memories of love... and now there's nothing but monsters waiting for him. You and me and those mockeries, Edmund." Istvan chuckled. "The sooner we beat it out of him the better."

A rack of keychains trembled.

Istvan stepped around the teller's counter. Kyra huddled in a ball behind it. Istvan tutted. "We aren't going to let him keep wearing that, are we?"

Kyra raised his head from his knees. "Hey!"

Ah, yes. That was anger, now. Sharp, and raw, so little of the weariness so common among most. The boy was still so young, and even his abrupt introduction to reality hadn't yet darkened him. It was such a striking contrast to Edmund.

"My dear Kyra," Istvan said, "I did tell you that we're the worst."

"Ignore him," said Edmund, drawing up behind him. "He's–"

Kyra bared his teeth. "You don't have to be a jerk about it!"

Istvan blinked. He looked at the boy a moment – his determined grimace, his scarred neck, his wild mass of hair, his absurd dress – and then he broke up laughing.

Don't be a jerk? That was all he could say to the spirit of the Great War? A complaint, for a child; a child who had foolishly chosen to escape relative safety in favor of allying with his own erstwhile captor; a child who thought he could extract promises from a man who drew power from language, who had studied law, who didn't want to believe that anything that he said was true; a child who didn't fear ghosts the way he ought.

Oh, things would only grow worse before they ever grew better. The boy had so much to learn, and so little chance of surviving it. The mockeries might return at any moment.

"Stop it," said Kyra.

Istvan took off his glasses to wipe at his eyes, still laughing.

Edmund swore, glancing from Kyra to the museum and back to Kyra again. He gripped the brim of his hat. "Istvan, if you can't–"

Kyra struck the floor with a fist. "Stop it!"

The door blew open. A rack of ornamental glassware shattered. Cracks spidered across one of the windows. A vicious wind ripped through both museum and gift shop, catching up layered dust, handkerchiefs, scarves, hats, dry leaves, and bits of shotglass, hurling them in every direction as keychains toppled from stands and hanging pictures fell from the walls. Another door elsewhere in the building slammed. The roof creaked.

Istvan immediately regretted laughing at a child who had once torn him to pieces and scattered him to the winds. "Er–"

The Conduit shouted over him. "You're afraid of me now, huh?" He got to his feet, holding onto the side of his dress as the building itself began to shake. "You going to attack me now, huh?"

"I wasn't–"

"You weren't what? You weren't what? You're a doctor! I know you're a doctor! You aren't supposed to be like this! I don't remember you acting like this! You were... I thought I could trust you! I thought I'd... I thought we could–"

Edmund interposed himself between them, still holding onto his hat, cape flapping wildly. "Istvan, get out."

"What?" Istvan said.

"Get out," Edmund repeated.

"What about the mockeries?"

"I don't care about the mockeries. Don't come back until you're ready to be civil."

Civil? It was the truth! It wasn't Istvan's fault that Kyra was hysterical – the boy had to learn, one way or another, and the sooner the better. The alternative was nothing but suffering, and they both knew it. Istvan held out a hand. "Betrayal so soon?"

"Out," Edmund repeated. "Go cool down. You're not thinking straight."

The pressure in the air mounted. Edmund winced. Blood trickled from one of his nostrils. Something cracked; something that sounded like glass. The windows?

Istvan backed away. He hadn't fought for this place only to see it destroyed, as satisfying as that might be. How could Kyra withstand the forces he wielded? How could Kyra turn on him like this, after Istvan had tried to free him? After he had defended him?

Ready to be civil, indeed. This was intimidation. No more, no less. Kyra would have to learn that force didn't always work.

Oh, yes, let Edmund see to the boy. He'd done a wonderful job thus far.

"You can't fly," Istvan informed him.

The wizard nodded. "You'll just have to come back later, then, won't you?"

Istvan spread rotten wings and shot through the nearest window. Out. Up. Skidding past the impaled mockery on the towers outside, and a dive down to skim along the brush-choked river. He didn't need either of them, anyway. Not civil, was he? Not thinking straight, was he?

And yet... he knew he wasn't. They were right. Both of them.

He hated that. He hated that he could be manipulated, that he had to be awful, that he couldn't stop himself, that he was what he was and yet he couldn't rely on that as an excuse forever. It wasn't fair.

Why did Kyra have to be deviant? Why did the boy have to know about Pietro Koller?

Hadn't the Susurration tortured Istvan enough?

Edmund's head was imploding. He was almost sure of it.

"Kyra," he said, voice distant to his own ears, spots dancing before his vision, "Kyra, can you shut that off?"

The Conduit collapsed onto the counter. The pressure – air, gravity, mental power, whatever it was – collapsed with him. The winds spun out and faded. Merchandise fell like rain. Kyra clutched his head where metal prongs met flesh, shaking, his eyes screwed shut as tears ran.

"I thought they were done chasing me," he croaked. He swallowed, and as he trembled, the air trembled with him. "Where are we? Was that some kind of magic that brought us here, and am I dead?"

Edmund patted his pocket. Watch. Needed his watch. "Niagara Falls, yes, and no. That isn't how it works."

"It is, though," said Kyra. "Teleporters take you apart, atom by atom, and then make a copy of you. The original ends up dead. That's the only way for it to work."

"That isn't how mine works," Edmund said.

Kyra mumbled something unintelligible into the counter. His shoulders shook. Blue lights sparked across the headband he wore: the same deep sky color as the guiding lines at Barrio Libertad.

Edmund wiped at his nose and found blood on his fingers. Great.

The most powerful Conduit in Big East was now his problem, the most powerful city-state in Big East would be discovering that shortly, and Niagara was a death trap just across from a cult given direct access to Shokat Anoushak's secrets of immortality. Also, Istvan wasn't going to come back. That had been it. It was over. Thirty years of friendship, thrown away. What was Edmund supposed to do now?

Statues. He'd been so stupid.

He looked to Kyra. "I'm sorry," he said. It didn't seem like enough. "I'm truly sorry. Just about everything we've done lately has been… in a word, fubar." He leaned on the counter beside the kid. "That means messed up. Worse than messed up. You didn't deserve to be in the middle of this."

"I'm the one who got me here," Kyra mumbled.

Edmund squinted at the cracked window. Another thing to fix. Right now, it didn't seem like he'd ever get to it. "I studied Shokat Anoushak," he said.

Kyra stopped trembling.

"I studied her for twenty years," Edmund continued. "I have copies of the earliest Innumerable Citadel records, in the original Arabic, brought over here from Iran. If anyone this side of the Atlantic can call themselves an expert on her, it's me." Edmund thought back to the cult report outside the New York City zone, the block of concrete propped up and crudely chiseled, and concentrated on breathing.

Statues. Of course it would be statues. So much of the Immortal's magic revolved around the inanimate, warping and blurring the distinction between creature and construct, granting life where there was none. Her monsters were proof enough of that. If she could somehow transfer her own soul – linger, just long enough, to find a new vessel sculpted in her likeness…

During the Wizard War, she had always ridden personally into battle. She'd been impossibly strong, never tiring. Fearless. Inhuman. Was what Edmund had seen of her – her skin, pale and weatherbeaten, dark paint masking deep-set eyes of brilliant emerald – nothing more than wax and crystal?

He grimaced. "Kyra, what's in Toronto? Your cult?"

"Yeah," came the response. Then, a moment later, with more conviction, "but it ain't mine. We gotta stop them. And if they bring her back, we gotta figure out how to kill her again."

Edmund hoped he was wrong. All they had on this was Kyra's word, and maybe a few mockeries. The kid could still be delusional. There was still a chance. "Why is this so important to you?" Edmund asked him. "You don't have to do this. You escaped. Why do you want to go back?"

Kyra let out a breath. He pulled himself up, an awkward operation given his height and lankiness, and brushed his fingers across the milky covering of his headband. The lights had died to a mere flicker, just visible under the surface. "Why do you think?" he said.

"I don't know. That's why I'm asking."

"She destroyed the world, Mr Templeton! She took away everything! And they want to use me to bring her back? They went through my *head*. They got it all jumbled up. I hear things sometimes. Smell things. If Shokat Anoushak hadn't done what she did, I don't know where I'd be, but it wouldn't be here, OK?" Kyra looked down at the counter, his hands flat against it. "Who are you guys, anyway?"

Edmund tried not to fixate on the anger in the request. After what he'd been through, the kid deserved the benefit of the doubt. "I'm the Hour Thief," he said. "I'm part of the–"

"How come you can do whatever you want? You

said that you're the Twelfth Hour, and the Hour Thief, and all these other things – what does that mean? And what's the deal with Dr Czernin? Are you two… friends, or what? You don't even seem to like each other, and I don't know what's wrong with him, either. Is it because he's a ghost? Did you really lock him up, too?"

Edmund held up his hands. "One thing at a time."

Kyra flinched. "Sorry."

"Don't apologize."

"Why not? I messed up your building." He looked away, all bravado suddenly drained, and leaned on the counter again, seeming much older than he was.

Edmund studied his features, in profile. He was darker than the Barrio Libertad councilman; darker than Janet Justice, even. His face was long, narrow, and sunken from malnutrition, as lean as the rest of him. A few wispy hairs sprang from his chin. The bruises from earlier – one on his jaw, another on his left cheek – still hadn't faded. The angry scarlet of recent burns circled his neck.

The kid was in it for revenge. Pure and simple.

"I'm the Hour Thief," Edmund began again. "I'm a wizard, and I work for the only group of wizards in Big East. That's the zone from Boston to DC. I don't know how you know Istvan, but he's a friend of mine. Or was. I hope he still is." He shook his head, staring down at the counter rather than at the mess of toppled souvenirs and broken glass. "And, yes, we had him chained up once. He's what we call a sundered spirit – he's more than the ghost of a person, he's the ghost of a war. He's dangerous. We didn't know if we could trust him."

Kyra watched him out of the corner of his eye. He didn't say anything.

"That's the same reason I put you in that place,"

Edmund continued. It wasn't the whole truth, but it was part of it. "We thought you might be dangerous. We didn't trust you. We haven't seen a Conduit like you before."

"That's what you call it?" asked Kyra.

Edmund nodded.

"Am I one of hers? Did the Immortal make me?"

Oh, boy. Now that was a question. That was a good question. There hadn't been any Conduits before the Wizard War. Grace had never said anything about being experimented on, or targeted: she had simply changed, maybe in the same second that Mexico City fell.

Edmund hedged his bets. "We don't think it was deliberate."

Kyra sighed. He turned around, his back to the counter, and clasped his hands together before his chest.

"I told you I studied Shokat Anoushak," Edmund added. "There's more to that story. When she came back, the Twelfth Hour made me Magister. Kind of like the wizard president. I didn't beat her, but I fought her until someone else did. Her name is Mercedes Hahn. She's the Magister now. She's the one who summoned the Susurration, which is what lured Shokat Anoushak and most of her armies in Big East somewhere where she could be destroyed."

"The robot fortress," said Kyra.

"Providence. That's right."

"They told me that the wizards were responsible for the Susurration. That you guys made it, and didn't tell anyone."

Edmund glanced back at the broken glass. He didn't want to talk about that right now. He'd said enough. "That's about right. Say, how about I find a broom?"

The kid shrugged.

Edmund stepped out around the counter, brushing past the register. There had to be a broom closet somewhere. More to the point, he had to figure out where Kyra was supposed to sleep. If the kid was going to stay here – unless and until the People's Council fought to get him back – he had to have somewhere decent.

And then there was the fact that Kyra couldn't stay here alone, either…

Edmund concentrated on not slipping. "Sit tight," he called.

"OK," came the unenthusiastic response.

Edmund rounded the corner to the bathroom, stepped inside, shut the door, pictured his own living room, and snapped his watch.

He had a pair of spare blankets in the hall closet. He didn't need two pillows, when it came down to it. He could give up one of those spare toothbrushes he'd packed away in the stash below his sink, as well as a box of dental floss, a travel tube of toothpaste, and some hotel soap. It wasn't his original stash, of course – he'd given most of it away in the early days after the Wizard War – but he'd made it a point of good practice to pick up toiletries wherever he found them, and he ranged further than most.

Food… well, he hoped Kyra liked potatoes.

He rolled it all up in one of the blankets as Beldam watched him suspiciously from the couch, and then teleported back to Niagara.

Kyra jumped when he walked through the front door. "Hey, I thought you–"

"Don't worry about it," Edmund said. He still wasn't familiar enough with the layout of the museum to teleport inside; better safe than sorry. He adjusted his grip. "I did see a broom closet back there. In the meantime, this is for you." He set the rolled-up blanket on the counter. "Pick a spot to hang your hat."

Kyra stared at him.

"To sleep," Edmund said.

Kyra looked down at the blanket, which was already doing its best to unroll itself.

"You're staying here," Edmund explained.

"Oh."

"I'll be staying here, too. There's a lot of work to do on this place and I don't want to leave you by yourself."

The Conduit swallowed, blinking like he was holding back tears. He nodded.

Edmund watched him gather up the blanket and its contents, feeling a little at a loss. The kid looked overwhelmed. It had to be overwhelming. Magic, and everything it implied, had been almost too much to handle when Edmund himself started. Going from the Susurration's false paradise straight into the arms of a Shokat Anoushak cult, after the end of the world as anyone knew it, was hard to imagine.

He thought of the lake on the back forty, a puddle compared to the one that Kyra wanted him to cross. He sighed. "It won't get any easier," he said.

Kyra froze.

Edmund ran a hand through his hair: the left side, where the grey was recent, and shouldn't have ever been. "It never does. You just get tougher."

Kyra brought a hesitant hand up to his chest, clenched in a fist over his breastbone as though holding back his heart.

"I'm sorry," Edmund said. "We got off to a bad start. I

know you have no reason to trust me, and I know you have your own demons. I'm sorry this place isn't much, and if I could take you anywhere else, I would, but..."

The words died on his tongue. He had somewhere else. He could. His house hadn't had any guests but Istvan in years. The only thing stopping him was fear.

No – fear, and practicality. He couldn't afford any accidents. Not that close to the Twelfth Hour. Not after seeing what Kyra had already done here, and to the Demon's Chamber, and to Tornado Alley. The kid couldn't be trusted. He couldn't be taken anywhere else.

"How old are you?" Kyra asked.

"Thirty-five." The words were automatic. They felt hollower than usual.

"Oh."

Edmund turned, suddenly feeling very alone. "Let me go get that broom."

CHAPTER SEVENTEEN

Istvan winged over New Haven, streaming bitter poison. The sun shone down on him, harsh and distant, little comfort to those buried in sudden snow below – the crashing front of a grey storm rolled in from the Atlantic. The first snow of winter, well before winter was due.

It didn't matter anymore. New Haven wasn't home to him. It had never been anything but a prison, the anchor that held him back. First, the Twelfth Hour, and then...

Get out.

Niagara wasn't Edmund's. Istvan had done most of the work. Edmund had no right, none at all, to demand that Istvan leave.

Get out. Don't come back.

It hurt. It oughtn't to have hurt, but it did. Istvan was invincible – he didn't have to take any of it, he didn't have to listen, or care – and yet here he was, aimless, already back to New Haven without thinking about it. Like he were reporting back. Like he were under order. He'd always returned to New Haven, to Magister Hahn, to the infirmary that wasn't truly his but that he'd claimed. Did he truly know how to do nothing else?

Had he been enslaved for so long?

Edmund had won. Edmund always won, in the end.

He was always right, especially when he was wrong. And now Kyra – poor Kyra, confused, tormented, scarred by Istvan's own impotence in the face of the wizard's cruelty – would trust him.

Istvan snapped his wings shut and dove. Mist gave way to the shock of freezing cloud, ice sleeting jagged through him, snowflakes buffeted in great whirling gusts like flocks of sparrows disturbed. Breaking through to the world below revealed a scene smothered: the storm had come rapidly, and thoroughly. The stone spire of the Twelfth Hour sped towards him and then past, light spilling from its windows. The courtyards bustled with frantic figures pulling down drying racks, shooing chickens, ducking in and out of doorways that slammed. Others fled the fields, hauling carts that left doubled trails in the sudden white.

No one was prepared. Some probably wouldn't live through the winter, just like last year. Of course they dreamed of Barrio Libertad – what had wizards ever done for them, but mitigate the misery the greatest wizard of the age had caused?

Past Edmund's house, sheltered only by the distant shores of Long Island, the fishing fleet tumbled and tossed in the waves.

Istvan flew a broad circle around them. Some of the crews spotted him, and pointed – shouted, pleas and curses – but he couldn't do anything to help them. He wasn't Edmund. They would have to make it back on their own.

He turned back towards New Haven, towards the bonfire set burning on its shore, and alighted on the sand. Those hurling driftwood on the flames waved at him. Had he seen the fleet, they asked. Could those at sea make out the fire?

"I've no idea," he said.

He turned away. He walked down the beach. No one followed him.

The stones were still there, of course. The children weren't. The tide was out, which meant he could walk further down towards the water than before. He passed the carved monolith of a head without comment.

He picked up a stone.

Not thinking straight. Not himself. Not civil, and not suited for company. Too many memories, and robbed of the ability to hide those he most cared about. Kyra could name Pietro Koller. That alone was a revenge more thorough than Istvan had ever suspected the Susurration could enact. The only thing worse would have been telling Edmund.

Unless, of course, it had. Unless, of course, he somehow knew already, and was only pretending that he didn't, smiling that pleasant smile to hide his revulsion.

Istvan threw the stone at the water. It tumbled through his hand, instead, and clattered onto the rocks.

He shouted the worst curse he could think of.

A wave rippled. Something beneath it, something sleek and immense, with the flash of a staring eye. Krakens, they said.

Istvan leapt at it. Stare at him? Mock him? Attack those boats who were turning back already, whether they could see the fire or not? Live in the harbor, slapping back stones and smug about it while New Haven starved and Edmund was infuriating and Istvan couldn't be at ease without murder–

He hit the water. Dull reddish-purple flesh flashed white, tentacles rolling and twisting around him, a gout of blue spilling from the creature's mantle where his blade bit into it. Not real blood at all. It spread like a cloud. The water dropped off this far from the shore, dozens of feet down, and that was where the creature lunged.

That didn't help it.

The kraken made no sound, not once, as Istvan hacked it apart. It felt pain as its limbs fell away, but it didn't seem anxious. It stared at him, reproachfully, as the light receded above them, and when it was over, Istvan only found himself floating beside its torn-up remnants feeling like his lungs were full of water (which they were) and like he was swimming in kraken blood, ink, and offal – which he was. That none of him was real or solid didn't matter.

It was, on the whole, the least satisfying thing he'd ever done.

He slogged back to shore. Perhaps the beast would wash up, later, and someone would eat it. Perhaps he would be able to rid himself of the feeling of breathing blood, eventually. He hated things sloshing through him. He knew he hated it. Why had he gone after something underwater in the first place?

The people at the bonfire – a man, a woman, and a young woman who might have been their daughter – stared at him as he stomped out of the surf.

Istvan flicked water off his knife, hoping that the handle wouldn't stain. Black might be acceptable, but not blue. Why did krakens bleed blue?

"Did you…" the women began.

Istvan sighed. "I killed a kraken, that's all."

Silence. Nervous glances at the water.

"Are they OK?" the man asked.

The fishing fleet. Of course. They were looking to guide in the fishing fleet. That's what the fire was for. "I saw some of the boats, earlier," Istvan said. He sheathed his knife. "I... I'll go check on them. I imagine they'll be coming in soon."

He could do that, at least. That wasn't underwater.

"The kraken wasn't doing anything," he added, feeling somewhat guilty.

The family didn't seem to know what to make of that.

"OK," said the woman.

Istvan chided himself. They were worried. The krakens had taken boats before. The storm would only get worse. Unlike Edmund, he couldn't dally so long as he liked.

He took off.

It wasn't the most awkward afternoon Edmund had ever spent, but it was close. He and Kyra swept up the debris, righted fallen shelves, and tossed broken tourist knickknacks into one corner. The cracked window would need repair. Edmund found and put the heat on once it grew cold, and as darkness fell he encouraged Kyra to find a place to bunk.

"What if they come again?" the kid asked.

"You'll be inside and they won't find you," Edmund replied, without much conviction. "Besides, you won't be alone out here. I'm staying, too, remember?"

Kyra cast a nervous glance at the windows. "They found me before."

"Maybe," Edmund said. He leaned the broom in one corner. "Go find yourself a place, anyway. If something dives out of the sky, I'll deal with it."

Kyra took his blankets and disappeared, and,

moments later, Edmund heard the rumble of the elevator headed down to the generators. Great. It was obvious, in hindsight – the generators were built into the dam, not on top of it, and the place was naturally sturdier – but he'd have rather had Kyra well away from any machinery.

Too late now.

He cast a glance towards the windows himself, half-hoping to see Istvan, but of course the ghost hadn't returned. He'd probably gone back to Triskelion. He wouldn't be back. Edmund would have to do everything himself.

He tried not to think about how well he'd handled the night before.

First thing first: get through the rest of today, and into tomorrow. Then figure out what to do about this Toronto business and get back together with the team. He had a place, Mercedes had a plan, and they had to start work on it sooner rather than later. The weather would only hold up for so long.

Kyra had mentioned monsters. The Twelfth Hour had its own monster. William. The Tyger. If he were really from up north, maybe he could be of some help figuring out how to reach–

Something screamed.

It was faint, distant, with an edge to it. Harsh. Metallic. For one terrible moment Edmund wondered if Kyra had already broken a generator.

Then the fireball plummeted from overhead and slammed into the treeline.

Edmund shut off all the lights. He shut off the heat. He let down the blinds, locked the door – for what good it would do – and bolted for the elevator. They were not staying here. Not tonight. Not with things falling from the sky. He'd served in the Pacific. He'd had enough of things falling from the sky.

With Istvan on patrol, he might have felt better. Without Istvan...

Without Istvan...

Edmund spent a few moments to beat back sudden panic. All of forever. Really all of forever. That was a hell of a long time to be alone. He'd thought he'd resigned himself to that, and maybe he had, once, but...

The elevator doors slid open. A chime sounded. He closed his eyes a moment, focusing on not breathing so hard, and then stepped out onto the upper catwalk. The generator room was cavernous, almost two stories high, with four churning generators evenly spaced across its length that made a hell of a racket. Not the best place to sleep, anyway. "Kyra," he called, "change of plans."

The kid jumped up from below, hugging the blankets to his chest. "Did you see them?" he demanded, "Did you get them?"

"I saw them. I don't know what they're doing and I don't know if they know about you, but I need to ask you one question."

"Yeah?"

Edmund hurried down the stairs, each step a crash on bare metal. "Can you hold it together for one night?"

Kyra blinked at him. "I think so?"

"That's what that tiara is, right? That helps? Diego gave that to you?"

The Conduit touched two fingers to the milky surface of the band around his head. It wasn't glowing, now. That was probably good. "How did you know?"

Edmund reached the bottom of the stairs, wondering

if he was really hearing more crashing above or if it was just the generators. Or his imagination. "I... knew another Conduit. Now hold tight." He fished out his pocket watch. "We're going to my place."

"Wait, are we doing that teleport thing again, because–"

Edmund snapped his watch shut. Archaic coordinates shifted to match, satisfying the compulsive neurosis of a creature outside of reality. The world dissolved and reformed itself into his living room. Beldam, back on the couch again, cast Kyra a wary eye.

"OK," Edmund said. He unclasped his cape. He tugged it off his shoulders, walked over to the hat rack, and hung it up. His hat went on top of it.

OK. It would be OK.

He straightened the hat on its peg.

"You have a cat," whispered Kyra.

Edmund turned. "That's Beldam."

The Conduit hadn't moved from the middle of the room. He was still holding the rolled-up blanket. "Does it talk?" he asked.

"No. She's a cat."

"Oh."

Edmund waited a moment for further questions, but none came. Kyra wandered over to the couch as though hypnotized, put the blanket on the coffee table, and sat down next to Beldam, drawing up his knees. The cat flicked an ear at him but stayed put.

"You OK?" Edmund asked.

Kyra nodded, toppling slowly sideways onto the arm of the couch.

Edmund glanced back to see what he might be staring at, but there was nothing there but the umbrella stand. "You sure?"

Another nod.

Well, it had been a busy day. For both of them. The kid would recover. Kids were tough. It would be fine. Kyra could sleep on the couch and then they'd figure out the rest tomorrow morning. The house would be fine. It could be warmer, but...

Edmund went to the front window and pushed a curtain aside.

Blizzard. In September. Right.

He started towards the kitchen – and the thermostat. "Tell you what, Kyra. I'll go make us some supper."

"You got a lot of books," came the response.

Edmund paused. "I'm a librarian."

"You can read all these?"

"Most of them."

Kyra hugged his knees tighter, the hem of the dress from Barrio Libertad brushing the floor below him. "Can I pet the cat?"

"If she'll let you."

"'kay."

Edmund turned on the heat and busied himself in the kitchen. Potatoes it was. Potatoes it would probably be for a good long while, if winter had decided to come already. He'd have to check back at the Twelfth Hour and see if anyone needed a refresher on harvest and storage. He'd also have to check the cisterns, and...

He dipped water out of its storage barrel and put it on to boil. "By the way," he called into the living room, "we don't have working plumbing. Don't use the bathroom. If you need something, let me know, and I'll show you where to find the outhouse."

"I'm OK," said Kyra.

"Well, when you're not, tell me." Edmund glanced

out the kitchen window, barely able to make out where his makeshift water catchment and storage seemed to have already frozen over. This was going to be a long night. "I'm going to bring some things in."

It took almost two hours. The storm tore through his coat like he wasn't wearing it. Snow had already piled a foot high in front of his door. Some of the pipe for the shower setup in the backyard would have to be repaired. The herb garden, set in its own box near the back hedge, was a complete loss. It had struggled from the start – much closer to the house itself, and nothing would grow – but he'd hoped the rosemary would live, even if nothing else took root. He hadn't had time to take better care of it. Now that he did... too late.

Once he was finished, he checked to see if the potatoes were boiling.

"You're done?" asked Kyra.

Edmund held his hands over the stove. "For now."

He spent some time so he could feel his fingers again. No good working in a kitchen with stiff fingers.

Footsteps fell on the kitchen tile. "How are you so fast? I didn't even see you."

Edmund shook out his hands. "Magic." The tongs hung in their place near the stove; he took them down, picked out the potatoes, and set them on the cutting board.

Kyra came up beside him, pointing. "That," he said. "Like that. Stuff don't boil that fast. You have to wait for it."

"I do. You don't." Edmund got out a paring knife. "Go ahead and sit down."

"But–"

"Magic, Kyra. It's magic. I'll explain later." He started

cutting up the potatoes. "Now go have a seat."

The Conduit retreated. The chair he pulled out was the one with its back to the front door. Istvan's.

Edmund tried to focus on the potatoes. The food that he'd spent some of his reserve time on, for no reason other than convenience. What would Istvan have thought? Not even a day, and already Edmund had fallen back into old habits. A moment here, a moment there, compressing minutes and hours between the time spent with company. Luxury spending. No need to keep anyone waiting. He had time. He always had time.

He looked down at the knife in his hand, smeared with starch. His stomach twisted.

He put the knife down. Think of something else.Plates. They needed plates. Plates, and forks, and something to drink, and there were plenty of other things to discuss that weren't about him. They didn't have to talk about him.

Kyra didn't have to know everything. He was just a kid. He was… he…

Hm. That was a good place to start.

"I have a question, if you don't mind," Edmund said as he set the food on the table. "What do I call you?"

Kyra looked up from patting Beldam. "What?"

"You were quick to insist on 'she' on the elevator. Is that right?"

"Yeah."

Edmund laid out the forks. He hadn't misheard, then. He'd wondered about that. "So… Kyra, the person I'm speaking to, right now – you're a girl?"

"Yeah."

"Have you always been this way?"

Kyra looked at him strangely. "What's that supposed to mean?"

Well. That solved that mystery. "Never mind. I was just making sure."

Kyra nodded. "Thanks."

Edmund sat down and picked up his fork. He'd dealt with stranger things, and – as consequences of Shattering went, if that's what this was – at least it was harmless enough. If it was something else... well, he wasn't a doctor. No reason to start worrying until she started speaking in Scythian.

"Why'd you only cut the stuff on my plate and not yours?" asked Kyra.

"I was hungry."

Istvan couldn't help with frostbite. He'd never been able to help with frostbite. His presence only made it worse, chilling spirit in addition to flesh... but cold wasn't the only cause of injury this night, and the rest he could do something about.

"I'm glad you're here," said Roberts.

"You oughtn't have tried to pick up that entire cart," said Istvan. "And you know that ice collects on that step."

Roberts shrugged.

"Don't do that."

"Sorry."

There were hooks to pry out of flesh. Burns from ropes and flame hurled suddenly before the wind. Concussions, cracked bones, and sprained ankles from falls. No one had expected the storm to come on so fast. The rush to proof the town against it, and to bring the fleet home, had its risks. That the vast majority of injuries were beneath Istvan's skill – as a surgeon, the best in the world – didn't matter.

He was a doctor. Even Kyra had said so.

"Lucy still isn't back," Roberts said, doing his best to hold very still.

Istvan put in the last few stitches above the man's eyebrow. "I'm sure she's telling everyone that I'm a god-king and attempting to incite armed rebellion."

"Sounds right."

"I expect the region to dissolve into bloody infighting within the week, and I'm wondering if I ought to go there, claim my title, and put a stop to it." Istvan drew his knife and cut the thread, tying off a knot. "Then, perhaps, I'll free all those slaves, give them amnesty, and conquer my way to Tornado Alley."

Roberts stared at him a long moment. Then he cracked a weak, lopsided smile. "Sure."

Istvan dropped the needle onto a nearby plate.

The nurse's smile faded. "Wait, are you serious?"

"Roberts, I need you to avoid heavy lifting for the next week and then check back here. I'll go put your information on file."

"Doctor–"

Istvan grabbed the other man's broad shoulders. "Don't you dare worry about me, because I am far, far from the one who needs it!"

Roberts, to his credit, didn't flinch. "You went to Triskelion," he said.

"No heavy lifting," Istvan repeated. "If you try anything else, I will know."

"Where's Mr Templeton?"

Edmund. Bloody Edmund. He was at Niagara, most likely. With Kyra. Reaping the benefits of the siege while, again, Istvan was stuck in the Twelfth Hour infirmary. Istvan was always stuck in the Twelfth Hour infirmary. In the first months of the Wizard War, its walls had been his only glimpse of a world beyond the Demon's Chamber – and he'd been grateful for it. He'd been grateful for anything Edmund could spare.

Istvan hadn't chosen it. He hadn't chosen any of it.

Large hands settled roughly where Istvan's shoulders would have been.

"Go find Mr Templeton," said Roberts.

Istvan bristled. "Why?"

"I know you. Go talk to him. You'll only get angrier and angrier if you don't, and no one wants to deal with that."

The man's eyes were watering. The infirmary had gone very quiet.

Istvan let go of him, leaving bloody handprints that faded. He was doing it again. He couldn't… he wasn't… it was never like this in the old days, when he had no one to hold him back, to… to return to, to…

He backed up, wreathed in the thunder of distant guns.

"I'll put in my own information," said Roberts – and, though his face remained impassive, and the worry was legitimate, disappointment and exasperation boiled below, the resentment of one who knew he shouldn't speak his mind.

Istvan fled.

Nothing halted him at the infirmary's double doors, and no one questioned him as he sped over their heads to the exit. It was early morning, the sun just rising. The storm still raged. If he were to navigate by the Black Building, he would have to climb above the clouds and hope that they weren't deep enough to obscure its spire.

He'd failed. He'd failed them all. If he couldn't stay calm at the infirmary – if he couldn't keep himself from yelling at Roberts, from lashing out at anything that moved, from being cruel, from not thinking… what kind of doctor was that? What kind of person was that?

Roberts had lost a daughter. Roberts had compared Kyra to his own child, and vowed to do what he could for him even in the face of a decision he couldn't change. Roberts knew what Istvan was – and still had the courage to speak to him, still worked alongside him, still expected better of him.

Triskelion. You went to Triskelion.

Istvan severed a tree branch as he took wing. It toppled into the snow with a crack and a thud: another innocent victim.

Statues.

Flesh of stone. Skin of wax. No more mortal needs or frailties. Superhuman physicality: strength, endurance, toughness. Really all of forever, without taking anything from anyone to do it. An alternate route to immortality.

Edmund stared at his ledger.

He wanted to know more. He wanted to know how she'd done it. He wanted to know how much Shokat Anoushak had changed, and when, and how. Was it the process that made her inhuman, or was it time? Could it be staved off? If Kyra was right, would the reborn Shokat Anoushak be the same person?

Was Kyra right?

Could someone else replicate it? Could Edmund…

He swallowed, mouth gone dry. He would never have to patrol again. Never have to do what he'd done again. He'd be completely self-contained, completely self-sustaining – not a scavenger reliant on others. No more Niagaras, not ever. Not ever again.

But… he couldn't. He didn't know enough. He didn't know how it worked.

Not yet.

His one and only encounter with Shokat Anoushak flitted through his mind, the Immortal wheeling over the remnants of Providence atop a beast with wings like razors, reinforcements rising wherever her arrows fell. She wore the regalia of a Scythian queen, archaic and colorful. She'd looked down at him as the city burned.

Run, she'd said, and her voice sounded as though she stood beside him, speaking words in a language two thousand years dead. *Run, and keep running as the jaws of fate and madness close on your throat. That's all that awaits you.*

Run.

Edmund closed his ledger. He managed to put it back in its place, though his hands shook, and to get the cap back on his pen. Better not to know. Always better not to know, especially when you wanted to know more.

Don't ask.

Don't ask.

He wished Kyra hadn't said a word. He should have stopped her. He couldn't sleep.

He couldn't sleep.

If Edmund was at Niagara, that meant north to Barrio Libertad and then west to…

Istvan paused, hovering above the main road that led from the Twelfth Hour to the coast. No. No, wait.

Edmund was here.

What was he doing here? He was supposed to be at Niagara! Where was Kyra? Had he left the boy there, alone – with not even a promise to return, because

Edmund so rarely made promises – all so he could spend the night in his own bed?

Istvan dove for the house. Smoke spiraled from its chimney. He swung in through the kitchen window, folding his wings to avoid clipping them on the appliances. "Edmund!"

A chair scraped backwards across the tile, accompanied by a wash of sudden dread.

"Edmund, what on earth are you–"

The wizard held up his hands. He seemed to be wearing a bathrobe; difficult to tell exactly, in the poor light. "Shhh! Cut the fireworks!"

The sound of snoring drifted from the living room. Istvan peered around the corner. A roughly human-sized bundle lay curled up on the couch, swathed in thick blankets. A cat sprawled on top of it, purring.

Kyra.

Oh. Oh, no.

Istvan tried to damp down the distant racket of gunfire. If the boy woke suddenly, startled, in the middle of New Haven... well, Istvan had enough to be blamed for already. He wasn't about to have a tornado devouring Edmund's house be his fault, too.

"Edmund," he hissed, "what are you doing here? Why is Kyra here?" He looked at the table. "Why are you reading in the dark?"

The wizard reached out to shut the book. "The mockeries came back."

"So?"

"One of them fell out of the sky while I was watching. It exploded, Istvan. Maybe they were fighting Kasimir's troops again, I don't know. It wasn't safe."

"So you brought Kyra to your house?" Istvan asked.

"Yes," said Edmund.

Istvan put his hands on the table. "You ran?"

"Yes."

What was the point of Niagara, if Edmund was just going to take people to his house? What was the point in building anything if Edmund was always kept just going home? Why not run everything out of the house, while they were at it? Clearly anyone could be allowed inside, never mind their documented hazard to life and property and the close proximity of unwitting neighbors, and it was perfectly normal to chain a child to a pillar and then later invite him over for tea and games. It was all perfectly acceptable if Edmund did it!

"Before you yell," Edmund said, "let's go somewhere we won't wake Kyra."

Istvan snorted. "Oh, it would be awful if something happened to this place, is that it?"

Edmund didn't answer. Instead, the wizard extricated himself from his chair and started down the hall, stewing in a well-seasoned medley of exhaustion, dread, and self-hatred. It was typical of him, and yet there was a strange... fluidity to it, walled back by the sort of tingling horror the man reserved for grappling with eternity, the kind that led to fits and panic if left unchecked.

Istvan didn't feel bad for him. Not at all. Istvan was still angry at him, and deservedly so, for Kyra's sake if no one else's.

What had he done, after Istvan left?

The other man paused at the junction between bedroom and bathroom, paused, and then sighed and pushed the door to the bedroom open. "Here."

"Now I'm permitted, I see."

"Unless you'd prefer to talk in the bathroom, yes."

Istvan brushed past him into the room and turned on the desk lamp. The sheets were still made up, as though Edmund had never slept in them. A bottle and a glass, inevitably, sat on the bedside table. No sign of the time ledger. Istvan had only ever seen it when it was open, never closed – or nothing that looked right, anyhow. There were plenty of other books stacked above the desk.

Edmund stepped in and shut the door behind himself.

"I won Niagara for you," Istvan said.

The wizard sat on the bed. "I'm aware."

"I gave you a way to get your time back. I took care of Kyra. I protected you from the Susurration, I was forced to unleash the War on it, and I've spent the last two months trying to make reparations – and what have you done? Nothing!"

Edmund glanced at the door. "Istvan–"

"You held endless meetings," Istvan continued, "you went on patrol by yourself – for yourself – every night, and when the Magister asked you to go on a proper mission, you complained. You imprisoned a child, Edmund, and made me keep him in a coma. I've done everything for you. Everything!" Tears welled: foolish tears, impossible tears, relics of a past long gone. Weakness, when he least needed it. His vision swam. "And now that you've gotten your time back, you expect to be lauded for all your hard work even as you run away, again?"

"I didn't–"

"You expect Kyra to forgive you? You expect me to forgive you?"

Edmund sat very still, both hands clutching the edge of the bed. He looked terrible: he hunched, his shoulders drooped, his face was drawn, and wan, and still not fully healed. He clearly hadn't slept at all.

Istvan tore off his glasses. He didn't care. He'd been used, taken for granted, ignored, taken for a monster – and none of it had mattered until he was free. He thought he'd been happy, chained. He deserved it, after all. The wizards were in the right. Edmund, at least, had spoken to him. Visited him. Never tried to free him.

Not until the War would be useful as a weapon. Not until they had no other choice.

Istvan would do anything for him. Istvan was his best friend. Istvan loved him, and loved him enough to never breathe a word of it.

And then he went and put Kyra in Istvan's chains.

Istvan couldn't face him any longer. He turned, and went to the window. Snow blew past, outlined by the lamp on the front of the house; a light not visible save as a diffuse glow in the storm.

"I'm sorry," said Edmund.

Istvan folded his arms.

"What did Lucy tell you at Triskelion? After I left?"

As though that's what started it. No problems at all until Lucy gave him ideas, hm? Istvan sighed. "She said that I'm an 'ending spirit,'" he said, still staring out the window. "Her world – where all of the Triskelion armies are from – they have things like me. Sundered spirits. I don't know how many, but they understand them, and they have a place for them, and they…"

"They treat them like god-kings," said Edmund.

"Edmund, Lucy said that I've a wisdom no one else does. She said that clinging to who I am – who I was, the dead man named Istvan Czernin – is halting a… a sort of transcendence. She said that I'm more than my parts, my memories. I'm an ending spirit of War, and if I go back there, I'm entitled to command every soldier they have. Even Kasimir's forces are mine, by right."

A long silence.

Istvan wiped at his eyes. He wished he could remember more details, but they slipped away; they always did. He was positive he'd ruined a great deal before coming back to himself. That Edmund didn't despise him was a wonder.

"You don't believe all that, do you?" the wizard finally asked.

He wanted to. Oh, he wanted to.

Istvan turned. "Are you going to do what Kyra asked of us? With Shokat Anoushak, and Tirunto, and whatever else?"

"Toronto."

"Edmund, I don't like that you brought him here. I don't like that you're trying to win him over. I know that I... I said some things to him, and that I could have been better, but Edmund, he remembers me! He remembers things that I..." Istvan drew a false breath. "Please, tomorrow, if you do nothing else, leave us alone for a time so that I can speak with him."

Edmund rubbed his face. Then he leaned forward, elbows on his knees. "Triskelion was a mistake."

Now he–

Only after he had time did he–

Istvan slapped a skeletal hand on the desk, soundlessly. "Of course it was a mistake! You listened to me! You should never listen to me!"

The wizard shook his head. "No," he said. "No, I should listen."

"I'm the last person you ought to–"

"Istvan, I should listen a lot more than I have been. Grace had a point, you had a point, everyone at the

meetings had ideas, and I was..." Edmund looked
down at the palms of his hands. "I was scared. I still am.
Mercedes wants to turn Niagara into a prison. I don't
know what to do with Kyra. I keep panicking over all
this talk about Shokat Anoushak, and I was afraid that
we were over, that you'd take off back to Triskelion and
I'd never see you again, or that I'd have to fight you
again."

He clenched his hands into fists. "Istvan, I've never
been so close to running out of time. I've never made
anything this big. I'm a librarian. I don't know how to
do this."

The man meant it.

Istvan tugged the desk chair sideways and sat in it.

"I'm not asking you to forgive me," Edmund said. "But
I'd sure like some help figuring out what to do next."

Something changed in the tenor of the house. A
subtle change, fuzzy and uncertain, a shift from one state
to another. Brief confusion and then a dawning shock.

Istvan looked from the door to Edmund's wretched
expression. "Well," he said, "I think that starts with
Kyra."

CHAPTER EIGHTEEN

Breakfast went well, Istvan thought.

"I'm sorry about your table," Kyra repeated.

"It's fine," said Edmund.

"It looks like it's only three pieces. I can help fix it."

Edmund finished hanging up the last of the cookware. "Don't worry about it," he said, voice flat.

Istvan bent to pick up a fallen fork. The house was still intact. That was progress. Besides, Kyra had seemed surprised and frustrated more than angry. Perhaps he didn't know how fast Istvan was. In fact, past his lack of revulsion for Istvan's appearance, the boy didn't seem to know much about his abilities or modern history at all.

"I'm still sorry," Kyra muttered, tracing the burns on his wrists.

"I was trying to be civil, I truly was," said Istvan. "What did I say?"

Kyra huffed a long sigh and went back into the living room, where he threw himself on the couch.

"Stop harping on the dress," said Edmund.

Istvan set the fork on the counter. "Why? He can't wear that. Don't you have anything his size?"

"No."

"Doesn't anyone?"

"No. And Kyra's a she, all right? We talked last night."

Istvan watched him straighten the cooking knives. "Edmund, that's ridiculous."

The wizard snatched up the fork and put it in the sink. "That's how it is. I don't know what's going on, but it isn't worth fighting over. Besides, Istvan, you're already stranger than a body and consciousness that don't match up."

"Can we just go?" called Kyra.

Edmund strode robotically past Istvan, picking his way over the wreckage of the table. It was almost as though the damage were Istvan's fault, which was ridiculous because Istvan wasn't the one who had brought Kyra to the house in the first place. The man had known what he was risking, it could have been much worse, and they were both lucky that Kyra hadn't seemed inclined to create another storm like the first time.

"She," indeed. The boy was a crossdresser, was what he was. Istvan was not stranger than that.

At least they'd settled some things about Niagara. It might not have been an ideal base of operations, but it did lie just across Lake Ontario from where Kyra wanted to go. Toronto. The place Diego had extracted a promise to visit from the man who rarely made promises. Istvan hadn't realized that the city – or the Greater Great Lakes fracture – was that close.

"Come on," called Edmund. "If we're going to go scout out Kyra's cult, we need to leave now. Otherwise, we'll be flying back to Niagara in the dark."

Istvan followed them both into the living room. Edmund already wore coat, hat, mask, and cape, because he had a terrible habit of spending his ill-gotten time on frivolities. Kyra carried a rolled-up blanket with a pillow inside, a rubber band holding back his hair. One of Edmund's old cold-weather jackets stretched over his shoulders. Beldam wound around his feet.

"So," said Istvan, drawing closer. "If this doesn't work, ought I go find–"

The cat hissed and shot past him.

"–a boat, somewhere?"

"It's gonna work," said Kyra. "I promise."

Edmund pulled out his pocket watch. "Ready?"

Istvan shrugged. Kyra squeezed his eyes shut, turning his head away as though facing a firing squad, and then nodded.

Brass clicked on brass. A moment later they were at Niagara, again standing in front of the museum in a cold drizzle. Scorch marks marred the building's face. The nearest dead mockery lay where it fell, sparking as water ran through its innards. A new plume of smoke rose from the trees. Kyra took off immediately for the museum and its gift shop.

"OK," said Edmund, "I'll be back in less than a half-hour, if we're lucky."

Istvan fanned his wings. He was to make a quick circuit of the area, just to be certain. "You have told William where we're going?"

"Of course."

"And how we're going there?"

Edmund sighed. "I'll be back."

He vanished.

Istvan tried to shake away some of the rain – in vain – and then leapt skyward. The museum and the dam it sat on receded below him, merely one part of a larger complex that included the entire artificial lake and its central, bridge-connected island. Kasimir's camp sprawled into the forest along the outer edge. A second dam lay on the other side of the river, of roughly equal size and equally below capacity. Marks along its edge indicated where the river had been higher, once.

Now, mockeries. There was the one that slid down the dam, the one on the island, the one in the woods, the one that had fallen into the lake, the ones that had fled… and the newcomer, also in the woods.

Istvan took off in that direction. It wasn't far – only a few miles over thickly forested terrain, divided by trails bearing signs and scenic overlooks as well as the highway – and he made it there in only a few moments, landing where the trees had split and shattered.

There were two of them.

He slid down the wave of earth thrown up by the impact, stepping over rivulets of oil. The mockeries lay half-buried, entangled in a bizarre embrace. The first was the usual helicopter-type, with a single rotor, toppled on its side as the smoke billowed from where its windows had smashed in. A faint sound almost like screaming emanated from the interior. Two broken blades jutted upwards, the others snapped off.

The second creature was jet-black, sleek, with strange angles and broad wings – an airplane, but shaped more like a boomerang than any airplane Istvan had ever fought. It was much, much bigger than the first one… and it still moved, metal popping with heat, flipped onto its back with one wing curled over, bat-like, in a way that shouldn't have been possible. One of the first mockery's claws dug into where its cockpit probably was.

Istvan frowned. Fighting? The two of them had been fighting?

He prodded the bigger one. It generated a harsh

metallic grumble, muffled in the dirt. Its surface trembled beneath his fingers, consumed in a strange, distant agony.

He had never seen two mockeries fight each other before. Had one of them gone mad?

"Wait here," he said.

The big one grumbled again. It didn't look as though it could right itself on its own, much less disentangle itself from the grip of the other mockery. Its shape was strangely familiar.

Istvan nodded and took off. The flight back to the museum was short, and he landed on the grass beside the front entrance.

"Kyra?" he called.

No answer.

Istvan pushed his way inside. A rattling came from the back; he passed a bathroom and then found an open closet door. He peered inside. "Kyra?"

The boy froze. He was knee-deep in boxes, in the process of pulling down a roll of packing tape from cluttered shelves. The blankets were nowhere to be found.

"What are you doing?" asked Istvan.

Kyra hugged the tape to his chest. "Fixing the window."

Istvan blinked. "The window?"

Kyra gave him a betrayed look. He stepped over the boxes and tried to edge past him, smoldering with what was probably frustration. It was still so difficult to read him with Istvan's usual level of precision. "Excuse me."

Istvan stepped out of his way, not sure what else to do. He knew that he'd caused an uproar. He knew that he'd been awful to everyone, that he'd said things he oughtn't have, that he'd hurt both Kyra and Edmund without thinking about what he was doing. Edmund had always shrugged it off: you were drunk, it's fine, I know how it goes. Let's both pretend it never happened.

But Kyra?

How was Istvan supposed to start over with Kyra, after all of that? They had only spoken briefly while he was sober, in the Demon's Chamber, and while it had been a well-meaning start, it hadn't even worked, and–

The odd tearing sound of tape off the roll split his thoughts.

Istvan returned to the front part of the building in time to see Kyra drawing a long strip of the substance over a crack in the glass he hadn't seen before. Had that broken when they fought?

"Kyra," he said.

"Yeah?"

"Do you ever recall seeing two mockeries fighting each other?"

The Conduit shook his head. He pulled the roll of tape downwards, crouching and pressing the ribbon against the glass.

"You're certain?"

A shrug. "They chased me. That's all."

Istvan gripped his bandolier. Oh, there was nothing for it. He had to ask sooner or later, and despite what Edmund so often said there were some things that it was better to know. "Please, tell me what you remember of Pietro Koller."

Kyra pulled down harder, a sudden tug that peeled away some of his previous work. He glanced at Istvan out of the corner of his eye. "You going to attack me again?"

"No."

"You sure?"

Istvan backed up three steps. "I promise that I won't attack you."

Kyra patted down the tape. "It's just pieces," he grumbled. "It's all just pieces. I don't know what you want. He was a… a guy. With a moustache. You danced with him once. I guess he's dead now, too."

Istvan's heart sank.

"Why does it matter?" Kyra continued. "Why'd you pull a knife on me for that?"

Oh, he shouldn't have asked. It was so long ago, and yet the Susurration had dredged it up like it had just happened – like everything they had ever done was new, like they were living it again all over. Gone. Only Pietro's image, used against him.

Dead now, too, for the second time.

Istvan turned his wedding ring around his finger. "Kyra, why are you staying?"

"What?"

"Why are you staying with us after everything we've done to you?"

Kyra dropped the roll of tape. It dangled, twisting. "You said there ain't anyone else," he said. "You promised you'd help."

"We did, but–"

"You guys are really powerful, and you can get places really fast, and you do whatever it takes to win. Besides, Mr Templeton said that he's fought her before. You beat her before." He clenched his fists before him. "If you did that, you can do it again."

"But the way we've treated you–"

"It don't matter."

Istvan almost stepped towards him; then checked himself and stayed where he was. He doubted proximity would help anything. "What do you mean it doesn't matter?"

"None of it was real anyway. None of them were real. It was fake. It was all fake, and it's stupid to care about fake people. OK?" Kyra snatched up the tape. "Just let me fix the window."

The screech of unrolling tape filled the room again.

Shattered. Shattered, and then enthralled by the Susurration before that. A life – perhaps most of his life – tailored to his expectations, even as the real world fell apart around him, and then a deluge of memory that wasn't his.

This time, Istvan did step towards him. "You aren't fake."

"Yeah, well, you keep changing your mind, and you tried to attack me, and you won't listen to me, and you're dead."

"Kyra–"

"Stop acting like you know me."

But Istvan knew what it was like! He knew the Demon's Chamber, he knew the shock of having too many memories, he knew how it was to come suddenly into power in the middle of war, he... he hadn't done anything to convince Kyra that he was worth listening to. Quite the contrary.

He rubbed at his wrists. "I'm sorry."

Kyra laid out the last strip of tape and finally turned to face him. "What's wrong with you? I don't know what you're going to do. Ever. You tried to help me, and then you do that, and then you..." He touched one of his burned wrists. "What's wrong with you? How are we supposed to beat the Immortal if you keep doing this?"

Back to Shokat Anoushak again. The boy seemed driven by little else.

Istvan sighed. "I'm a spirit of War," he said. "To me, suffering is like a terribly powerful drug, and when you last saw me, I'd just killed a lot of people."

A long pause.

"Oh," said Kyra.

"You know how it is that you remember so much about Shokat Anoushak? I'm just the same, but with my war. The Great War."

"Were they bad people?"

"Not really."

Kyra drew a shaky breath. "I'm gonna put the tape away."

"I'm sorry," Istvan said. "I wish that I had a better answer."

The Conduit walked past him, giving a wider berth than before. He seemed dazed, distant, moving automatically rather than giving his place in the world any thought. The edges of him – the Shattered reflections, emotions colliding into cancellation – grew blurred and muddied, once again making him difficult to discern even as he moved in plain sight. It was as though he were an entire city, and hid within himself.

"Is there anything I can do to make it up to you?" Istvan asked.

Kyra pulled open the closet. He stood there a moment, considering. "Stop making fun of my clothes and don't call me a boy," he said. He glanced back, eyes narrowed. "And help me win."

•••

Ice cracked beneath Edmund's boots as he arrived back at Niagara, the grass withering. He could see his breath and feel the inside of his nose solidifying. He wouldn't have been surprised if the storm at New Haven had actually come with him.

Behind him, William Blake, the Tyger, let out an inquisitive growl.

"Right," said Edmund. "Wait here. I've warned Kyra, but I don't know how she'll take it at first."

The beast nodded. He raised himself to his hind legs, bear-like, and peered about as snow condensed and fluttered around him.

Edmund hurried to the museum. This trip was going to be a long one. "Istvan," he called, pulling the door open, "Kyra, we're here!"

"Oh, good," said Istvan from somewhere above him.

Edmund looked up. The ghost was sitting on the roof, legs dangling over the edge. He looked more disheveled than usual, like he'd been slogging through mud. Edmund glanced back inside, but nothing seemed out of place or more broken than before. "What happened?" he asked.

"Nothing." Istvan pushed himself off, wings flickering into view, and landed soundlessly near him. "We only talked."

"And?"

"He doesn't like me at all."

Edmund sighed. "Well, that's part of your problem."

"What?"

Edmund shook his head and stepped into the building. "Kyra?"

"I'm here!" came the response. "I'm almost done!"

"Done with–"

The Conduit emerged from the back rooms, wearing a souvenir hoodie and wool hat, with bulging canvas souvenir bags slung over both shoulders. "OK," she said.

Edmund raised his eyebrows. "What's all that?"

Kyra looked at the floor. "Well... if we need tape or rope or something, they had a bunch in the back, and I even found some snack bars that fell behind the shelves." She reached into one of the bags and held one up. "See?"

Edmund had no idea how long those things could last, and he didn't want to find out. "Right," he said. "Remember, this is just a fact-finding excursion. How long are you expecting us to be gone?"

"I dunno." She peered at the wrapper. "I hope these are still good."

"Let's hope. Come meet William."

Kyra followed him back out, never looking at Istvan. She had to turn sideways to fit both bags through the door. What else had she packed?

"Right," said Edmund. He backed up to present the Tyger, who now crouched on the grass in an obvious effort to seem smaller. "William, Kyra Stewart. Kyra, William Blake, also known as the 'Tyger.' He's our resident mockery and monster expert." Edmund glanced back at him. "No offense."

The Tyger bared saber teeth, picking out letters one at a time before holding up the screen strapped to his foreleg. Green letters glowed on its face.

none taken

Kyra stared at him.

"He's friendly," Edmund said.

"He was human," added Istvan. "They all were. We thought that her monsters had lost themselves in the change, when she did whatever she did but... we were wrong." He looked away. "We didn't know it, either, until William came along."

Edmund grimaced, rubbing at his upper arm where the scars hadn't yet faded.

Kyra edged closer to the Tyger, shivering. "I've seen things like you," she breathed. "They stood at the doors. I didn't know you could talk."

She reached a hand towards him.

William backed up, shaking his great head, and then crouched back down on the grass.

keep your fingers, he typed.

Kyra pulled her hand back. "Sorry."

the true question, he continued, *have you seen things like you?*

She blinked at the screen. Then, slowly, she shook her head.

Edmund frowned. She had met Grace, hadn't she? She must have, at least once, while Barrio Libertad was holding her. Grace was a Conduit, too – they had that in common. Although, granted, Grace couldn't cause nearly as much destruction on as wide a scale, was over twice Kyra's age, held a powerful position, and remembered well what the world was like before the Wizard War.

As far as Conduits in general, well… the sample size left something to be desired. At least Kyra wasn't talking about a vault full of them in Toronto. Small favors.

The Tyger emitted a rolling growl. *comrades in mystery, we*

A smile crept across Kyra's face. "I guess so."

you chose your name?

"Yeah! A- At least the first part. You like it?"

fitting. i myself am a poet

"Really?"

A cold finger tapped Edmund on the shoulder. <Edmund,> Istvan murmured in the soft drawl of his Viennese German, <We're going to need a new plan. What we have is not a good idea.>

Edmund glanced back at him. The ghost jerked his head towards the museum.

Kyra and the Tyger were still holding their strange half-silent conversation. Edmund held up a hand. "Excuse me, you two. This won't be long."

Kyra gave them a suspicious look, but William simply nodded.

Edmund followed Istvan back to the overhang before the door. "This plan was never a good idea," he said, once they were far enough out of earshot. "Why back out now?"

"There were two mockeries in the woods, not one," said Istvan. "One of them is still alive."

"Still alive? And you left it?"

"Yes, I left it. It's tangled with the other one. Edmund, they were fighting each other. Kyra claims he–"

"She."

Istvan sighed. "–she hasn't seen anything like that before, but what do we have to rely on for any of this, aside from what Kyra says? If both of those mockeries are from the same place, we might be flying into some sort of... monster civil war, and unless Kyra somehow shows much more restraint, everything there will see us coming."

Edmund rubbed at his face. Warring mockeries? Monster factions? The Greater Great Lakes still had its fair share of beasts, unlike Big East, but nothing had spilled over before and everyone assumed that they weren't that smart. Maybe mockeries were territorial if left to their own devices?

But, then, there was the Tyger…

"You're certain that you can't teleport us?" Istvan asked.

"Yes," Edmund said. "I never went to Toronto before the Wizard War, I sure don't want to try blindly aiming for it now, and moving everyone in jumps across that lake is too much of a risk."

"So you would rather show up as part of an immense obvious water tornado directed by someone who may not even be able to control it."

Edmund sighed. He didn't like it, either; Istvan knew he didn't like it, but it was still better than the alternative. The idea of trying to get a boat past whatever might be in that lake – with shores touching both spellscars and the epicenter of the fracture zone – gave him nightmares. "You're the one who argued for giving Kyra the benefit of the doubt on this, Istvan."

The ghost crossed his arms, looking across the grass at Kyra and the Tyger. He still seemed a little bedraggled – frayed uniform seams, dulled buttons, barbed wire rusted and tangled – and Edmund wondered what, exactly, he and the Conduit had talked about while he was gone. Whatever it was, it must have hit home.

It was good to see him like that, in a way. It meant he cared. It meant the real Istvan, the man and not the war, was back. He wasn't going back to Triskelion. He wasn't going to buckle under and believe whatever line Lucy told him about being some kind of divine commander: he was better than that. Edmund had banked everything on that. Edmund liked Istvan.

"I'm glad you're with us," Edmund said.

Istvan turned his wedding ring around his finger. "Someone has to scout ahead."

"We figured it out," called Kyra. She waved at them. "Mr Templeton, I think I can move you and Mr Blake without freezing you up."

Edmund grimaced. Crossing Lake Ontario was a hell of a trial run. He wasn't looking forward to this trip. "That's great," he called back. "We're done here, too."

He looked to Istvan; the ghost shrugged.

"The worst it could be is a wash," Edmund said, to him and maybe to himself. "If it goes south, I'll get us back." He started towards the others. "Come on."

Istvan followed, and Edmund knew now how much he'd taken that for granted.

Edmund could and did get them all to the shoreline. Scrubby grass greeted them, waterlogged, growing from sludge. Cold rain drizzled, flash-freezing when it came anywhere near the Tyger.

Edmund turned up his collar.

The steel grey of Lake Ontario stretched out before them. To the north, it dimmed and hazed into a thick fog. To the west, the shoreline curved away towards the Greater Great Lakes spellscars, mud flats dotted with shipwrecks half-sunk in the reeds, or maybe flocks of tall, thin shore birds; hard to tell. To the east – towards the Big East spellscars – wind-driven waves grew to dangerous heights, sharpening into razor edges, a frozen sea that seemed to crash and collapse when you weren't looking directly at it.

He tried to imagine that he wasn't hearing the faint, plaintive blare of a ship's horn. There couldn't be shipping on this lake – not any more.

"All right," he said. "Kyra, what do you want us to do?"

The Conduit walked up to the edge of the water, ignoring the muck sucking at her shoes. She let out a breath. She rubbed her hands together. "Dr Czernin should fly ahead and make sure we're going the right way," she said. "That way I won't get lost again. You and Mr Blake, uh… just…" She shrugged. "Just don't move too much, OK? And don't freak out. I've picked up way bigger things than you guys."

"I remember," said Edmund, which he did very well. All of those bigger things had been whirling around the periphery of the storm, crashing into each other and getting torn to shreds, as opposed to safely floating in the center.

Kyra had once torn Istvan to shreds.

Edmund swallowed. They had a backup plan. He could get them back if disaster struck. He kept telling himself that. He wished it wouldn't have to happen over a lake.

A tapping, claw against key.

Edmund glanced at the Tyger. He'd briefed him about this, and the beast had agreed to come anyway if it meant a hope of finding others like himself, but agreeing and doing were two different things when you were staring out at it.

a request, said the screen.

Edmund raised his eyebrows.

The Tyger reached out and plunged a paw into the lake. The water froze instantly around it. He gave an ineffectual tug, gave Edmund a significant look, then wrenched the limb free with a crack.

if accident, he typed, *tow an iceberg home, please*

Edmund imagined the Tyger frozen inside an ice cube, floating helplessly towards the Hudson. "Right," he said.

Then, because it seemed important to ask, he added, "How long can you survive frozen like that?"

long enough to visit spain

"I promise I won't drop you," said Kyra, who had admitted at breakfast that she hadn't tried to carry anyone other than herself before. "I got this."

"I'll be off, then, I suppose," said Istvan. He set a hand on Edmund's shoulder, switching to German again. <If anything goes wrong,> he said. <I'll know.>

Edmund steeled himself. "I know."

Istvan took wing, scattering mud and wire. He circled them once, then darted out over the water and back – getting his bearings, no doubt. He was an experienced flier who had crossed oceans before. They didn't want to end up in Tornado Alley or somewhere else equally far off course.

The Tyger padded up closer to Kyra, rain ripples solidifying to ice that cracked beneath him. He showed his screen to her; she smiled. She resettled the bags slung across her shoulders.

"OK," she said.

She started to dance.

Edmund blinked.

It was no more than a gentle rhythm, at first: a bobbing of the head, and then a shifting of the shoulders, side to side. The Conduit held up her hands before her, drawing and pushing at the air in slow circular motions. Her feet stayed planted where they were: in the mud.

It wasn't complicated, and it wasn't especially graceful, and the rain and cold and bags she was carrying did nothing to enhance it...

...but the wind began to stir.

Not like before. Not near them, not wildly, in every

direction. The waves in the lake began to lap sideways. The grass behind them rustled, bending and waving in the opposite direction. Edmund's hat stayed where it was. The Tyger's fur barely ruffled.

A startled shout reached them.

Edmund squinted at the fog bank where Istvan had gone. A trail of green-yellow gas led to the ghost himself, whipped sideways and whirled in an arc that sucked the fog after it. The leading edge of the wind drew up water, tore up sand and reeds, dragged both over land and then over the lake again, rapidly building into a tornado of frightening speed. The rush of blown grass became a roar.

Kyra kept up her strange samba, moving her arms in wider and wider circles. She was mouthing something – counts? beats? – to herself, sometimes adding snatches of a tune, and seemed oblivious to Istvan's distress.

Edmund edged closer to her, careful to stay just out of accidental collision distance. He knew that Conduit abilities came easily, even naturally, channeled from somewhere or something else. He knew that they could erupt with immense force when under duress. He knew that controlling them was a matter of concentration and conscious restraint more than anything.

He'd never seen Grace dance. He'd never even seen her try to link any kind of art to what she did. She was an engineer: she'd set up experiments for herself and tested her limits during the Wizard War. She had her gauntlets to make sure she didn't go overboard. She'd described the mindset she needed as "awesome mode."

This was... different.

He held onto his hat.

Istvan clawed his way out of the storm and landed

beside him. "I'll wait, then," the ghost said, irritably shaking out wings missing most of their feathers. He glared at Kyra. "What does he think he's doing?"

"She," said Edmund. "Don't distract–"

Kyra made a sound that suggested a trombone fanfare, or something else with the same downwards slide. She flung out both arms straight in front of her, spun around like a top, and then jumped.

Edmund's feet left the ground. His stomach lurched. He tried to catch himself – it felt like he was falling backwards – but there was nothing to grab onto.

He found himself upside-down and accelerating upwards.

"What," said Istvan, somewhere below him.

Edmund checked: he was still holding onto his hat. Good. His cape was blowing up and sideways. A turn of his head revealed the Tyger in a similar predicament, slowly tumbling end over end.

"OK?" called Edmund.

aaaaaaaaaaaaaaaaaasxdf, typed William.

Edmund had to agree with that. He tried to get himself back upright, but miming an astronaut didn't work and he wasn't anything with wings. At least it didn't seem like the blood was rushing to his head. He squeezed his eyes shut, fighting down the urge to throw up.

"Yeah!" shouted Kyra over the howl of the storm. "I told you! Hey, Dr Czernin, go ahead, OK? I got them."

"They're upside-down," said Istvan.

"They are? Oh. Uh."

"I'm all right," lied Edmund. If the Tyger had a response, he couldn't see it.

This was going to be a long trip.

CHAPTER NINETEEN

"I took lessons," Kyra explained, arms held out in a mid-air balancing act, "Miss Murphy's School of Dance. I went every Friday."

Istvan frowned, keeping easy pace with the eye of the storm. They were still going the right way – he had flown up and out three or four times now to check their position – and the entertainment of the hour had turned to idle conversation, shouted over the wind. "The Susurration gave you dance lessons?" he asked.

"No, Miss... yeah. I guess." The Conduit went silent a moment. What looked like half a ship sped by in the whirl of water that surrounded them. "I guess it did lots of things."

Istvan glanced at Edmund, who was now canted over sideways like he was riding a palanquin – the best he'd managed the whole way. The wizard shrugged, looking only slightly ill. "What the Susurration tried to pull on me was ideal," he said, "not perfect."

"I went to school and everything," Kyra continued, sounding much less sure of himself. "I went camping. I went to a space museum, and did a practice mission, and got to be on the astronomy crew. I went to church, and I was in the choir, and..." He trailed off. "Anyway, the dance thing: it helps, is all. Once you get the beat going, it's easy." He waved at the storm. "All I got to do is keep count, now."

"She," Istvan reminded himself. He was to use "she." Think of the matter in terms of a misplaced spirit, rather than a delusion or a sickness. Edmund, at least, was wholly convinced that was what it was. Istvan wasn't so sure, but... oh, he was tired of being corrected.

"What church?" asked Edmund.

"Baptist," Kyra replied.

"That so? I was raised Methodist, myself."

n/a, typed the Tyger, passing by in a slow orbit meant to keep him and his wintry presence at, if not a comfortable distance, at least a more comfortable one from everyone else.

They all looked at Istvan.

He sighed. Of course the Susurration would have omitted certain lessons from her religious instruction. Not a word about how her peculiar mannerisms ought to be stamped out: that would have been distressing, and the Susurration hadn't permitted distress. "Catholic."

Kyra tilted her head. "They do everything in Latin and stuff, right? How was that?"

"Dreadful." Istvan glanced up at the rushing top of the funnel, where the sun peeked just over the edge. It was getting to noon, and they had been travelling for some time; surely they had to be close. Perhaps the fog had finally burned away? "I'm going to go check our heading again."

He pulled up, spiraling around and around with wind that buffeted ever fiercer. The top spun into clouds and spray, water drawn up hundreds of feet in the air and then hurled outwards together with mud and weed and bits of fish. If the level of the lake were still the same as before, he would be surprised. He was almost certain that they had run over at least one finned monster.

The funnel finally spat him out, a true waterspout that roared along at a pace that a motor vehicle might have been proud of. Rain fell around it for almost a half-mile.

Istvan flew higher up above it, trying to get a better view. The fog had cleared, finally, and…

Goodness.

He averted his eyes from the far shore, just to be sure that he wasn't imagining anything, and then looked at it again.

A tower. Toronto had its own tower. Just as Big East had the Black Building, the Greater Great Lakes offered a pale white spire: an immense, ridged, pearlescent structure that might have been carved of marble, with light sparkling off faint, glistening filaments that trailed down off it.

The city itself stretched across the shoreline, mirage-like, its structures difficult to count or hold in mind but always stark against the snowy bulk of a vast advancing sheet of ice: a glacier that Edmund, nor Kyra, had ever mentioned.

The Greater Great Lakes. A fracture zone.

A deep fracture zone.

Istvan dove back towards Kyra's storm. They couldn't make landfall so close to the epicenter. Even approaching what was left of New York City was dangerous; if Toronto had its own tower, it might be the same way.

All this time, he'd thought the Black Building was the only one.

"Edmund!" he called, "Kyra! There's another tower! We have to turn…"

The storm sank lower beneath him. What was Kyra doing? He trimmed his wings closer to his sides, falling faster to keep up. The central eye opened before him, a great whirlpool in the air, and he managed to reach the others just as the storm jerked off course, suddenly wheeling hard left. Edmund zipped past him with a yell, tumbling end over end.

Istvan beat his wings furiously to keep from being slammed into a screaming wall of wind and water. "Kyra! Did you hear–"

A bridge rose before him, water cascading from concrete pillars. An acid green glow lit up the storm. Istvan careened through a row of suspension cables, shot over the broken hull of an oil tanker, and swerved around the sudden jutting face of a clock tower with most of its roof missing. Wreckage, in motion. Ruins, drawn together and crushed into shapes resembling vertebrae, radio antennae for bristles, slabs of glass and concrete for scales.

Green lightning boiled across its surface. A shoulder rolled below, impossibly vast.

The Greater Great Lakes hadn't lost all of its monsters.

Istvan sped through one window and out another and caught up to Kyra. He – she – floated in the central axis of the storm with clenched fists, hunched like a prize fighter, directing its path with great windmilling sweeps. The Tyger and Edmund sped around her like errant moons, turned and tossed like leaves, the former clawing ineffectually at the wind with all four paws and the latter tangled in his cape and hunched into a ball of abject terror: Edmund had never, ever managed well around this much water. That he was still here at all was a miracle.

"Kyra," called Istvan.

The Conduit spun them away from looming claws the size of ships. The storm shuddered. Great splashes came from below, parts of the monster or parts of their own conveyance falling, Istvan didn't know.

They were still losing altitude.

He darted above her. "Fly up," he shouted. "Fly up!"

Kyra flailed desperately at the air, eyes wild.

A shadow fell over the sun. Another roar – somehow even deeper than the storm, crashing, shattering, like an avalanche given voice – thundered through the funnel, louder and louder, splitting it from the top down in a shower of rain and cloud and descending fog.

Kyra clapped her hands over her ears.

She fell. The others fell with her.

Istvan dove after them. They couldn't fly. None of them could fly but him and Kyra, and she'd be hard pressed to survive the impact. Edmund couldn't operate in such blindly disorienting conditions; unless the wizard somehow managed to pull himself together at the last moment, it was up to Istvan, and Istvan couldn't catch anyone.

Only Kyra could do that now.

Istvan grabbed at her wrist. He shouted at her to follow him, though he doubted she could hear him. He did his best to drain off as much fear as possible in so few moments.

Then he pulled up as hard as he could.

The Conduit stared up at him, blinking as skeletal wings beat around her. She was still falling, of course – Istvan couldn't lift anyone, no matter how he tried – but a new clarity sparked in her eyes. Perhaps she was reminded of their second meeting, in the Demon's

Chamber. Perhaps the uselessness of a ghost's wings momentarily slipped her mind. Perhaps he had given her just enough room to breathe.

Or perhaps the jaws rushing down at them were encouragement enough to move quickly.

She closed her eyes. Her lips moved, a silent beat – one, two, three, four – and then she whirled her free hand in a circle and yanked it upwards.

The wind surged. The funnel spun itself back together, collecting fog and foam, tearing pieces off the horror that loomed around them. Kyra's fall slowed, halted, and then reversed, accelerating upwards, straight for the jagged vastness of the descending maw. Istvan looked down just as Edmund and the Tyger shot past him, sucked along in the Conduit's wake. He hadn't known that tigers could make sounds like that.

A wall of water rushed after them. It was as though Kyra were dragging the entire lake into the sky. There were fish in it.

Istvan flew back up after her. "Kyra!"

Kyra made a fist and punched upwards.

Edmund soared through the air. He didn't know how high he was, he didn't know where the others were, and he wasn't sure what had happened. The horizon tumbled around his head. The crash and roar of storms and monsters fell behind him, replaced only by the rush of wind. He couldn't feel his fingers. He clutched his hat in a death grip. His stomach debated whether or not to throw up again, even though there was nothing left to throw up.

Sunlight shone down on him. Sunlight, instead of endless water.

Well, at least he could be sure that the fall wouldn't kill him. It would probably break most of his bones, but it wouldn't kill him. Maybe he'd even fall on land instead of into the lake.

He squinted through fogged goggles. The grey expanse rushing toward him looked like it was probably lake.

Dammit.

He was still here, though, wasn't he? He hadn't run away this time. He'd stuck it out. He'd been useless, sure, but Istvan couldn't tell him off for running away.

He'd stuck it out.

It was... it was something. It was really hard to think.

A sickly yellow-green contrail sliced across the sky, accompanied by distant thuds and booms: artillery fire, where there shouldn't be any. The contrail looped up, then turned a circle and...

Istvan dropped down from above like a fighter jet, barely moving his wings. "Are you all right?" he called.

"No," Edmund said truthfully.

The ghost pointed. "Aim for that beach. We'll meet you there!"

Beach?

Edmund tried to get his eyes to focus. Beach. Right. That was probably that strip of white, where the water stopped. That was a big tower. Had Toronto always had a tower? He pried some fingers off his hat and rummaged around for his pocket watch.

It wasn't there.

His blood went cold. "Istvan—"

The ghost peeled away from him. "The chain, Edmund!"

Edmund looked down. "Oh."

He fished the watch back up from where it dangled, spinning, its chain attached to one of his lower buttons as always. It felt good in his hand. Good old chain, doing more than just looking decorative.

Watch secured, he eyed the beach again. It wasn't far, and was getting closer all the time. It looked like a stretch of yellowish sand, leading up to some bluffs with buildings on top. The skyline hurt to look at.

Well, he had to land somewhere.

He made the proper offerings to exchange the coordinates for there and here–

–and then fell up and sideways and banged his back on rocks and rolled into a snowbank before finally coming to a stop, wishing he'd realized that the beach was both steeper than it looked and not sand. This was going to hurt tomorrow. This hurt now.

"Mr Templeton!" called Kyra.

Edmund coughed. He spat out snow.

"Mr Templeton," Kyra repeated. "You gotta go get Mr Blake!"

No.

Oh, no, no.

Edmund tried to get up and only succeeded in falling onto the battered planks of an old pier. A finned reptile paddled by, eying him curiously.

He was not going back out there again. If the Tyger was stuck in an iceberg, the Tyger was stuck in an iceberg. They could fetch him later. It didn't have to be much later, but later. Besides, that monster was still out there – and probably worse.

No, the lake could have him.

Kyra sloshed through water that was only calf-deep to her. She'd somehow managed to hold onto her souvenir bag, which was impressive under the circumstances. "Mr Thorston–"

"Fine," Edward snarled. He hauled himself upright. Now he was even wetter, and even though the water wasn't cold, it...

...wait. Something wasn't right.

He turned to look up at the bluffs and wished he hadn't. There was something frightening about seeing a glacier looming where there hadn't been one before. Where there had been buildings before. Where, suddenly, there were buildings again, longhouses with racks of fish set up to dry.

"I tried to tell you," called Ivan. The ghost landed beside them in a rush of feathers and choking oil smoke. "We can't stay here," he said. "We're terribly close to that tower, and if it's anything like New Amsterdam–"

Deep fracture zone.

Oh, hell.

Edwin looked around, picked a spot at random further down the coastline, and snapped open his pocket watch. Silver glinted in the sunlight. "Hold on."

It took four jumps before the landscape stopped changing.

By the time they reached what had once been a ferry terminal, he had all of his names straight again, it was snowing hard, something they couldn't see was screaming and circling above them, and he was on the verge of taking them all back home and vowing to never leave his house again. Istvan had been right. They should have stuck to Niagara. Kyra had no idea what she'd gotten them into.

"What about Mr Blake?" the Conduit asked for the third time.

Edmund finally managed to get the magazines burning. "He'll be fine."

"No, he won't."

"Then maybe you shouldn't have dropped him!"

Kyra flinched. She drew her arms to her chest.

The fire flickered: there was a draft coming from somewhere. Edmund blew on the flames, wishing Istvan would come back from checking the perimeter. No one lived here, and if the tile ended up scorched no one would notice. The Greater Great Lakes belonged to monsters. That was it. This was no place for ordinary people, even if they were cultists. William hadn't had to come. He shouldn't have. Wanting to find more of his kind was understandable, but not when his kind was made by Shokat Anoushak. Istvan didn't go around looking for more sundered spirits, did he?

Edmund had told William that he wouldn't let him fall. Edmund had been worse than useless in that vortex.

"Kyra," he said, "do you really have any idea where we're supposed to be going, or was getting here the full extent of your plan?"

The Conduit sat down on one of the cheap metal benches, not looking at him. Snow blew past the piers and passenger bridges of the terminal in a flurry. She muttered something.

"What was that?"

"We're looking for the crystal building," Kyra muttered.

"And where is that?"

No response.

Edmund tossed another magazine on the fire as a metallic scream echoed through the far end of the terminal. Great. He'd asked, earlier that morning, if she knew what she was doing. Oh, sure, she'd said. No problem. We just have to get there.

This was the last time he took a fifteen year-old on their word. This was serious.

"Kyra," he said, "William wanted to help you. He came because he sympathized with your situation. He was not obligated in any way, shape, or form, but he came, anyway."

The Conduit drew her knees up on the chair, hugging them.

"He wanted to help you," Edmund repeated.

"I know." Her voice was a whisper.

Edmund dusted his knees off and stood, reminding himself that getting angry wouldn't solve anything. He should have grilled her more on the details before they left. He wasn't used to working with kids. Kids shouldn't be involved in things like this. "You stay here," he said. "Istvan and I will figure out how to get William back."

Kyra looked uneasily out the window again. "Stay here?"

"We won't be long."

"But–"

"No."

"But I can help!" She pulled her bag off the seat next to her and started to rummage through it. "I can try again! I won't drop anyone this time, I promise!"

"No," Edmund repeated. "Istvan should be back any minute, and–"

"I put this together!" said Kyra. "You can't leave me here! He'll know!"

Edmund frowned. "Who?"

Something slammed into the roof.

Kyra yelped. Edmund reflexively sprang for her, meaning to get her out of the way if something fell. Instead, he received a blunt hammer to the chest – a sudden wind, out of nowhere – and discovered himself airborne for the second time in less than an hour.

"Sorry!" called Kyra. "I'm sorry!"

The light fixtures trembled. Dents punched themselves across its surface, two lines of them spread far apart.

Edmund spent a moment to catch his breath and teleported back to the floor before he hit anything else, redirecting the momentum into a roll that, while undignified, did the job of preventing any further harm to his vitals. Getting back up was harder. That landing on the beach had been murder.

Metal claws sliced through the roof, ripping it up and peeling it back. An angular shape reared stark against the snowfall, matte black, its blunt head and broad wings suggesting a bat made of folded paper. Origami, in the Japanese style. Headlights blazed down at them.

Edmund forced himself back upright. Mockery. He'd never seen one like this before. Was it the same one that had been following them and screaming outside this whole time?

A tooth-rattling scream confirmed that suspicion.

"Go away!" yelled Kyra.

Edmund grabbed at his hat before he lost it and grabbed hold of one of the benches just in case. The windows shattered. Burning magazines blew in all directions. The mockery snapped backwards, its lights cutting a path through the snowfall instead, black wings spread far past the hole it had made. It was huge; mostly wings, but huge.

A ghostly horror shot through the falling glass. Istvan. Where had he been?

"About time," Edmund shouted.

"Wait!" the ghost called. "Wait, it wasn't hostile! Kyra, stop it!"

"I am stopping it," she yelled back.

He held up his hands before him, beating against the wind. "No, stop attacking it!"

Edmund gritted his teeth. This was the same Istvan who had massacred a fortress only two days ago. Now he decided to swing to the other extreme? After the thing had already torn up the roof? "What do you mean it wasn't hostile?"

Istvan landed next to him, crouching and folding his wings, poison streaming from him. "It was circling. I followed it. It didn't land until just now, it didn't do anything when I got closer to it, before, and it's the same kind of mockery I saw crashed with the other one. The two that were fighting each other! I think I've seen it before!" He grabbed at Edmund's shoulder. "If there's some sort of monster war, we should see what this other side is, don't you think?"

"Istvan, the mockeries don't think."

"Well, that's what we thought about the Tyger, wasn't it?"

Edmund thought of William trapped in ice. "And look where that got him."

"Kyra," Istvan shouted again, "Kyra, stop attacking it! Let's see what it does!"

The Conduit glanced from the mockery to them and then back to the mockery. She had managed to get a storm wind rushing up through the hole in the roof, around through the broken windows, and back up again, and now part of the terminal was on fire and the rest was rapidly filling up with snow. Edmund doubted her eyes could get any wider. The band around her head lit with traceries of bright blue.

Istvan drew his knife. "If it tries to attack us, I'll deal

with it," he said to Kyra. He gestured with the blade. "Now come over here next to Edmund and leave the creature be."

The mockery managed to hook a claw around one of the overhead beams, pulling itself down against the wind. That grating shriek tore at Edmund's eardrums. Metal creaked and bent: how long could the roof hold this thing's weight?

"Give it a try, Kyra," Edmund called.

If Istvan was right, and two different kinds of mockery had been fighting each other... well, if worst came to worst, it would be no worse than things were now.

The Conduit cast another fearful glance up at the mockery and then took a step backward. Cinders whirled past her. She winced, putting a hand to the side of her head. It seemed harder for her to stop storms than to start them – maybe there was something about them that wanted to be used, or channeled, just as Grace's innate electricity sought to leap for metal.

"There you are," said Istvan. He started forward as the wind began to flag, one arm raised, interposing himself between Kyra and the creature above her.

Edmund readied his pocket watch.

The wind sputtered out. Kyra staggered. The roof groaned, now thoroughly misshapen. The mockery lowered itself down to peer through the hole it had made, its lights sweeping across Istvan and then to Kyra. It worked its wide angular jaws. Then, folding its wings in that strange paper-like fashion – they were metal, but attached to the rest of its body indistinguishably, as though the entire creature were wing – it pushed itself through the gap.

The claw that settled on the floor was almost as

large as Edmund. It was single, bat-wise. The rest of the mockery that followed filled the terminal, a mass of black angles and shielded antennae, indistinct shapes swirling through a useless cockpit... and he finally realized what it was. Or, rather, what it was modeled after.

A stealth bomber.

No wonder they had never seen one before.

Edmund winced as it turned its brilliant gaze on him. This could go badly very quickly. "Evening," he said, feeling a little foolish.

The mockery opened its mouth.

Lights poured out. Hundreds of tiny, twinkling lights, like fireflies.

Istvan tensed. He'd seen lights like these in the Wizard War: great clouds of them, swirling around and into supposedly safe structures, setting everything that burned alight and melting through barriers with a touch. They weren't something he could kill, or even slow; in those days, barring a ward set up by one of the wizards, the best recourse had been simply to run.

"What are those?" asked Kyra, backing away. Snow billowed through the broken windows, tumbling more sideways than it ought; the flames licking at the corners of the terminal flickered.

The cloud danced around Istvan a moment, and then darted towards the window in a rush like a school of fish. The mockery closed its jaws, raised its head up on its almost nonexistent neck, and made a deep thrumming noise.

That still wasn't an attack. It hadn't attacked anything but the roof, so far. That was vastly different than most mockeries, wasn't it?

"I found your twin," Istvan told it.

It settled itself more comfortably on the tile. It didn't seem to have rear legs: only a rear strut, like a tail but jointed. The mist inside its cockpit roiled, flashing with traceries of green. Its headlights fastened themselves on him.

Istvan glanced at Edmund. The wizard looked as though he intended to bolt at any moment. It had been Edmund's idea to try to capture one of these creatures, not so long ago, and it had been Edmund who killed it; was it so awful to actually try something other than violence? Istvan had done enough killing in recent days. Never mind how much Lucy might want him to go back.

Never mind how much he might want to go back.

He made a show of sheathing his knife in the glare, squinting up at the mockery. He held up his hands. "We're only here for answers," he said.

The headlights snapped off. The glittering cloud swept back around before the mockery, forming a shifting curtain of light that rolled like waves. A circle rotated across it, with a gap in the center – where one mote remained stationary, and three others circled around it.

"Hey," said Kyra.

A shape that very much resembled a pair of jaws closed on the circle. It spun apart, sending the four motes in all directions. The curtain collapsed into a cloud that rushed upwards, the headlights switched back on, and the mockery stared at Istvan expectantly.

He frowned. "Well."

"That's us," said Kyra. "That's us. It's like it was above us, like a weather map. Did you know they could do that?"

"No," said Edmund.

Istvan thought of William and his screen. Pictures? This mockery could make pictures? Had they always been smart enough to do that, or was it only this type?

Kyra set her bag on the floor and dug through it. "I'll make a picture," she said. "I brought markers."

"Make a picture on what?" asked Istvan.

"The floor, I guess. They're permanent."

The mockery turned its gaze towards her, drifting snow glittering in the beam. Istvan couldn't make out much of anything from it: none of the mockeries seemed to have emotions like those of living creatures. He knew that Edmund couldn't take time from them. How intelligent could something like that be?

Diego, too, was a machine…

"Do you understand what I'm saying?" he asked.

It glanced at him, then returned its attention to Kyra as she set about scribbling some monstrosity on the tile.

Istvan looked to Edmund.

The wizard shrugged. "I don't think it does." He nodded at the cloud of lights. "I wonder if this kind might have been the delivery mechanism for the fireswarms. They always did seem to come from somewhere high up."

"But using them to communicate?" asked Istvan.

"Maybe Shokat Anoushak wanted reports."

The mockery emitted a grating shriek and pinned its gaze on Edmund. Its wings shifted and stretched, one crashing into a terminal wall. The cloud above whirled into a tight spin, flaring red with sudden heat. The mists in the cockpit coiled over what seemed to be flashes of teeth and eyes.

"My mistake," said Edmund, backing up.

Istvan stepped between it and him, knowing that it

would do little good but feeling better about it regardless.

Kyra sat up on her knees and waved both arms. "No," she shouted. "Over here. Look over here. Look at this." She pointed at the tile.

The mockery made a sound like popping metal, not taking its headlights from Edmund.

A cold wind buffeted it. "Hey! Look!"

It snapped its head around – and paused.

Istvan tried to get a better look at what Kyra had drawn. Snakes? A sort of... knot of snakes? Perhaps dragons, of the Eastern sort? Two of them had horns. They were terribly crude, hasty single-line figures, tangled into each other and put in a circle with odd markings scribbled beneath it.

A jolt of surprise and dread to his left suggested that Edmund knew what it was.

"Edmund–" Istvan began.

The mockery screamed. It crouched as though to lunge.

Kyra draw a line through the shape.

The mockery stopped screaming.

Kyra scribbled the shape out entirely, then sat back up again. She pointed at Istvan and Edmund, then jerked a thumb at herself, and finally slammed a fist down on top of the mess she had created. "If you got a leader," she said, "take us to it."

CHAPTER TWENTY

Istvan couldn't recall the last time he had ridden anything that flew. He had ridden horses before – long ago, in the Boer War – but he didn't remember ever trying anything similar with a mockery. Standard procedure had been simply to be rid of them. The mockeries had been flying roadblocks, really; not nearly so entertaining as foes that lived.

Well. Things did change.

This mockery even had something like saddles along its metal back: a row of them, shrugged into the metal once it accepted them aboard. Shokat Anoushak's people had been horseman, nomadic raiders, fearsome mounted archers, and she herself was no exception. Perhaps she had designed all of her creatures to carry a rider if need be.

"I hope you realize how lucky it was that you pulled that stunt with a marker," Edmund told Kyra, leaning forward to be heard. The cloud of lights that followed them lit his face with a red-orange glow, keeping the cold at bay and even melting some of the snow as it fell; Istvan imagined even that concession to comfort was welcome.

"All I had was a marker," came the reply. "I thought

it would be OK."

"If you'd used something else, and been a little more precise, it wouldn't have been," said Edmund. "You can't go sketching things like that on a whim."

The Conduit hunched in her seat. "It worked."

"There's power in language, Kyra, and symbols are a kind of language in themselves. They say things. The right ones can even draw down attention from things. The next time you see a building with a fleur-de-lis or some other decoration, think about that."

"Lots of buildings have decorations," Kyra pointed out.

"Exactly," said Edmund.

Kyra glanced back over her shoulder. "You're not saying they're all magic, are you?"

"No." The wizard crossed his arms. "But they could be."

Istvan sighed. All he'd been able to glean about the symbol was that it had something to do with renewal, life, perhaps immortality – Edmund was vague; he said that he'd only found parts of it in his books, that it was only ever depicted in part – and that it, was of course, one of Shokat Anoushak's magics. Sometimes Istvan wished he knew more about all this, but whenever he said anything, Edmund only ever told him that such wishes were dangerous.

Istvan still didn't know what exactly the other man had done to receive his own abilities. Only that it had involved a blood sacrifice, and something had come from a lake, and that the rest was so awful that somehow even trying to recall the details could send Edmund into a panic. Something about gods.

And now Kyra, evidently, had produced concrete

proof that the Shattering had translated some of Shokat Anoushak's knowledge to her intact. It was no wonder that the cults were getting worse.

"Edmund," he said, "while this is all very interesting, I should go back and look for William. This is why we brought him. You and Kyra can see to whatever this is; I'll notify you once I've located him."

The wizard looked back at him. "We're not splitting up."

Istvan thought of the Tyger, abandoned so near to the tower, drifting about with that enormous monster still in the bay. "We already have."

"Let's not make it worse."

"That's a rule," called Kyra. "Never split the party."

"What do you know?" Istvan called back. "I don't like leaving a man behind, is what I don't like, and you're the one who lost him in the first place."

"Well… it's a rule," Kyra replied. "That's all. I didn't make it. We don't have to follow it, either, it's just there."

"We'll get him back," said Edmund.

"How?" asked Istvan.

"Not by you going out yourself. I'm not…" The wizard drew a steadying breath. "Listen, Istvan, you can't move him. If we're doing anything, I'm the one who will have to go out there."

Of course he would. Him or Kyra, though Istvan doubted Kyra had the precision to pick up a living being from outside the funnel without hurting him. They had told the Tyger that they would get him across. No matter what was happening now, they still had an obligation. "Edmund, I don't see how–"

"Istvan, I can't fly. It's a big lake. It's snowing. It's starting to get dark. I don't like leaving him there any more than you do, but I'm not equipped for this. Maybe we should have looked for a boat." The wizard sat back in his saddle, exhaustion seeping from every pore. He sighed. "If you're right about this monster war thing, maybe we can ask for help."

"I'd go if you let me," grumbled Kyra.

"You're not going," said Edmund.

She patted the mockery's broad back. "We could ask the airplane monster."

"It's not as smart as you think it is."

The mockery let out a grating shriek.

Kyra leaned over further to stroke the beast near its cockpit. "It's plenty smart. You're hurting its feelings, Mr Temp–"

They pitched forward. Edmund grabbed at the strap of Kyra's bag, slung over her shoulder, to keep her from falling off. Istvan held on tighter to the bar before him. He wasn't sure that he liked aerial riding at all: he could do all of this much more easily himself, and more comfortably besides. He was probably faster, too.

But it had seemed rude to refuse when the mockery produced three saddles...

The icy ground rushed towards them. The snow had piled so high it was difficult to make out what lay beneath it: buildings, certainly, but split by great flat barriers, a sheet of white pressing forward to crush all in its path.

"Should have brought better gloves," grumbled Edmund.

Istvan wished he could lend anyone his own coat. If not for the lights that yet kept pace, like tiny embers, both Edmund and Kyra would have frozen long ago.

The Greater Great Lakes fracture did have a glacier, after all.

The mockery sped towards its advancing edge, dropping lower and lower. The cityscape that led up to it swept into a sinuous collection of hills and towers, none of them matching, most of them ruined. It seemed to be mostly new construction: rows of identical houses, box stores, church spires here and there, a sprawl rather than the dense skyscrapers of a city center.

One of the rubble-strewn hills shifted, rising like a crocodile peering out of water. Snow banks tumbled. It opened an eye that sputtered green lightning.

"Does Big East have those?" whispered Kyra.

Istvan winced as their mockery let out another scream. "We did."

"What happened?"

"We killed all of them."

"You did?"

"Me? No." Istvan thought of Lucy, reciting titles like "the star-tower beast of dread Chicago," and sighed. "Well, some of them. With help. What did you think those great bloody skeletons were around Providence?"

"Oh," said Kyra.

The city-beast closed its eye again, and relaxed back down under the earth. Istvan had seen them erupt from nowhere, burrowing through solid rock as though it were air, always seeking more structures to add to their form. Were all of the ones in Toronto so... docile? Save the one in the lake, of course.

"Watch the sky," murmured Edmund.

Istvan squinted. Dark shapes moved against the clouds.

The glacier rose towards them. It wasn't a wall so much as a mountain, its slope gradual but inevitable, cut through with fissures. The mockery angled towards one of them: a gash in white, other lights glinting in the advancing darkness. There didn't seem to be anywhere to land.

He tried to peer over the side, but the mockery's wings were too broad. It was almost all wing. There was no side to peer over.

"These weren't the ones who took you?" Edmund asked Kyra.

The Conduit shook her head.

"They all look the same to me," said Istvan, pulling himself back upright. "How would you know?"

"That," Kyra replied, pointing at the glacier. "I don't remember that, and I probably would, right?"

Istvan looked to Edmund.

The wizard shrugged. "Just thought I'd ask."

Istvan thought of the sigil again. Mockeries weren't bright enough to fake hostility, were they? Its reaction to the mention of Shokat Anoushak had seemed quite genuine, for a wholly unnatural creature, but...

They slowed. The roar of engines quieted, then petered out. The mockery's wings fanned, their strange angles and sharp edges stark against the onrushing ice. They were gliding – gliding directly towards a steep cliff riddled with holes, from which light poured like a multitude of stars. Mantis-like shapes scuttled across its surface.

They weren't going to land. Not the way the others were likely expecting.

"Hold on," Istvan called. "Hold on tightly!"

The ice sped towards them. The mockery tilted upwards, wings flaring, stalling just before it struck the surface. Its claws connected with a jarring crack. Flecks of ice showered down, cascading into the glacial canyon below.

Istvan realized he was hovering rather than staying seated like he ought. "All right?" he asked.

Edmund clung to the barred saddle horn, digging in his heels to keep from slipping off. He was missing his hat. No – it was crushed down and folded between his arms, evidently not worth the trouble to keep on his head. "Great," he said, which was a lie.

"I'm OK," said Kyra, in the same predicament.

The mockery loosed a low hiss and began pulling itself across the cliff face.

Edmund was done with flying. He didn't care how it was done: if he didn't have to fly ever again, anywhere, he'd be happy. He wasn't even supposed to be here. None of them were. His job was at Niagara, not deep in a foreign fracture zone that still crawled with monsters.

And did it crawl. Did it ever.

The mockery took them to the nearest opening in the cliff face, clambering halfway inside and then pausing just long enough for Edmund to pry his fingers off the saddle horn and get both himself and Kyra to what passed for solid ground. The roar as it took off again shook the cave. The lights – and their heat – went with it.

A bare tunnel awaited them.

Istvan alighted beside him, the thunder of his presence probably doing the ice no favors. It was so cold that Edmund could barely make out the smell of poison. Not that the ghost had to worry about anything like that: Istvan didn't care about cold, didn't care about heights, and didn't care about hunger or exhaustion. Istvan was probably having a grand old time.

"Cheater," Edmund muttered.

Istvan turned empty eye sockets on him. "What?"

"Nothing." Edmund looked to Kyra, who was standing

some distance off, shivering. She'd managed to hold on to that bag, through everything. "Kid. You wouldn't happen to have any of those snack bars still on you, by any chance?"

The Conduit blinked at him. Her breath steamed before her. "The food?"

"The food," Edmund confirmed. "Good idea, by the way."

She looked away, seeming embarrassed. She set the bag on the ground and began rummaging through it, still shivering.

Edmund unbuttoned his cape and shrugged off his overcoat. He offered it to her. "Here."

"What? No, no. I'm good."

"It'll make me feel better," Edmund said.

"Well…" She pulled out a snack bar, looked at it, then held it up. "Trade?"

"Deal."

Edmund took a bite as Kyra put on his coat. Almonds and chocolate. He hadn't had chocolate since…

He checked the packaging. Far too many sixteen-letter words for his liking.

He shrugged and took another bite. Preservatives were a wonderful thing.

Istvan heaved a sigh. "Shall I go on ahead?"

Edmund pretended that the cold wasn't bothering him. "No. We're right behind you. Kyra, how's the coat?"

The Conduit finished buttoning up the front. It seemed to fit, more or less, except for the fact that the kid was almost a foot taller than Edmund and the hem didn't reach as far as it should. "It's OK. Pretty warm."

Edmund nodded. "Good."

Istvan sighed again and started for the tunnel. He was

wearing his military greatcoat, now – an elaborate number with embroidered hems and the same flower insignia along the collar as his usual jacket. After all his time in the Alps, the glacier had to almost feel like home to him.

The tunnel wound down, gently, curving side to side as if it had been bored by a giant worm, slippery in the center where other feet must have trod. Edmund held up his telephone for light, however faint. The bluish glow of the screen did nothing to make the place seem warmer.

"No welcoming party," muttered Istvan.

Edmund didn't answer. One procession to a throne room had been enough.

His screen blinked. He checked it. Power low. Great.

"Hey," said Kyra. The yellow beam of a pocket flashlight blazed before them – then sputtered, and died. Kyra frowned, and shook it. The light didn't return.

"You tried," said Edmund. "Working batteries are a trick."

"What else do you have in there?" asked Istvan.

Kyra shoved the dead flashlight back into the bag. "Took everything I could find. It's the end of the world, right? It's what you're supposed to do. Why didn't you guys pack anything?"

Edmund didn't have the heart to tell her that every journey, when you could teleport, wasn't far from safety and resupply. He hadn't packed extra anything in years. Come to think of it, he hadn't gone on any kind of long-term mission for as long as he could remember. That had been more Istvan's field, and a ghost wouldn't remember to bring food.

"Overconfidence," he said.

Kyra slung the bag back over her shoulders with a huff.

Edmund wondered if he shouldn't head back to get another coat... but a bare tunnel wasn't the best marker, and he didn't want to miss a return teleport in the middle of enemy territory. He didn't usually mean to stick around when things took a turn for the worse. Always easier to leave, regroup, and come back later. Always easier to run.

Istvan was right.

They pressed on as the glacier cracked and shifted around them. Edmund's battery power fell lower and lower. The cold settled into his limbs and stayed there. He couldn't feel his nose.

Finally, firelight flickered across the ice.

The tunnel opened into a broad, low-roofed chamber with rounded walls. A bonfire burned in the center of it, propped atop a slab of concrete. Water dropped from the ceiling. Heaps of plastic tubs and packing crates lay stacked atop each other, coated in frost, numbers scrawled clumsily across their sides.

Near one of three other entrances crouched a blue-furred cross between tiger and bear. It was sorting a collection of scrap wood into two piles.

"William?" asked Edmund.

The beast turned, crouching with a growl. One of its ears was torn off. Icicles dripped from its muzzle. Not William. Kyra hadn't been kidding about seeing his kind before. It seemed William *was* from up north, after all.

Edmund held up his hands, shifting unobtrusively closer to the bonfire. "Sorry. We've lost a friend."

Yellow eyes shifted to Istvan.

Edmund glanced over. The ghost had killed who knew how many of Shokat Anoushak's creatures during the Wizard War. Had word of him made it all the way here?

Istvan removed his hand from his knife handle. "We should like to talk," he said. "One of the fliers brought us here. The great angled black one. We're from Niagara." He glanced back up the tunnel. "We... have some questions."

"We're here to stop Shokat Anoushak," Kyra chimed in.

"Quiet," Istvan hissed.

The beast paused a moment, tilting its head. It looked back and forth between Istvan and Kyra. Then, it bared its teeth. It reached out a great paw, flexing its claws to full extension.

K, it scratched into the floor.

Friendly. Not disturbed by the notion of stopping its creator. All good signs. It was about time anything started looking up.

Edmund rubbed his hands together. Maybe soon he'd be able to feel them again. "Is there someone we can talk to?"

y

"Thanks."

np

The beast shoved aside one of its piles of wood and ambled towards one of the other entrances, jerking its head.

"What did that last one mean?" whispered Istvan.

Edmund shrugged.

"They're rebels," breathed Kyra. "Monster rebels."

"We'll see," Edmund told her, trying not to sniffle as his nose defrosted. He called after the departing beast, "Mind if we warm up a little, first?"

A shrug.

Edmund edged as close to the fire as he dared. Maybe he could make himself a torch. Anything was better than nothing. Were all the northern monsters cold-loving? Or, if they were hiding here against their will... did that mean this was one side of a civil war, or a band of refugees?

Was Shokat Anoushak back already?

He shook his head as the bottom dropped out of his stomach, fighting back fluttering terror. Later. Find out what they knew. Don't get ahead of himself. Besides, if the Immortal was back already, it would be a damn sight more obvious.

Wouldn't it?

"All right?" he asked Kyra.

"They'll help us get William back," she replied. She gave a firm nod, moving closer to the fire. "If he's one of them, they'll definitely help us."

"We don't know who he was," said Istvan, keeping his voice low. He gripped his bandolier, watching the waiting beast with narrowed eyes. "He doesn't know who he was."

Edmund looked around for a length of wood he could use. "Maybe they will."

A mansion lay buried beneath the ice.

Edmund cringed as they emerged beneath the vast dome that sheltered it, ton after ton of glacier pressing down over their heads. The building was Victorian, enormous, a sprawling estate of narrow windows and long halls. Fires burned along the advancing edge of the ice, set along what had likely once been magnificent gardens and was now nothing more than a collection of dry hedge remnants and the glittering skeletons of trees. What was keeping it all up, he couldn't imagine.

Swarms of glittering lights milled in the air, drifting like stars beneath the dome.

<Do you suppose they're hiding?> asked Istvan, in German, casting a glance at the beast padding before

them. <Is this a refuge?>

Edmund shrugged, unknowing. This was a more elaborate refuge than most. He didn't think the Twelfth Hour could have pulled off something like this.

Their guide paused before the mansion stairs. It jerked its head at the doors above them, then sat. A fine sheen of frost crackled across the ground.

"Thanks," said Edmund.

The beast shook its head.

"Can you use the lights?" asked Kyra, pointing at the motes drifting above them.

Another shake of the head. A claw scraped a word into the frost:

go

Edmund glanced at Istvan. This was about as deep into enemy territory as they could get, if this went bad. And getting back... well, they'd already left William floating for over four hours. He hadn't seemed worried about suffocating, but the less time he spent in the harbor, the better. If only it hadn't started to get dark. If only it wasn't so cold.

If only it hadn't had anything to do with the lake.

"I'm going back if they aren't helping," said Istvan. He started up the stairs.

"Sorry," muttered Kyra.

Edmund didn't respond. There wasn't anything left to say that he hadn't said already. He followed Istvan up and got the door open.

A swarm of lights met them, glowing with welcome heat. The mansion's furnishings seemed intact, aside from some upholstery damaged by water, and if he didn't look out of any of the windows, Edmund wouldn't have known it sat under a glacier in the first place. There was even a fire lit.

"This is even nicer than your house, Mr Templeton," said Kyra.

Edmund squinted at a china cabinet. "It's much nicer than my house."

"Hello?" Istvan called.

The lights whirled around the three of them and then darted off through a far doorway, down a broad hall.

"Well," said Istvan. "You'd think that they could come to us."

Edmund shrugged. He didn't even know what "they" were. Finding a community of Shokat Anoushak's creatures was strange enough. Expecting anything seemed ungracious.

The mansion was, despite first appearances, far from deserted. A stag paced down one of the halls. Stone lions guarded a conservatory. A trio of golden birds, with sparkling trains like a peacock, stood on a dining table, pulling apart a chunk of oily meat. The lights darted everywhere, in and out open windows, turning slow circles around chandeliers. Footsteps sounded on the floors above them. Snorting and scuffling came from behind closed doors.

No speech. None of the beasts could form so much as a single word.

It was eerie. Big East had no surviving creatures from the Wizard War: anything that appeared came from outside, or arose from the influence of the surrounding spellscars. All of the originals – those not already killed in the fighting – had died at Providence with their master, leaving nothing but ash and glass.

Would they have formed a society of their own, given the chance?

The lights led them up a spiral staircase, funneled

into a thin stream, and sped through a pair of tall double doors, one of them cracked slightly open.

Oh, boy. Edmund took a breath and led the way inside.

The room must have been a study, once. Across the back stretched a full wall of glass, looking over the gardens and the ice looming above. In the center, the lights danced around a larger-than-life sculpture of an owl, stiff and crude, carved from dark wood, its eyes blank and staring circles of mother-of-pearl. Ash and shavings lay heaped on the floor around it.

Edmund looked closer. No, there were bones in there, too. Most of them much smaller than human. Most of them.

Istvan drew up to one side of him, warily. Kyra hung back: the abundance of strange beasts was making her more and more nervous, despite her initial enthusiasm, and Edmund couldn't blame her.

Neither one said anything, so Edmund broke the silence first. He was the wizard here, after all. He faced the owl and took off his hat. "Evening."

The owl stared at him, the oily sheen of its eyes seeming to shift color.

He tried a smile. "I'm Edmund Templeton, the Hour Thief. We're from the Twelfth Hour, down south, and we're here to investigate rumor of a cult. We were hoping you could help us."

"Ain't a rumor," Kyra muttered.

"Isn't."

"Edmund," Istvan huffed as the lights drew closer.

Edmund wasn't sorry. The kid had to learn proper grammar someday. Best to start sooner rather than later. "These are my friends," he continued. "Dr Istvan Czernin and–"

Glowing motes met wooden feathers. The owl blazed into a pillar of fire.

"Woah," Edmund shouted, instinctively, jerking backwards and holding out a hand to shield Kyra. The heat seared his eyes. The ash billowed into a white cloud, settling on every surface. He blinked through fogged goggles as skeletal wings beat against the fire… which then spread wings of its own.

"You are the storm that bypassed harbor," came a crackling voice, neither male nor female, harsh and rasping.

"Harbor?" Istvan demanded. "We weren't looking for–"

The owl's eyes glowed within the flames. "None brave the north so long as harbor remains. This is our defense, and our prison."

Edmund coughed. Harbor. Not harbor, Harbor.

The monster in the lake. It had a name.

"We had a reason," he said. He turned to get Kyra to the fore. The kid knew her Shokat Anoushak stuff. If any time was a good time to explain things in gruesome detail – or show off that symbol again, preferably with a few intentional errors – it was now. He looked around. "Kyra?"

The doors swung slowly on their hinges.

"I'll find her," said Istvan. The ghost shot through the doors, half-airborne, his feet barely touching the floor.

Edmund was left alone with the owl. It folded flaming wings, crouching on its perch.

"So," he said. "Can I get a name?"

CHAPTER TWENTY-ONE

The Conduit hadn't gone far. Perhaps she feared running into another of the beasts: one of many prowling the mansion, unpredictable, sometimes indistinguishable from decoration. They had captured her, she claimed. If not these, then others. It had to be a trial to endure their presence now, friendly or not.

Even so, that was no excuse to run.

"Kyra, you can't leave," Istvan informed one of the couches in the next room over.

"Ain't leaving," came a voice from behind it, where she had somehow wedged herself. She seemed fond of small spaces, which was odd for such a large and lanky frame.

Istvan sighed. "Get out from there."

"No."

A strange thrumming came from the door. Istvan glanced over his shoulder. One of the golden birds peeked around the frame. He tried to shoo it away. It stayed put.

Well, at least Kyra couldn't see it. He crouched near where she had hidden. "You were excited to meet these creatures, weren't you? You know that they're odd. You're the one who asked to see their leader, remember?"

"But..." she began.

"What if he's offended?" Istvan asked.

Kyra burst into tears. "I don't know! I don't know! I messed up everything and now we're stuck under a glacier and they're everywhere, and if they haven't beaten her yet how are we supposed to do anything?"

Well. This was inopportune.

Istvan checked to see if the bird was still there. It was. Now there were two of them. He held up a wing, spreading it across the gap between couch and wall for privacy's sake. "Kyra–"

"They got that big thing in the water, and they still can't win?"

Istvan grimaced. They couldn't afford this right now. The proper time to fall apart was after the crisis was over, not while trying to determine precisely what it was and certainly not while in enemy territory. The Conduit had been doing so well for her age, too – she hadn't destroyed anything, yet, and that was nearly a miracle.

Granted, no one had been expecting the sculpture to set itself alight and speak. Edmund could take it in stride, of course, but Kyra was new to this business. Istvan had dealt with young people before. Not this young, usually, but... sometimes.

"Remember," he said, "this was only an expeditionary jaunt. None of us knew what we would find."

"What if William's dead? It's my fault if he's dead!"

"We don't know that yet. You yourself wanted to see if these beasts would help us. You can still do that, you know."

Silence.

Istvan tried to make out better detail in the tumult: fear, of course, but of what shade and seasoning? It was so much easier to hold conversations like these when he knew the trouble. Was it… shame?

Oh, it slipped away – whatever else the Shattering did, it seemed to tug impulses in a hundred different directions, magnifying common woes into overpowering tides and splitting confusion into self-canceling paralysis. To be young, and so damaged; perhaps Edmund had a point in humoring her eccentricities. *Her*.

Though that did seem to be one of the few things she was certain about…

"There was a burning one there, too," Kyra mumbled.

Istvan frowned. "There?"

"The other place. Toronto. It asked me things. It pulled stuff out of my head."

Ah. Well. That would make the owl creature even more off-putting.

"I shall make certain it doesn't try anything," Istvan said, trying to sound as reassuring as possible. "And if it does, I expect that it won't for long." He reached a hand towards Kyra's hiding place. "Come along, now."

Something in the Conduit's tenor changed. "Could you kill it?"

Istvan found himself wondering if the owl had a hollow inside or if it were solid wood. Or was the creature proper the fire itself? "I don't know. Possibly."

"Would you? If you could, I mean. You said you killed tons of people."

He had. So what if he had? So what if it were less murder and more slaughter, so great was the disparity between what he could do and what an ordinary man could do – that it wasn't fair at all, that as much as he told himself that they had been soldiers, that they fought well, that they died bravely, they had still died and it had been easy to kill them.

Kyra still wasn't coming out from behind the couch. They couldn't afford this. Edmund had to be wondering where they were. Edmund hadn't produced any results on his own. Breaking the siege was what Kasimir had asked in exchange for Niagara. Istvan had wanted somewhere to keep Kyra that wasn't the Demon's Chamber. Magister Hahn had been adamant that Edmund find something, and find it quickly. Nowhere else could have been won in so short a time.

Niagara was a prize, and now it was theirs. That was what mattered. If Istvan had been chained, he couldn't have solved that problem, now could he? He would have had to think of something else. He would have... he would have thought of something else.

What was that idiom about a hammer?

Istvan's outstretched hand was fleshless and bloody. He couldn't manifest wings in any other state. "Kyra," he said, "Edmund needs you to help him negotiate."

She didn't respond. A sniffle suggested that she was finished with her outburst, at least. Oh, she ought to have stayed at Barrio Libertad. Istvan and Edmund could have done this themselves much more easily, save perhaps for the journey across the lake, which would have taken much longer. Perhaps the encounter with the bat-like mockery may have gone differently, as well. It was too late to speculate.

"Kyra," Istvan repeated. "See this through, hm? I know that we haven't always been the best of allies, but in that room, with that flaming creature, I'll be right behind you." He thought back to their unfortunate second meeting in the Demon's Chamber, and sighed. "With my knife ready, if that helps."

The couch shifted, scraping an inch or two away from the wall. Istvan stood as the Conduit rose from behind it, all elbows, not looking at him. She re-buttoned the top button of Edmund's coat. The remaining bag she slung over her bony shoulder with a clatter. The birds at the door chirruped and fled.

"Sorry," she said.

"No, I understand," replied Istvan, thinking of the young men and, occasionally, women he'd met in Indochina, fighters no older than Kyra herself. More often than not they hadn't fared well, either. He'd done his best.

Kyra grimaced. "You'd be fine whatever happens. You're a ghost. You're bulletproof. They can't kill you."

"I wasn't always."

"You are now."

It was true. It had been true for a long, long time. Istvan shrugged. "That does help, yes," he conceded. He waved a hand towards the door. "Let's find Edmund, hm?"

Kyra wiped at her eyes, jaw set. "Don't tell him."

"I won't."

She stumped off.

By the time Istvan saw her back to the room with the owl, Edmund had retreated to the far side of the room and the flames had blazed nearly to the ceiling: a great bonfire in the shape of the statue that was, those huge pale eyes swiveling in a smoldering head at every motion. Heat haze shimmered across the windows. It was blinding.

"That wasn't us," Edmund repeated. He had taken off his hat and looked ready to remove his jacket, as well. His hair stuck to his forehead, sheened with sweat.

"Even if it was, we're not looking to do it again."

"Not looking?" spat the fiery owl, its voice hissing sparks. "Would you? Could you?"

"I don't know. You'd have to ask Diego. He's the one who built the weapon, and he's the only one who knows how he did it. We're not here to destroy you or your people." The wizard looked over at Istvan and Kyra, relief breaking over his face. "There you are!"

"Yeah," said Kyra, faintly. She leaned against the frame of the door, face turned from the heat. "Yeah, we're back."

"We're all right," Istvan offered.

Edmund nodded. "Good." He looked to the owl. "Marat, this is Kyra Stewart. She's your storm. We're here on her initiative."

Marat hunched its head on its shoulders, fluffing burning feathers as its eyes remained blank and unblinking. It stared at Kyra.

She swallowed. She tried to say something, but no words emerged. She shrank away, her breath coming harder than before, her limbs trembling.

Istvan set a hand against her back. She flinched. She could have retreated further, backed up through him... but the cold of his touch seemed to be enough, and he was glad for that. "You aren't alone," he said.

Kyra wiped at her forehead. The heat was getting to her already.

"We had a rough trip," Edmund explained to Marat.

The creature's talons dug glowing cracks into its perch. "Why return?" it hissed, its gaze still fixed on Kyra. "The south is a haven for your kind. You are no exile. There is no place for you here."

The south? Big East? Any true haven for humans

would have been anywhere but a fracture zone – out past the spellscars, in the sparse expanses, where most had fled and relative normality yet reigned. Places like Tornado Alley, where the most anyone had to worry about were storms.

Though… Big East was the only fracture zone cleared of monsters…

Istvan looked to Edmund, the shock of a new idea rattling in his mind. Big East had no monsters. If the creatures of the Greater Great Lakes knew that, and knew that Shokat Anoushak was killed there, and didn't know how it happened, why, they must be terrified of their southern neighbors. "Edmund, is that why they haven't invaded?"

"Hsst," Edmund replied, motioning for him to keep his words to himself and glancing nervously at Marat.

The great owl ignored them both. It waited for Kyra, its flames lapping at the edge of its ash-piles, staring as only a creature with no eyelids could.

Kyra mumbled something.

"Speak," ordered Marat.

"'m here for her," Kyra said. She stared down at the floor a moment longer, took a breath, and then tried to make eye contact with the fires. "I'm here for the Immortal. She's coming back, and I'm here to find her and kill her."

Embers showered through the air. "You?"

"Yeah. Me. And these guys. They're a big deal." She pointed at Edmund. "That's the Hour Thief. He fought her in the Wizard War. He's magic, he has super-speed, and he knows all her weaknesses, because he studied everything she left." She jerked a thumb behind her. "And this is Doctor Czernin. He's unbeatable. He can come back from anything, and fly, and kill entire armies."

"I'm also a surgeon," Istvan added, feeling that her assessment wasn't quite fair.

"Yeah, he's that, too." She indicated her headband. "And this is from Barrio Libertad. They're the ones who vaporized her with a superweapon. It's pretty neat. They can see you right now."

Marat jerked backwards on its perch.

Istvan stared at the headband. "They what?"

Edmund buried his face in his hands.

"It was just in case," said Kyra, as though it were the most obvious thing in the world. She squinted at Marat. "So. We got all that, but we ain't here to fight you unless you're with her, and your flying monster didn't seem like it was. We need some help. We lost someone. Could you send one of your airplanes to go look for him?"

"Leave," came the reply.

Kyra stared at it, bravado faltering. "But–"

Marat snapped its wings open, blazing to twice its former size. Ash billowed around it. The curtains caught fire. "Leave this sanctuary!"

Kyra covered her eyes. Blue traceries flashed across the surface of her headband. Edmund had said it was for her powers. He said she'd told him it was for her powers. It was supposed to help her control them, just as Grace Wu's gauntlets guided her blows. Did it, really? Had it all been a ruse?

The Conduit turned, eyes wild.

"Don't–" Istvan began.

She dashed through him, one arm held before her, swinging around the doorframe and slamming her back on the wall that now separated her and the inferno. She slid down against it, breathing hard.

Edmund hurried around to them, coughing.

<I thought you asked about the headband,> Istvan said, in German. Edmund was so paranoid about Barrio Libertad; he had, surely.

<I didn't,> Edmund replied.

<Why–>

<I made assumptions. You make sure Kyra doesn't take off.> The wizard turned to Marat, switching back to English. "Our friend is one of yours," he said. "A blue bear-tiger with breath like ice. He fell in the lake when Harbor attacked us."

Marat tilted its head.

Edmund put his hat back on. "We'll be looking for him. Thank you for having us."

The owl folded its wings, swiveling its head to the other side. It shifted on its perch. "Come," it said. "Show us."

Istvan thought of what Kyra had said. The other burning creature hadn't only asked questions. It had "pulled stuff" out of her head. That didn't sound like conventional interrogation. "Edmund," he began.

"I'll be fine," the wizard replied. He took a breath, coughed again, and then approached the fire.

Marat lifted a glowing talon.

"This sucks," said Kyra.

"You can't make threats like that in the middle of a negotiation," Istvan replied, "and you can't reveal things like that without telling your allies first. How long has he been watching? I know that you don't trust us, and there is no reason you ought, but we came all this way, and perhaps they might have told us more if you hadn't gone immediately to the last option."

Edmund watched the ghost pace back and forth across the ticket-taker's office, a blurry figure trailing flickered wings. Everything hurt. His vision still wasn't quite straight. Cold from the ferry terminal's broken windows seeped under the door. They had been here for almost a half-hour now, after an uncomfortable return ride from the glacier, and only now did it feel like the lava was almost finished threading its way through his brain.

Marat, and all of its ilk, had been Shokat Anoushak's information gatherers. Her mappers. Her interrogators. It all depended on where they were, and what form they took. When nothing more was needed, they'd burned evidence to the ground. No one had ever thought the glowing lights were anything more than clouds of quick and easy arson.

Kyra sat slumped at the desk, arms crossed on it, her chin propped atop them. She still wore her headband; which still had no obvious lens or anything else that would indicate its additional function. Possibly its only function.

"There's... gradation, Kyra," Istvan continued. Barbed wire wrapped itself around the nearby chairs, bloodied and coated in rust. "You have to be patient for diplomacy. You don't say all of it all at once!"

"Yeah," the Conduit said. "Sure."

"Kyra, I know you were frightened, but–"

"Doctor, you're telling me I did bad? I ain't never killed anyone. I didn't get you burned up, and I didn't lock anyone up, and if I said I had a camera, you'd have said to get rid of it."

Edmund closed his eyes and rubbed at his temples, trying to clear his mind of jumbled fires. Marat hadn't been kidding around when it asked where, how, where,

where, who… He hoped it had only taken what it needed to find William. He had a feeling it hadn't stopped there.

Didn't matter now. It was getting harder to keep secrets by the day.

"It isn't the camera," he told Kyra. "It's who gave it to you."

"Mr Espinoza was nice," she said.

"Does the thing actually help regulate your powers?" Edmund asked.

Kyra didn't reply.

Edmund opened his eyes again. The Conduit had her head laid sideways on her arms and was glaring out of the service window into the wrecked lobby, where snow fell through the hole in the roof. The fires from earlier had gone out long ago.

"You said you'd help me," she said.

Istvan came to a halt. "We are!"

"No, you're not. You keep asking me to do things, and I try to do the things, and then when they don't work, you tell me I did bad. I don't know how to do this stuff, OK? That's why I got you guys! You're supposed to be the best at this and then you don't do anything!"

Edmund glanced at Istvan. The ghost threw his hands up.

Edmund pinched the bridge of his nose. What did the kid want? She'd had a plan – she said she had a plan – and so they'd let her run with it. Let Kyra give it a shot her way. It was the least they could do to make up for how they'd treated her earlier. Edmund was never going to live that down.

"What do you want us to do?" he asked.

Kyra sighed. She made a fist, pounding it slowly against the service window. "I don't know. Make a plan, or something. I don't even know what you guys can do or what all your deal is – you don't explain yourselves, ever, and you keep talking in German or something when you don't want me to hear. Don't you have… you know, the other guys? The Twelfth Hour? Why aren't they helping?"

Istvan leaned against the closed door to the office. "We haven't told them."

The Conduit sat up. "What? Why?"

Edmund tried to think. There were a lot of reasons. Good reasons. The kid's claim hadn't seemed credible, at first. She was Shattered, after all: that was a medical issue. It made people erratic. No reason to act without more information, so he hadn't.

Then the situation had blown up in his face. Barrio Libertad got involved. Mercedes had her say. Triskelion happened. No, Edmund had let Triskelion happen, and it hadn't just happened – it was Istvan, doing what he did best. Istvan, freed and told he should rule instead of obey.

And then Mercedes pretended she didn't know what they'd done. As long as they had Niagara, it didn't matter. *You're training more wizards, Mr Templeton. I expect results. No more excuses.*

"You aren't supposed to be here," he said.

Kyra looked away.

"I know Diego released you. I know that this is important. But he let you go against the will of his own people, and we aren't supposed to have you, either." Edmund ran a hand through his hair. "We – I – should have given you to Barrio Libertad in the first place, and it was a mistake that I didn't."

"They didn't believe me," she mumbled.

"That's fine."

"If you do, why ain't you throwing everything you got at it? Why ain't you doing everything you can? She's coming back, Mr Templeton. You fought her. You know what she does! Why haven't you told anyone else?"

Istvan pushed himself away from the door. "Because you're damaged!"

She flinched.

Edmund held up a hand. Not now. This wasn't going to help. "Stop it."

"No." Istvan stepped towards the Conduit, form flickering. "Kyra, you must understand. I know that the Susurration made you think that the world is fine, and fair, and reasonable, but it isn't."

Oh, hell.

Edmund wobbled to his feet. "Istvan–"

"Let me finish," roared the specter. He turned back to Kyra, expression hard. "Kyra, you are a child. You are a Negro. You are ill, and don't know to be ashamed of it. You are tall, and loud, and dark, and you insist on being what you aren't, and you frighten people – and then you can go and conjure those storms, and destroy whatever you like."

Kyra knotted her hands in her lap. She looked at the floor.

This wasn't going to end well. This wasn't going to end well at all.

"That's enough," Edmund said, barring the other man's way.

Istvan stepped through him.

"Kyra, no one knows what to do with you," he continued. "No one knows where you ought to be. You haven't even tried to hide! You arrived all of a sudden, shouting about Shokat Anoushak, wild and Shattered and wearing that bloody dress, and that is unforgivable. That is more frightening than your storms." He leaned closer, setting a hand on the desk beside her. "If you keep carrying on as you have, the world will destroy you. If you understand nothing else, understand that."

Kyra balled her hands into fists.

"I'm sorry," said Istvan. "That's how it is. That's how it always has been."

He turned. He glanced at Edmund, and it was a strange glance, not apologetic but not quite angry, either. The ghost crossed his arms and leaned back against the door, staring off into the snow.

"Great," said Edmund.

Kyra got to her feet. "That's it?" she said. "That's what you're worried about?"

Edmund sighed. Now Istvan had gone and done it. There were things you didn't say, and you didn't say them for a reason.

He rubbed at his face. He wished his head would stop hurting.

Kyra looked back and forth between him and Istvan. The ghost wouldn't meet her eyes.

"That's stupid," she said.

"That's how it is," Istvan replied.

"Look outside! If that's how it is, you're OK with how it is out there, too? Full of monsters? All the buildings falling down?" She waved at the ticket window, the hole in the roof, the snow drifting over the remnants of Shokat Anoushak's sigil. "How is the world anything like it was when you got people who can summon storms, and when there's wizards and magic, and when anything like that old world ain't even real?"

"There have always been wizards," Edmund muttered.

"Yeah, whatever! They won't help me because I'm black? Or because I'm a girl? Or because I'm tall? That's stupid!"

"Kyra, it isn't that. It's—"

She threw her hands up. "OK, so it's all of it. And I sometimes wreck things. But you haven't even tried talking to the Twelfth Hour? You haven't told them where we're at?"

Edmund sat down again. He rested his elbows on his knees.

He didn't know. He didn't know anymore. Did it matter what she was? Maybe. He might have knocked her around less if she hadn't seemed older, if she wasn't so dark, if he hadn't been under the impression that he was facing a grown man who happened to be black. None of that was her fault.

It was over. He didn't want to talk about this.

"We were trying it your way," he said.

"I didn't want to make it worse," Istvan said.

Kyra stared at them. "Whatever," she finally said. "Will you tell the other wizards now?"

Edmund let out a breath.

"I got this on camera," she added.

The rest of the breath came out as a wheeze. Damn Diego. Should have known. All of Barrio Libertad was probably watching, given how the fortress felt about privacy. Grace, too. She had to know everything, now.

Edmund eyed the headband. He couldn't ask Kyra to take it off. They'd see that, too, and it would seem like he was hiding something.

"I'll tell Mercedes," he said.

"Who?"

"Magister Hahn. Leader of the Twelfth Hour."

Istvan sighed. "The wizard president."

"I'll drop you and Istvan at Niagara," Edmund continued, "and we'll go from there. I won't mention last night. You weren't supposed to be in New Haven." He thought of the disaster averted, the blessed fact that his house was still standing. "Besides, that flyer Istvan found might still be–"

A shriek rattled the building. Grating. Metallic. The roof in the lobby beyond groaned and buckled, the blunt head of the stealth bomber creature nosing through it and shining its blinding gaze down at them.

Kyra bolted for the door. "Finally!"

Istvan jerked out of her way as she pulled it open and dashed through. The bomber swiveled its lights towards her, pulling itself through the hole in the roof and setting one great claw and then the other on the broken tile.

Edmund got up. "Istvan, what the hell were you thinking?"

The ghost straightened his bandolier. "You can't pretend that the boy won't suffer. If he'd been raised in reality, he'd know that." He watched Kyra run up to the bomber. "You learn early."

Edmund frowned. Istvan complained about his own appearance quite a bit, but had nothing to worry about on that front, and he'd insisted more than once that the Twelfth Hour locking him away was completely justifiable. What leg did he have to stand on, saying that?

Except… in the cable car…

No. No, that opened up too much trouble. Too much thinking. That had probably been nothing more than the violence talking. Like a drug. It got to him, and made him strange, like he'd been acting all the way to Triskelion and into the siege. He'd done it during the Wizard War, too.

"What?" asked Istvan.

Edmund shook his head. "Never mind."

Istvan grabbed his shoulder. "What did I say?"

"It was about Beldam," Edmund lied, though Beldam had come up in the same awkward conversation and so he hoped there was enough truth to it to make the claim seem sincere. "I'll tell you later."

He looked out the window again. A very familiar blue-furred figure was disembarking the plane, accompanied by a swarm of glowing lights. "Oh, good. They found William."

Istvan followed his gaze. "Ah."

That had been fast. Shockingly fast. Those lights – Marat? – could probably cover miles of ground, searching for someone, and then the airplane creature could pick up whatever they found. The Twelfth Hour needed a system like that.

Now the only risk was whether William would hold the long wait against him.

Edmund headed into the lobby. "William. How are you holding up?"

The beast turned. Ice sheened his fur, a brittle coating that melted in the glittering glow surrounding him before re-freezing moments later. He held up his screen. The glass was cracked, and no words appeared on it. He shook his head.

"Here," said Kyra. She handed him the marker.

William shook his head, growling. He swept aside the snow before him with a great paw, then watched as ice crept over the tile in its place.

"That marker isn't going to stick," Edmund said.

"Oh," said Kyra.

"Carve in the ice," Istvan said, arriving behind him. "That's what the other one did." He took out his knife, knelt, and scraped a gouge in the surface to demonstrate.

The Tyger nodded.

"Sorry about the wait," Edmund told him as he set about clawing clumsy words into the ice sheet, knowing that the apology alone wouldn't be enough for leaving him to bob helplessly in the lake for those long hours.

A shrug.

Kyra patted the bomber's steel wing-claw. "Thanks for getting him back."

The creature screamed its harsh scream. She grinned up at it, wincing.

William backed away, and pointed.

I'M AN AGENT – WHO KNEW!

CHAPTER TWENTY-TWO

Right. Of course he was. The kid was a walking surveillance tool and the tiger was a spy. That's how the world worked now.

Edmund sighed. He was tired of ice. He was tired of water. He was tired of no one telling him anything until they were sure that it was the worst possible time. He wanted to be able to talk to Istvan again without anything being complicated or strained. He missed complaints about unimportant things, like the wallpaper. If he had his way, he was never going to visit Canada again.

He knew he wasn't going to get his way.

It took almost an hour for William to painstakingly scratch out his story. He was a Greater Great Lakes creature, as they had suspected. Shape, abilities, and design all varied by region. Marat – or another fire, it was unclear – had performed some kind of memory erasure before sending him off to investigate Big East, its lack of monsters, and its murder of Shokat Anoushak. Nothing save his likely origin could be traced back, ensuring some measure of safety from whatever had destroyed Providence.

They had counted on curiosity eventually drawing him back. If that failed, they had two surviving stealth flyers. If he were killed... they would have their answer.

William wasn't the only project, either. Every beast in the Greater Great Lakes was afraid. They were all former slave soldiers, with only vague memories of humanity. They were splintered into dozens of factions, none agreeing on how to go about life after the Wizard War, and all they knew about their southern neighbor was that everyone like them in it was dead. Shokat Anoushak was dead. They were free, and terrified that they would be the next target.

Then came Lord Kasimir's beachhead at Niagara.

As far as William could tell, that had been the last straw. The appearance of an army so close to the heart of the Greater Great Lakes convinced several parties that they were mere months away from invasion.

The storms appeared not long afterward: Kyra, fleeing across the lake.

Kyra's cult wasn't just crazy. They were probably desperate. They might well think that the only sure defense against what the Wizard War had unleashed was the Immortal herself: killed once already, and returned again in glory. The most powerful wizard to ever live. Their creator. Maybe they even thought that they could convince her to show mercy to her "children."

Nothing Edmund had ever read suggested that would be the case.

"Why are you allowed to tell us any of this?" he asked.

William pointed at Kyra, then tapped a claw against his head.

The headband. Barrio Libertad. Marat knew now that there would be no hiding, and was trying a different gamble. Their agent had returned intact, more or less, and there was nothing left to lose.

Edmund sat back against the outstretched wing of the bomber. Marat's lights circled its head in a glowing halo, and it was the only place warm enough to be tolerable as the night's chill ate through his jacket.

He was tired.

Was he ever tired.

"Kyra," he asked, "do you remember how you were captured?"

The Conduit shook her head. She sat beside him, on the side closer to Marat, and was still wearing Edmund's coat. "Just what I already told you. I was... It was confusing. Really fast. I guess they must have taken me over the water, but there's just this... mess."

She shook her head again. She was flagging badly, starting to nod off and then snapping upright again when spoken to. Still awake, but forced to fight for it. She seemed to have forgotten about the last snack bar, clutched in one hand and laid over her knees, opened but untouched.

"A blur," said Istvan. "A jumble. Too many memories."

Kyra shrugged, not looking at him.

The ghost sighed. He sat by himself, leaning down from one of the benches, the Tyger sprawled on the ice before him. He had said very little since his outburst earlier. Edmund wished he could stop worrying about him. "Can beasts be Shattered?" Istvan asked.

N, scratched William. *ONLY HER WORD – NONE OTHER*

Edmund nodded. The cult would have needed someone else, then, if they were going to take advantage of Shattered memories. Kyra. Rochester, too, was across the lake.

...but it was spellscarred. It had been for eight years.

Which meant that either she wasn't from there after all, had been somewhere else, or had somehow survived in the spellscars all this time. Maybe she'd been out of the city when the Wizard War hit. She would have been maybe seven years old, then.

He rubbed at his temples. It didn't matter, anyway. The Susurration would never have let her remember anything so traumatic: it had probably rewritten her entire past, and they would never know where she was really from. She would never know. Just like William. Every beast in the Greater Great Lakes was rebuilding an identity from scratch.

What a kick in the head.

"What are you going to do now?" he asked William.

A single hovering glow melted the surface of the scratched ice, and then retreated. William froze it again just by reaching over it.

STAY

That's what Edmund was afraid of. "You're sure? What about Mendoza?"

William paused. His ears flicked.

NOT FOREVER, he amended.

"We ought to tell the Magister," Istvan murmured.

"I'll do that," said Edmund. "William, will we have any way to contact you?"

The Tyger made a low rumbling sound. He raised his head to look at the orbiting lights of Marat.

The motes spun away from the bomber, whirling down and across the lobby before coalescing into a pair of wide, blank, staring eyes. They blinked once. Then the shapes rushed apart, flowing towards the bomber again. The creature opened its jaws. Marat's lights streamed into it.

The bomber loosed a creaking growl and shifted, lowering itself closer to the ground. Its ridged back formed itself into a row of saddles. Another flight. Marat express. The place where Kyra had sat even had extra bars to hold onto.

It seemed they would be entertaining guests.

"Yesss," whispered Kyra.

Edmund smiled a fixed smile. "Thank you," he said. "But I'll get myself home."

Istvan and Kyra rode back across the lake, without Edmund. Strictly speaking, neither of them needed to make use of the mockery's services, but Kyra had insisted and, so far as Istvan was concerned, if Marat were to come back with them, keeping it (them?) and the aircraft creature company was the polite thing to do.

It did, however, carry the disadvantage of leaving him alone with Kyra.

The child wouldn't speak to him. She had refused to even look at him. She sat in the saddle before him, with Edmund's empty seat between, and dozed. Yes, she was tired, but Istvan knew it was more than that.

He'd hurt her. Again. And no matter how much he told himself it was for her own good – she had to know, she had to understand how it worked, she had to be prepared and strengthened for the suffering she would endure simply for being – he couldn't help but think of what he'd been told, long ago. He was a disgrace. A sinner. A moral deviant at worst and an inherited defect at best, something that ought to be weeded out for the good of the species.

And he could hide it. Kyra had no hope of that.

Kyra didn't know she ought.

What would it have been like, growing up like that?

An idealized upbringing. Always fair, always in her favor. No one to tell her she shouldn't speak back to her betters, or that she shouldn't dress how she liked. No consequences for looking the way she did. No questions when she declared, against all evidence, that she was a girl, and would be treated as such.

A fantasy. None of it real. All of it gone. The Susurration had done her more damage than she would ever know, letting her run wild like that.

So why was Istvan almost jealous?

He let her sleep. It was a short trip back to Niagara, accompanied by the soft halo of the lights that kept them warm, and Kyra seemed to have forgiven Marat for the acts of its associate so long as it stayed with the airplane creature she loved and went nowhere near the statue that burned in its bed of ash. Children were easily appeased, but had memories for hurt as long as anyone's.

She probably thought Istvan had betrayed her. Twice.

They hummed along under a cloudless sky studded with stars. As they stooped lower, the far shore came into view: a sudden darkness, where the reflections on the water ended; a ragged gash in the night, torn by trees, and edged by the faint glow of Niagara's remaining lights. In moments they were circling over the dam complex, descending in broad spirals... and then Istvan realized.

Niagara didn't have that many lights.

The glow came from the south. From the wreckage of the city proper. From further down the road, in a winding line – and it was moving.

Their mount gave a shriek. Marat had noticed, too.

They wheeled southward.

"Whu–?" asked Kyra.

"Hold on," Istvan told her.

She looked around wildly, likely still half-asleep. The mockery had produced additional surfaces to secure her to before they left, for that reason. Perhaps she was expecting another sheet of ice.

Instead, she received a blast of cannon fire – directly past their heads.

Warning shot.

Oh, it wasn't. They couldn't have come all this way. Lucy couldn't have done it already, and brought others with her...

Istvan leapt from his saddle, spreading tattered wings.

"Hey!" shouted Kyra.

"Stay away!" Istvan shouted. "All of you!"

"What is it? Who are they?"

Istvan darted around the mockery as it pulled up, engines straining. "An army," he said. He hesitated. "Possibly mine."

Kyra blinked. "What?"

He dared not say anything more. He dove towards the newcomers. The convoy. The line of baroque tanks, flanked by a swarm of smaller vehicles, driving ahead of what looked to be an entire locomotive and several dozen cars somehow freed of their tracks. The din was tremendous; the taste of dread and misery overwhelming. Smoke and dust streamed from their passage, a rising plume that reflected the glow of a hundred lights.

It couldn't be anyone else.

A shout went up as he descended. Searchlights arced skyward. He selected the lead tank and dropped, landing beside its turret, spattering it with phantom mud and bullet scarring. "What is this?" he demanded. "What's happened?"

The two figures in armor holding fast to its sides flinched away. One reflexively reached for a weapon, halting the gesture just in time to transform it into the customary slam of fist-on-breastplate. Both tried to kneel. It didn't quite work in their position, but they did incline their heads and crouch somewhat lower.

"None of that," he snapped. "Tell the rest of your men not to fire at the mockery."

Another salute. Searchlights continued to sweep the sky, but a number of turrets lowered back to their usual ground-facing arcs. The other warrior held up a hand, and they slowed, the terrible grinding of treads and other things on pavement quieting as the rest of the convoy followed suite.

Istvan wished such immediate obedience wasn't so gratifying. "Now, what's going on?"

Silence.

"What's going on?" he repeated. "Answer me!"

"A coup, my lord," one of the warriors said, speaking as though Istvan had dragged the words from him with a hook and radiating an odd mixture of shock, self-recrimination, and terror.

Istvan stared at him. "What?"

"Kasimir denied the Banner-Bearer's right-of-spirit. He has turned his back on the mother country. He cast her out and cursed your name. She has led the faithful these days and nights to join your service, that you may come into your power and establish new and righteous conquest on this earth."

The convoy rumbled to a halt.

"Hail, Devil's Doctor," boomed a familiar voice.

Istvan looked up, heart sinking. It was. Oh, it was.

Lucy strode across the road towards him, clad in

full armor, its plating scuffed and dented, stained with what might have been oil. She carried a simple sky-blue standard. The customary crest on her helmet now boasted a long horsehair plume, akin to that of Lord Kasimir.

"What have you done?" Istvan asked, faintly. Not all the way to Niagara. Not here. Not now. Marat was still circling above, watching, and Barrio Libertad, too, through that bloody circlet. What would Edmund think?

What would Kyra think?

Lucy dropped to a knee before the back of the tank. "Hail, Lord of the Long War," she continued. "Hail, Ravager of the Pale Beast, Ender of Complacency. I bring to you your spearhead, your first arrow, your sharpened blade. We departed in grace, as would be your wish; we come to you now to guide your transcendence."

Istvan tried to remember anything that she said to him in Triskelion that might have led to this. They had spoken of Kasimir but only to note that the warlord had hoped to retain Istvan as an ally. They had spoken of the siege, but only as a test of Istvan's abilities. He still didn't know why Kasimir had wanted the place and its guardians destroyed. Hadn't there been a statue, somewhere in its depths?

Kyra had mentioned statues.

Istvan stepped off the tank, landing on the pavement beside the warrior woman. "Why?" he asked. "Why now? Was it only the fighting that proved all of this to you, or was there something more to it?" He folded his wings and they dissipated, taking the rest with them; he didn't want to prove her point by appearance. "Who were those people in the mountain?"

"Fools," Lucy replied.

A metallic scream rang out. Istvan glanced at the sky. Black wings plummeted towards them, haloed in glowing motes like stars, blazing lights sweeping across the convoy.

Lucy shot to her feet, raising her rifle.

Istvan darted before her. "Don't!"

A strange cry came from behind them, a many-throated and melodic bellow with a high, piercing edge to it. The locomotive rose up off the ground, serpentine, gaping blunt jaws. Coals burned within it. A great plume of smoke and fire shot into the air.

That was how the train ran on the road. It was a mockery. The entire train was a mockery. Terror boiled off it just like the smoke: were there people in those cars?

A pair of warriors leapt off a nearby vehicle and ran at it, shouting in their own language, armed with long poles that glowed like hot pokers. They jabbed at its sides. The train hissed and lowered itself back to its wheels.

Marat's flier landed at the head of the convoy with a crash, claws digging into the pavement. It turned to cast wary headlights on the other mockery. The warriors before it raised their weapons but didn't fire.

Kyra peered out from behind its head. "Wow."

Lucy held up a fist. "My lord, what shall be the fate of this child?"

"Nothing," Istvan told her. "That's Kyra. He... She is one of ours."

"And the mockery?"

"An ally."

Lucy put her rifle away. The rest of the warriors followed suit. "In time," she said, "you will form mighty alliances. Heed those who speak within you."

Kyra slid off the mockery's back. "Wow," she repeated.

She walked nervously past the tank, breezes buffeting the smoke and exhaust around her, and stopped a short distance from Lucy. "You're really Doctor Czernin's army?"

"We are pledged to eternal service," Lucy boomed.

"Why? He's kind of a jerk."

Istvan imagined Edmund's reaction to discovering that their charge had been cut down by a hail of concentrated gunfire. He interposed himself between them. "Er – don't mind Kyra. She doesn't know what's happened." He leaned closer to the Conduit, dropping his voice. "Be polite if you want to live."

"I'm recording," said Kyra.

"I know."

Lucy approached them, planting her banner on the ground and waving off the tank's attendants. "Understand, child," she said, kindly. "Your master is an ending spirit. He is no man. He is multitude. He is Lord of the Long War, the first we have discovered in this world. What you see before you is only the shell of what will be. You should be honored to stand in his presence."

Kyra frowned.

"She isn't property," muttered Istvan.

Lucy glanced back at him, and nodded. "Of course, my lord."

He knew he should say more. He knew he ought to protest the whole of it, that it was based on a philosophy – a religion! – that would only lead to pain. Triskelion was a ruin, its people so militaristic that their homeland couldn't have been much better. If that was the will of an ending spirit, he didn't want to be one.

And yet... the fact remained that these people held a wholly different view of sundered spirits. What they were. What they could be. They had a place for him, a plan for him: that it involved vaulting to the status of god-king was almost secondary to the simple notion of anyone, anywhere, celebrating him for what he was. What if they knew something he didn't?

He couldn't meet Kyra's eyes.

"Child," Lucy continued, "you are truly blessed. These tales are yours. You need only ask, and I will tell them."

Kyra nodded, slowly. "O-kay."

"I'm sorry," Istvan said.

"You kidding?" she replied. "We got an army!"

"Istvan," said Edmund, "what the hell?"

Istvan froze.

Edmund strode through smoke, a caped shadow against the many lights of the convoy. He wore his top hat. He held his pocket watch. He was shivering, and exhausted, and in shock: but the anger was enough to carry him forward, and the fear enough to propel him from behind.

Grace Wu stalked beside him.

Edmund. Edmund, they came of their own initiative. It was their idea. I didn't know. I didn't know anything.

I let them do it. I never denied what they said.

"Doc," called Grace. She clenched her hands into fists. The panels of her gauntlets clicked and locked. Sparks crackled across the metal. "Gig's up."

At least fifteen Triskelion rifles immediately pointed in her direction.

Edmund kept his hands tucked in his pockets. "I don't know what you expected."

Lucy – it was Lucy, though with some unfamiliar additions to her armor – leveled her banner like a spear, which on closer inspection, it was. Scarlet lights flashed behind her visor. "No further, Scion of He-Who-Watches-in-Walls," she boomed in her strange accent. "This is sovereign ground. You have no right here."

Grace paused where she was. "Where's your boss?"

"I answer to no mortal," Lucy replied.

Grace shifted her gaze to Istvan. "You kill him with the rest, Doc?"

"No," said Istvan. He stood just behind the lead tank, near Lucy. His translucent form was hard to make out in the harsh glare of so many headlights, but it seemed like he'd rather be anywhere but there: he was turned sideways, not looking directly at Grace or Edmund, gripping his bandolier. Clouds of poison seeped across the pavement.

Behind him, Kyra edged away, trying to retreat. Edmund couldn't blame her.

"Kyra," called Grace, "stay put. We'll get you out of here."

The Conduit froze. She turned and straightened, taking a deep breath... and then didn't seem to know what to say. She swallowed. She glanced back and forth between Grace and Istvan, then looked back to the bomber mockery perched at the head of the convoy. The creature made a low creaking noise. Some of Marat's lights drifted closer.

Kyra reached a hand back and leaned against the tank treads, her breath coming harder. She stared down at nothing.

Edmund had seen that look at Barrio Libertad. They should never have let a kid get herself involved in this. What was Istvan thinking, letting her anywhere near these people? They were mercenaries, killers, slavers:

whatever they were doing here, it wasn't going to be good, and Kyra shouldn't have to see it.

She shouldn't have to know exactly what they'd done.

Edmund took a step forward. Some of the rifles shifted to point at him. He smiled, tightly. "Istvan, could I have a word?"

He had fought Triskelion soldiers before, more than once. He didn't need permission for passage. He knew how they operated: if they fired off gas grenades here, he'd be ready, and those rifles would be useless. They couldn't touch him. Istvan knew that.

The ghost glanced at him, but didn't hold eye contact long. He sighed. "Let him through," he murmured.

Lucy made a curt gesture. All of the rifles returned to pointing at Grace.

"Thank you," said Edmund. He crossed the distance between them, cape snapping in the cold wind, keeping his hands in his pockets.

It was never easy. It was never simple. This entire fiasco had been a mistake. If Istvan was somehow behind this, Edmund was about ready to call it quits. Let Grace take the lead. Let Barrio Libertad do whatever they wanted.

Sorry, Mercedes, we lost. We lost the second I locked Kyra in those chains.

We lost the second you put me in charge.

Grace let her lightning sputter out. She propped a hand on her hip. "If that's how it is," she said to Lucy. "Fine. We can do it that way. How much do you know about your old boss's dealings with Barrio Libertad?"

Lucy flipped her banner-spear back upright and planted it on the ground. "Such dealings are null, Scion.

Your courage is misplaced."

"I don't think so. Let's talk about what's installed on your tank, and maybe a couple of your soldiers." Grace put a finger to her ear. "Wait, no – actually, most of your equipment. That's going to make this hard for you."

Lucy stepped towards her. "Hollow threats! Those were Once-Lord Kasimir's prizes, Scion, not ours. We destroyed them prior to our passage!"

Edmund stopped beside Istvan. <I hope you didn't have anything to do with this,> he said in German. <Kasimir's little campsite was enough.>

Istvan still wouldn't look at him. <They were coming up the road when we arrived.>

<That isn't a 'no.'>

Istvan shook his head. He was watching Grace.

Edmund sighed. Of course he was. He wasn't like Edmund, who had to remember to look away from her. <I didn't bring her,> he explained. <One of Barrio Libertad's drones was waiting in the museum. She jumped me when I opened the door.>

They knew the real state of Niagara, now, wreckage and all. They'd called his and Mercedes' bluff. He couldn't get away from them.

Couldn't get away from her.

<They've been watching everything,> he continued. <Whatever Kyra's seen or heard, it's all public now.>

Istvan swallowed. He looked ill.

<Istvan,> said Edmund, <the one thing they don't know about is the specifics of what happened at Triskelion. What Lucy told you. What's she doing here? What are we supposed to do about all these people?>

"You're doing the German thing again," said Kyra.

Edmund looked back. The Conduit stood just behind

Istvan, arms tucked to her chest in the strange way she did, tall and thin and dark against the night. She was hunched, her shoulders drooping; like the weight of the whole Triskelion convoy sat on her back. Pale smears marred the waist of Edmund's loaned overcoat, dust and alkali rubbed off the tank's dirty sides.

"Wasn't supposed to be like this," she added.

"You weren't supposed to leave Barrio Libertad," Edmund told her.

"Mr Espinoza let me go."

Edmund thought of all the trouble that could have been avoided. Like this. This, right now. No Kyra, no confrontation with Barrio Libertad, no need to rush finding a base of operations, no Triskelion. They could have dealt with Shokat Anoushak on their own time. They'd done it once before.

Kyra's fault. If she'd just kept her mouth shut.

"And Diego shouldn't have defied his own people," Edmund said, because he couldn't say the rest. He eyed the headband she still wore. "Was that camera his idea, or did Grace put you up to it?"

Kyra pressed her hands more tightly to her chest. "It was just in case."

"Did Grace put you up to it?"

"I only saw her once. She wanted to help me learn my powers."

That wasn't an answer. He was tired of not getting answers. No one ever told him anything until it was too late, and then when he did his best to fix it, he got criticized for it.

He raised his voice. "Kyra, did Grace–"

"No!"

His hat blew off, the sudden wind forcing him

backwards. Istvan winced. Lucy and Grace paused their argument, the former catching at her cape and the latter holding up a hand to shield herself against a hail of dirt and grit. Some of the soldiers turned rifles on Kyra. It took a moment for the smell of exhaust and chlorine to creep back into its place.

Kyra bolted.

Gunshots split the air.

Oh, hell.

Oh, hell, he hadn't meant for that to happen.

The sound yet rang in his ears. Only a moment. It only took a moment. A half-second lapse of judgement, and a kid could die. That was it.

Edmund tackled her to the ground.

"Don't fire," Istvan roared. "Don't bloody fire!"

Broken feathers beat around his head. Wetness seeped into his sleeve. A distant, mechanical clanging swept past his ears. A light like an approaching train. A fireball burst above them.

Kyra screamed. Edmund covered his face.

Oh, hell.

CHAPTER TWENTY-THREE

Pain seared through Istvan's senses.

Marat's mockery charged with a deafening shriek, ripping up pieces of road. Five soldiers crashed to the ground beside him: three on their backs, two sprawled in odder positions. Three from inside the tank, two from perches on its hull. The tank itself had vanished. Parts of the rest of the convoy went with it, men and vehicles both flashing out of existence with the same clamor: Barrio Libertad's technological teleport, turned against its allies.

The shape of a massive owl blazed in the sky.

Istvan hovered above the prone forms of Kyra and Edmund, all semblance of humanity torn from him. It came to this. They had let it come to this!

He'd not refused Lucy's overtures. He'd not stopped Edmund. He'd not told Kyra to stay with the mockery. He'd accepted that it couldn't have gone any other way.

He couldn't be hurt.

"Happy now, Doc?" yelled Grace. She leapt for him, fists crackling.

Lucy caught her arm and slammed her down onto the pavement. Shots skipped off her body armor. Someone threw a grenade.

Istvan lunged through the smoke. "You will not," he shouted. "You will not! If you're going to listen to me, you bloody well listen to me! Put down all of your weapons! All of them!" He drew his knife, wheeling about. Smoke turned to poison where he touched it, flashing with the memory of artillery. "If anyone wants to fight, you're fighting me! I won't have it!"

A Triskelion soldier stumbled past him, spotted him – and then fell to his knees, arms shielding his head, trembling in terror.

Istvan threw his knife on the ground. "Stop it! I'm not what you're after! I'm not... I'm not whatever you thought I was. Get out of here!"

The soldier fled.

Grace appeared before him, obscured in the drifting clouds, shafts of light and dark casting her face into shadow. She wiped blood from her mouth.

"I don't want this," Istvan told her. He clutched at his ribs, where she had blown them apart in the Demon's Chamber. "I never wanted this."

"Doc," said Grace.

"I don't–"

The Conduit gritted her teeth. "Stop yelling and go see to the kid."

He stared at her.

"And come back to the fortress later to get your flower embroidery," she added. She unlocked her gauntlets and stalked away, back into the smoke.

See to the kid.

See to her.

Yes. Yes, he was a doctor. He could do that.

He should have done that already.

Istvan whirled about and arrowed towards Kyra and

Edmund, the child's pain like a beacon in the smoke. Two more soldiers fled from his shadow. A more disciplined group rushed their more lightly-armored fellows – those who had been drivers and gunners for tanks now vanished – to some semblance of cover. Shapes belonging to no living man flashed and faded in the mists, blind and drowning. The train mockery bellowed, sounding its eerie whistle.

A wall of flame greeted him. Sparkling lights danced around it, igniting everything they touched. Marat.

Istvan stepped through.

Kyra lay on the road gasping. In shock. Blood soaked her left sleeve. Edmund hugged her to him, pressing a bunched corner of his cape to the wound. His hat lay abandoned on the cracked asphalt. The flying mockery crouched over them, headlights blazing down.

Edmund glanced up at Istvan's approach, eyes haunted. "Just grazed," he said. "It just grazed her."

Istvan knelt beside them. "Let me see. And hold her arm up."

"Just grazed," Edmund repeated. He raised her arm higher, keeping his bloodied cape pressed tightly against it. "I was fast enough. This time I was fast enough."

This time. Not before. Not when it had been Istvan doing the harming.

Istvan edged closer, unbuttoning his surgeon's cuffs. "Kyra," he murmured, "I'm going to have a look. This will feel very cold."

Kyra nodded, her eyes squeezed shut.

"I'm sorry," he added. "Be brave."

He reached for the wound. The fabric of Edmund's cape and jacket scraped through his fingers. Blood welled below, thankfully not enough to indicate that her brachial artery had been severed. The muscle was torn, yes; the flesh traumatized, yes; but she wouldn't bleed to death. A graze it was. How many antibiotics did the Twelfth Hour yet possess? Their supply had been stretching perilously thin, last he knew.

However–

"Find me a medic," he shouted in the general direction of Lucy's troops. "Or at the very least a field kit!"

"Istvan," said Edmund, "they'd have to run through the fire."

"Then they can run through fire!"

Kyra swallowed, shuddering. "I'm gonna die, huh?"

Istvan traced along the bone, siphoning away what pain he could. Oh, it brought back memories. Gunshots were their own horror, distinct from the trauma inflicted by his own blade; it had been some time since he'd treated one. "No," he said. "No, you aren't."

No breakage. No fractures. No…

He paused. He checked again. Oh. Oh, that wasn't good.

"What?" asked Edmund.

Istvan withdrew his hand and picked himself up. "Where's that kit?" he shouted. He stalked towards Marat's wall of flames. "If you can control that at all, let them through. Now."

Edmund kept hold of Kyra's arm. "Istvan, what is it?"

Istvan sighed. Oh, Edmund had been lucky, all these years. Never struck anywhere important. Escaping death by a miracle. It wasn't his time. It was never his time. All part of his magic. Istvan, himself, had never been so lucky in life. He'd been a mere mortal. As was Kyra.

"Nerve damage," he replied. "Nothing severed, but there is damage."

He didn't mention the rest. The possibility that her arm might be paralyzed from the elbow down, or left weak and fumbling. The pain, bone-deep, that could last for months, or years. He'd never recovered feeling in most of his left side. Even now, he couldn't move part of his face. He'd died a morphine addict.

One wrong move, and life could change in an instant.

"But I have to fight her," said Kyra. Her eyelids fluttered. "I gotta be able to fight her."

"You will," Istvan told her.

Edmund gave him a sharp look.

"I'll make certain you fight her," Istvan said, and he meant it. Kyra had come all this way. She'd endured so much. She'd put every fiber of her being into reaching a single goal – and if the thought of facing Shokat Anoushak herself was all that she had left, all that she dreamed of, the only reason she could grasp to keep living, very well. She would have her fight. He couldn't deprive her of that. They would take her back to Toronto in a cast, if they had to.

The flames parted. A pair of Triskelion soldiers rushed through, one carrying a large satchel marked with a scarlet circular symbol that seemed strangely familiar. Istvan had seen it before. In the mountain fortress. Splashed across the shoulder-plating of a man who could barely stand, caked in gore.

Istvan tried to remember anything past that, and couldn't. He'd let the medic live, he thought. He hoped.

He snapped orders at the two soldiers: stop the bleeding, treat for infection, move her somewhere warmer. Edmund could take them to Niagara proper, if necessary. They slammed fist to breastplate and hurried over to Kyra, setting the satchel down and unrolling a length of gauze. It wasn't ideal, but the Twelfth Hour infirmary was likely still overworked after the storm and if they took her to Barrio Libertad, they would never be able to get her out again.

Istvan had done more with less before. He hoped he wasn't making a foolish mistake.

Lucy strode through the flames. "Your people stand ready for retribution," she boomed. "The Scion of He-Who-Watches-in-Walls cannot escape with this insult."

"Miss Wu didn't shoot Kyra," Istvan said.

"Her appearance incited—"

"Find who did it." He took two steps back towards Edmund and Kyra, and then a thought occurred to him. The train. The column of soldiers alone couldn't be radiating so much misery, and Triskelion was home to more than its masters. He looked to Lucy. "Have you brought slaves?"

"Only those we could provision, my lord."

Istvan raised a hand, found himself at a loss for words, and then lowered it. "We'll be speaking about this."

It got worse. It always got worse.

Lucy inclined her head. "Of course."

He turned away.

The fires abated. The lights that were Marat rushed in a glowing mass towards the waiting mockery, which swallowed them and then took flight in a clap of thunder.

The generators churned in the darkness. They were loud but steady, a reminder that there was more beyond their one room alone, and they still ran at far below capacity, fed by a river choked with debris. It was the only place to find respite now that Lucy's troops had reached the dams, even without a good number of their tanks and armor. At least Grace Wu was nowhere to be found.

Edmund had left, as well. His clothes were bloodied, he'd have to talk to Mercedes about Marat and Kyra's cult in the morning, and he could bring back more supplies; plenty of reason to return to New Haven for the night. Istvan agreed. Sleep well, he'd said.

Kyra had refused to budge.

Now Istvan sat beneath the catwalk to the elevators, knees drawn up. The Conduit lay on blankets beside him, flat on her back, left arm bound stiffly from shoulder to elbow. She couldn't bend it, he'd made sure. He wanted to avoid any further damage.

Hypocrisy, perhaps.

He leaned back against the wall. Slaves. Over two hundred slaves, packed into that train. His. All his, Lucy assured him. Just as the army was his. They weren't about to negotiate the matter and they weren't leaving. Every man, woman, and child in that train had been captured in raids throughout the mountains. Could he repatriate them? Ought he, given the hellish conditions there? Would Barrio Libertad take more refugees?

If he led Lucy and her people to Toronto – took advantage of their zeal, their firepower, to put an end to this Shokat Anoushak matter for good – wouldn't that be abusing power he never asked to be given? Wouldn't that be playing into what they expected of him?

Even armies had as much right to peace as anyone. Especially armies. Lucy and her forces had threatened Kasimir's stragglers with death if they didn't leave immediately or join the coup.

Kyra let out a long breath. "What if it's all fake?"

"Pardon?" asked Istvan.

"Fake," Kyra repeated. "A trick. Nothing real. What

if it's... this is all stupid, right? None of this should be happening. None of this."

Istvan squinted at her in the darkness as she turned over onto her good side.

"Maybe I was supposed to die," she added. "Then I could wake up."

Oh. Oh, no.

He shifted closer to her. "Don't think like that."

"What do you care? You don't even think I should exist."

"Kyra, I don't–"

The words caught in his throat. He didn't think that; he truly didn't! Would he have seen to her if he thought that? Would he have tried to free her from the Demon's Chamber if he thought that? It was only all the rest, that was a problem.

All the rest.

"If this is about earlier," he said, "I was telling you the truth. I know you don't want to hear it, and that you don't believe me, but that's how it is. It isn't that I don't think you ought to be here. I was only telling you what you have to know so that you... so that you won't be..."

Concussed. Chained. Shouted at. Driven to tears. Forced to confront terror, over and over. Shouted at again. Told that her very existence was an affront to others.

Shot.

"...hurt," Istvan finished.

"This place sucks," said Kyra. "I want to go home." She curled up more tightly, voice drifting. "I just want to go home, OK? I'm really tired."

The painkillers. It had to be the painkillers. She knew "home" was a lie. She knew there was no returning. She had been so adamant; she couldn't give up on them now.

"Kyra," he said, "you've been an inspiration, and I mean that."

"'kay."

"Don't lose hope. Don't let it crush you. Giving in is... it might seem like the answer, but it isn't. I've lost someone. I know. It doesn't solve anything, it doesn't bring them back, and it leaves nothing but grief for those around you."

No response.

Istvan propped his elbows on his knees, wishing the Conduit were easier to read. He hadn't realized how much he'd come to depend on the taste of emotions rather than the turn of expressions. "Kyra, I'm sorry. I'm sorry for what I said. I still don't understand you, or why you think the way you do, but... I'll try. I promise I never wanted you to be hurt."

A yawn. "Why were you dancing with Mr Koller?"

He hesitated. The headband. It was still watching. Listening.

Kyra waited a moment, then turned back over, pulled off the headband, and shoved it under her pillow. "You loved him, didn't you?"

Istvan sighed. "Yes."

"Is that how it is with Mr Templeton, too? Is that why you hang around him, even though you guys fight all the time?"

He couldn't answer that. He looked away.

"You're scared," Kyra said, as though it were a revelation. "You're this... thing, and you're scared!"

The nerve. She had no idea what it was like. She hardly knew him. A stray memory here and there, stolen against his will, did not an understanding make.

He wasn't afraid; he only knew the consequences. It was better for Edmund not to know. Even Edmund himself would agree with that. The man never wanted to know anything that was the slightest bit unpleasant.

Istvan was protecting him. It wasn't fear, it was duty.

He pushed himself up. "Do get some rest," he told Kyra. "I'm going to find a way for you to accompany us to Toronto, when we return."

"Scared," she whispered. She made an odd sound, like a chuckle, then fluffed her pillow and lay back down upon it. "Me, too."

Istvan departed.

Edmund's table was still broken when he went to eat breakfast. It had only been a day since Kyra had stayed at his house. Only a day since they planned a trip that had gone well off course, and visited a couple of questionable stops, to boot. A long, long day.

The storm beat at his windows. If there was sun, it wasn't trying hard enough.

Edmund scrubbed the blood out of his jacket. Kyra's blood. He shouldn't have pressed her. This was his fault. It was always his fault. It didn't matter what it was.

He shook his head, wishing for a moment that Istvan were there and then remembering what fresh hell the ghost had brought down on Niagara. It was his soldiers – wanted or not – that had shot Kyra. It was his idea that had taken them to Triskelion in the first place. His cruel, bloodthirsty nature that he hadn't resisted.

But it would be Edmund's fault for not restraining him. Istvan was his responsibility. Mercedes would be sure to remind him of that. Edmund had freed him, and the consequences were on his head.

It couldn't be the mark of a good man to miss having his best friend in chains.

He'd dreamed of statues.

He left for the Twelfth Hour as soon as he could bring himself to put the jacket back on. It would need a more thorough washing, later, just like everything else.

The crowds outside had dispersed. No one wanted to stay in the storm for long. There were more important things to do than worry about politics. Inside was a madhouse: heaps of clothes and blankets piled against the shelves, produce rushed to storage, laborers huddled around overtaxed radiators, stranded representatives from the Magnolia Group trying and failing to reach their brethren, disgruntled chickens pecking at boxes.

"Hey, it's the Hour Thief," someone called.

They rushed him. How many monsters are there? Who's this kid? Why were you up north when you could be helping us? You're still living in your own house? We could use that army here! Who did you kill? Shokat Anoushak's coming back? Why weren't we told? What's going on? We're freezing here. Help us!

Help us.

Edmund backed up and met another crush of bodies. Faces bobbed before him, frowning, shouting. He didn't recognize them. He'd never learned names. During the Wizard War, they'd died too quickly for him to remember, and in the years after that he'd always worked alone. Alone, or with the one other person who couldn't be killed.

He couldn't breathe. He almost tripped over a stray chicken.

The faces pressed closer, demanding. Why wouldn't he share his teleport? Who would be chosen to become a wizard? He was supposed to be the good one – the one who'd seen them through the Wizard War – the one who could be trusted. Why was he keeping them in the dark? Why wasn't he standing up to Magister Hahn?

Why–

A liar! Just like the other wizards–

How could you chain up a kid? You got her shot!

He fled.

The Demon's Chamber shouldn't have been his destination, but it was. He didn't go inside. Someone had put yellow tape over the door. Air whistled through the gaps between wood and stone.

Edmund sat on the cold steps and tried to catch his breath. Barrio Libertad. Barrio Libertad hadn't kept their mouths shut. More pamphlets. More defamation. More truth where it hurt the most, handed out without any thought to people who didn't need to know. What was next, magic itself? Were they going to take matters into their own hands? Were they going to break into the vault?

He had. Long ago.

He never should have stolen that book. He never would have lived to see the Wizard War, much less what came after it. He never would have become a target for so much hatred. Why weren't they mad at Istvan?

Footsteps sounded on the stairs.

Edmund stood, wobbled, caught himself on the wall, wiped at his eyes, and straightened his suit jacket. He took a breath and then started up the stairs towards the newcomer, business-like. "I'm sorry, I can't answer questions."

"Wasn't asking," said Janet Justice.

Edmund managed a brittle smile. "Janet."

The computer expert stopped three steps above him, effectively blocking the way in the narrow stairwell, and crossed her arms. She held a folded piece of paper in one hand. The silvery curves of her earrings glinted in the orange glow of the Demon's Chamber. She was black, like Kyra, and it shouldn't have mattered. "Looking for the Magister?" she asked.

"I was, yes."

"She left for Barrio Libertad. You're the highest authority here, for now."

Edmund nodded, slowly. Had Barrio Libertad called Mercedes to a summit, or had she decided to go on her own? He wouldn't have wanted to stay here, either, if he were in her position. "I see."

"Good job," Janet added. Her voice held no approval.

"I'm glad you think so," he said.

She thrust the paper at him. "Here. I found your crystal building."

He blinked. "My what?"

"Kyra mentioned a crystal building. I checked to see what the satellites have on Toronto. This was the closest I could find."

Edmund took the paper and unfolded it. It was printed in black and white, warm to the touch, a photograph of the northern city from far above. The Wizard War had devastated the ground, but not the sky: many satellites still functioned, if you could find the machinery to talk to them.

One pale, angular structure was circled in yellow marker.

Kyra had never spoken to Janet, as far as Edmund knew.

"Pamphlets?" he asked.

"Broadcast," she replied. "Never thought I'd listen to a radio program."

"How long?"

Janet flashed a humorless smile of her own. "All day. Good talking to you, Mr Templeton." She turned around to start back up the stairwell, bracing a hand against the cracked stone.

He took a step up. "I'm doing the best I can."

"Those people feed you," she said.

Her footfalls receded, leaving him, once again, alone.

He sank back down. He took off his hat and stared into it.

What would it be like to be made of stone and metal sheathed in wax and porcelain? What would it be like to not have to take anything from anyone? What would it be like to never dream again, to never drown again, to never tremble at the thought of forever?

No one would have to feed him, then. Those people in Triskelion wouldn't have had to die. He wouldn't have been so desperate. He would have made better decisions.

He'd finally stop running.

CHAPTER TWENTY-FOUR

It fit her well enough.

Istvan stepped back, inspecting the overall effect. Kyra was taller than most of the Triskelion force, and so there were some gaps at the joints, but for an overnight effort, it wasn't bad at all. It was certainly better than that dress.

"Try walking," he advised.

The pair of soldiers to either side of her retreated, bowing as they went.

Kyra stretched. The blue-grey steel of the breastplate had dents in it. The helmet had a visor and little else; not intended for a full motorized suit of armor, but for lighter auxiliaries. Armored shoulders flashed in the grey light of the morning sun. Her cape – they had insisted on a cape – fluttered bright scarlet.

She took a hesitant step. The boots only barely fit her. Their rough soles brushed dew off the grass.

"Seems OK," she said.

Her left arm was strapped to her chest, immobilized. She hadn't been able to move her fingers that morning. Istvan knew that such things could remedy themselves, in time, but didn't hold high hopes. It was more than likely that the combination of dubious drugs and his own pain-siphoning presence was all that kept her able to move – or think – at all.

Lucy strode up beside him. "We shall fully restore Kasimir's encampment while you bring a third death to the Immortal," she boomed. Her blank visor tilted towards Kyra. "Let your wrath spare nothing, favored one."

Kyra nodded an uncertain nod. "Yeah. Thanks."

Istvan looked to the encampment that lay across the dam's artificial lake, past the island where the wreckage of a mockery still lay tangled in electrical wire. A solitary creature had struck during the night; to its detriment. Small figures labored among the ruins, clad not in the brilliant finery of soldiers but in the drab grey of the slave force. He had ordered them freed, but the army treated them little differently. Now they were prisoners. They had nowhere to go.

He wished Lucy hadn't brought them. It was one thing knowing that Triskelion was built on their backs, that the coal that powered tanks and forges had been hauled from the earth on their shoulders; it was another, seeing it. It was always easier to use people when you didn't have to see them.

He'd... he'd find somewhere for them. In the meantime, he did have to admit that Niagara needed repairs done, and better defenses established, just in case. He'd figure something out.

Kyra walked a slow circle, cape streaming behind her, then shaded her eyes from the sun, now at a considerable angle from the horizon. "Is Mr Templeton coming back, or what?"

Istvan hadn't seen the wizard since the night before. He was starting to wonder the same thing. "Any moment, I expect."

The Conduit kicked at the grass.

Istvan sighed. "Perhaps he–"

Helicopter blades thundered overhead.

Dozens of rifles pointed at the sky. The train mockery, chained along the road to Niagara city, let loose a gout of flame. Kyra shouted: a great gust blasted upwards, tearing at the grass. Lucy dug her banner-spear into the ground. One of the other soldiers fell over.

The attacking mockery wobbled, speeding around for a second pass. It was a double-bladed affair, quite large, with bright red and yellow markings. It had its skids folded up. Shark teeth gaped at its front.

Istvan spread ragged wings and leapt at it. How many monsters could the north possibly muster? And where was Edmund, anyhow? The wizard should know better than anyone that they were wasting time.

The mockery roared above him. Istvan drew his knife, looped around and over the creature, tilted into a dive that dodged the first set of propeller blades, and–

–startled eyes, very human, met his own.

The machine blew through him, a rush of cold metal and plastic and blood and blazing heat and more metal. He floundered in its wake.

Grace Wu was in there.

Painted on. The teeth were painted on. It wasn't a mockery at all.

Barrio Libertad had a helicopter?

Gunfire cracked, four or five shots at extreme range. Istvan made sure all of his limbs were where they ought to be and then dove back to the dam, speeding low over the Triskelion forces. "It's friendly! It's friendly! Let her land!"

Much of the grass near the museum and gift shop was

clear: a broad sweep that followed the curve of the dam. That was where Grace landed, the downdraft sending waves rippling through dry stalks. No sooner had the helicopter's skids touched the ground than she bounded out, clad in her usual outlandish attire. "You have to evacuate."

Istvan alighted near her as Lucy and her two attendants hung back, forming a perimeter. "We do not," he said.

"Oh," said Kyra, "it's her."

Grace stared as the younger Conduit strode stiffly towards the landing site, resplendent in borrowed Triskelion gear. Then she shook her head, and turned back to Istvan. "Where's Eddie?"

"Not here."

She mouthed a curse. "He's not in New Haven, either. Janet was right."

Istvan frowned. "What?"

"Never mind. Listen, it's coming for you. It's less than two hours away."

"What does Janet have to do with–"

"Harbor." Grace glanced at Kyra. "That's its name, right?"

Kyra nodded, mutely. She scanned the horizon with wide eyes. Bits of grass skimmed away, carried by a new wind.

Grace pulled her goggles off. "Harbor is crossing the lake, right now. You have to get everyone out of here."

Istvan stared at her. Marat had said Harbor was a… a prison creature. It guarded the border. What was it doing, moving south? The tanks weren't going to do any good at all against something like that. They had no support out here. Even Istvan could hack at a beast so large for days without slowing it. The last one he fought was at

Barrio Libertad, and the fortress was... well, a fortress. With great turreted batteries.

"How?" was all he could manage.

"They're on our side," said Kyra. She hugged her good arm to her chest. "They said they were on our side!"

"Are you sure you haven't seen Eddie anywhere?" asked Grace.

Istvan shook his head. "No. No, I haven't. Excuse me."

Grace gave him a look. "Oh, sure."

"They're on our side," Kyra insisted.

Istvan hurried over to Lucy, dropping his voice. "You wouldn't happen to have brought any Bernault devices with you, perhaps? Maybe ten or twenty of them?"

The warrior woman shook her head. "Kasimir guards such weapons in his deepest vaults. To regain them would require a mighty campaign."

"We haven't any time for that."

"No," she agreed. "We do not. Not unless the Hour Thief grants us his power to move between moments, as he did the once-prisoners of our old foe."

Istvan grimaced. Edmund wasn't there to do any granting in the first place, never mind whether or not he could compress an entire military campaign into a few hours, which Istvan doubted. The man would never do anything like that again, anyhow. Giving away that much time could have killed him.

Grace had said he wasn't in New Haven. Not at the Twelfth Hour, or anywhere nearby. Where was he? What did he think he was doing?

"I can try hitting it," Kyra said. She made a fist with her good hand. "I hit it once. Maybe it'll listen if I get its attention?"

"Kid, you have one arm," Grace informed her.

"I can do it!"

Grace gave Istvan a look that suggested he'd given Kyra too many painkillers.

"Take me in the helicopter," Kyra continued. "If I don't have to hold us in the air, I could do more, maybe. And Dr Czernin can fight, too."

Lucy eyed the conversation. "We will hold our ground, should you will it," she said. "We are no strangers to such beasts."

Istvan shook his head. Without better weapons, that would be little more than pointless massacre. "No. Fall back into the woods, if you can. It will probably go after the dam and then the city – they always do."

"You will give up your prize so easily?"

"The dam doesn't matter! I don't want you all getting killed!"

Lucy took a step backward, then struck fist to breastplate. "Thank you for your mercy, my lord. We will prepare to fall back at once."

She strode away.

Istvan folded his wings. Mercy, indeed. He'd won the dam with blood in the first place. How quick they were to praise him. How quick he was to let them.

Grace Wu waved him back over. "Doc," she called, "what are the odds that Kyra's cult is behind this? I only know what we got from the logs; did you and Eddie discuss anything else off-camera?"

Istvan approached both of them again, letting his worse aspects fall away and thinking of Kyra's damning comments on Pietro. Not off-camera. Not all of it. "Marat said that Harbor is a prison creature. He didn't seem able to control it. I would imagine that only Shokat Anoushak knew how. As for the cult…" He tried to imagine what

Edmund might say. "They do know some of what she knew. Perhaps this is part of it."

"What if we're too late?" asked Kyra. "What if she's back already?"

"Don't get ahead of yourself," said Grace.

"What if Harbor's a distraction?" Kyra continued. "We should go to the crystal building. How fast is your helicopter? Do you think we could find Marat and get help?"

Grace opened her mouth, then closed it. She glanced up at the sky and its gathering clouds, cast Istvan another look of aggravation – *what did you feed this kid?* – and then popped the door of the helicopter open. "Come on. Both of you. We'll talk in the air."

They lifted off as Lucy's army began to break camp.

"No, I'm not supposed to be here," snapped Grace over the whine of rotors. "I'm supposed to be back on Shattered round-up duty. You think the Council wants anything to do with you guys? You think we don't have our own problems?"

The helicopter jolted. Storm clouds streamed past the cockpit windows. The lake below them churned into house-high waves, steaming where lightning struck it, whipped into fog and froth by Harbor's passage.

"I didn't know Barrio Libertad had aircraft," Istvan said.

"We have lots of things. It doesn't matter." She dipped them lower, gaze flicking between altimeter and cloud bank. "If they're not going to do anything, I will. I'm not letting you get the kid shot again."

Kyra, in the back, fumbled with her seat harness one-handed. "We have to be low enough now. Come on, open the doors! Let's go get it!"

Grace gave Istvan another look.

Lucy had asserted that it was "mostly" morphine. Istvan was beginning to suspect the rest consisted of combat stimulants. When they got back, he was going to find a Triskelion medic and insist on a much more thorough translation of those labels.

"It was the best medication we had available," he muttered. "Would you rather we gave her nothing?"

Grace rolled her eyes. "You're not fighting Harbor," she called over her shoulder. "Sit down."

Kyra, undeterred, leaned forward, straps dangling from her shoulders. She gripped the corner of Istvan's chair and stared out at the lake.

"Sit down," Grace repeated.

The younger Conduit squinted. "What are those lights?"

"Lightning, I would imagine," said Istvan, because Harbor was covered in lightning, after all. "Now, Kyra, you really ought to–"

"No, no," said Kyra. "Little lights! Turn back around!"

Grace gritted her teeth. The helicopter shuddered as she brought it back around, knuckles white on her controls. The horizon tilted. Harbor's storm bank spun below and then settled, the beast's green lightning cracking through brief gaps in the fog.

"I'm not getting any lower," said Grace.

Istvan tried to make out any of Kyra's lights, and couldn't. "I could have a closer look," he suggested.

Grace shrugged. "Knock yourself out."

He drew his feet up onto the seat. "Kyra, please sit down," he said. "You can take my place if you like, but you do need to be strapped in."

"I can fly," Kyra muttered.

"Yes, and you'll fly straight through the canopy if you hit a bad stretch. Where will Miss Wu be then, hm?"

Grace snorted. "I'll–"

Istvan hurled himself through the window.

The cold of the glass gave way to the cold of the open air. He snapped open his wings. The fog rolled below him, and he dove into it. Harbor's great back crashed through the water like an island in motion, its tallest towers a crest that rose above the spray. It wasn't swimming: it was walking along the lake bed, and Istvan feared the waves that would strike the shore when it arrived.

Why it hadn't swam through the Earth to emerge below Niagara in moments, as others of its kind had done to other cities, he wasn't sure. Perhaps its masters could only tell it to move, and so it had moved in the simplest way it knew how.

As he dipped lower for a closer look, a mote of fiery light darted past him. It turned a circle, as though inspecting him, and then flew away, joining another of its kind in the fog. He knew those lights.

"Hello?" he called.

A familiar metallic scream answered. Shadows flitted through the fog. Then, strange-angled wings rushed towards him, edged in fire.

Istvan dodged out of the way. "Marat! What's–"

A second mockery sped after it. Then a third, and a fourth. They were ungraceful things, their limbs twisted, their steel hides pocked with rust and burn marks. One had wings of stretched canvas attached to the shell of an automobile – a travesty that never ought to have flown at all. Still, its maw was sharp and jagged, and its headlights burned with the same feral intelligence as its siblings.

Marat's sleeker beast dove for Harbor's towers. Wind whistled through the holes torn into its back edge.

Istvan chased after it. "Marat!"

Lights spilled from the mockery's jaws, streaming over its back and wings, etching lines of fire across the metal.

GO

Were they trying to stop Harbor? Marat had pulled information from Edmund's head, before, and Kyra said that its kind were scouts and interrogators: could it stream into Harbor, as well, and turn it back?

And these other mockeries...

Istvan pulled up and away, drawing his knife. He'd never seen mockeries so crudely constructed. Or... had he? Imitations. They had to be. Imitations made by the cult. He could at least give Marat a fighting chance before he returned to Grace and Kyra.

Canvas parted easily. He'd learned that in his war. The beasts rolled and slashed and snapped at him – dropping from above, barreling up from below, streaming smoke that blinded, darting in and out of the fog – but he'd dealt with their like before, and it was a long, long way to fall.

Where was Edmund? If Janet Justice had told Grace that she'd seen him, why? Did she not trust him? He should have come back. He should have been with them. He'd promised that he would return. Had Grace checked his table at Charlie's?

Oh, if he were hiding... or hurt...

Istvan looked up from the spinning fragments of a wing to meet the next challenger – and then ducked as a circle at the front of its cockpit burned cherry-red, molten metal spraying from a hole that hadn't been there before. It tumbled away. It hadn't even managed a scream.

Grace Wu's helicopter, shark teeth and all, hovered where it had been. A peculiar mirrored device protruded from under its nose. She waved from the cockpit.

Well, now.

Istvan darted back inside to discover that Kyra had taken up his offer of the copilot's place; he settled into one of the rear bucket seats. "It's Marat," he said. "They may have a chance of turning it back."

Kyra pumped her good arm. "I knew it! Now we have to go to the crystal building!"

Istvan glanced at Grace. There was no guarantee that Marat would or could stop Harbor, but neither could they. Not without something like the Bernault devices. But going after the cult already, and without Edmund? He was the only one who knew anything about magic. He was the only one who knew anything about Shokat Anoushak in any great detail. He was their wizard! They wouldn't even be able to understand her, if she were truly returned.

Which... she wasn't, of course. They would have known if she were. She would have already started destroying the world again. That was what she did, after all.

"What was that melting cannon?" Istvan asked.

"Your tech people sent me the location," Grace admitted.

They looked away from each other.

The helicopter rose on whining rotors, lifting them back up and out of the fog. Something clunked below them: the cannon's mechanism perhaps, retracting.

"I tried calling Eddie," said Grace. "Never picked up."

"Can't you find telephones?" Istvan asked. "Janet could."

Grace shook her head. "Either his phone's dead or he pulled the battery out."

Kyra frowned, watching the other Conduit. Then she twisted around in her seat to look at Istvan. She had very dark eyes, and some of Triskelion's restless, artificial energy seemed to have drained from them. "We have to go," she said. "We don't got time for this."

"We would if Edmund were here," Istvan snapped.

She flinched.

He didn't have to taste the hurt to know it was there. He was getting better at reading her, however slowly. He sighed, looking out the window. "I'm sorry."

She turned back around. She didn't reply.

Istvan twisted his wedding ring around his finger. Edmund ran. He always ran. Istvan had always been there for him. The man could stand to be more consistent in returning the favor. Edmund had chained him away for thirty years, after Istvan had murdered his friends in front of him. The right thing to do. Istvan couldn't begrudge him. Kyra couldn't understand.

"We need him," Istvan said. "Kyra, Edmund has been dealing with this sort of mess for much longer than you've been alive. We don't know how to counter anything we might find. We don't know enough about this cult's magic."

"I do," Kyra muttered.

Istvan froze. Did she? Could she?

"I got myself out," she continued. "I can get you and Ms Wu in."

Grace glanced over her shoulder at Istvan – a measuring glance – and then reached up to flip an overhead switch. Dark traceries etched themselves over the glass before her as though they had always been there. Map lines.

"OK, kid," she said, "you've got yourself a job. Show me where to thread the needle."

"This is a cool helicopter," said Kyra.

Grace throttled up. "It's pretty great."

Istvan watched Harbor's waves roll past as they sped towards Toronto.

His boots crunched on the snow. Cold pricked at his flesh, wind cutting past his collar. His own breath steamed his goggles. He kept his hands in his pockets. He'd gotten the blood out of his coat, at least. Much better than having no coat at all.

This was it, then. This was where to find her.

Edmund peered up at the mirror-bright walls. They tilted at uncertain angles, outwards and then inwards again, strange angular towers clustered together. He couldn't tell if they had windows or not. It was like the building couldn't decide if it was one structure or several. Like it couldn't decide whether or not it wanted to fall over. It was trapped, suspended mid-catastrophe.

He took the stairs.

When the beasts crawled down from the towers, and the railings rose up like serpents to block his path, and the space between sculptures opened empty eyes, he smiled. His lips cracked in the cold.

"I'm here for the Immortal," said the Hour Thief. "Would you mind sparing me a few moments?"

CHAPTER TWENTY-FIVE

They rushed at him.

He was faster.

The railings erupted and he ducked just in time. Ice crackled along their metal length as they uncoiled. Frost tumbled over his cape. Three stairs passed beneath his feet. He reached the first landing, spun away from claws that gouged the stairs behind him, and spotted a pair of glass doors ahead. The entrance.

Something blazed green in the corner of his vision. The air thrummed around him. A shadow fell over the stairs. A crack, like broken bone–

He snapped his watch. The world rewrote itself. The atrium rose three or four stories above him, a maze of stairwells and walkways that crossed at uncoordinated angles. One of the nearer ceilings reflected his own face a dozen times. Some were older than others. He tipped his hat at them.

<You shouldn't be here,> they responded in Old Persian.

"I know," he said. He glanced back at the door to see its handles unwinding, frost crackling across its threshold. "Care for an audience?"

The faces blurred and rippled. A black shadow appeared

inside the mirrored surface, swimming, skeletal.

Glass became water.

Edmund hurled himself away. It crashed down beside him, liquid that returned to glass and then became molten, a corona around black bones. Don't look at them. The space between them hurt to look at.

Spattered glass burned holes in his cape. He burned time taken from dead men, interposing minutes where they had no business being: enough to cross the atrium, flee past a gallery of colored shards, and pause for breath between water fountains.

He needed to go down. She would be down, surrounded by rock and ore and clay: the stuff that statues were made from. She might have been a rider, and an archer, one who favored flying steeds, but in the end, she was a maker of monsters. A monster herself. An immortal architect of her own creation.

Go to the source.

He only had to go through this once for answers. He only had to run a little while longer. He'd stolen knowledge he shouldn't have once already.

"You can't catch me," he shouted down the hall. "She might have been the first, but she isn't the only one. You can't stop me from reaching her."

A smooth skittering answered him, like marbles on tile.

Edmund readied his pocket watch. "Believe me, you can't."

The guardian rounded the corner.

<Immortal,> it said in his own voice.

Edmund tried to look at a spot just to the left of the being rather than figure out where it began and where it ended. "That's right. I'm the Hour Thief. I spoke to Shokat Anoushak before she died in the Wizard War. If she's back – if your Lady of Life has truly risen again – I want to meet her."

<You covet her secrets.>

He swallowed. He could see himself reflected even at the edge of his vision, distorted mirror-images that lengthened and vanished along skull and ribcage as the creature moved. "Always have," he said.

Molten glass hissed.

<If I drowned you,> it said from behind him, <how long would it take you to die?>

Water dripped, trickling in thin rivulets around his boots. The fountains. Some part of the creature was coming through the fountains. Oh, hell. He might be talking to a being that occupied the entire building: anywhere touching glass or plumbing. No wonder it had found him again so quickly.

Edmund didn't dare turn his head. "I'm not here to fight. I'm here for answers. If you want to keep this up, we can, but I'd rather not waste your time."

<You are not wanted here.>

"I know. I'm here anyway. Is she?"

No reply.

Other creatures appeared further down the hall, peering around the corner. One lizard-like being clung to the ceiling.

Edmund focused on the pocket watch he held ready in his right hand. One wrong move, and he could be back home. No one the wiser. This wasn't the bad idea it seemed to be. He had to know. That was it. That was all. It wasn't a crime to be curious.

He had to know.

"If I'm in the wrong place," he said, "all you have to do is say so. If Shokat Anoushak isn't here, I'll go. That's a promise. I don't make many promises."

The creatures looked to each other. Some traced signs on the floor or in the air. The guardian remained where it was, implacable, molten glow dimmed but not gone. They had all been human once. How long would they live, now? How long would those bodies last? How long would it take them to go mad?

They still weren't answering. If they'd done it, if they'd really resurrected the Immortal, wouldn't they be proud of it? Wouldn't they be shouting it from the rooftops?

Instead, nothing.

Nothing.

Edmund took a breath, mostly steady. It wasn't true, then. She was dead. She wasn't coming back. There was no other way. This had all been a fool's errand, and he was a fool for thinking anything good would come of it. A fool for hoping. Istvan would never approve. Istvan wouldn't understand.

If he found out that Edmund had done this – if he found out that the Hour Thief was looking for a way out, another way to cheat Death her due... well, Edmund had gone too far once already. Knowing that he would again would be too much. The last straw. Istvan hadn't chosen what he was. Edmund's predicament was of his own making.

Cowardice. It all came down to cowardice.

Shokat Anoushak was dead, and there was nothing more for it.

Edmund held up his hands. He should have been relieved. If he'd been a better man, he would have been. "All right," he said. "That's fine. I was mistaken." The words felt like he had to drag them out of a pit. "I'm sorry," he added.

He flipped open his pocket watch, knowing all the while that he'd be back. He'd only promised to go, not to never return. Kyra was still on her mission. He couldn't leave the kid high and dry. Not again.

No one would have to know.

The creatures from down the hall ceased their debate. The glass guardian rippled, the forms of its fellows sliding across its mirrored surface. Then it stepped past Edmund and into the wall, melting into the surface with a hiss, black bones receding and vanishing as though sinking out of sight into the ocean. The stink of molten rock seared his nostrils.

His own voice echoed through the building. <It is decided. Stay with us, immortal. Our Lady is changed, weary and reluctant, but she would not deny you enlightenment.>

Edmund's pocket watch fell from nerveless fingers.

The cult swept him up.

Grace Wu landed the helicopter in what had been a city park, touching down between oaks and playground equipment. The skids sank into deep snow. They couldn't take the machine any closer without risking detection, and without Edmund, they couldn't afford direct confrontation. Not with Kyra wounded. Grace was a fine fighter, but she couldn't catch bullets. Istvan, of course, couldn't catch anything at all. No Edmund meant no insurance. No Edmund meant no hope of escaping disaster.

Kyra could level buildings, but she wasn't immortal. She wasn't a weapon. All she wanted was to see this through – to finish her mission – and it was up to Istvan to help her do that.

And Grace. Grace always made everything her business.

Toronto's white tower spiraled heavenward above them as they unloaded supplies, its smooth and strangely scalloped sides occupying an unnerving stretch of the horizon and ascending beyond sight. It was close – perhaps too close – and Istvan hoped that even a cult of monsters wouldn't want to risk operating too near the heart of a fracture zone. Their names hadn't changed yet, had they?

They had set down as far away as they could…

Istvan scanned the sky again from his position atop the helicopter. No mockeries. If they'd been spotted, the cult was being quiet about it.

"OK," said Kyra. She slung a duffel bag over her good shoulder, visored helmet flashing in the sun. Much like Miss Wu, she cut a colorful figure against the snow: they wouldn't be losing track of her anytime soon. "We have to look for the hole I left."

"The hole," Grace repeated, picking up a bag of her own.

"Yeah. In the ground. They dug tunnels all under here. That's how we get in."

"Uh-huh." The older Conduit slogged her way towards the edge of the park, pushing through snow that was thigh-high to her and knee-high to Kyra. "What makes you think they haven't sealed it? You've been gone, what, two weeks? More than that?"

Kyra followed her trail. "I don't know, it was a pretty big hole."

Istvan eyed the snow, imagining it slithering through his kneecaps. He could fly over all of this. He could be at the crystal building in moments. It would be easier, and faster – and, with Harbor on its way, they could use some speed.

But he couldn't take the others with him. He would be alone, and Grace and Kyra would be stranded out here. Miles away. Walking targets.

Bloody Edmund. Didn't the man realize how much they relied on him?

"You coming?" called Kyra.

Istvan sighed. He slid down from the helicopter. The snow sank through his legs, slithering through his kneecaps precisely as he'd feared.

To think, he could have brought an army instead.

Grace led them across the park, under an overpass crowded with rusting vehicles, and down a road lined with row after row of shops and malls. Not another soul to greet them. Faded pictures remained on display: smiling women in woolen hats, colorful drinks, children's books and television characters with enormous eyes, advertisements for acupuncture, foods that Istvan remembered seeing in Indochina. Most of the signage was in Chinese. More cars lay under a thick covering of snow in vast parking lots, frozen to the ground.

He imagined the cult stealing outside to scavenge for parts, cutting up those vehicles to create mockeries of mockeries. "I thought this was Canada," he said.

Grace averted her eyes from the frosted windows of a nearby truck and the still shapes inside. "It is."

Kyra watched the sky.

Istvan wished Grace hadn't come. She had been helpful, yes, but she was only part of this because she had forced her way into it. She hadn't been with Kyra in the Demon's Chamber. She hadn't gone with them to investigate Toronto. She was a hero, an icon: a veritable national institution representing the region's greatest power. She didn't understand what it was like, being locked up. Being feared. Being hated. She had no stake in this.

He drew closer to her, dropping his voice. "Miss Wu, if you aren't supposed to be helping us, why not deliver the warning and then depart? What's going on at Barrio Libertad?"

"Politics," she muttered.

"Oh?"

"I'm not leaving you alone with the kid again, and that's not a popular opinion. Let's go with that." She checked the back of one of her gauntlets, knocking snow from between the seams. "Looks like we're only another mile and a half out."

Istvan squinted but couldn't make out anything that looked like a map.

"It was by a river," said Kyra. "I remember there was water. I flew over a river." She shook her head, drawing a deep breath. She tripped over a buried curb.

Istvan threw out a hand–

–and Grace caught her. "Careful," she said.

Kyra steadied herself. "You're not my mom," she muttered.

"Your mom told you to be careful running around in plate armor with spikes on it? Kid, I wish my mom was that cool."

"I'm OK," Kyra grumbled. "We can do this." She smoothed her cape. "Ms Wu, I… I'm sorry. For running away from you. I know you didn't have to come. You're a big deal, too, right? Barrio Libertad's own superhero?"

For a moment, Grace didn't reply. She let Kyra go and checked her gauntlet again, a dark and resentful fear welling from her. "Yeah," she said. "That's me. Resistor Alpha."

Istvan frowned.

Kyra resettled her duffel bag. "Thanks for coming. I mean it."

Grace nodded and forged on ahead. Kyra trudged after her, favoring her left side. The sweetness – a subtle thaw, languorous and delicate – was unmistakable.

"Kyra," Istvan said, "the painkillers are wearing off, aren't they?"

She shook her head. "I'm OK."

Istvan moved up to walk beside her, snow or not. He knew lies when he heard them.

Down it was.

In the basement loomed the remnants of other exhibits. Cases of porcelain. The mask of a jackal. Hanging lanterns that cast no light. Strange tubes of painted glass. A more classical display awaited restoration, abandoned on a table, surrounded by brushes and oils: paintings crusted with the passage of time, never to reclaim the brilliance of their original colors. The others rested on shelves or lay half-packed in boxes, waiting for a curator that would never come.

Edmund reached down to pick up a fallen label. The item it belonged to was nowhere in sight. There was nothing sadder than a collection with no one to keep it.

He had to focus on the small things instead of what was actually happening.

Alive. Shokat Anoushak was alive. They'd done it. It could be done.

It felt as if the room were spinning. Shapes moved around him: fur and scale, stone and metal, chimeras that never spoke a word but watched him as they descended, pressed close as brothers. He was theirs now, and they knew it.

He put the label in a pocket. The beasts carried him away. Through a service door – another basement – and then into bare rock, a passage melted by acid or flame. Its surfaces glistened like wet bone. Like glass. Water trickled along the ceiling, a river running upside down that flashed hints of molten intelligence.

He reminded himself to breathe.

Alive. Alive.

<We are her children,> the water whispered. <We are her newmade people. We are the secret-keepers, those of shattered shards made one.>

The tunnel pitched sharply downwards. Edmund stumbled. Beaks and cables reached to steady him. Something too deep to hear rumbled in his chest. Phantasms flickered at the edges of his vision.

Shattered. Kyra was Shattered. Who had first coined that term? What was shattered had once been a whole, like a vase or a window: that was part of the definition. But who had been whole? Kyra? Or someone else?

<Our Lady endures so long as she remains in memory. Memory can be graven in stone.>

The water grew louder. Falls. The only light came from those creatures that bore lights: beams from eyes and screens, motes that danced between antlers. The congregation. That's what it was.

"I shouldn't be here," Edmund said, but he couldn't convince even himself, and nothing else heard him. It was getting harder and harder to keep from shaking.

<There is a difference between words spoken and written. One remembers, clarifies, listens. The other is. Thus do the old empires fall.>

They pushed him. The lights blurred, green replaced

with ember-orange: lights like those of Marat. Rock bit
into his knees, scraped the palms of his hands. He wore
gloves for a reason. He'd be hurt if he didn't. The falls
thundered in his ears.

This was bad. Why had he done this? He shouldn't be
doing this.

He picked himself back up, brushing off his pants–

–and came face-to-face with Shokat Anoushak al-
Khalid.

His knees wouldn't hold him. He toppled back down,
stumbled away, heart racing, clutching his fists tightly
to keep himself from reaching out. Real. She was real.
Seeing was enough.

His back struck a pillar. No further.

The Immortal loomed from a great outcropping
of cracked and mottled granite, burned smooth: a
commanding figure, seven feet high, clad in bright riding
tunic and tall feathered crown. Gold ornaments in the
shape of strange beasts twined around her neck, seeming
to shift and melt into each other. Flowered trim glittered
at wrists and hem. A sword and quiver hung from her
belt. The regalia of a Scythian warrior-queen.

Dark paint marked eyes that glittered like emeralds.
Eyes that were emeralds, and maybe always had been.
No wax. No pretenses. Stone through and through. She
emerged from the rock like a ship's figurehead, one with
it, her hands and feet sunk into it. A waterfall tumbled
from a broken cavern wall behind her, cascading over
fallen boulders and flowing around her outcropping and
away, carried by grooved channels.

Edmund couldn't form words.

She spoke for him. <So.>

Scythian. A language two thousand years dead. The

only way to learn it in the modern age was to study the works the Immortal herself had penned. No other texts survived. <So,> Edmund managed.

She studied him a moment, dispassionately. <How do I know you?>

He blinked. How could she not remember? She'd spoken to him, before her death. She'd called him, personally, by title. She knew who he was. What he was. <I'm the Hour Thief. I studied you. I fought your armies. We spoke, once.>

The carved figure before him remained silent and unmoving, as only a statue could. Shokat Anoushak. Alive. Alive, for the third time. What did that do to a person?

He tried to keep his voice even. <I'm immortal,> he continued. <You knew that. You once told me to run, and to keep running, forever. That running was all I could do. Fate and madness. You know these things. I listened.>

<Hm,> she said.

That was all. She sounded as though she'd misplaced a cup of tea.

Edmund pushed himself back to his feet, slowly. She didn't remember him. She really didn't remember him. He wasn't sure how to feel about that. <That's why I'm here,> he said. He took a breath – now, or never – and looked her in the eye. <I want to know how you did it.>

She chuckled. It was a low, rehearsed sound. <Ask every king and sage who sought to be remembered, for I am of their making. I am memorial and tribute, an obelisk in the sand: a tale that lies in wait, locked inside dead matter. So long as there are graven records, so shall I be.>

Oh. Oh, boy.

What had the water said? Shattered fragments made one. The difference between spoken words and those on a page or a monument. His own magic relied upon spoken language: asking and receiving, oral contracts, an understanding that didn't always go both ways. What Shokat Anoushak was saying was...

Edmund swallowed, dizzy again, trying to comprehend the sweep of history. She predated so much of what he took for granted. Most everyone was literate, now. Had her language even possessed a written form during her lifetime?

Had she invented it?

<Those who tell stories on the wind alone have the right of it,> she added, dispassionately. <They knew better.>

He glanced over his shoulder at the tunnel from which he'd come. The cult remained there, watching, lit by their own bodies. A steady stream of water trickled around his feet. Why were they still here in Toronto? Why not finish what she started?

<I don't understand,> he said. <Why do you hate written language? Why destroy our cities? Why...> He struggled to find the right words, <...cover all the nations with monsters and rip open the world?>

She gazed at him a moment. She hadn't taken one step from the stone: he was beginning to wonder if she could. <You do not agree with these things?>

<No!>

She smiled. <Then, Hour Thief, we are of one accord.>

CHAPTER TWENTY-SIX

Edmund stared at her. He hadn't heard that right. He couldn't have. He'd probably lost something in translation – all he knew of Scythian was what he'd read, and there were probably any number of inaccuracies in his understanding.

This was Shokat Anoushak. This was the woman who had, for all intents and purposes, put an end to civilization as they knew it. No warning. No ultimatum. Mexico City hadn't known they were a target until they sank beneath the lake. The rest of the world had no time to prepare for what was coming.

And now she didn't "agree" with what she herself had done?

<I don't understand,> he repeated, feeling like an idiot but unable to articulate any better response.

<You have lived only one life,> she replied. <I have lived many. They are a tale to me, as I expect to one day be a tale to others. All that I am is inscribed in stone; did they not tell you this?>

Edmund shook his head. <I don't see–>

<No one can escape, Hour Thief. No man. No woman. None can hold fast to defiance forever. This is the truth, as I have lived it.>

His words died in his throat. Panic clawed at his

stomach, worming up his ribcage, and he clasped his hands together behind his back before they could start shaking. That wasn't what he wanted to hear. Oh, hell.

Oh, hell.

Shokat Anoushak continued, relentless, remorseless. The emeralds of her eyes glittered beneath the gold leaf of her crown, sunken deep into the stone. If she noticed his discomfort, she didn't remark upon it. Or didn't care. <I am not the first. I am not the last. I am a story engraven, memory in waiting. Each of me suffers her eventual fate, for this is immutable, but I continue. This is true immortality: not life, but lives without end.>

Edmund couldn't breathe. It felt like the cavern was collapsing in on him. It felt like he had to run – but there was nowhere to go, and his legs wouldn't carry him.

He couldn't find his pocket watch.

<I didn't destroy your cities, Hour Thief. That was another life, blasted by the centuries. Her reasons were her own.> She turned her head, finally releasing him from her gaze. Her voice softened. <I am but a prisoner here, in her shadow.>

Shock jolted him from terror.

The stone.

She couldn't move from the stone.

They hadn't finished her. The cult. They hadn't finished her, on purpose, before they revived her – created her – whatever bringing back a being who could exist again and again in different iterations might be called. They weren't stupid: they'd hedged their bets, and trapped the Immortal within her own form.

Edmund looked back at them, once more. They were still watching, dark shapes crowded in the mouth of the tunnel, glimmering where the light from Shokat

Anoushak's prison struck metal or scale. The light.

He looked up. Glowing motes hovered near the cavern ceiling. Yellow-orange, like those of Marat. Shokat Anoushak's own interrogators.

They wanted knowledge without the risk.

If anyone deserved this, it was her. She'd killed more people than anyone in history. She'd kicked history off its course, and normality along with it. No one knew if the fracture zones would ever recover. Nothing would be the same again.

But... if what she said was true... if the one before him now had to be told of the devastation secondhand...

<Do you move your soul from body to body?> he asked.

She chuckled. <There is no such thing.>

He swallowed. His hands grew clammy again: once more, he forced himself to quash the urge to run. Either she didn't know, or didn't care. He didn't know which was worse. The original Shokat Anoushak must be long dead. How could she still think of herself as one being? Could there be more than one of her at once?

What would happen to him?

Edmund tried to get hold of himself. One thing at a time. The cult. He had to focus on the cult. He had his answers. He should leave, and leave now.

But... when would he get another chance?

He'd already seen others imprisoned. He'd done it himself. He'd never expected to find Shokat Anoushak – if it was her, truly her – in this kind of position. Willing to talk. Willing to answer questions.

If this one wasn't mad, what might she be able to tell him?

<Ah,> she said. <You understand.>

•••

Istvan had made a terrible mistake.

Kyra was flagging, and flagging badly. She favored her arm constantly now, hunched to one side. She moved more and more slowly. She weaved as she walked. She'd been shot just yesterday. She shouldn't have been allowed on the field at all.

She struggled on, but even Grace Wu was starting to look concerned.

Istvan should have sent them both away. He should have gone alone. He couldn't be trusted with operations like this: he wasn't a leader anywhere but the surgical theater, and even there he had his critics.

If Lucy's army fell to Harbor, it would be his fault.

If Edmund had come, they wouldn't have these problems. If Edmund had come, they would have done things right. If Edmund had come...

"Kyra," Istvan said, "does it feel as though I'm pressuring you?"

She wiped at her visor as snow whirled around them, a sudden flurry that had struck as they crossed the last highway. They couldn't see more than five feet ahead. "What?"

"Pressuring you," he repeated. "You don't have to do this. We can take you back. I don't want to force you to do anything you don't want to do – you're in no condition."

"We're already in a snowstorm," she said.

"We can go back," he repeated.

She gave him a reproachful look. "You can if you want."

"Here," called Grace from up ahead. She waved an arm, her outline barely visible. "I think I found it!"

Kyra followed the older Conduit's trail. Istvan

followed Kyra. He had to stay close to make sure the pain didn't become overwhelming, and he wished he weren't so grateful for it. It was impossible to lose her.

Near Grace Wu, the road simply ended, mid-lane. A steep incline vanished down into the fog. Boulders, pieces of concrete, and the twisted wreckage of cars lay scattered about, softened by snow. A rushing hiss came from somewhere beyond sight, like falling water. Istvan couldn't make out the river, if there was one.

"Yeah," said Kyra. She wiped at her nose. "Yeah, that's it."

"How are we doing this?" asked Grace, kneeling down on the edge and running a hand across the broken roadway. "Slide down and hope for an opening?" She scooped up a handful of pebbles and let them trickle between her fingers. "I could try moving some rock, if we need a little more precision, but I'll have to get a good look at what's there, first. I'm good, kid, but I'm not you."

Kyra stood there, staring down at the pit. The jumble of her presence – discordant responses, first one feeling and then another, subtleties crowding over one another – offered little elaboration beyond fear. Nerves. A sense of unease, self-doubt, and exhaustion that was wholly to be expected.

This was where she'd escaped, after all. Perhaps the first use of her power. Istvan imagined that he would feel the same, were he to return to the Italian Alps.

"I could go see if there's a way in," he offered.

Grace set down and unzipped the bag she carried, drawing out a long metal coil. "You wouldn't know what to look for."

Istvan propped a thumb in his belt. "A hole, I should think."

"And then what, if there isn't one? You'll tell me 'there's rocks'?" Grace shook her head. "No good, Doc. I'll handle this."

Kyra mumbled something.

Grace picked up the coil like a lasso. "What?"

"Don't touch the water," Kyra repeated. She kept staring at the pit. "I dunno if it can see you, 'cause it's the river, but don't touch it."

"Er…" said Istvan. He glanced at Grace. They had both dealt with Shokat Anoushak's magic during the Wizard War, but neither one of them were trained in these matters. That would have been Edmund's job. Bloody Edmund. No wonder those people at the Twelfth Hour were so insistent on learning magic themselves: there wasn't always a wizard around to help them. Wizards couldn't be counted on.

A wizard had done all this in the first place.

Grace shrugged: she was, presumably, already used to things watching her that oughtn't be capable. Like walls. "No water. Got it."

She tossed the coil. It unraveled into the wind, unfurling small projections along its length and flattening itself like a ribbon before it side-slipped downwards: an odd, very long sort of kite. Grace connected its other end to her gauntlet and gazed at a spot just above it intently.

"It's like one of those jungle snakes," said Kyra.

Grace nodded, gaze never leaving that one small spot. "Bingo."

Kyra set her own bag down, then leaned against it wearily, cradling her bandaged arm. She closed her eyes. "Cool."

Istvan knelt beside her. She still didn't seem able to move her fingers, and all this jostling about wouldn't help it. She shouldn't have been here. Oh, he'd made a mistake. No crusade was worth disfigurement and paralysis.

Nothing he did was ever "cool."

"Dr Czernin?" said Kyra.

"Hm?"

"Can you... do the thing?"

He sighed. He took hold of her arm, directly over the bullet wound, and did his best to draw off all the pain he could. It wouldn't help heal it. He never should have let it happen. It was sweet, all the same.

After a few moments, Grace nodded to herself. She reeled in her coil-kite, rolled it up, and put it back in the bag. "OK. You two. You want the good news or the bad news?"

"I like good news," said Kyra.

"That's too bad, because I got both."

Kyra made a face. "Oh."

Grace flashed a smile. "Good news: we have an entrance point! Bad news: it's underwater. The river's running right down into it. Here's our options." She held up one finger, and then another. "Go for a swim, or rip the roof off. We could also look for another way in, but we have maybe a half-hour before Harbor makes landfall and breaks all the Doc's tin soldiers. Which will it be?"

Istvan thought of their surroundings torn up and whirled into a great funnel like he'd seen in Tornado Alley. Kyra could do that, it was true. But in her condition?

Then again, a swim would be little better...

"What if there's others?" Kyra asked.

Grace zipped her bag shut. "Other what?"

"Prisoners. Shattered people." The younger Conduit peered over the edge again. "I can't choose what gets ripped up, Ms Wu. It all goes."

Grace sat back. "You know, if you'd stayed put–"

"I'm not an experiment, Ms Wu."

Istvan raised his eyebrows. Well, now. "Pardon?"

Grace rolled her eyes. "We had a disagreement. I'm over it." She stood, dusting off her gauntlets. "Look, Kyra, it'd be nice to have more than two options, but we're out of time. If there's other prisoners, you'll just have to be careful. And that sucks, I know, but having no flexibility sucks. If you're a hammer, we have a hammer. Unless you want to swim. Which, I'm fine with that, but your doctor might have other ideas."

Kyra pointed at Istvan. "Send him."

Grace opened her mouth, then shut it again. She eyed Istvan speculatively.

Istvan stepped back. Him? Alone? The entire cult was probably down there. What if he lost himself? The others would be left entirely in the open, and he might not come back. He'd already carved his way through one stronghold blasted into the rock. "Er, Kyra, I don't think–"

"Just go look," she said. "You don't gotta fight anything."

Don't have to fight. Right. Yes. He could do that. Scouting. Not so often underground, or into a hive of cultists, but… he'd done it.

"You'll be OK," said Kyra. "You're invincible."

Istvan felt ill. Through the rock. He'd have to go through the rock. What if there were other prisoners? How were they supposed to get them out without Edmund?

"I'll be quick," he said.

Grace tossed him a lax salute.

Istvan closed his eyes, turned his face away – and dove into the pit. Don't touch the water, for it had eyes. Rock was better. He could pass through rock instead. It was no trouble at all. Like swimming in particularly thick molasses. He could do this.

He struck gravel.

It felt as though he'd fallen into liquid sandpaper. It scraped at his throat, his lungs. No light. The damp mustiness of earth. He couldn't tell which way was down, or if he were moving at all. He had no heart to beat, or breath to catch, and the tiny scrabblings of worms were too faint for his ears; even the waterfall, wherever it was, had fallen silent. He tried to orient by Grace Wu's fading presence: her worry, her irritation. Kyra was much more difficult to locate.

The rock poured into him, blinding, choking.

Then something caught at his awareness. A faint thread, a distant richness: a strangely familiar feeling, old regret and older dread with the consistency of a fine bitter chocolate. And… something else. Something ancient. Something that drew all fears into itself, crushing them into empty space.

It couldn't be.

Istvan tumbled from the ceiling. Motes of light danced around him. He spread flayed wings, gasping in a breath by habit.

A man in black whirled to look up at him.

Istvan faltered. "Edmund?"

The motes blazed into flame.

The specter's empty eye sockets stared down at Edmund. Istvan had no face – not right now, not always – but the agape jaw was enough.

What was he doing here? How had he known?

What did this look like?

"Wait," Edmund called. "I–"

The lights closed on the other man, swarming, piranha-like. A knife flashed. No use. Istvan dove down, twisted across the chamber, beat at the assailants with wings set aflame, scattering phantom feathers across the granite–

No. No, no, no.

Edmund chased after him, waving both arms. "Istvan, wait!"

The specter cast one last glance at him – at Shokat Anoushak – and shot back up through the roof.

Edmund slipped on a too-smooth rock. Spent a moment to catch himself – couldn't halt his momentum – and ended up stumbling into one of the grooved canals, soaked up to one knee in frigid water. He stumbled back out of it with a curse.

"Istvan!" he called again, though he knew it was no use. His fingers searched again for his pocket watch; it had vanished from its place, and its chain with it. "Oh, hell," he added. "Oh, hell."

The congregation scattered, some up the tunnel and others spilling over the canals and toward him. The crawling lizard-like creature. The spearing bird and its razor wings. A beast with stars sparkling among its antlers. Signs and signals he couldn't read passed back and forth between them, in scraped hooves and blinking glances: their own silent language, invented out of necessity.

"Wait," Edmund said, holding up his hands, "I had nothing to do with this."

The water rose from the canal before him. Murky

shapes swam in its sudden depths. A molten glow glimmered around ribbed and angular darkness, coming closer. <You lied,> it hissed in his voice.

Edmund backpedaled. "I didn't!" Where had he dropped his watch? He needed his watch. It was so much harder to focus without his watch. "Istvan wasn't supposed to be here! He shouldn't have known! Listen, I didn't tell anyone where I was going. You can have your swarm up there attest to that. This was personal. I never said a word. I don't know why he's here!"

<You keep an interesting collection,> commented Shokat Anoushak.

"He's not a collection," Edmund snapped. Istvan was a friend. His best friend. The only friend he could keep.

A friend he'd abandoned without warning, and who had just caught him with the enemy.

The glass guardian drew closer, water from the falls running across the ceiling and congealing into its mirror-bright surface as the rest of its bones emerged from wherever it kept itself. Far too many arms swept outwards and hardened into scythes.

Edmund swallowed. "I didn't lie to you," he repeated. One of the buttons on his jacket was missing. The one that normally held his watch chain.

He couldn't leave now. This was maybe the only chance he'd get. He had so many questions. He'd studied Shokat Anoushak for so long, and now she was right here: alive, trapped, and willing to talk. Maybe the cult was onto something. It would have been fine if Istvan hadn't showed up. It would have all been fine!

Rock cracked. Dust showered from the ceiling.

The guardian paused.

A new tributary spouted from the waterfall. A thud

came from above, and then a strange, scouring rush, like wind. New seams crackled across the stone.

<So, my children,> said the Immortal, <you didn't dig deep enough after all.>

Edmund covered his head.

The ceiling came apart with a roar. Shards of rock showered across the remaining congregation. Sun and snow and biting cold poured into the cavern–

–along with an entire river's worth of water.

It crashed against the granite. Edmund bolted for the tunnel entrance. The guardian flared molten and dissolved, melting into the advancing wave, a sheen rippling across its surface. Cult members struggled within it, swept away.

Shokat Anoushak merely laughed.

The river slowed – hardened – halted. Ton after ton of stone spun upwards, hurled into the air. What had been a cavern was now a sinkhole, coated in ice.

A tall and lanky figure floated high above, clad in bright armor and a bulky backpack, right arm outstretched. Around her flowed a scarlet cape. Beside her hovered Istvan, cloaked in poison and thunder. Grace orbited with the wind, flailing, armed with a pair of duffel bags and sheer bravado. It couldn't be anyone else.

The eye of the storm.

Kyra.

"Gently," Istvan advised. "Gently!"

Kyra wavered in the air, barely balancing one-armed. "I'm trying. I can't go any lower." Her eyes darted from the exposed cavern to the rim of the new crater and back again. More earth tore from below and spiraled up around them. "I... I don't think I can land down there without ripping it up."

"How did you land before?" Istvan asked.

"I never landed anywhere before!"

Grace Wu shouted something about a grappling hook – it was difficult to make out her voice over the wind.

Istvan looked down again. Edmund was safely in the cavern mouth, holding onto his hat. Good. The cult seemed to be having trouble regrouping. The statue of Shokat Anoushak was partially submerged in the now-frozen river. How such a thing had happened, he had no idea, but at least they wouldn't have to worry about Edmund drowning.

Captured. This whole time, the man had been captured! That was the only explanation for his absence – surely he would have returned to Niagara, if he were able. Had they taken his telephone? Could the cult somehow block his teleport?

Never mind that he hadn't seemed relieved to see Istvan. There... there had to be a good reason. Perhaps they had tortured him. Perhaps he was drugged, or...

Istvan shook his head. No, first they had to get down there. Put an end to this.

Kyra dipped lower again. A new layer of rock disintegrated. She pinwheeled, trying to regain altitude. "Hey! Hey – what if I just dropped us? Could we float down?"

"What?" shouted Grace.

"What about the rocks?" asked Istvan.

Kyra gritted her teeth. "I guess they'd get dropped, too. Uh. Miss Wu!"

"What?"

"Can you punch rocks?"

"What?"

Istvan tried to gauge the distance to the cavern floor. It was much too far to fall safely, but not far enough to open a parachute. Unless...

The river shifted. Strange reflections rippled across its frozen surface.

He blinked.

Kyra yelled. She whirled about and punched down with her good arm. The wind twisted crazily, shearing sideways, gouging the frozen waterfall out of the cavern wall. Ice turned to spray. Molten droplets flew past and through him, some striking Kyra's armor.

Glass? The river was glass?

"On the edge," Grace called, zipping past overhead. "Land on the edge! I'll rappel..." She waved a grappling hook, partly removed from one of the bags, as she sped out of earshot again.

Kyra steadied herself again, looking around wildly. "Did I get it?"

The rest of the river rose up behind her. It had a skull.

Istvan shouted a warning. He lunged. His blade struck water. He couldn't cut water. How was it water again? "Kyra!"

It snapped her up. Mirror-brightness rippled along the creature's length as it twisted, falling back towards a now-liquid lake where the ice had been.

It was turning back to glass, with Kyra inside.

Istvan dove after it as the storm disintegrated. Dust, rock, parts of cars, and building foundations tumbled around him. Grace Wu plummeted past with a yell. Istvan couldn't catch her. Istvan couldn't catch anyone. "Kyra!"

The young Conduit kicked ineffectually. Bubbles streamed from her mouth. She grabbed hold of strange black bone, and kicked again. New storm winds ripped through its length, severing it in three places, and it collapsed.

They fell together, in sudden rain.

CHAPTER TWENTY-SEVEN

Edmund appeared.

Istvan gaped at him. "I—"

The man grabbed for Kyra as she fought with her parachute – and missed. He tumbled past at a precarious angle, with a barely audible curse, and then vanished again. He hadn't had his pocket watch with him.

He could teleport. He wasn't trapped here at all.

Istvan looked around for Grace Wu and caught a glimpse of Edmund flickering in and out of existence near her, as well. Her parachute was starting to... no, it was unfurling already, it was...

Her odd snake-like kite coil floated over to them, the lens of a camera glinting at its end. She shouted.

Istvan wasn't certain what happened after that, precisely. Kyra took hold of the coil, he knew. Grace Wu's parachute seemed to have opened remarkably quickly. Kyra did something with the wind. It all happened when he wasn't looking: he glanced back and forth between one and then the other, and then somehow, they had managed to get both parachutes open before they struck the cavern floor, and had reached the shelter of the entrance tunnel before the storm detritus smashed down where they had been.

Just in time.

Just enough time.

Istvan clawed his way out of the rubble. Dust and snow whirled around him. Rivulets of water and molten glass trickled down into the ground. Shouting and flashes of light came from somewhere close by. Edmund must have given Grace time enough to get both her and Kyra out of danger, trusting that she would do something useful. Of course he couldn't do the same with Istvan. Granting time to the dead would be resurrection, and that was beyond his powers.

The fighting, wherever it was, died down. A voice – a woman's voice, one Istvan didn't recognize – called out. He turned, squinting. He didn't know that language.

Shokat Anoushak rose from the wreckage. Her once-fine garments were torn, her crown missing. A web of cracks split her face. She had no hands. Her presence was a well. A pit. A pool so deep and so pure that it fell away, bottomless, bitter as ash.

Istvan backed up, knowing that barbed wire and artillery would give him away. Kyra was right. Kyra had been right about everything.

Shokat Anoushak knelt down and plunged the stumps of her wrists into the wreckage. Green lightning sparked around them. She smiled.

"You," shouted Kyra.

The Conduit staggered through the dust. She looked very much worse for wear, her armor scorched and dented. Her boots slipped on loose stones. She had only one good arm to steady herself – and yet she struggled on anyhow, glaring at the risen Immortal with hate in her eyes. "You ain't going nowhere!"

The wind followed her. She raised her hands.

Edmund hurtled himself at her, tackling her to the ground. "No! You can't!"

Istvan flinched away from the scuffle, glancing back at Shokat Anoushak. What was Edmund doing? Was he enthralled? Why was he here, after all? If he could escape, this entire time, and hadn't...

Why hadn't he told them? Why had he gone alone?

Kyra yelled. A sudden blast knocked Edmund away – and then he wasn't there. He stood behind her. He wavered, unsteady on the rubble. The young Conduit turned to face him instead, fist raised. "Mr Templeton, what are you doing?"

"Edmund," said Istvan, unable to articulate much else.

Oh, he wasn't. He couldn't have. He was better than that.

He had to be better than that.

Edmund closed his eyes, then opened them again. "I need her," he said. He held out his hands. They shook. "I'm sorry."

His only chance. The only way. He couldn't let this go. He couldn't let Kyra finish what she'd come to do. He couldn't let Istvan stop him. He couldn't let anyone stop him. Grace was already out of the way.

Shokat Anoushak had to live.

She had to live, so the Hour Thief could live forever. No matter what it took.

It hurt to look at Istvan.

"I'm sorry," Edmund repeated.

"Why?" Istvan asked. Flesh crept back over bare bone, his face a mask of horror. "We expected you. We thought that you were lost, or hurt, or captured. I thought..." His wings drooped. "Edmund, why?"

Edmund swallowed. "Counterbalance," he said, his own voice sounding alien. "It's what Mercedes would want. Someone who can threaten Barrio Libertad." Numb. He'd gone numb. "Politics, like the Cold War. It's just politics."

Good reasons. Logical reasons.

Shokat Anoushak straightened, flexing hands of loose rock and scrap held together by sheet lightning. A layer of water flowed up her stone form, rippled, and solidified over it, mirror-bright: a second coating, a skin that covered the cracks. Dozens of silvery braids cascaded down her back. She cast her gaze over those assembled, a molten glow flickering behind the emeralds of her eyes.

Edmund wiped his hands on his jacket, trying to hide the shaking.

"That's stupid," announced Kyra. "You're stupid." She brought her fist back up, snow spinning around her in a sudden flurry. "I'm taking her out."

Istvan stared at him a moment longer, then looked away. The memory of artillery thundered. "Harbor is attacking Niagara," he said.

Edmund froze. Harbor? *The* Harbor?

Something hit him in the back. Sparks lanced up his spine. His muscles seized. He tried to teleport, tried to reach for the coordinate-offerings that would get him out of the vice grip that closed around him, but lights popped before his eyes and he was almost positive he was having a heart attack. It wouldn't kill him.

"A parachute, Eddie?" yelled Grace. She pushed him down. "Really? You're going to try to tangle me in a parachute?"

He couldn't form any words that weren't garbled.

"I did not resign for this," she added. "I did not come all the way out here just so you could join Team Evil. Kid, take it away."

<I made you,> said Shokat Anoushak.

Gravel slithered. It sounded like someone stumbling.

"What?" demanded Kyra.

<Your power. Did you think it was an accident?>

A pause. The wind whistled in his ears.

"Don't listen," called Istvan. "Whatever she's saying, it isn't true."

Kyra answered him, after another long moment, "I dunno. Makes sense to me."

Edmund tried to make his lungs work again. Kyra understood Scythian. Great. He twisted in an attempt to get a better view of something that wasn't the ground, but Grace held him in a headlock, and only clamped down tighter. She was inhumanly strong; he wasn't going to win this by force.

"Listen to me," he managed to wheeze. "This is a new being you're talking to. She didn't do what you think she did."

Grace snorted. "Bullshit."

"She doesn't even remember the Wizard War, Grace!"

"Why do you need her?" asked Istvan.

Edmund faltered. He'd said that, hadn't he. He shouldn't have said that. He shouldn't have come. He already knew too much. He had to get out of this headlock before they did anything else. Get out, get the others away, and then go from there. It was too late to turn back now.

If they didn't forgive him, fine. He didn't deserve it.

"OK, Miss Anoushak," said Kyra, finally, "what do you want?"

<An answer,> replied the Immortal. Her tone was even, calm, almost conversational. <You are not like the others. You were never unwanted, formed by forces even my past life couldn't control.>

Edmund closed his eyes. He didn't need his pocket watch. It made things easier, was all. He could still win this.

Shokat Anoushak continued, <You, Kyra, are not Shattered, but Shatterer. My first work. Breaker of prisons, the wind through chains. Will you act as I made you?>

Edmund teleported.

Kyra stared, free hand creeping up to clasp at the sling across her chest. The snow fell around but never on her.

What the Immortal was saying to her, Istvan had no idea, but he was certain it was nothing good. Why would anyone like that bother speaking, unless there were some motive? Why deal with lessers at all, if she were so beyond them? The Susurration had wielded words like a weapon; surely Shokat Anoushak was no different.

He held his knife at the ready. "Kyra, don't listen. She can't be–"

Grace Wu struck the rubble with a curse. Edmund was gone.

Oh, no.

Istvan leapt to protect Kyra. Edmund was fast: too fast. If the wizard tried to get at her, it would be almost impossible to stop him. Istvan couldn't touch him if he didn't want to be touched.

Edmund got there first. So did Grace.

They struck with a flash. Stones flew. Grace lunged,

gauntlets crackling; Edmund flickered, sliding just past the edge of vision. Charged punches never reached him. Istvan couldn't make out the motion between: both of them seemed to maneuver in bursts, one with uncanny deftness and the other with explosive energy.

Istvan landed beside Kyra, who was doing her best to cover her face. Gravel skittered off her armor.

"Shatterer," she repeated to herself. "Breaker of prisons."

Oh, she was losing herself already.

Istvan folded his wings around her. Lightning cracked. Edmund and Grace Wu vanished, golden light dissipating where they had been–

–and only Edmund returned.

Shokat Anoushak said something in her ancient language. The man flinched. She gestured to the sky. Glowing motes, like those of Marat, descended in the snow. An odd skittering came from the cavern entrance; a whine, like rotors, came from above. Glass crept up the cavern walls.

Reinforcements.

"I'm sorry," Edmund said, clutching his side. His cape smoked. "Istvan, I'm sorry, but you both have to leave."

"Where's Miss Wu?" Istvan demanded.

"Somewhere safe." Edmund reached for Kyra. "I don't expect you to forgive me."

His hand passed through one of Istvan's encircling wings. The feathers, after all, weren't truly real. A ghost could provide no barriers.

Istvan had no other options.

He threw himself into him. Through fabric to flesh, chilled by the cold air, slick and trembling. Through flesh to bone and organs. Muscle twisted. Nerves misfired. Blood rushed through his veins, burning hot. A shout vibrated in his throat. The frantic fluttering of Edmund's heart became his own. Fear and exhaustion turned to sweet terror.

They toppled, thrashing. Striking the rubble lit up a constellation of pain. Istvan gasped. It was dizzying. Intoxicating. He sank into the other man's spine and nerves, working outward, quelling the convulsions muscle by muscle, tendon by tendon. He tried to be gentle. He didn't want to hurt him.

He'd never done this before, and he imagined Edmund would never want to again.

Another thing to never talk about.

Finally, they lay on the ground, sweat-soaked, breathing hard. Dust caked Edmund's nostrils. Snow fell on him. The world lay sideways, through blurred vision.

On a wall of broken rock and concrete stood Kyra, surrounded by approaching foes, facing Shokat Anoushak al-Khalid. Alone.

Istvan couldn't move to help. It was all he could do to keep Edmund pinned.

The Immortal held out a hand. Her words sounded like a question.

Kyra breathed in, deeply. She kicked a stone. She glanced at Edmund and Istvan, balled her hand into a fist, then looked to Shokat Anoushak... and smiled a fierce and tired smile. "You got a weird sense of humor."

She began to dance.

CHAPTER TWENTY-EIGHT

Grace came for them in the helicopter. Edmund evidently hadn't sent her far. There was plenty of room to land: what had been a modest cavern had become a vast open pit, its edges pulverized, the buildings surrounding it leveled by hurricane winds. Of Shokat Anoushak, no sign. She could have taken shelter near Kyra, in the eye of the storm, but she hadn't.

The Immortal hadn't said a word as the winds took her.

"I did what she wanted," said Kyra, by way of explanation. Then she climbed into the back seat of the helicopter, curled up, and went to sleep in full armor.

Istvan couldn't fault her. She'd earned it. She could worry about what she'd done – what she'd destroyed, who she had killed – later. Power had consequences, and there was more than stones buried in the rubble. He wished he had learned more about them.

For now, Kyra could rest.

"What do we do with him?" mused Grace. She leaned against the helicopter, eyeing Edmund. The man lay on the ground, freed from Istvan's shackles but unmoving. He breathed. His hazel eyes were open and fixed on a point somewhere on the now-distant cavern wall. He was awake – aware, even; he'd flinched when Grace landed – but otherwise unresponsive, hemmed in by flitting terrors. It was as though he simply had no motive force left at all. As though he'd broken.

Had he struck his head, after all? It had been so difficult to keep track of every nerve, cut off every impulse, fight every twitch and jerk and scream...

Istvan brushed three fingers across Edmund's arm. He didn't move.

Siding with Shokat Anoushak. Oh, why hadn't he said anything? What had driven him to this? Could there have been another way?

Why hadn't he said anything?

Istvan looked to Grace. "Can you put him in the helicopter?"

She nodded.

They made for Niagara. Kyra slept in the back; Edmund lay secured in the cargo bay. Grace and Istvan shared the front seat, in a long silence. He couldn't recall the last time they had spent so long together amicably. Probably never.

It seemed to require some acknowledgement, at least.

"I know we haven't always gotten on well," he began.

"Don't start that," Grace replied. "Just because I resigned doesn't mean we're friends. I'm not ready for that."

"You resigned?"

"Yup." She didn't seem entirely happy about it. "Barrio Libertad's the top dog now, Doc. The Susurration's gone. We're free. We don't need a symbol like Resistor Alpha anymore." She paused, quashing uncertainty and bitter betrayal, then continued, "it was about time for a change of scenery, anyway. I bet Eddie knows the feeling."

Istvan frowned. How did one resign from being a people's hero? It had been a formal title, true, but something must have gone wrong. "Where will you go?"

She jerked her head to indicate Kyra, asleep in the back. "Wherever the kid goes. I'm the only Conduit that's been studied. I'm a professional. She needs a teacher." She brought up her odd map again. "Besides, what she does isn't just wind, Doc. It's something else. I want to know what."

Istvan watched the waves below. More Grace Wu. He'd dealt with worse, he supposed. She had been useful.

"Before you ask," Grace added, "the People's Council never liked how close I am to Diego. They would have gotten rid of me sooner or later."

"Ah."

She set her jaw. "Politics."

They sped towards the opposite shore. The waves grew in height, a mist setting in. Still no Harbor. Istvan tried not to worry. If the beast had meant to reach the dams, it probably could have by now... but Lucy was competent, and would surely have followed orders to retreat. Wouldn't she?

It was odd, to worry more about Lucy than Edmund.

"There," said Grace.

The helicopter wheeled. A broad trail of broken trees and gouged earth led inland. Silt filtered down the river, spilling into a fan of muddy brown at its mouth. Rain clouds gathered over the devastation.

Istvan's heart sank. Marat hadn't stopped Harbor, after all.

Grace followed the trail as it led up into the river, tore

away part of the canyon wall, and turned westward... and kept turning, curving back towards the lake, dredging a new branch of the river as it went. Miles of it. It reached the churning edge of the spellscars, reversed, and finally, in the midst of what had likely been a small port city, they found a skyline where none had been before. A clock tower. A bridge. Docks, crushed into one another, lightning skittering across their metal fastenings.

Harbor lay partially submerged, its towers tilted to one side. Dead fish floated in the water around it. Birds darted between the wreckage. If Istvan didn't know better, he would have thought the creature were sunning itself.

"Well," he said.

"Is that a train?" asked Grace.

Istvan squinted. It was. Trains didn't usually trundle through the woods, but there it sat on a bluff, like a metal centipede. Small armor-clad figures waved up at them.

"How about that evacuation," Grace said. "Guess it was told to hit your army, after all. Wonder why it stopped."

"Maybe it just likes the water," Kyra murmured, sleepily.

A dark, broad, bat-like aircraft dipped down from the clouds high above them. It waggled its wings. Marat.

"Never mind," said Grace. She flashed it a thumbs-up.

Istvan gave Marat a nod, then turned to look at the back seat. "You're awake."

"Mm-hm," Kyra agreed. "Hurts."

He sighed. "I know. We'll see you looked after."

"And Mr Templeton?"

Istvan brushed at his bandolier. It was easier not to think of that. He didn't know what to do about that. All this way, and the man hadn't attempted to teleport out or even move: he was still back in cargo, like a potato sack. "Edmund, as well."

Kyra paused. "Did I do OK?" she asked.

Grace chuckled. "Are you kidding?"

"Of course," said Istvan. "Of course you did. You were very brave."

Kyra sat up, cradling her arm. She peered out the window – at Harbor, at Marat, diving in close to flank them – then down at the helicopter seat. "There were still people down there," she said. "I mean, cult people, and monsters, but you said they were all people, once. Like the tiger."

"Don't beat yourself up," said Grace. "It was us or them."

Istvan said nothing.

Kyra sighed. She looked out the window again. "It was what she wanted," she repeated, quietly.

"What did she say to you?" Istvan asked. "Shokat Anoushak. What did she tell you, before…" He trailed off; they both knew. They had another point in common, now.

Kyra shook her head. "Don't matter."

He nodded. "I won't–"

"I had a family. They were real to me." She drew her knees up. "I'll… I'll figure it out. I'll be OK."

The helicopter thrummed. They turned back towards Niagara.

"Let's find your army, Doc," said Grace.

Metal beneath him. Metal above him. The rattle of an engine. It should have worried him – the closeness, the motion – but Edmund couldn't bring himself to feel anything. He couldn't think anything. He couldn't move anywhere but in a spiral. Down, down; nine circles, ending in ice.

He'd never meant to.

Too late.

Didn't matter. Nothing did. Shokat Anousak had known that. That was the secret. Live long enough and become the villain. He'd known it would happen, someday.

He'd never meant to.

Too late.

Someone opened the back hatch. Light flooded in. Words. He remembered words. She'd said them, and there was nothing else. His pocket watch was gone.

He deserved it. He deserved everything that happened to him.

Grace reached for him. "Come on, Eddie. Up you go."

Edmund stared at the wall. "I'll walk," he said.

"My lord! You return in glory!"

"Yes, well–"

Lucy slammed fist to breastplate. She and the others assembled dropped to a knee.

"–something to that effect," Istvan finished. He watched Grace help Edmund out of the helicopter. The man seemed only half present, moving as though cement encased each limb. He gathered his cape in one hand. He wouldn't look at Istvan. Kyra leaned against the machine's side, blinking wearily.

"Your orders were clear, my lord," Lucy continued, "but as we fell back, the beast followed. Retreat was no option. Yet, you wished our lives safeguarded, and as we are obedient, I sent a diversionary force of slaves to taunt the beast at river's edge, armed with the–"

"You what?"

"–steel hide of our mockery, and the promise of freedom, should they survive." Lucy tilted her head. "Word has said that new warriors will soon join our ranks. The beast is routed. Does this not please you?"

The beast routed. Niagara saved. All good things, yes.

But... the rest... oh, why were these people so...

Istvan tried to find words. "They aren't slaves. No slaves. I told you to free them. All of them. Wasn't that an order, as well?"

"Our former slaves remain free, my lord. We located a small band of survivors in Niagara city, down the way, and pressed them into service."

"Don't do that."

Another salute. "Yes, my lord. Shall we still recruit them as warriors? It was a mighty deed they performed on your behalf."

Istvan clenched and re-clenched his hands, wishing there were someone else – anyone else – to make these decisions. He didn't know! He still didn't know what to do with the first group! He'd had no chance to talk to anyone, yet, and Harbor was still nearby, and other groups in Toronto undoubtedly wouldn't like Triskelion forces remaining here, and Edmund was all but a walking corpse, and–

And–

Oh, there was so much.

Istvan looked around. Grace Wu led Edmund to the museum, and parked him there, like a carriage. The man slid down the wall and sat back against it, staring at nothing. Kyra stood off near the helicopter, almost dozing, as a medic saw to her wounded arm. Istvan ought to be doing that. He ought to be doing what he used to do, not... not this.

He grimaced. Oh, the Triskelion army wasn't going to take this well. "I'm not a god-king," he said.

Lucy glanced up at him.

"I'm not one of those wise spirits," he continued, "an ending spirit, like you said. I don't want to trample upon your religion – and I do still respect your people – but I... I wasn't thinking clearly, when you told me." Istvan fiddled with his bandolier. "I was drunk. I'm very sorry, but you're mistaken."

The warrior woman paused a moment, then stood. She picked up her banner-spear. She strode closer to him, and planted it in the ground. "I know the signs," she replied, not unkindly. "You are mighty beyond the power of men, are you not? You did die, and return, did you not? This is not a matter of religion, my lord. It is simple truth. You are an ending spirit. That this world does not yet recognize your right of dominion is no fault of yours. These nations have endured but a single Wizard War, and so have had no need for the protection and counsel of your kind."

He stared at her. Their world had seen more than one Wizard War? Was that why they were so harsh, so embittered? Desperate enough to pledge allegiance to creatures of blood and terror?

"Patience," Lucy continued. "You have already shown mercy, my lord. The true wisdom you seek will come, in time."

"But–"

"I shall see to our defenses. Kasimir will not permit

our people to remain apart for long. Should you find yourself with doubts, it is my duty and honor to address them: ask what you will, in times of quiet, and I shall answer." Lucy turned about and snapped an order. Her guard scattered. She took up her banner and pointed with it. "Now. Visitors await you in our encampment. They requested to see your companion, the Hour Thief, as well. Look for the central tent."

Istvan's protestations flew out of his head. "Visitors? Who?"

"Magister Hahn of the Twelfth Hour, and a representative of He-Who-Watches-in-Walls, our once-benefactor."

Ah. Diego. Edmund would be so pleased to hear that.

A sense of loss struck him. Edmund. The man currently sitting in a doorway, staring at nothing. The man who had to be coaxed to move, lifted bodily from where he'd fallen, who hadn't acknowledged Istvan's presence at all since Toronto, since… their entanglement. Istvan hadn't known any other way to stop him.

He tried not to think of the warmth of blood. The shock and sweetness of impact. It shouldn't have been any different than anyone else, and he shouldn't have had to do it.

Edmund's fault. Edmund's fault, for abandoning him.

Istvan sighed. "Of course."

Lucy saluted one final time and strode away. If only he shared her conviction. If only he could understand the orders she was giving. He'd have to study their language, now, whatever it was. It couldn't be more difficult than Vietnamese.

It had taken him years to learn Vietnamese.

•••

"It's a matter of perception," said Magister Mercedes Hahn. She leaned back in a camp chair, turning a pen between her fingers. The tent wasn't spacious, but it did keep off the light rain that had begun to fall. "Everyone knows what happened in your encounter with Shokat Anoushak, and knows your part in it. It raises too many questions."

An orb hovered beside her, ramshackle, painted bright red and yellow. Its lenses swiveled as she spoke. The things were swarming all over New Haven now, she'd said. They'd made a deal, she said.

Edmund stood where he'd been told and listened. That was what he did. He couldn't do anything else. Couldn't be trusted with anything else.

"Everyone knows?" asked Istvan. "Who is everyone?"

"Everyone," Mercedes repeated. Her gaze flicked to the orb. That was where she'd been that morning. Barrio Libertad.

Always Barrio Libertad.

The orb sputtered with static. "I need her," it said, in Edmund's voice. "Counterbalance. It's what Mercedes would want. Someone who can threaten Barrio Libertad." Its lenses clicked into a new configuration. "Politics, like the Cold War. It's just politics."

Edmund reached for his pocket watch. His fingers found an empty pocket.

"So," Mercedes continued, voice flat, "we've come to an arrangement. Mr Templeton, you're taking an extended leave of absence. The Twelfth Hour will be conducting an investigation. We regret our lapse of judgement and seek to do right by our citizens in this trying time; allying, if need be, with those we might not always agree with. Niagara is, as of now, abandoned."

"What?" demanded Istvan.

"You heard what I said, Doctor. That's the line. We're sticking to it."

So. That was it. That's what this was about. Try a project, put a problem person on the project, blame them if it fell through. And had it ever fallen through.

Edmund had been Magister. He was famous, held in awe if not beloved; one of the few surviving wizards, the one who'd led the rest against Shokat Anoushak. He was the senior statesman at the Twelfth Hour. He could get away with anything, and everyone knew it.

Now he was the guy who'd chained up a kid and palled around with evil incarnate.

Istvan swept an arm through the air: at the tent, at the dam, at the museum and its damaged windows. "We fought for this, Magister. Killed for this!"

Edmund closed his eyes.

"You killed for it, Doctor," said Mercedes.

Istvan paused. "Er – well, mostly, but–"

"You protected it."

"That was only a few flyers, and Harbor wasn't–"

"You found allies with a stake in it, and an army to staff it. You have your first recruit, a teacher for her, and a successful trial-by-fire."

Edmund's eyes flew open. Oh, hell.

Istvan looked like he'd been caught in headlights. "Magister, you just said that we were abandoning Niagara."

Mercedes smiled, tightly. "That's the line."

Istvan just stared at her.

Edmund turned his hat in his hands. She wasn't

giving up her idea. Instead of a second headquarters, the Twelfth Hour would gain a place far out of the way, hidden from prying eyes: somewhere to put Conduits, cultists, monsters, and everyone else who caused problems. A prison. A factory for new wizards, founded on the simple principle of expediency. The Twelfth Hour didn't have enough new ones in training and never would if they didn't make changes.

He couldn't imagine what she'd bargained for such a deal. What did Barrio Libertad gain from it? What was the Twelfth Hour going to lose?

"I won't do it," said Istvan. He crossed his arms. "I'm not manning some sort of secret outpost."

"Consider it a trial," Mercedes replied. "If you successfully build a functioning community here, it won't stay secret. You will have oversight. You'll have support from both the Twelfth Hour and Barrio Libertad. Holding Niagara has become a point of common interest, believe it or not." She raised an eyebrow. "Or would you prefer that we appoint your friend Lucy?"

"Goodness, no! She would turn it into a labor camp!" The ghost glanced around, as though checking to be sure that Lucy wasn't present, and then continued, "there must be someone else. What about Grace Wu? She said that she's resigning from her post, why couldn't she–"

Mercedes remain unmoved. "Will your army listen to Ms Wu, Doctor?"

Istvan's scarred face twisted. He fiddled with his bandolier.

"Will they?"

"...no," the ghost conceded.

Edmund sighed. He considered protesting, himself,

but in the end he knew it wouldn't matter. It wasn't up to him, now. "If I'm not needed here," he said, "I'll head home."

Mercedes glanced at him. "Don't expect to stay at New Haven, Mr Templeton."

He halted. He'd always lived in New Haven. He'd lived in New Haven for his entire adult life, since the Second World War, since he'd graduated from college. Over seventy years. "Excuse me?"

"You're under investigation," she repeated. She pointed her pen at him, seeming very small in her camp chair. "You won't be staying in New Haven. You're free to pack what you like, but I expect you to be based out of Niagara for the foreseeable future."

"You're taking my house," he said.

"It's for your own protection."

Edmund curled his hands into fists. He didn't need protection, and she knew it. "Are you taking my cat, too?"

She gave him a look. Barrio Libertad's orb swiveled in his direction.

"You're not taking my cat," he muttered.

Why was everything his fault? Why was he the one to lose it all? He'd made bad decisions, sure. He wasn't going to argue that. He deserved what he got, but there had to be a limit. Mercedes wasn't stripping anyone else of their house, was she?

He glanced at Istvan.

The ghost didn't meet his eyes. "You know that I always enjoyed visiting."

Istvan didn't have a house. Right.

Edmund put both hands in his pockets, not feeling

any better. It was the worst thing, being angry and having no one to point a finger at but himself. What was he supposed to do now?

"I'll go pack, then," he said, "before a mob breaks down my door."

He strode for the tent flap.

CHAPTER TWENTY-NINE

Istvan chased after him. They had to talk about what had happened. They had to repair things, somehow: there was too much else at stake, too many other people affected, to allow Edmund to carry on like he was.

Unfortunately, Edmund was much faster, and he had a head start. He could teleport without his pocket watch. Istvan could only fly.

So he did. He knew where the man was going.

Kyra remained with Grace Wu. Asleep again. Gathering her strength. She would be fine, for now, if "fine" included a bullet wound that might not ever heal fully. Perhaps she would be awake when Istvan returned, and responsibility for Niagara might somehow fall to someone else in his absence.

He sped over the spellscars and their nauseating fluidity, landscapes that blurred. Edmund couldn't be left alone. Oh, he was worst when he was alone.

The spellscars gave way. Foothills. Forests. The grey blocks and ragged streets of the outskirts – a stretch of mismatched, crumbling skyscrapers – steam from the Generator District – and then New Haven, and the stone mountain of the Twelfth Hour, and the Black Building sharp across the bay.

Istvan dove. Over the snowy streets trundled Barrio Libertad's machines, making repairs and ferrying crates. He swung through Edmund's patched kitchen window. "Edmund–"

A box crashed to the floor. "If you can't help pack, get out."

The living room. Istvan hurried past the table. "Edmund, I'm glad that you're speaking again. I was terribly worried. I'm sorry, and I wish that it never happened, but we have to..."

The wizard stood before his bookshelves, cape thrown off, hat missing, hair disheveled, and Beldam the cat twined around one leg. The box lay before him, dropped on its side. Books lay stacked on every surface, partially sorted, hundreds of them. Istvan hadn't realized he owned quite so many.

"Hell," Edmund muttered.

Istvan edged into the living room. Beldam shot away with a hiss. "I'm, ah, sure you'll be able to move them."

"Doesn't matter."

Istvan waited, but Edmund said nothing more. He just stood there, one hand in a jacket pocket, looking down at his books.

Oh, there was no other way.

"Why did you go to find Shokat Anoushak?" Istvan asked.

Edmund shook his head.

"We had a plan," Istvan continued. "We were counting on you. I thought we were going to do better, after the night before, and..." He swallowed. "Edmund, I don't know what to think. We've always been... we're close friends. I trusted you."

The wizard knelt down to right the box. "Well, maybe you shouldn't have."

"I don't like not trusting you."

"I'm a thief. It's in the handle."

Istvan stepped over a pile of books. "Edmund—"

"I knew this was coming," the wizard replied. "I hoped I'd last longer. I've had nightmares about this, Istvan. What she said to me. The cult. I would have stayed. I've lived long enough, and that's it – it's over. It's all over."

He started methodically stacking books again.

Istvan thought of Kyra, who had torn apart Shokat Anoushak alone, with one arm, after being shot, imprisoned, shouted at, disbelieved, dismissed, and mocked – all by allies. She wasn't even supposed to be who she was. He'd told her so. He still didn't understand her. He still wished she weren't so inconvenient.

"This isn't about you," Istvan said.

Edmund dropped a book in the box. "Don't give me that."

"You can't go and do whatever you like. Neither of us can. Don't you realize that if anyone gets hurt, it isn't us? It's never us!"

The wizard picked up another book, anger and old fears mixing into a familiar and not unpleasant spice. "It isn't," he finally agreed. "It's never us. And you know what that means?" He stood, finally facing Istvan. "It means I'm the only one left. Every time. Always." He let the book drop. "You know that better than anyone."

The Ukraine, all those years ago. Edmund the sole survivor of ten. Istvan's fault. Oh, he knew. He'd never forget.

"What about the people that died?" Istvan asked.

Edmund looked away. "I'm not arguing this with you."

Istvan reached for his shoulder. The other man flinched.

Too soon.

Istvan backed off. "It may not be fair," he said, "but that's how it is. We're powerful, Edmund. You're powerful. Immensely so, even if it doesn't always seem it. Think of Harbor – it can crush people without noticing, and we're just the same. We have to watch our step. It's easier if you listen."

Edmund pushed aside a stack of books and sat on the couch.

"To the screaming," Istvan added, wondering if he were taking the metaphor too far.

"Yes. I get it."

Istvan wished he could sit next to him. Instead, he remained at some distance, twisting at his wedding ring. "Edmund–"

"Why do you keep coming back?" the wizard asked. He dropped his head in his hands, rubbing at his eyes. "I can't be trusted. You said so yourself. I'm the one that put Kyra in chains. I helped put you in chains. I sold you out to Shokat Anoushak. They're calling me racist. They're taking my house. Why bother with me, all this time?"

Thirty years. Injustice for injustice. It had been easier when they could ignore it: pretend that they were on equal ground, that Edmund hadn't held Istvan's chains once before and still held every authority over the one he claimed to be his best friend.

It was different, now.

"I love you," Istvan said. "That's why. I've loved you for years, even though you're aggravating and I've often wished that I didn't." He crossed his arms, reflecting how stupid it was to feel as though his stomach fluttered. He was a ghost. He didn't have one. "And, before you ask, yes, I do mean it in every sense."

Edmund didn't move for a long moment. "Ah," he finally managed.

Istvan waited a moment longer, then turned. "I expect you want me to leave, now. That's all right – I can't help you pack, anyhow. I only... I wanted you to know."

Why, he couldn't imagine. He oughtn't have. This was Kyra's fault, somehow. Deviance. It was rubbing off. He only wanted to show Edmund–

To convince him–

Oh, this had been a mistake.

"I hope we can remain friends," Istvan added, awkwardly. There were books everywhere. He had to make it through the books to escape. Why did anyone need so many books?

"Wait," called Edmund.

Istvan did, halting near the kitchen, hating himself. He shouldn't have said anything. He'd stayed quiet all this time, and now it was ruined.

The wizard came up beside him, threading the maze with ease. "Istvan," he said, "whatever you did behind closed doors is your business."

Polite. Measured. Acknowledging the truth, and shuffling it away. Of course. Istvan had known him far too long to hope. He hadn't expected anything else.

The fluttering was gone.

Edmund sighed. "All I can say is it explains some things. I'm not letting what we had – have – go because of something like this. And… I'm sorry."

Istvan looked at him. Hazel eyes, always tired. Trim sideburns. A shock of grey at his left temple. Slim and graceful, brilliant with language, so often callous and stubborn. Always thirty-five, at a cost.

"If you ever side with Shokat Anoushak again," Istvan told him, "I will kill you."

"That's not a bad idea," said Edmund.

They stood, a moment, beside each other. It felt like revenge.

Now that the other man knew, it would always remain in the back of his mind: reframing Istvan, casting him in a new and unflattering light, raising questions he wouldn't dare ask. He would look away; bite his tongue. Try again to trust Istvan just the same as before.

Try to trust a war; a war that loved him. It couldn't be done.

But he would have to think about it.

Edmund ran a hand across his face. "Look, I'll… I have to pack. None of this is going to move itself."

"I'm sorry for what I did," Istvan said, thinking guiltily of that last confrontation before Shokat Anoushak. "I knew no other way to stop you."

"Just save a place for me, all right?" asked Edmund.

"Always." The return trip to Niagara seemed much shorter.

Istvan found Kyra on the edge of the dam's artificial lake, near one of the guard towers left over from Kasimir's occupation. Grace Wu was with her. Marat's mockery crouched over them, the matte-black angles of its strange flattened body sheltering them from the rain. A bright patterned blanket lay on the ground. A guard stood watch. The whole formed a pavilion, of sorts.

Atop the tower, the rain turned to hail: the Tyger waited there, inspecting the encampment and taking notes. Marat's lights floated around him. Triskelion's recently liberated slave force labored just across the water, felling trees for palisades.

Istvan landed far enough away to not be startling.

"You don't have to stay here," Grace was saying. "After what they did to you, I'd take off, too."

"It's close to the glacier, though," Kyra replied.

"Kid, have you ever lived in a glacier before? I'd do it. It might be cool." A pause. "Might be *cool*...? No?"

"You already used that one," said Kyra.

"But seriously," Grace continued, "you'd have to careful or you'd freeze to death."

Istvan skirted the water's edge, walking towards them. "Kyra. How are you feeling?"

Kyra sat up. Or, rather, tried to. After a moment, she laid back on the blanket, wincing. "Hi, Doctor Czernin. I'm OK."

"Thought I heard some familiar gunfire," said Grace. She sat to the other Conduit's left, legs crossed, gauntlets laid beside her. One of her duffel bags formed a sort of back-rest. "You should have another look at her arm, Doc."

Istvan let wings and poison dissipate. The sound of distant artillery faded. He looked up at Marat's mockery. The beast peered down at him with lit headlights – they always seemed to glow, day or night – and emitted a grinding rumble.

Istvan hoped that was a positive sign. He looked to Kyra. "I've spoken to Magister Hahn and I should like a word with you. I'll check your arm, as well." He waited for Grace to excuse herself. When she didn't move, he added, "Miss Wu, if you don't mind?"

Grace eyed the laborers, then the guard.

"It's OK," said Kyra.

The older Conduit sighed. "Fine." She pulled herself up. "I'll just go chat with some of your press-gangers, ask after their families. Maybe see how bulletproof I am."

Istvan winced. "I've ordered them to–"

"Yeah, I know. That's great. Which reminds me, I meant to give you this." Grace unzipped the duffel bag and pulled a length of cloth out of it. "I got it back from Barrio Libertad before they burned it."

His embroidery. With the field of flowers, and the house. The one he'd made in the Demon's Chamber, while waiting for Kyra to wake.

He took it. "Thank you."

Grace shut the bag again and strolled off.

"What is it?" asked Kyra.

Istvan checked for damage – no threads were loose, it didn't seem stained – and then knelt beside her, handing it over. "I meant this to be yours. I suppose it was... lost in transport."

She hitched herself up, laying it out on the blanket to inspect. She was back in civilian clothes, now; armor with spikes on was, unsurprisingly, far too uncomfortable to rest in for long. He didn't know how Lucy's people did it.

"I'm going to have a look at your arm," he said.

"OK."

He traced the wound. The Triskelion medic had done a

fair job. Nothing seemed infected, and any contaminants from Toronto had been washed away. But that damaged nerve... oh, it was another matter. It would need work.

"You made this?" asked Kyra.

"I did."

"You got all the different flowers right. I know these – look at the petals."

Istvan tried not to think of the Demon's Chamber. It was broken, now. No one else would be put in it ever again. "Kyra," he began, "the Magister expects you to stay here. Niagara is to be a joint facility between the Twelfth Hour and Barrio Libertad. A training site, of sorts. She thinks of you as our first recruit. I've been put in charge – the army listens to me, and..."

The Conduit put the embroidery down.

"...you don't have to stay," said Istvan.

She drew her knees up. She looked better after some sleep, but she would need much more time to recover. There was still dust in her hair. "You got the shape right," she said. "Not just a cartoon flower. You put in the structure."

Istvan sat down near her. "I've seen a great deal of poppies, Kyra."

She set the embroidery down. "I don't get you," she muttered.

"I'll tell you whatever you would like to know," he said, and he meant it. After what he'd told Edmund, everything else was easy.

Kyra set her jaw. She flicked an ant off the blanket, pulled off her headband, and stuffed it under Grace's duffel bag. "Am I human?"

He frowned. "Pardon?"

"She said she made me. Shokat Anoushak. She said I'm some kind of prison-breaker, something she did on purpose. Ms Wu keeps saying I'm like her, but what if I ain't? Even the stuff I remember weren't never real, or mine. Some of it, anyway. Most of it." She rubbed at her bandaged arm. "I ain't a robot or something, am I? It's real blood, right?"

"It seems real to me," Istvan said, somewhat baffled. Shokat Anoushak had been made of stone. Most of her creations weren't truly living. Yes, some were flesh and blood, like the Tyger, but they had been human, before, and...

And...

Istvan sat back. Did they always have to be monstrous? Did the changes have to be physical, or could someone like William be made, who seemed normal yet carried a blizzard with them? How would Shokat Anoushak have done that while fixed to a stone?

"Yeah," said Kyra. She lay back again, pulling at the duffel bag to make a serviceable pillow. "You get it."

The creature above them rumbled. Its metal skin trembled, shaking away rain.

"You aren't a monster," Istvan said.

Kyra put her good hand behind her head, looking up at the mockery's smooth underside and folded landing gear. "I've been thinking. I'll stay here with you guys, but only if I'm allowed to go to that glacier whenever I want. I don't have to fly if that's a problem – I can go with Shade. OK?"

"Shade?"

She pointed up.

"Ah." Istvan doubted he could pry her away from the

beast. "I imagine we can allow that, yes. So long as we know where you are."

"And some other things," she continued, gaining courage, "I don't belong to nobody, so you can't fight over me. You don't yell at me for stupid reasons. I want to know what's going on, and if you're gonna keep talking in German, you teach me German. OK?"

He couldn't hold back a smile, ruined though it was. "I can do that."

Kyra nodded, closing her eyes. "Then we're good."

She still wasn't at ease, or without questions, or free of pain – far from it – but it was a start. Certainly much improved from their first meeting.

A made Conduit. Imagine. No wonder she hadn't wanted to say anything to Grace Wu.

"You're gonna make this *not* a slave camp, right?" Kyra asked.

Istvan glanced back at the laborers on the shore. That. Oh, they had to figure out what to do about that. "Kyra, if it stays a slave camp, you've my permission to personally tear me into pieces again."

"I will."

"I'm sure. I'm counting on it." He thought of Edmund, and Shokat Anoushak. Always best to have balances. He didn't know if it were possible to build something fair on war and murder, but it would be worse not to try. Istvan stood. "Rest. We'll see if we can get that arm fixed."

"Maybe I could get a robot arm," she mumbled.

"Don't you have one already?"

Kyra flashed a smile. "Maybe. It would be cool, though."

He couldn't argue with that. Grace Wu undoubtedly

would have ideas, as would Lucy. That was a frightening thought. "I'll see what I can do, at any rate," he said. "Edmund will be coming by with furniture. Don't spend all night out here, hm?"

Kyra waved him off. "Sure."

Istvan turned to go. Oh, there was so much to do. The weather wouldn't stay fair all year, the factions in Toronto would all need contacting, Lord Kasimir would be on the march for revenge, more than likely, and they needed to secure a reliable food source before winter set in...

Could they repair the dams? Could they do it all in time without forced labor?

"Hey," called Kyra, "you're good guys now, right? We're the good guys?"

Istvan paused.

"We better be the good guys," said Kyra.

He wondered what to tell her. The world was complicated, and cruel, and didn't play favorites. They had made mistakes. They would always make mistakes. The entire premise of Niagara, both coming here and staying here, was questionable.

But... Kyra already knew all of that.

Istvan nodded. "We had best be."

"Paige Orwin delivers in this wild debut about
Time and War teaming up to battle the evils of
eternal peace."
– ALIS FRANKLIN, author of *Liesmith*